QUENTINS

QUENTINS

Maeve Binchy

McArthur & Company
Toronto

First published in Canada in 2002 by
McArthur & Company
322 King Street West, Suite 402
Toronto, Ontario
M5V 1J2

National Library of Canada Cataloguing in Publication

Binchy, Maeve
    Quentins / Maeve Binchy.

ISBN 1-55278-308-1

    I. Title.

PR6052.I46Q46 2002   823'.914   C2002-903024-2

The publisher would like to acknowledge the financial support of
the Government of Canada through the Book Publishing Industry
Development Program (BPIDP) and the Canada Council for our
publishing activities.

Printed in Canada by Transcontinental Printing Inc.

10 9 8 7 6 5 4 3 2 1

To my dear good Gordon.
Thank you for a lifetime of generosity, understanding and love.

PART I

Chapter One

When Ella Brady was six she went to Quentins. It was the first time anyone had called her Madam. A woman in a black dress with a lace collar had led them to the table. She had settled Ella's parents in and then held out a chair for the six-year-old.

'You might like to sit here, Madam, it will give you a full view of everything,' she said. Ella was delighted and well able to deal with the situation.

'Thank you, I'd like that,' she said graciously. 'You see, it's my very first time here.' This was in case anyone might mistake her for a regular diner.

Her mother and father probably were looking at her dotingly, as they always did. That's what all the childhood pictures showed, anyway ... complete adoration. She remembered her mother telling her that she was the best girl in the world, and her father saying it was a great pity he had to go off to the office every day, otherwise he would stay at home with the best girl.

Once Ella asked why she didn't have sisters and brothers like everyone else seemed to. Her mother said that God had only sent one to this family, but weren't they lucky that it was such a wonderful one. Years later, Ella learned of the many miscarriages and false hopes. But at the time the explanation satisfied her completely, and it did mean that there was no one she had to share her toys or her parents with and that had to be good. They took her to the zoo and introduced her to the animals, they brought her to the circus whenever it came to town, they even went for a weekend to London and took her picture outside Buckingham Palace. But somehow nothing was ever as important as that first visit to a grown-up restaurant, where she had been called Madam and given a seat with a good view.

The Bradys lived in Tara Road, in a house which they had bought years ago before prices started to rocket. It was a tall house with a big back garden where Ella could invite her friends from school. The house had been divided into apartments when the Bradys bought it. So there was a bathroom and kitchenette on every floor. They had restored most of it to make it a family home but Ella's friends were very envious that she had what was like a little world of her own. It was a peaceful, orderly life. Her father Tim had a twenty-two-minute walk to the office every day, and twenty-nine minutes back on the return journey, because he paused to have a half-pint of beer and read the evening paper.

Ella's mother, Barbara, only worked mornings. She was the one who opened up the solicitors' offices right in town near Merrion Square. They trusted her utterly, she always said proudly, to have everything ready when the partners arrived in at 9.30 a.m. All their mail would be on their desks sorted for them. Someone to answer early-morning phone calls and to imply that they were already at work. Then she would go through the huge collection in what was called Barbara's Basket, where they all left anything at all to do with money. Barbara thought of herself as a super-efficient book-keeper, and she controlled the four disorganised, crusty lawyers she worked for with iron rules. Where was this receipt for transport undertaken in the course of a case? Where was that invoice for the new stationery that someone had ordered? Obediently, like small boys, they delivered their accounts to her and she kept them in great ledgers. Barbara dreaded the day when they would all become computerised. But it was still far away. These four would move very slowly. They would have liked the quill pen to work with had they been given a choice!

Barbara Brady left the office at lunchtime. At first she needed to do this in order to pick Ella up from school, but even when her daughter was old enough to return accompanied only by a crowd of laughing girls, Barbara continued the routine of working a half-day only. Barbara knew that she achieved more in her four-and-a-half-hour stint than most others did in a full day. And she knew that her employers realised this too. So she was always in the house when Ella returned. It all worked out very well. Ella had somebody at home to provide a glass of milk and shortbread and to listen to her colourful account of the events of the day, this drama and that adventure. Also, to help her with what homework needed to be done.

This system meant that Tim Brady had an orderly house and a good cooked meal to return to when he got back from the investment brokers where he worked with ever-increasing anxiety over the years. And when he came home every evening at the same time, Ella had a second audience for her marvellous people-filled stories. And the lines of care would fall gradually from his face as she followed her father around the garden, first as a toddler then as a leggy schoolgirl. She would ask questions about the office that her own mother would never dare to ask. Did they think well of Daddy at the office? Was he ever going to be in charge? And later, when it was clear to Ella how unhappy her father was, she asked him why he didn't go somewhere else to work.

Tim Brady might have left the office where he was so uneasy, and gone to another position, but the Bradys were not people to whom change came easily. They had taken a long time to commit to marriage, and an even longer time to produce Ella. They were nearly forty when she arrived, a different generation from the other parents of young children. But that only deepened their love for her. And their determination that she should have everything that life could possibly give her. They did their basement up as a self-contained flat, and let it to three bank girls in order to make a fund for Ella's education. They never did anything just for themselves. In the beginning a few heads were shaken about it all. Was there a possibility that they did too much for the child? some people wondered. That they would spoil her totally? But as it happened even those who had forebodings had to agree that all this love and attention did Ella no harm at all.

From the start she seemed able to laugh at herself. And everyone else. She grew into a tall, confident girl who was open and friendly and who seemed to love her parents as much as they loved her.

Ella kept a photograph album of all the happy events of childhood, and wrote captions under the pictures: 'Daddy and Mam and the Chimp at the zoo. Chimp is on left', and would peal with laughter at it every time.

Even at the age of thirteen when other children might have

wriggled away from scenes of family life, Ella's blonde head pored over the pictures.

'Was that the blue dress I wore to Quentins?' she asked.

'Imagine you remembering that!' Her father was delighted.

'Is it still there?' she asked.

'Very much so, it's got smarter, more expensive, but it's certainly still there and doing well.'

'Oh.' She seemed disappointed to hear it had become expensive. Her parents looked at each other.

'It's a long time since she's been there, Tim.'

'Over half her lifetime,' he agreed, and they decided to go to Quentins on Saturday night.

Ella looked at everything with her sharp young eyes. The place looked a lot more luxurious now than the last time. The thick linen napkins had an embroidered Q on them. The waiters and waitresses wore smart black trousers and white shirts, they knew all about every dish and explained clearly how they were cooked.

Brenda Brennan had noticed the girl looking around with interest. She was exactly the teenage daughter that Brenda would have loved to have had. Alert, friendly, laughing with her parents and grateful for being taken out to a smart place to eat. You didn't always see them like that. Often they were bored and sulky and she would tell Patrick later on in the night that possibly they had been lucky to escape parenthood. But this one was every mother's dream. And her parents didn't look all that young, either. The man could be sixty, he was tired and slightly stooped, the mother in her fifties. Lucky people, the Bradys, to have had such a treasure late in their years.

'What do most people like best to eat, are there any favourites?' the girl asked Brenda when she brought them the menu.

'A lot of our customers like the way we do fish . . . we keep it very simple, with a sauce on the side. And of course many more people are vegetarian nowadays, so Chef has to think up new recipes all the time.'

'He must be very clever,' Ella said. 'And does he talk to you all normally and everything while he's working? I mean, is he temperamental?'

'Oh, he talks all right, not always normally; then of course he's married to me, so he has to talk to me or I'd murder him.' They all laughed together and Ella felt so good to be treated as one of the grown-ups. Then Brenda moved on to another table.

Ella saw both her parents looking at her very intensely.

'What's wrong? Did I talk too much?' she asked, looking from one to the other. She knew she was inclined to prattle on.

'Nothing's wrong, sweetheart. I was just thinking what a pleasure it is to bring you anywhere, you get so much out of everything and everyone,' her mother said.

'And I was thinking almost the very same thing,' her father said, beaming at her.

And as Ella went on to high school she wondered if it was possible that they might care too much about her. All the other girls at school said that their parents were utterly monstrous. She gave a little shiver in case suddenly everything went sour. Maybe her parents wouldn't like her clothes, her career, her husband? It was going dangerously smoothly so far. And it continued to go well during what were meant to be the years from Hell, when Ella was sixteen and seventeen. Every other girl at the school had been in open warfare with one or both parents. There had been scenes and tears and dramas. But never in the Brady household.

Barbara may have thought the party dresses Ella bought were far too skimpy. Tim may have thought the music coming from Ella's bedroom too loud. Ella might have wished that her father didn't turn up in his nice safe car and wait outside the disco to take her home at the end of an evening, as if she were a six-year-old. But if anyone thought these things they were never said. Ella did complain that her father fussed over her too much and that her mother worried about her, but she did it lovingly. By the time Ella was eighteen and ready to go to university, it was still one of the most cheerful, peaceful households in the Western Hemisphere.

Ella's friend Deirdre was full of envy. 'It's not fair, really it isn't. They haven't even got annoyed with you for doing science. Most parents refuse point-blank to let you do what you want.'

'I know,' Ella said, worried. 'It's a bit abnormal, isn't it?'

'They don't have rows, either,' Deirdre grumbled. 'Mine are always on at each other about money and drink . . . everything, in fact.'

Ella shrugged. 'No, they don't drink, and of course we rent out the flat so they have plenty of money . . . and I'm not a drug addict or anything, so I suppose they don't have any worries.'

'But why are they all on red alert about everything in *my* house?' Deirdre wailed.

Ella shrugged. She couldn't explain it . . . it just didn't seem to be a problem.

'Wait until we want to stay out all night and go to bed with fellows, then it will be a problem,' Deirdre said with her voice full of menace.

But oddly when that happened it wasn't a problem at all.

In their first year at university, Ella and Deirdre had made a new friend, Nuala, who was from the country and had her own flat. Right in the centre of the city. So whenever anything was going to be too late or too hard to get home from, the fiction of Nuala's flat was used. Ella wondered if they were truly convinced, or did they suspect that she might be up to some adventure. Perhaps they didn't want to know about any adventures, so they didn't ask questions to which the answers, if truthful, might be unacceptable. They just trusted her to get along with everything as they always had. Occasionally she felt a bit guilty, but there weren't all that many occasions.

Ella never fell in love during her four years at university, which made her unusual. She did have sex, though. Not a great deal of it. Ella's first lover was Nick, a fellow student. Nick Hayes was first and foremost a friend, but one night he told Ella that he had fancied her from the moment she had come into the first lecture. She had been so cool and calm while he had always been over-eager and loud and saying the wrong thing.

'I never saw you like that,' Ella said truthfully.

'It's got to do with having freckles, green eyes, and having to shout for attention as a member of a large family,' he explained.

'Well, I think it's nice,' she said.

'Does that mean you fancy me a bit too?' he asked hopefully.

'I'm not sure,' she said.

He was so disappointed that she couldn't bear to see his face. 'Couldn't we just talk a lot instead of desiring each other?' she asked. 'I'd love to know about you and why you think science is a good way into film-making, and, well . . . lots of things,' she ended lamely.

'Does that mean that you find me loathsome, repulsive?' he asked.

Ella looked at him. He was trying to joke, but his face looked very vulnerable. 'I find you very attractive, Nick,' she said.

And so they became lovers.

It was less than successful. Oddly they weren't either upset or embarrassed. They were just surprised.

After a few attempts they agreed that it wasn't all they had expected it to be. Nick said that it was his first time too, and that perhaps they should both go off and get experience with people who knew all about it.

'Maybe it was like driving a car,' he said seriously. 'You should learn from someone who knows how to do it.'

Then she was fancied by a sporting hero, who was astonished when she said she didn't want to have sex with him.

'Are you frigid, or what?' he had asked, searching for an explanation.

'I don't think so, no,' Ella had said.

'Oh, I think you must be,' said the sporting hero in an aggrieved manner. So then Ella thought it might be no harm to try it with him, since he was known to have had a lot of ladies. It wasn't any better than with Nick, and there was nothing to talk about, so it was probably worse. She had the small compliment of being told by the sporting hero that she most definitely wasn't frigid.

There were only two other brief experiences, which, compared to Deirdre and Nuala's adventures, were very poor. But Ella wasn't put out. She was twenty-two and a science graduate; she would find love sooner or later. Like everyone.

Nuala found love first. Frank, dark and brooding. Nuala adored him. When he said that he wanted to join his two brothers in their construction business in London, she was heartbroken.

This called for an emergency dinner at Quentins. 'I really and truly thought he cared, how could I have been so taken in, so humiliated?' she wept to Deirdre and Ella when they settled at their table.

It was meant to be an Early Bird dinner, where people came in at six-thirty and left by eight. It was intended for pre-theatre goers, and the restaurant hoped to be able to have a second sitting for the table. But Deirdre, Ella and Nuala showed no signs of leaving. Mon, the lively little blonde waitress, cleared her throat a couple of times but it was no use.

Finally Ella approached Mrs Brennan. 'I'm very sorry. I know we are meant to be Early Bird and the cheaper menu, but one of the birds at our table has a terrible crisis and we are trying to pat down her feathers.'

Brenda laughed despite herself and despite the people waiting in the bar for the next sitting.

'Go on then, pat her down,' she said good-naturedly.

'Send them a bottle of house red, with a note saying: "To help the crisis",' she told Mon.

'I thought we were meant to be dislodging the Early Birds,' Mon grumbled.

'Yes, you're right, Mon, but we have to be flexible too in this trade,' Brenda said.

'A whole bottle, Mrs Brennan?' Mon was still confused.

'Yes, a very poor wine, one of Patrick's few mistakes, sooner it's drunk the better,' Brenda said.

They were overjoyed at the table.

'As soon as we get some money, we'll eat here properly,' Ella promised.

And they settled down to the plan of war. Should they just murder Frank now, or go to his house and threaten him? Should Nuala find another lover in the next two hours and taunt Frank about it? Should she write him a hurt, sad letter that would break his heart and unsteady his hand for the rest of his working life? None of these things proved to be necessary, because Frank came into the restaurant looking for Nuala. He was greeted with a great deal of hostility by the three girls. He seemed very bewildered. Yet they were ranged against him and there was no way of talking to Nuala alone.

'All right, then,' he said, with his face red and almost tearful. 'All right, it wasn't what I had planned, but here we go.' He knelt down and produced a diamond ring.

'I love you, Nuala, and I was waiting for you to give me an indication of whether you would mind coming to England with me. When you were so silent, I thought you wouldn't come with me. Please, do please, marry me.'

Nuala stared at him with delight. 'I thought you didn't love me, that you were leaving me,' she began.

'Will you marry me?' he said, almost purple now.

'Frank, you see, I thought you wanted a career more than . . .'

A vein was moving dangerously in Frank's forehead.

'I was so upset I had even been looking up jobs in London . . .'

Ella could bear it no longer. 'NUALA, WILL YOU MARRY HIM . . . YES OR NO?' she shouted, and the whole restaurant watched as Nuala said that of course she would, then everyone cheered.

Deirdre and Ella were to be the bridesmaids three months later.

'Maybe I might meet my own true love at Nuala's wedding,' Ella said to her mother. 'I'll certainly be hard to miss in this awful tangerine-coloured outfit she has insisted we wear.'

'You look well in anything,' Barbara said.

'Come on, Mam, please. We look like two things dressed up to sell petrol in a garage or to give away sweets for a charity.'

'Nonsense, you're much too hard on yourself . . .'

'Deirdre was saying that again only the other day, she says you both give me everything I want and praise as well, that I'm a spoiled princess.'

'Nothing could be further from the truth.'

'But Mam, you don't even nag me about not going to Mass.'

'Well, I will if you like, but what good would it do? Anyway Father Kenny says we should look after our own souls and not everyone else's.'

'It's late that Father Kenny and the Church have decided that, what about the Crusades and the Missions?'

'I don't suppose you're going to tell me that you think poor Father Kenny was personally involved in the Crusades and the Missions,' Barbara said with a smile.

'No, of course not, and I will be polite and respectful all during the wedding ceremony, though I think Nuala's crazy to go for the whole church thing.'

'So when the time comes for you, we won't have to alert Father Kenny?'

'No, Mam, but by the time the time comes for me, it could be the planet Mars that might be the in place to get married.'

Ella didn't meet her true love at Nuala's wedding, but Deirdre did meet and greatly fancied one of Frank's married brothers, who had come over from London for the wedding.

'Oh, Deirdre, please don't. I beg you, put him down,' Ella had said.

'What on earth do you mean?' Deirdre's eyes were wide open with innocence.

'I'm worn out covering for you and that fool of the first order, delaying photographs and everything until the bridesmaid comes back dishevelled with one of the ushers, what *are* you thinking of?'

'It's okay, it's a bit of a laugh. Nuala would laugh too – will laugh, in fact.'

'No, Deirdre, you've got it so wrong, that's her brother-in-law now. Someone she'll be seeing with his wife twice a week in London. Nuala won't laugh, and what's more, she won't know.'

'Oh, God, you're so disapproving! That's what people *do* at weddings, that's what weddings are *for*.'

'Adjust your dress, Deirdre, more piccies to be taken.' Ella had a voice like steel.

'What do you mean, adjust my dress?'

'Well, pull it down at the back, it's all caught up in your knickers.' Ella had the satisfaction of watching Deirdre's worried face as she beat around hopelessly at the back of her dress, which was, as it happened, not caught up at all.

At the wedding, Ella met Nuala's cousin, a woman she had not met for years. She was just about to leave her job as a science teacher; did Ella know anyone looking for a job?

Ella said she'd love the job herself.

'I didn't know you were going to teach,' the woman said, surprised.

'Neither did I, until this minute,' said Ella.

Her parents were very surprised at the news also. 'You know you can go on at university and take more degrees, the money is there for you,' her father said, nodding towards the downstairs flat, where the three women bankers were happy to pay for the privilege of living in a good address like Tara Road.

'No, Dad, really, I've been to the school, they're nice. They don't mind I've no experience. They seem to think I'll be able to manage the kids; well, I'm tall physically ... that's a help, if it comes to arm wrestling,' Ella said with a smile.

'You got a good degree as well,' her mother reminded her.

'Yeah, well, that helped, I suppose – anyway I just have to do this teaching diploma, which means lectures in the evenings ... and since the school is over that way near the university, I was thinking ...' She wondered how to put this to them. That it was time to leave home. They took it very calmly.

'We had wondered if you'd like to live in the basement flat eventually?' Her father was tentative.

'You'd be free to come and go like the bank girls there are,' her mother said. 'Nobody to bother you or anything.'

'It's just the distance, Mam, it's not about people bothering me. You never have.'

'You know, days could go by without your having to see us, just like the tenants. And there are big, strong walls ...'

She knew this was their last plea, then they would give in. 'No, I'm not worried about your hearing my wild parties, Dad. Honestly, it's only to make it all quicker and easier. And I'll be at home often, even staying for whole weekends if you want me.'

The deal was done.

'I don't believe you, your own place *and* a room at home, that's pure greed. Why should you get it all, Ella Brady?' Deirdre said.

'Because I'm reliable, that's why,' Ella replied. 'I'm no trouble. I never have been. That's why I have such an easy life.'

And it all did go easily. Ella liked the school, the other young teachers warned her of the pitfalls, the staffroom bores, the danger of getting sucked into campaigns, how to cope with parent–teacher meetings, how to lobby for better equipment for the lab. She liked the children and their enthusiasm. It seemed only the other day that she was in a classroom on the other side of the desk. The lectures were easy too, and she found herself a flat in a leafy road only five minutes from the school.

'I feel free here somehow, independent,' Ella explained to Deirdre.

'I don't know why you bothered, you got your meals served to you back in your parents' place, and it's not as if you ever brought a bloke in here, by the looks of things.'

'How do you know?' Ella laughed.

'Well, have you?'

'No, as it happens, but I might.'

'See?' Deirdre was triumphant. 'I don't know why you feel so free and independent, I really don't.'

And in a way, neither did Ella know. She thought it had something to do with not having to think about her parents' marriage. They were old now, in their sixties, and they still clung to work rather than retire like other people of their age did. They could sell that big house in Tara Road for a fortune and buy a much smaller place. Then Mam would not have to go in anxiously to the law firm where she suspected that she was being kept on from kindness. Dad would not have to go to what he saw as a changing world of money men.

They got on well together. Surely they did? As she had so often told Deirdre, they never had rows. Suppose they were to turn the house back into apartments, then the rent that would bring in would mean they could retire. She would say nothing yet, just let the idea develop.

She went back home to see them for supper at least once a week and every Sunday as well, but she never stayed over. She said she studied better in the flat. Some months later, she made the suggestion that they should let her room.

Never had anything fallen on such unresponsive ground. They were astounded that she should even think of it. They didn't want to retire. What would they do with their days?

Suddenly Ella's legendary laughter left her. She saw a very bleak future ahead. Imagine what desperate lives people must lead if these two, who were meant to be Happily Married, couldn't even bear the thought of being side by side at home instead of going to jobs which they found tiring and anxiety-creating.

'I'd prefer to be a nun than have a dead marriage,' Ella told Deirdre very earnestly.

Deirdre worked in a busy laboratory where she knew a great many men.

'You might as well *be* a nun, the way you live,' Deirdre said. 'In fact, I think you are one in plain clothes.'

And as time went by Nuala still kept in touch from London. She had decided not to get a job after all, but instead to work in the company as a receptionist. Frank said it was better to keep all the family secrets within the family, she wrote.

'What family secrets does she mean?' Deirdre wondered.

'Probably that her brothers-in-law are screwing everything that moves in there,' Ella suggested.

'Very droll.' Deirdre still wondered what they could be hiding.

'Oh, for heaven's sake, Dee. Remember them at the wedding in their sharp suits and their eyes never still, moving around the room? Those fellows have never known what it was like to keep proper books or pay proper tax in their lives.'

'You think all builders are unreliable, that's your prejudice.' Deirdre was spirited.

'No, I don't, look at Tom Feather! His family are above-board. Lots of them are. It's just Frank's lot make me shudder.'

'If you're right, do you suppose they have our pal Nuala drawn into it all?' Deirdre wondered.

'Poor Nuala. I'd just hate to be wrapped up with that lot,' Ella said.

'Now funnily enough, I'd find being wrapped up with Eric, that eldest brother, no problem at all,' Deirdre laughed.

'You might get your chance, they're going to have a family gathering here in Dublin for Frank's parents. We're invited,' Ella read at the end of the letter.

'Great. I'll get one of those suspender belt things.'

'No, Deirdre, you won't, it's only three years since the wedding, they won't have forgotten you. We'll keep well away from Frank's family.'

The party was very showy. There were even columnists and photographers at it. Frank and his three brothers posed endlessly as an Irish success story. They were photographed with politicians, celebrities, with their parents and their wives.

'It's very fancy for a fortieth wedding anniversary, isn't it . . . all this razzmatazz. I think that the old folk look a bit bewildered,' Deirdre said.

Ella pushed her sunglasses back on her head to study the party more seriously. 'No, they're well able for it, the mam and dad, for them it's a triumphal celebration. It's "Look at what a success Our Boys have made in life".'

'Why don't you like them, Ella?'

'I don't know, I really don't, to be honest.'

'Do you think Nuala's happy?'

'I think so, a bit hunted. But she got what she wanted, so I suppose that's happy.'

Ella always remembered that remark because just as she was saying it a man beside them was jostled against her by a press photographer. 'Please, Mr Richardson, can we have you in the group?'

'No, thanks all the same, but this is a family party. It's not appropriate.'

'It would make sure we got it in the paper?' The camera man was persuasive, but not enough.

'No, thanks, as I said, I'd really much prefer to talk to these two lovely ladies.'

Ella turned at the calm, very forceful voice. And she looked at Don Richardson, Financial Consultant, whose picture was indeed often in the newspapers. But they had never done him justice. He was good-looking certainly – dark curly hair, blue eyes – but he had a way of looking at you that excluded everyone else in the room. Ella knew she hadn't imagined this because out of the corner of her eye she saw Deirdre shrugging slightly and moving away. Leaving her alone with Don Richardson.

Ella had never been able to flirt. Her friend Nick said it was a weakness in a woman. Men just loved that come-on look from under the eyelashes. Ella was too up-front he said, lessened the magic somehow. She wished she had listened to Nick. Now for the very first time she wanted to know how to do it.

Even if she had five minutes with Deirdre – but her friend had gone to hover in the danger area of Frank's brothers.

It turned out not to be necessary.

He held out his hand to her with a great smile. 'Ella Brady from Tara Road, how are you? I'm Don Richardson. It's such a pleasure to meet you.'

'How do you know my name?' she croaked.

'I asked a couple of people, Danny Lynch, the property guy, he told me. He lives near you, apparently.'

Ella heard herself saying, 'Yes, well, near my parents, actually. I've moved out of home, you see, and I have my own place.'

'Why am I very pleased to hear that, Ella Brady?' he asked. He hadn't stopped smiling and he hadn't stopped holding her hand.

Chapter Two

Ella got home from the hotel somehow on her own. She thought afterwards that she must have taken a taxi, but she didn't remember it. She sat down and looked around her for a long time before she took stock of it all. This was not happening to her. This was the stuff of silly movies or magazine stories, which had to have the love-at-first-sight theme running through them. Don Richardson was just a known charmer, a professional who made his money by saying Trust Me to people, by holding their hands for a little too long, by letting his eyes lock into theirs. There was obviously a Mrs Richardson in the room tonight, maybe a history of several of them. There were little Richardsons at home all of whom would need quality time. Ella Brady was *not* going to go down this road. She had mopped the tears of too many friends who had told her fantasy tales of men who were going to leave their wives. She would not join their number. Women had an amazing capacity to fool themselves, Ella had seen it over and over. She would never be part of it.

He was waiting outside the school next morning. Sitting in a new BMW and smiling as she approached. Ella wished that she had dressed better. But he didn't seem to notice.

'Are you surprised?' he asked.

'Very,' she said.

'Can you sit in for a moment? Please,' he asked.

'I have to get to class.'

She sat in his car. She wanted to make some kind of joke, some wisecracking remark that would disguise how nervous and excited she felt.

But she decided to say nothing at all. Let him explain what had to be explained.

'I'm forty-one years old, Ella, married for eighteen years to Margery Rice, daughter of Ricky Rice, who is theoretically my boss, or at any rate the money in our company. I have two sons aged sixteen and fifteen. Margery and I have a dead marriage – it suits both of us to stay together, at the moment anyway. It certainly suits her father and it suits our two sons. We share a home out in Killiney, by the sea. I also have a business flat in the Financial Services Centre.

'Margery spends most of her day golfing or running charity events. We live entirely separate lives. You would be breaking up nothing, nil, zilch, zero, if you were to say that you would have dinner with me tonight in Quentins at around eight.' He put his head on one side as if waiting for her argument.

'I'd like that, see you there,' Ella said, and got out of the car. She felt her legs shaking as she went into the staffroom. Ella Brady, who had never taken a class off in her teaching life, went straight to the Principal and said she had to leave the school at lunchtime, it was an emergency. She booked a hair-do, a manicure and a leg wax. She bought fresh flowers for her flat, changed the sheets and tidied the place, examining it with a critical eye. It was probably a wasted effort. But it was wiser to be prepared.

'You got your hair done,' he said as she joined him in one of the private booths at Quentins.

'You went home and changed too. Long trek out to Killiney and back,' Ella said, smiling.

'Separate lives, Ella, either you believe me or you don't.' Don had an extraordinary smile.

'Of course I believe you, Don. Now that that's out of the way, we never have to mention it again.'

'And do I have to get anything out of the way? Long-term loves, jealous suitors, possible fiancés in the wings?'

'Nothing at all,' she said. 'Believe me or don't.'

'I totally believe you, what a wonderful dinner we are going to have,' he said.

The evening passed too quickly. She reminded herself over and over that there must be no brittle jokes about it being time to send him home.

He had dealt with that side of it already. They were meeting as free agents or not at all. He told her about a lunch they'd had in the office today with outside caterers for the first time, and how it must be the hardest job on earth preparing and clearing up after businessmen who all wanted endless vodka and tonics without letting their bosses see just how much they were knocking back.

They were marvellous kids, he said, ran the thing like clockwork, he'd get them more work. Didn't even want to be paid in cash, said they had some accountant who went ballistic over VAT and everything. Ella said that she thought everyone did.

'Sure they do, of course they do. I was only trying to give these two at Scarlet Feather a break.'

'Oh, Scarlet Feather, I know them! Tom and Cathy, they're great people,' Ella said, pleased they had someone else in common.

'Yes, they seemed fine. I'd hire them again. They're not going to get rich quick, but that's their business.'

He seemed for a moment to think less of them because they weren't going to get rich quick. A shadow came over it all. Maybe Rice and Richardson only liked people who made lots of money.

'How do you know the builders, Eric and his brothers?' she asked.

'Oh, business,' he said quickly. 'We handle a few investments for Eric and the boys. And you?'

'My friend Nuala is married to Frank, the youngest brother,' she said.

'Some small city. Imagine you knowing that catering couple as well. Anyway, Angel Ella, now tell me about your lunch.'

She told him about the elderly teacher who was afraid they would all get radiation from the microwave, and the sports teacher who had lost his front tooth biting into a hard French roll. She told him about the Third Years sending up a petition about school uniform being a danger to girls as they were maturing, since it made them objects of ridicule. None of these things had happened today because Ella had been racing around getting her flat cleaned and her body prepared for what might lie ahead. But as stories they were real incidents from other lunchtimes in the staffroom, and they made him laugh. And with Don Richardson it was going to be important to keep him laughing.

If you wanted to be his friend or whatever there would be no place for moody.

No place at all.

He drove her back to her flat.

'I enjoyed this evening,' Don Richardson said.

'Me, too.' Her throat was tight and her chest constricted. Did she ask him in? They were free agents. Or was it sluttish? And why should it be sluttish for the girl, not the man? She would wait and take her timing from him.

'So, since I have your telephone number, maybe we can go out again, Angel Ella?' he said.

'Yes, please.' She kissed his cheek and got out of the car while she still had the strength to do so.

He waved and turned the car.

She would not spend *any* time wondering would he drive eleven miles south to Killiney and the dead marriage or one mile north into the city to the bachelor pad.

She let herself into the flat and looked accusingly at the vase of expensive fresh flowers she had arranged before she had left.

'Fine lure you were to get him back here,' she said.

The flowers said nothing.

Maybe I should get myself a cat or a dog, something that might grunt at me when I come back here alone, Ella thought. But then she might not always be coming back here alone.

It was her father's birthday next day. Ella had bought him a gift voucher for a hotel in Co. Wicklow. An old-fashioned place with a big, rambling garden. When she was a child, they sometimes drove down there for Sunday lunch. He used to point out the flowers to her and she would learn the names. Ella remembered her mother smiling a lot there, sitting and pouring out afternoon tea in the garden.

Maybe it would be a nice peaceful place for them to go and stay. The voucher covered dinner, bed and breakfast. It could be taken up any time in the next month. Surely they would like that?

They loved the idea, both of them. Ella felt tears at the back of her eyes to see such gratitude.

'What a wonderful gift, just imagine it,' her father said, over and over.

Ella wondered why had he never thought of such a thing himself if it was so great. Her mother was delighted too.

'The three of us all going down to Holly's *and* staying the night!' she said.

Ella realised with a shock that they thought she was going with them as well.

'So when will we go?' Her father was excited now like a child.

'A Friday or a Saturday?' she suggested. She couldn't ruin it all now by explaining that she hadn't meant to come with them.

'You choose,' Father said.

Don wouldn't ask her out on a Saturday, that would surely be family time.

They fixed to go the following Saturday. Just as Ella was about to call the hotel and make the booking her mobile phone rang.

'Hallo,' Don Richardson said.

She noted that he hadn't said his name. It was arrogant in a way to assume that she knew who it was. But she was no good at playing games.

'Oh, hallo,' she said pleasantly.

'Is it okay to talk?' he asked.

'Oh, it's always okay,' Ella said, but she got up and moved out towards the spiral steps down to the garden at the same time. She gave an apologetic shrug to her parents as if this were a duty call she had to take.

'I wondered if you'd like to have dinner Saturday?'

She looked behind her into the sitting-room. Her parents were examining the brochure for Holly's as if it were some kind of map of a treasure trove. She could not cancel it now.

Ella held on to the wrought-iron rail. 'I'm so sorry, but I've just arranged something, literally in the last few minutes, and it would be a bit difficult, you see, to . . .'

He cut her off.

'Never mind, it was on the off chance, there'll be other evenings.'

He was about to go. She knew she must not begin to burble at him but she was so very anxious to keep him on the line.

'I *wish* I didn't have to . . .'

'But you have,' he said crisply before she could cancel her parents' outing and go with him wherever he suggested. 'So catch you again.' And he was gone.

All during dinner her heart felt like a stone. And later, she helped her mother with the washing up and they had the most extraordinary conversation.

'Ella, you couldn't have done anything that would please your father more, it's just what he needs. He's been very pressured at work.'

'Then why didn't *you* take him to Holly's, Mother?' Ella hoped her tone was not as impatient as she felt inside. Her mother looked at her, amazed.

'But what would we have done there together, just the two of us looking at each other? We might as well just stay here looking at each other if there was to be just the two of us.'

Ella looked at her mother in shock. 'You can't mean that, Mam?'

'Mean what?' Her mother was genuinely surprised.

'That you don't have anything to talk about with Dad.'

'But what *is* there to talk about, haven't we said it all?' Her mother spoke as if this were the most glaringly obvious thing in the world.

'But if that's the way it is, why don't you leave him, why don't you separate?' Ella stood with the dinner plate in her hand. Her mother took it away from her.

'Oh, Ella, don't be ridiculous, why on earth would we want to do that? I never heard of such nonsense.'

'People do, Mam.'

'Not people like me and your dad. Come back inside now and we'll talk about this great visit to Holly's.'

Ella felt as if a light warm woollen blanket had been put over her head and was beginning to suffocate her.

She went to the cinema with Deirdre and for a drink afterwards. They talked normally as always. Or so Ella thought. Then Deirdre ordered another drink and asked Ella, 'They're serving sandwiches. Do you want one?'

'What?' Ella said. 'Oh, yes, whatever.'

'I'll get you one with mouse's dirt and bird droppings in it, then,' Deirdre said cheerfully.

'What?'

'Oh, good. Welcome back, you're awake again,' Deirdre laughed.

'I don't know what you mean.'

'Ella, you saw none of the movie, you haven't said a word to me, you've bitten your lip and shuffled about. Are you going to tell me or are you not?'

She had told Deirdre everything since they were thirteen, but she couldn't. It was odd, there was too much to tell and too little. Too much in that she had fallen in love with an entirely wrong man *and* that her own parents' thirty-year marriage, which she had always thought was very happy, was fairly empty. And yet too little to tell. To Deirdre it would all be simple. She would say that Ella should go for the man, married or not. Take what she wanted and not get hurt. And Deirdre would say that everyone's parents had rotten marriages, it's just the way things were.

'Nothing, Dee, just fussing, ruminating, being neurotic . . . that's all it is, honestly.'

'That's all it ever is, honestly, but you always tell me,' Deirdre grumbled.

'You've got such a great, uncomplicated way of looking at things. I'm envious.'

'No, you're not, you think I'm sexually indiscriminate, that I have a hard heart . . . come on, you're not envious.'

'I am. Tell me of your latest drama, whatever it was.'

'Well, I had a great session with that Don Richardson, you know, the consultant guy you see all over the papers. *Very* good he is too, insatiable nearly.'

Deirdre held her head on one side and watched Ella's face. After a few seconds she was contrite. 'Ella, you clown, I was just joking.'

Ella said nothing. She had both hands on her head as if trying to clear it.

'Ella! I didn't, I never even met him, you silly thing, I was only on a fishing expedition to see if that's who you fancied.'

Ella took her hands away from her face.

'And it seems as if I was right,' Deirdre said.

'How did you know?' Ella's voice was a whisper.

'Because I'm your best friend, and also because you couldn't take your eyes off him when he came up to you at Nuala's do the other night.'

'Was that only the other night?' Ella was amazed.

'Will I get a half-bottle of wine?' Deirdre suggested.

'Get a full bottle,' Ella said, some of the colour coming back to her face.

The next Saturday the Bradys left Tara Road in the middle of the afternoon so that they could take a tour of Wicklow Gap before going to Holly's. Ella was determined to do it well if she was doing it at all. Give them a day and night out to remember. Oddly, Deirdre had seemed highly approving that she had refused the date with Don for Saturday night. To have agreed would make Ella too available. He would call again, mark Deirdre's words, she knew about such things. Ella had brought a flask of coffee and three little mugs and they stood in the afternoon sunshine to admire the scenery. There was bright yellow gorse on the bare hills, and some flashes of deep purple heather. Here and there a thin vague-looking sheep wandered as if bemused that there wasn't more green grass for them to eat.

'Imagine, you can't see a house or a building anywhere and yet be so near Dublin, isn't it amazing?' Ella said.

'Like the Yorkshire Moors. I was there once,' her father said.

Ella hadn't known that. 'Were you there too, Mam?'

'No, before my time.' She sounded clipped.

'It's a bit like Arizona too, all that space, except it's red desert over there,' Ella said. 'Remember the time you gave me the money for the Greyhound Bus Tour? When Deirdre and I went off to see the world.'

'You were twenty-one,' her mother remembered.

'And you sent us a postcard every three days,' her father said.

'You were very generous. I saw so much that I'll never forget, thanks to you. Deirdre had to work for the money and borrow some, I don't think she's paid it all back yet.'

'Why have a child if you can't give her a holiday?' Barbara Brady's lips were pursed with disapproval of those who didn't take parenting seriously.

'And what is money when all is said and done?' said Tim Brady, who had spent all his working hours, weeks and years, advising people about money and nothing else.

Ella was mystified. But she remembered Deirdre's advice about not killing herself trying to understand them, there was probably nothing to understand.

Holly's Hotel was buzzing with people, most of them having driven from Dublin for dinner. But the Brady family had their rooms, time to stroll in the gardens, have a leisurely bath and then meet in the chintzy little bar for a sherry while looking at the menu.

'I must say, this is a marvellous treat,' her father said over and over.

'You are such a thoughtful girl,' her mother would murmur in agreement.

Ella told them that she loved looking at people in restaurants and imagining stories about them. Like that couple near the window, for example, they were drug pushers back in Dublin, just come for a nice respectable weekend to know what the Other World was like.

'Are they?' Her mother was alarmed.

'Of course not,' Ella said. 'It's only pretend. Look at that group over there – what do you think they are?'

Slowly her parents got drawn into the game. 'The older couple is trying to get the younger ones to go halves in buying a boat,' said Tim Brady.

'The younger couple is telling the older ones that they're bankrupt and asking for a loan,' said Barbara Brady.

'I think it's a group sex thing, they all answered one of Miss Holly's ads for wife-swapping weekends,' Ella suggested.

And they were all laughing at the whole crazy notion of it in this of all places when Ella looked up and saw Don Richardson and his family being ushered from the bar into the dining-room. He looked over and saw them at that moment. It would be frozen for ever in Ella's mind. The Bradys all laughing at one table and Don at the door holding it open for his father-in-law, his sons aged sixteen and fifteen, and his wife Margery who only lunched for charities and otherwise played golf. Margery, who was not large, weather-beaten and distant-looking, but who wore a smart red silk suit and had one of those handbags which cost a fortune. Margery, who was petite, smiled up at her husband in a way that Ella would never be able to do since she was exactly the same height.

Ella's father was very engaged by the menu. Would smoked trout salad be too heavy a starter if he was going to have Guinness, steak and oyster pie?

Ella wondered if she might possibly be going to faint. Was this a sign that since she had refused to go out with him Don had decided to play the rare role of family man? Was this self-delusion of the worst kind? Did he think less of her for being with her parents? Or quite possibly more? Would he acknowledge her in the dining room? Ella ordered absently and chose the wine. It was too late now to ask if they could eat upstairs in the bedroom. She had to face it.

In the dining room they were quite a distance from the Richardson party and it was the two teenage boys and their grandfather who faced them, the couple with the dead marriage had their backs to the Bradys.

Ella's parents were still playing the 'let's imagine' game about people. The two women over there were planning a shoplifting spree, her mother thought, or they were discussing putting their father into an old people's home. Ella's father thought they had hacked into a computer and made a fortune and were wondering how to spend it.

'What do you think, Ella?'

She had been thinking about the body language of Don and Margery Richardson as they sat together easily. They were not stroking each other or hand-holding but they didn't have that stiffness that couples often have when there is a distance. Like her own parents had. Every night except tonight when they seemed to be very relaxed.

'Go on, Ella, what do you think they are?'

She glanced briefly at the two retired women who obviously treated themselves out to a meal and a gossip twice a year.

'Lesbians planning which of them should be inseminated this time,' she said, forgetting she was talking to her parents rather than to Deirdre. To her surprise they thought it was very funny and when Don turned around slightly to look for her as she had known he would, there they were all laughing again. Ella felt a touch of hysteria. She wanted to stand up and scream to the whole restaurant that at best life was just one ludicrous, hypocritical façade. But you'd need to be a brave person to lose control at Miss Holly's. Ella thought that he would say hallo, stop by the table and say something smooth and pleasant. Just be prepared for it and behave accordingly. Nothing glib or too smart.

Her father removed his glasses and seemed pleased to be able to identify at least one of the fellow diners. 'My goodness, that's Ricky Rice, of Rice and Richardson Consultants,' he said.

'Oh, do you know them, Dad?' she asked, her mouth hardly able to form the words.

'No, no, not at all, but we all know of them. Dear Lord, do *they* have clients,' he said, shaking his head with envy.

'How did they get such great business, do you think?' Her mother was peering over at the table.

'Know all the right people apparently,' her father shrugged, his face defeated and sad.

Ella was determined to raise the mood. She asked them about property prices in Tara Road. One house there had sold for a fortune recently.

'Didn't you do well to buy a house there, Dad?' she said.

'We wanted a place with a nice garden for you to grow up,' her mother said. 'And wasn't it marvellous? Still is, of course.'

'But you don't live there any more,' her father said.

'No, Dad, not full-time, but I'll come back and see you as I will always do while you're there, or wherever you are.'

'What do you mean, wherever we are?' Her mother sounded very anxious.

Please, please, may he not look around again now and see them all frowning and anxious. 'I meant, Mam, that some day you'll want to sell Tara Road and buy a smaller place, won't you? Won't you?' She looked from one to the other eagerly.

'We hadn't ever thought . . .' her father began.

'Why should we leave our home?' her mother said.

'You know that guy Danny Lynch who used to live in Tara Road? He says this is the time to sell.'

'Well, he left his wife and children – he's no role model,' her mother said.

'No, but he is an estate agent.'

'Not any longer.' Her father spoke gravely. 'Apparently he and his partner got into a lot of funny business,' he said very disapprovingly.

'And anyone who would cheat on his wife like he did isn't worth listening to on any subject,' Ella's mother said.

There was a movement two tables away. Ella saw him stand up. She knew he was coming over. Make them laugh, she told herself.

It was a tall order. She had about thirty seconds.

'Don't mind me, Deirdre says that I'm obsessed by property. That's another game I play, I pretend houses aren't what they seem to be. Apart from Holly's Hotel here being the wife-swapping centre of Europe, I think Mam's law office is money laundering big time. And wait till I tell you what I think Dad's firm is up to . . .' She stopped just as he arrived at the table. It had worked, they were both looking at her with eager smiles to know what she would say next.

'Hallo, I'm Don Richardson. We met at Frank and Nuala's party this week.'

'Oh, that's right. Don, these are my parents, Tim and Barbara Brady.'

His handshake was so firm, his tone so warm, she felt nothing but gratitude to him. He was being so genuinely pleasant to two strangers. He was not speaking to this couple as a man who was about to seduce their daughter, betray his wife; she saw him as someone who had come to rescue the conversation. She explained it was her father's birthday; he explained that it was a celebration because his son had scored a winning goal in a match. In the few short moments that he stayed he managed to discover the name of, and praise, her father's firm, he even knew of the office where her mother worked when it was mentioned and said they were highly respected lawyers. And then he was gone.

They spoke of him admiringly.

'Very hard-working man. That's why he got where he is. People used to say it was all his father-in-law but the firm was nothing until he got into it,' her father said.

'And very easy with people too,' her mother said.

Ella felt it was very foolish to be as pleased as she was that they liked him. And she felt very pleased indeed at the way he smiled at her as he left the dining-room. She knew he was going to call her again soon. But she hadn't known that he would call her at midnight.

'I hope I didn't wake you,' he said on her mobile phone.

'No. I was reading, there's a kind of window seat here, I was actually looking at the shapes of the bushes and flowers more than reading.'

'Bushes? Flowers? Where are you?' He sounded confused.

'How quickly men forget. I'm in Holly's, we met here about four hours ago.'

'In Holly's?' He sounded very disappointed.

'Don, you know I am. Is this a game?'

'If so, I've lost,' he said.

'Where are *you*?' she asked.

'I'm parked in your road. I was hoping you'd ask me in for coffee.'

'So your son's celebration is over?'

'And your father's continues?'

'That's life, I suppose.' She was smiling now, he was outside her door back in Dublin. He had not gone back to his Killiney home with the wife in red silk. His ties to his home must be very loose, as he had said. He had driven all the way in to Dublin on the off chance of seeing her. He *must* fancy her.

'You could come in for coffee another night. Like tomorrow,' she said.

'Tomorrow's bad for me – a big political fund-raiser – I have to be there glad-handing people.' He sounded regretful.

'Oh, well.' She made herself shrug.

'Monday night?' he offered.

Deirdre had told her not to be too available. 'Bad for me, Tuesday or Wednesday are fine, though.'

'Tuesday then, I suppose, since it can't be earlier. Suppose I brought a bottle of truly lovely wine, would you cook me a steak?'

'It's a deal,' said Ella, who wondered how could any human get through the number of hours between now and Tuesday at eight o'clock.

They had the Full Irish Breakfast, and Miss Holly came to talk to them. 'Nice to meet Don Richardson last night.' Ella's mother wanted to show that they were anyone's equal.

'Ah, yes, wonderful family man, Mr Richardson,' said Miss Holly, nodding in approval. 'You see it all in this business, Mrs Brady, believe me, so many of our so-called business leaders don't have the same standards as they used to, no indeed.'

'Brings his family here a lot then, does he?' said Ella in a strained voice, stabbing at the sausage on her plate as if she wanted desperately to kill it.

'Well, no, he works so hard, you see. Usually it's just his wife and her father and the children, but Mr Richardson always rings and orders them some special wine, and when he can he's with them.'

'That's nice,' said Ella, suddenly feeling a great deal better.

She kissed them goodbye at Tara Road and refused to think about the fact that they might spend a lonely wordless afternoon now that she was no longer there to be the central point of their life. She had done her best to get them to sell this big place. To liberate some money so that they could go on a cruise, get a better car or whatever they might like. She knew that it wouldn't matter where they lived or how much money they had, they were not going to take their future in their own hands and make the best of it. Which was what she, Ella, was going to do. She was going to get involved with this dangerously attractive man, no matter how many turnings there would be in the road ahead. And if she got hurt then she got hurt, that's all there was to it.

Her phone rang. She pulled in to the side of the road but it wasn't what she had hoped. It was Nick, her old mate from college.

'Oh, Nick,' she said.

'Well, I've had warmer receptions,' he said.

'Sorry, I'm coping with traffic,' she lied.

'No, you're not, you fibber, you've pulled in, I'm in the car behind you.'

'Is this a police state or what?' she said and leaped out of the car to give him a hug.

'I saw you ahead of me and I wondered if you'd like a late lunch.'

'Like it? I'd love it, Nick.'

They sat companionably as he told her all about the dramas in his life and she told him nothing about the dramas in hers. Nick was such an easy person to talk to, such a friend. No need to explain anything or wonder about what he was thinking. It was all there on his handsome, freckled face and in his big green eyes. He was wearing a black leather jacket and sunglasses on his head. It would have been so uncomplicated to love someone like this instead of what she had got herself into. She looked at Nick affectionately. He would never know what she was thinking.

When they had last met he had just set up a small independent film production company called Firefly Films with two others and they were doing quite well. Much better than they had hoped. They still did a fair bit of bread and butter work like videos of weddings and advertising things, a lot of word of mouth. That's what it was all about in Dublin today – Nick had been able to point a job to Tom and Cathy who ran a catering company called Scarlet Feather. And apparently it had gone well so now Tom and Cathy in return had got him a job to film and edit a big fund-raising event tonight. Huge money, the guy wanted to pay in cash but, hey, that was okay too.

'Tonight?' Ella's eyes were dancing.

'Yeah, he wants a nice, neat fifteen minutes of the highlights showing as many celebs as possible and literally just the best sound bites, no long tedious speeches ... we could do it in our sleep.'

'Nick, can I come with you? To help. Please.'

'Hey, Ella, you don't want to be involved in any of this kind of business!' Nick was startled.

'Please. I beg you. I'll get you coffee, I'll carry your bags.'

'Why?'

'I just want to, we're friends. You wanted to have lunch with me and I said yes, why can't I say I want to go on this gig with you tonight and you say yes?'

'You'd be bored.'

'Please, Nick.'

'Okay, but you do get to carry my bags, do you hear?'

'I love you, Nick.'

'You love someone certainly; you're as high as a kite,' he said. 'But it's not me.'

She met them outside the hotel later in the evening. She hardly recognised Nick, he was so businesslike and efficient.

'This is Ella. She knows nothing but she's here to help,' he said casually.

Ella grinned. 'I always wanted to be in movies,' she said, joking.

'Well, you picked the wrong team, tonight's only video,' said a small, earnest-looking girl who did not at all like the tall, blonde Ella coming in on the act.

'Look, I promise I won't be in the way.' Ella concentrated on the girl, the two men were no trouble and couldn't have cared less about her. 'Just tell me what to do or to get out of the way and I'll do it.'

'Well, okay, thanks then.' The girl was gruff.

'What's your name?' Ella asked.

'Sandy.'

'Well, Sandy, I mean it, anything I can do?'

'Why are you here?' Sandy was blunt. She fancied Nick greatly and probably in vain. But as far as she was concerned, Ella was a threat.

'Because I'm keen on someone who's going to be here and it was the only way I could get in.' There is never anything as good as total honesty.

Sandy believed her immediately.

'And is he keen on you?'

'Not enough,' Ella answered, and they were friends for life.

She tidied away their gear into corners, got a pot of coffee from the kitchen, asked the office to let them have three photocopies of the seating plan rather than the one they had been given. And was in fact quite useful and helpful until she saw Don Richardson come in with Margery on his arm.

This time she wore dark green silk and what looked very like

31

real emeralds. She knew everyone and they were all kissing her on the cheek. Today was a Sunday yet she looked as if she had come straight from the hairdresser, she must have somebody come to her house. She was like a little porcelain doll. Ella felt tall, ungainly, sweaty, and out of place. From behind a pillar she watched as Don spoke swiftly to Nick telling him what needed to be done, where to position himself. And then she did no more to help anyone in Firefly Films, she stood there twisting a table napkin around in her hands and watching Don Richardson. He had said tonight was bad for him to meet her because he had to do a lot of glad-handing.

She wasn't even sure what the words meant.

Now she knew. It was shaking hands and at the same time gripping the other person's arm firmly above the elbow. It was looking into their eyes and thanking them for their support. It was turning to introduce them to other people with a fixed smile of gratitude. And Don Richardson did it very well.

Ella had no idea how long she stood there while others in the great dining room ate through a five-course meal. But Don didn't sit down either, he moved from table to table, talking here, laughing there, always nodding imperceptibly at Nick if he wanted him to turn the camera on groups. Margery sat at a table and talked easily with politicians and their wives. Margery's eyes never roamed the room looking for him, wondering was he hesitating too long at this table, laughing too animatedly with the two bosomy women who did not want to let him go. Was this because she knew how to play it? Giving him a long lead meant he always came home? Or had he been telling Ella the truth, that they really did lead separate lives?

There was dancing now, but Firefly Films' work was over. Don Richardson hadn't wanted to film any red-faced groping on the dance floor. The party supporters would want to see a video of themselves looking decorous, mixing with the party leader, with cabinet ministers and celebrities. That's what Nick and Ed and Sandy were going back to the office to do now, edit the video and copy it for Don Richardson. It had to be in his office next day by lunchtime. It would mean working all night.

'I don't suppose you're going to come and help us some more back at base, Ella,' Nick said, without any hope.

'I'd love to,' she said guiltily. 'It's just I have school tomorrow morning, you see.'

'Why did I know you were going to say that?' Nick gave her a brotherly pat on the behind.

Sandy wasn't jealous any more. As they packed away the equipment, she whispered to Ella, 'Did you see him?'

'Yes, I saw him.'

'Did he see you?' Still a whisper.

'No, no he didn't.'

'Are you glad or sorry you came?' Sandy had to know. Again total truth is very satisfying.

'A bit of both, to be honest,' Ella Brady said, and slipped out the back way before she might see Don Richardson hold out his hand and ask his tiny, emerald-wearing, estranged wife to dance.

She got a taxi home and stayed awake until 5 a.m. After two hours she woke groggy and bad-tempered. And when she got to her class, she didn't feel any better. 'If you know what's good for all of us, you lot must be no trouble today,' she warned the Fifth Years, who were inclined to be difficult.

'Was it a heavy night, Miss Brady?' asked Jacinta O'Brien, one of the more fearless troublemakers.

Ella strode so purposefully towards the girl's desk that the class gasped.

Miss Brady couldn't be about to hit a pupil, surely? But that's what it looked like. Ella stood, her face inches from the child's. 'There's always one in every class, Jacinta, one smart-arse who goes too far and ruins it for everyone. In this class you are the one. I was going to treat you like adults, tell you the truth – which is that I didn't sleep and don't feel too well. I was going to ask for your co-operation so that I could give you as good a lesson as possible.

'But no, there's always the smart-arse, so instead we will have a test. Get out your papers this minute.'

Ella gave them four questions, and then she sat there trembling at her outburst. She had said smart-arse. Twice.

This wasn't the kind of school where you said that.

She had meant to say smart aleck. Oh, God, why couldn't it be Tuesday? Then she could see Don Richardson that night.

But she got through the day and was relieved to get home.

'I understand you've started stalking him now,' Deirdre said on the phone that night.

'How did you hear that?' Ella gasped.

33

'It was in one of the gossip columns. I can't remember which,' Deirdre said. As usual Ella fell for it.

'What?'

'Oh, shut up, Ella, you eejit. I met Nick. He told me you wanted to crash Don's big fund-raiser with him.'

Ella began to breathe again.

'Some capital city this is, you can't do anything,' she grumbled.

'Well, you haven't *done* anything, have you?' Deirdre reminded her.

'No. Tomorrow night,' Ella said. 'It would have been tonight, but I remembered what you said about not being too available.'

'Can we meet lunchtime Wednesday?' asked Deirdre.

'No, that's my short lunch ... it will have to wait till after work.'

'Early Bird Quentins? My treat?' Deirdre offered.

'Early Bird starts at six-thirty. I'll be there,' Ella promised.

There was an old clock on a church tower near Ella's flat. It was just striking eight when he knocked on the door. 'I'm boringly punctual,' he said. He carried a briefcase, an orchid and a bottle of wine.

'I'm just delighted to see you,' Ella said simply. There was something about the way she said it that made him put down everything on the table and take her in his arms.

'Ella, Angel Ella, I'm never going to hurt you or be bad for you in any way.'

There was a catch in his voice as he spoke into her hair. 'Nothing bad is ever going to happen to you, believe me.'

And as she looked at him before she kissed him properly, Ella knew this was true.

They put the orchid in a long narrow vase, and got about the business of preparing dinner. He sliced the mushrooms, she made the salad. They had a glass of cold white wine from her fridge. And he opened the bottle of red he had brought before they sat down in the most normal and natural way, as if this was where they had always lived. She didn't ask him would he stay the whole night because she knew he would. They talked easily. He said he had enjoyed meeting her parents.

'They liked meeting you, too, but I expect everyone does,' Ella said.

34

'Does that mean you think I'm putting on some kind of an act?' he asked, hurt.

'No, I don't think it does, you do like people, and you make them feel as if there's no one else in the room. It's just the way you are ... even now.'

He looked round her flat. 'Come on, there is no one else in the room!' he said, laughing.

'No, it's a way you have, I expect you were great at the fund-raiser thing on Sunday.' Her eyes were bright.

'I don't know,' Don Richardson said thoughtfully. 'People had been generous, I was just thanking them, making them feel that they weren't being taken for granted, that the Party appreciated them. It wasn't meant to be all smarmy, just gratitude.'

'Glad-handing,' she said, remembering his words.

'Yes, I was sending myself up when I said that, it's just that I would have preferred to be with you.'

'You were very good at it, I saw you,' Ella said suddenly. She didn't know why she had made this admission. Possibly because she wanted no lies, no pretending. To her amazement he just nodded at her.

'Yes, I saw you, too,' he said.

She felt her face redden with shame. He had actually spotted her stalking him as Deirdre described it.

'Nick, the guy who did the video, he's a mate of mine. He wanted some help.'

'Sure.'

'Actually he didn't want any help, I just asked if I could come along too.'

'Did you, Ella? Why?' His hand rested on top of hers, lightly.

'I just wanted to see you, Don, I was very sorry too that we weren't meeting that night, to go to the do was the next best thing.'

He stood up and held her face in his hands and kissed her. 'I didn't dare to believe that might be true, Ella. I've thought about it over and over since then and prayed it was true.'

'And would you ever have said that you'd seen me?'

'No, it was your business that you were there, I'd never interrogate you. Never.'

'You were very good, Don, you were tireless.'

'No, I was very tired, I drove past this house on the way back to my flat, I saw your lights on and realised you were home . . . but . . .'

'But what?' she asked.

'But our date was for tonight. I didn't want to look foolish and over-eager.'

Her eyes had tears in them as she led him away from the table and to the bedroom. And it was everything that it had never been before, with Nick or with the sporting hero or the two one-night stands. Ella lay in his arms long after Don had gone to sleep. She was the luckiest woman in the world.

Next morning, she just offered him coffee and orange juice, and didn't fuss about breakfast. He seemed to like the lack of fuss. Possibly Margery and the boys made too much noise and crowded him out. Ella would never be like that.

She picked up a package of papers to take to school.

'What are they?' he asked, interested.

'Oh, I gave the Fifth Years a test yesterday. The good side of that is you have forty minutes' peace while they do it, the bad side is you have to mark thirty-three extra papers.'

He kissed her on the nose.

'I know nothing of your life, Ella Brady,' he said.

'Probably better to keep it that way, in case you keel over and die of boredom,' she said.

'You couldn't bore me.' He sounded very serious. 'May I come back tonight, a bit late-ish?'

'I'd love that,' Ella said. She had been forcing herself not to ask when they would meet again.

'I'm not tying up your evening on you?' He was solicitous.

'No, I'm meeting Deirdre for an early supper at Quentins. I'll be back by nine. Does that suit?'

'I'll be here around ten, I'll have eaten a very dull and sober dinner . . . a financial committee. I have to take notes and be alert so maybe I could drink a glass of wine or two with you?'

She gave a little shiver. Don Richardson who had homes in Killiney, in the Financial Centre and in Spain, was going to stay in her little flat two nights running. Last night in bed he had told her he loved her. It looked as if he meant it.

Ella managed to get through the day, and when she arrived at Quentins, Deirdre was waiting.

'Are you going to tell me everything?' Deirdre demanded before Ella said hallo.

'Not as much as you'll want to know, but I'll tell you a fair bit.'

'Tell me the main thing, the only thing, is he coming back for more?' Deirdre asked.

'He's going to stay the night tonight as well, yes.'

'He stayed the whole *night*. Oh my God!' cried Deirdre in such a loud voice that everyone in the restaurant looked over at their table.

'Thanks, Dee,' hissed Ella. 'Why didn't you ask for a microphone, then even the faraway tables could have heard you.'

'No worries.' They were consoled by Mon, the young waitress whom they both knew and liked. She had told them in the past about her unerring bad taste in men back in Australia, and how she had lost her heart and all her savings to a fellow in Italy. Deirdre and Ella had been sympathetic and said that it was pretty much a global problem. Men were the cause of most of the unrest and unease on the planet.

Mon had recently found a new love, she had confided. He was older and wiser and trustworthy. His name was Mr Harris.

Had he a first name? they wondered. He had, apparently, but Mon liked to think of him as Mr Harris at the moment.

'I hope your Mr Harris isn't here to be shocked by my loudmouth friend Dee,' Ella said in a low voice.

'No, he's not, and he wouldn't be shocked, but tell me, did that guy with the gorgeous smile and the dark blue eyes really stay the whole night?' Mon whispered.

'Dee, I will stab you very hard with something,' Ella said.

'No, don't stab her. No one heard except me and, anyway, the others are all tourists. It doesn't matter if they did,' said Mon cheerfully.

Don stayed that night and the next. On Friday morning he said he was going to Spain for a few days.

'I wish I didn't have to.'

'Enjoy it,' Ella managed to say. She didn't ask if it were business or family. She didn't want to know. But he told her.

'I look after a lot of property interests out there. I need to go out at least once a month, not a hardship posting, I agree. Sometimes the boys come if it's half-term or when they can get a day or two off school. But not this time. Still, I'll be back next

Wednesday and maybe we can go out for a meal. I don't want you getting tired of cooking for me.'

'I enjoy it, Don, truly I do, and perhaps, you know, it's wiser not to be out in public in the circumstances.'

He looked surprised. 'Honestly Angel, I told you there's no problem, it's separate lives.' He said it so often it had to be true.

But the next day some torment made her call the Richardson home in Killiney and ask to speak to Mrs Margery Richardson. She was prepared to hang up when the woman came to the phone.

'I'm afraid she's not here,' said the housekeeper. 'She's gone to Spain. She'll be back on Wednesday.'

'Nick? It's Deirdre.'

'Oh, I know, Deirdre. You want to join Firefly Films,' he said.

'No, I don't, but I'm worried about Ella.'

'Join the club.'

'No, seriously. She's not herself, Nick.'

'When are any of us ourselves?'

'Stop being flippant, it's not funny. This guy Don Richardson, where is he at the moment?'

'He's gone to Spain. He ordered another dozen videos, to be ready when he gets back. Main thing, he seemed pleased with them.'

'That's not the main thing, Nick, the main thing is ... Ella is miserable. Did he say it was business or going with the family?'

'How would I know? And what difference does it make?'

'So why is Ms Brady throwing herself off O'Connell Bridge?'

'No!' Nick cried.

'It's a figure of speech, she just won't be consoled.'

'Oh Jesus, this love business is terrible,' Nick said sympathetically.

'Tell me about it, Nick! I'm so glad I never bought into it myself,' said Deirdre.

'It's wonderful that Ella came to us for a whole long weekend,' Tim Brady said. 'Imagine, she's going to stay here until Tuesday.'

'Yes,' said his wife.

'Aren't you pleased, Barbara?'

'I'd be much more pleased if she hadn't asked us to say she isn't here and we have no idea where she is,' Ella's mother said.

'She says she wants to cut herself off a bit from the world, have a rest.' Her father believed the story.

'Yes, but some man has rung four times. He says her mobile is turned off, he's getting anxious and annoyed.'

'Trust Ella, it may just be some fellow she doesn't want to encourage. Does he say who he is?'

'No, and I don't ask him,' Barbara Brady said.

On Sunday the man on the phone did say who he was. 'Mrs Brady, it's Don Richardson here, we had the pleasure of meeting briefly in Holly's Hotel last week . . . I am most anxious to talk to Ella. I wonder if you could ask her to call me? I can give you the number.'

'Oh, yes, of course, Mr Richardson, I remember. Nice to talk to you again.'

'Yes, so if she's there . . . I wonder . . .'

'No, unfortunately she's not at home.' Barbara Brady hated telling lies. She knew she wasn't very good at it either.

'But she will be back sometime, won't she? I mean, you will see her, won't you?'

'Oh, yes, of course,' Barbara Brady said too quickly.

He dictated his telephone number and thanked her.

'Ella?' Barbara Brady knocked on her daughter's bedroom door. 'May I come in?'

'Sure, Mam.'

Ella sat hugging a cushion and rocking to and fro. She was red-eyed, but not actually crying.

'Don Richardson called again.' Her mother's voice was clipped. 'This time he left his name and number. He said that he was in Spain and I told him that I would give you the message and the number.'

'Thanks, Mam.'

'And are you having any supper?'

'No, Mam.'

'Or any plans to tell your father and myself what's going on?'

'None at all, Mam.'

'I'll leave you to your thoughts then.'

'I love you, Mam.'

'Three easiest words to say in the whole world, "I love you".'

'But I do!' Ella was stung.

'We will be downstairs when you love us enough to join us,' her mother said with her mouth in a very hard line.

'I don't suppose she could be involved with this Don Richard-son?' Barbara said to her husband in a low, frightened voice.

Ella's father was shocked. 'He's a married man, Barbara, married to Ricky Rice's daughter.'

'Of course, she couldn't be so foolish.'

Ella had come to the top of the stairs and heard this. She went back to her room and stared ahead of her for a long time. It was inconvenient keeping her mobile phone turned off but she didn't want to get any messages from him, and she kept the phone in her flat off the hook, too. She had forgotten about the school. There were two dozen red roses for her there on Monday.

'Stop hiding, I love you,' was the message.

Everyone in the staffroom had read it before she did. Their eyes were on her as she looked at the card.

'Oh, I never knew the Fifth Years cared so much,' she said with a laugh.

As she left the room Ella heard them talking about her. 'They must have cost a fortune, seventy to eighty euros,' said one. 'Bet he's married, otherwise he'd have put his name on the card,' said another.

Ella gritted her teeth and got down to work. She wouldn't have to think about him until Wednesday night. If he showed up.

He knocked at her door at 8 p.m. on Wednesday. He had no flowers, no wine.

'Hallo Don.'

'What's all this about?'

'I don't understand,' she said.

'Neither do I. I said goodbye to you here on Friday morning, I told you I loved you, you told me you loved me. Then I went to Spain on business and suddenly you won't take my calls and get your mother to lie for you. What's going on, Ella?'

'I don't know. What *is* going on?' she said.

'You tell me. I've been straight up all the way, you're the one playing games.' He looked very angry.

They were still on the doorstep.

'You have not been straight. You didn't tell me you were taking your wife to Spain.' Ella let the words tumble out.

'I took "my wife", as you call her, nowhere!' he shouted.

'Your wife is what she is,' Ella cried.

'I don't care. I will go the distance here on the doorstep, but on mature reflection, as they say, you may prefer to do it indoors,' he said.

Wearily she opened the door.

He marched into her sitting room as if he owned it and sat down. 'Okay Ella, tell me,' he began.

'No, you tell me. You said you were going to Spain on business and then I hear that you took your wife.'

'And how do you hear this, Ella?'

'It's not important, you did take her.'

'I did not take her, she decided to come at the same time, she owns half the house.'

'But you didn't tell me that she was going.'

'I didn't bloody know until she said she was going and anyway, it's not important. I don't have to tell you, you agreed to accept that we lived separate lives. You told me you agreed, that you believed that.' He looked bewildered and upset.

'Huh,' she said.

'What does that mean?'

'I don't know,' Ella said truthfully.

'You said it, so you must know. What do you mean? What are you asking me?'

There was a silence.

'What do you want to know?' he asked again.

Another silence and then she spoke. 'Did you sleep with her? Do you still have sex with her?' Ella's voice was low.

Don Richardson stood up. His face was working, she had never seen him so upset. 'I'm sorry, Ella, I'm really sorry. I thought I had made it all clear, I really thought I had come and told you the whole situation outside your school that day.'

'Yes, but . . .' she began.

'And I thought you said that you understood.'

'I thought I did but . . .'

'But you don't understand at all, you actually think that I could love you and have sex with Margery, you really do think that, don't you?'

'I think it's possible, yes.'

'Then you and I, we haven't much more to talk about, Ella, my angel, have we?' he said sadly.

'Do you?' she asked.

'Do I what?'

'Do you have sex with her?'

41

'Goodbye, Ella,' he said, moving towards the door.

'So it's yes,' she said in a heavy tone.

'It's no actually, but it doesn't matter. I won't stay where there's such suspicion. Someone must have hurt you very badly somewhere along the line to make you feel hurt and anxious like this.'

'Bullshit, Don Richardson, nobody hurt me before, nobody touched me before, I never loved anyone before. There's no mythical villain. You tell me it's a business trip and then I hear your wife is with you, what's so abnormal about being upset? Don't make me into some kind of freak.'

'And how exactly did you hear, might I ask?' His voice was ice cold.

It was the end. Ella knew it. 'Not that it matters, but I called your house, and I was told that the lady of the manor was in Spain.' Another silence.

'Thanks, Ella, thanks for everything, thanks for coming to spy at the fund-raiser, thanks for calling to check on my family's movements, thanks for jumping to conclusions, and most of all thanks for not believing me when I say I love you. I'm sorry – but then what exactly am I sorry for?'

She looked at him in horror as he stood there saying goodbye.

'Why should I apologise for being utterly honest from the start, telling you the score, telling you the truth, coming to meet your parents, calling them to say I was worried that you didn't answer your phone. Are these the actions of some kind of shit? No, I think they're what a man who loves you might do.

'But you know better. You have some different standard. I truly hope you find what you're looking for. You are a lovely girl, Ella. An angel in fact, and I'll always wish you well.'

He was nearly at the gate when she caught him, held his arm and pleaded with him to come back. People walking their dogs on the leafy road saw the blonde girl in floods of tears pleading with the tall handsome man.

'I'm sorry. Forgive me. I want just one more chance. I'm such a fool, Don, it's only because I love you so desperately. I'm just afraid to believe you love me. Come back, please, please.'

And if they had continued looking they would have seen the man leading her back into the lighted hall with his arm around her.

'Does all this mean he'll be moving into your place now?' Deirdre asked some days later.

'Of course not, don't be silly,' Ella said.

'Why is it so silly? It would save the rent on the place in the Financial Services area.'

'But he has to say he's somewhere. He can't say he's here,' Ella said as if it were totally obvious.

'No, of course not,' Deirdre said, confused.

'Why can't he say he's shacked up with Ella if it's a dead marriage?' Deirdre asked Nick later.

'Don't ask,' Nick said. 'I've found it much easier not to bring up cosmic questions like that.'

Chapter Three

The pattern of their life began then, at least three and sometimes five nights a week together. Ella saw no other friends in the evening because she was never sure whether Don might suddenly be free.

There were lunches, of course. Deirdre would voice the questions that Ella never spoke aloud. 'Is he going to leave her for you? He's practically living with you, for God's sake.'

'He can't leave, because of his father-in-law. I told you that.'

'Ricky Rice lives in the modern world. He's heard of divorce, he knows Don isn't in the family nest every night.'

'Why rock the boat? We're fine as we are.'

'And your parents, what do they think?'

'They're fine with it,' Ella shrugged.

'No, Ella, they are not. Nobody's fine with their little girl being the plaything of a tycoon.'

Ella pealed with laughter. 'I don't know why I have you as a friend. You try to unsettle me and you use ludicrous phrases. "Plaything." "Tycoon." For heaven's sake! You're so old-fashioned, so utterly disapproving.'

Deirdre took a sip of wine, and spoke in a rare serious moment. 'Actually, no, I'm not. I'm envious if you must know. I'd really love to be as absorbed and obsessed as you are.'

Ella said nothing for a moment. It wasn't like Deirdre to be so utterly honest. It demanded a similar honesty in response. 'Well, okay, if you must know, it's not at all fine with my parents.'

44

'How could it be?' Deirdre was sympathetic.

'Well, it could be if they allowed themselves to move into this century, Dee, if they just looked at the calendar and checked that it's not nineteen twenty-something.'

'They're no worse than anyone else of their generation.'

'Oh, but they are, even at school they don't go on that way.'

'Well, you can hardly tell the nuns you have a lover that lives in half the week.'

'There are hardly any nuns left, only a few old ones doing the accounts or the garden or something.'

'But isn't it called a convent?' Deirdre protested.

'Oh, they're all called convents, but that's not the point. Some of the staff are ancient, but they don't go round frowning and fretting.'

'Do they know, though?' Deirdre persisted.

'They don't *not* know. They don't ask, they don't mutter and have suspicions.'

'Well, they aren't your parents.'

'But they're in this century. It's all changed. You know when we were at school they used to say "Ask your mummy and daddy this" or "Tell your mothers and fathers that"? We don't say that any more. It's just not relevant. You can't assume that everyone has one daddy and one mummy at home.'

'So what *do* you say?' Deirdre was interested.

'We say: "Ask them at home." Can they have a dictionary, an atlas, sheets of graph paper. Whatever. Even the geriatric teachers accept that it's not magic happy families for everyone these days.'

'Still, you can't blame people for wanting the best for a daughter,' Deirdre said. She was worried about her friend.

'If I had a daughter, I'd want her to be happy, not respectable. That's the best anyone can have, to be happy, isn't it?'

When there was no reply, Ella spoke again. 'Deirdre! It's what you just said a minute ago! You said you envied me because I was so happy.'

'I said obsessed,' Deirdre said.

'Same thing,' said Ella.

Don brought some clothes and arranged them neatly in Ella's wardrobe. He used Ella's washing machine and ironed his own shirts. Sometimes he ironed her things for her too. Ella's father wouldn't have done that in a million years. 'Why not? I'm at the ironing board anyway,' he would say with a grin that melted her heart.

Every two weeks or so she invited her parents for a meal in her flat, always on a night when she knew he would be busy elsewhere. She didn't even have to ask him to move his clothes from her wardrobe and his electric razor from her bathroom shelf. He just put everything into a suitcase and covered it neatly with a rug. It was never mentioned, even when he was unpacking the case, when he would return late that night after her parents had left.

He always sounded interested in them and what Ella had to report. He remembered everything she told him. Even small, unimportant details. That her father liked seedless grapes because he was afraid of appendicitis. Don would buy some when her parents were expected. He remembered that her mother liked a particular perfume and he bought it in the airport in time for her mother's birthday.

'I'd like to meet them socially, you know,' he had said more than once.

'I know, Don, and they'd love you, but it's easier this way,' she would say.

'Is it all easy and happy for you, Angel?' he asked.

It was happy, yes, but easy, no. They asked too many questions.

'Ella, your father and I wouldn't dream of interfering in your personal life.'

'I know you wouldn't, either of you. What about more Greek salad?'

'But we do wonder: do you have enough friends and go out? I mean, if you are going to live in this kind of monastic seclusion here in this flat ... then why don't you live at home and save the rent?'

'What your mother is saying, Ella, is that we'd love you to have a home of your own.'

'And I do, Dad, and we're in it, having supper,' she said, eyes too bright.

'Your father and I were just hoping ...'

'Oh, we all live in great hope. Look, I'll clear this away. I have a lovely cheese and grapes. No seeds, Dad. No pips.'

It was getting harder and harder. She wished they could just meet Don. Socially. Without any statement being made.

It happened on a Sunday not long after that. Don was to go out to Killiney for the day. Margery's father had taken his grandsons out shooting. They had some pheasant and they were going to cook them.

'Savage kind of thing to do, going out killing small birds for fun,' Ella had commented.

'I agree with you. I never go shooting, as you may have noticed.' He held his hands up in surrender.

'You haven't time,' she laughed at him.

'Even if I had. Anyway, they say they're shooting them for food, and they are eating them,' he said as an excuse.

'Okay, peace, peace. I don't suppose that the chicken that ends up in the *coq au vin* for Sunday lunch enjoyed it all that much, either. Will you be late? I only ask because I was going to take my parents for an Irish coffee in that new hotel in town, in case you think I'd abandoned you.'

'Great idea. They'd like that,' he said. 'No, I won't be late as it happens, and I'm too arrogant to think you'd abandon me.'

In the new hotel she was pointing out some of the features to her parents, the paintings of politicians on the walls, the very expensive carpeted area which had been closed off from the public by a silk rope, when she saw Don. He had come in from Killiney by himself. He was looking for her, he was going to engineer a social meeting with her parents. She sat back and let it happen.

'We did meet in Holly's, didn't we? How are you both?' He looked from one to the other with pleasure. 'And Ella, great to see you again.'

She smiled and let him carry the conversation. Had they ordered? No? Good, then let him get them something. What about an Irish coffee?

Her parents looked at each other in amazement. That's exactly what they were going to have. How had he guessed?

Ella wondered what would happen if she said he had guessed because she had told him about it in bed that very morning. Nothing good would happen, so she didn't. She watched him move the conversation from himself to getting her parents to talk. He was alert and attentive to everything they said.

Ella watched him objectively. She let her mind wander. It was not an act, he did like these people just as he had liked the people at the fund-raising dinner, just as he liked the people in Holly's Hotel, at Quentins, and presumably everywhere. It was a wonderful gift and he used it well.

She tuned in again as he was talking to her father.

'I agree with you entirely. You can't ask people to buy stock that you would not buy yourself. That way you lose your integrity.'

'But, Mr Richardson, you wouldn't believe how greedy and impatient young people are these days. The old, safe options aren't good enough ... they want something fast, something now, and I have a terrible time urging a bit of caution.' His face looked sad and complaining, as it often did of late.

Ella heard Don speak in a slightly lowered voice. 'It's the same for all of us, Mr Brady. They all want the new car, the boat, the second home ...'

'Ah, but it's different for you over there in Rice and Richardson. You have high fliers going in to you, people who already have money.'

'Not so. We get all sorts of people who hear that we're good. It's a lot of pressure to be good every week. You're talking to someone who knows about it.'

Don Richardson was making himself the equal of her timid father.

'I think that every Monday morning,' Ella's father said sadly.

'Well, speaking about tomorrow, let me share something with you that I'm going to do myself first thing in the office ...'

Their voices were really low now. Ella heard mention of a building firm which just might be going to get a huge contract. It would be the nearest thing to a safe bet that they could offer to their demanding high fliers. 'If it's only a might ...?' Ella heard her father say fearfully.

'I wouldn't steer you wrong.' His warm voice was so strong and reassuring. Don wouldn't steer anyone wrong or lie to them. It wasn't in his nature. Please, may Dad be strong enough to take his advice. If Don said these builders were going to get the contract, then he knew they were. Don knew everything.

Naturally, the builders got the contract. And, amazingly, her father had actually passed on the tip and he was much more highly

48

regarded in his company than before. Her father told her happily that it had been a real act of kindness of that man to give him the word. And Ella forced herself not to sound too pleased.

Her mother said that the partners in the law firm where she worked couldn't believe that Rice and Richardson had recommended them to do some work. Nothing complicated, just run-of-the-mill testamentary and probate work, but it had done her no end of good. People used to think that it was almost time for her to retire, but not any more. Ella said it was only her mother's due.

Nick told Ella that Don Richardson must have a filing system in his head. At least twice a week they got a call from someone saying that Don had given them the name of Firefly Films. It was like a seal of approval.

And finally, the last citadel fell, and Deirdre said she liked him. 'You don't have to tell me this, Dee. I'll survive even if you don't,' Ella said with a laugh.

But no, Deirdre wanted to make her position clear. She had been in a trendy nightclub and Don had come up to her. 'Very far from all your domestic fronts tonight,' Dee had said to him.

'I know you disapprove of me, Deirdre, and in many ways I respect you for looking out for a friend. All I can say is that I love her, but I wouldn't be helping anyone or anything by leaving Margery and the boys now. Ella knows everything there is to be known.'

Deirdre looked almost embarrassed. 'I believed him, Ella. I bloody believed him. I even believed him when he told me he was entertaining people from Spain and they had insisted on coming to the nightclub. He does love you. You do have everything.'

'Not everything, Dee. Not the home and the babies,' Ella said.

'Don't worry about it. Women can have babies at sixty these days,' Deirdre had said cheerfully. 'You have over thirty years before you need to start getting broody.'

As the months went by, Ella felt she had known no other life. Soon those boys would grow up and they could think again seriously. But now? It was all fine, so why upset what was working well?

Don's part of the study was as tidy as he was. He used a mobile phone and got in the habit of moving out into the hall when he answered a call. The reception was better and he didn't interrupt the television or the music that they listened to. He had a few books on the wall shelves, and business magazines in the rack, but everything else was in a small laptop.

'Suppose you lost it?' she teased him once. 'Suppose we had burglars, or it was snatched from you in the street?'

'Backup,' he said simply. 'House rule: we all copy every single thing from that day's transaction on to a disk every evening.'

'And what do you do with the disks?' She was interested. 'Surely you could lose a disk just as easily?'

'What have we here, Ella? An investigation, a tribunal?' He laughed, but his eyes weren't smiling.

Ella was annoyed with him and showed it. 'Sorry, Don. Didn't know the little woman wasn't allowed to be interested. Forget it. Forget I even spoke.'

'Hey, Ella angel, you're being a little bit heavy,' he began.

'No, I'm not. If you asked me a question about school, I'd think you were interested and I'd answer you. I wouldn't accuse you of being part of a Department of Education hit squad.'

'I apologise.'

'No need to. Message received. Don't ask Don about his work. Okay, I'll remember.'

'You're very hurt,' he said.

'No, just a bit pissed off. I'll get over it.'

'Come here, please ... I beg you.' His eyes were pleading.

'What?'

He opened his little computer. The one that fitted in his briefcase. 'First my password. I want you to know that.' His face was very serious.

'Don, this is silly.'

'My password is "Angel". It has been since I met you.' He typed it in and the program sprang to life. 'Please, Ella, look at the headings. My life is your life. You are welcome to look at any of these at any time.'

'That wasn't what I wanted ... you were short with me, that's all.'

'See, here's Killiney, all the details about bills and expenses are there. Here's the boys' school fees and trust funds under their names, James and Gerald ... and here's travel, and here's Ella.'

'You have a file on me?' Her voice was a whisper.

'Angel, of course I have.' He pointed to a file called 'Brady'.

She was in tears now, but he took no notice. He was determined to explain everything, show her how open he was being with her.

'These are the day-by-day transactions in these files. These are the ones we put on disk, and since you wanted to know what we do with the disks, we post them back to the office. We all have little ready-stamped envelopes. Now, Ella, you know the password, anything you want to know is there, but don't ever tell me again that I am secretive. That's the last thing I am.'

'How can I tell you how sorry I am?' she asked through tears.

He stroked her hair. 'Angel Ella, I'm the one to be sorry if I sounded sharp to you. I get people asking me questions day and night. It's such a relief to be with you, you don't.' His face was full of remorse.

'I'm such an eejit,' she sniffed.

'I love you, Ella.'

'I know,' she said. 'I don't deserve you.'

'Your father wouldn't dream of asking you, but then you know me. I'm such a busybody, Ella. It's just that we wondered, do you see a lot of that Don Richardson?' Barbara Brady's voice trailed away with the enormity of her intrusion into her daughter's life.

'Oh, I run into him a lot around the place, yes. Any problem with that?' Ella looked a long, clear look at her mother.

'No, no, none at all. It's just that he is married, and all that sort of thing.'

'What sort of thing exactly?'

'Well, married, I suppose, and with children. Two sons, I heard.'

'Ah, that's nice for him then.'

'Ella, you know we want the best for you.'

'As I do for you and for Dad, too.' Ella's smile was radiant.

'Will you come to Spain at half-term?' Don asked her.

'I'd love to, but won't it be ... difficult?'

'No, not remotely. I'd love to show you the coast.'

'I'd love to see it. I pay for my own ticket, though.'

'That's silly, Angel. I have a ticket for you.'

'Leave me my pride and dignity. Won't I be staying in your house? Isn't that enough?'

'Well, no, I thought we'd stay in a hotel. Easier.'

'Sure.' But Ella was quiet.

'I chose it for you in case you were uneasy about staying in what is in many ways a family house.'

'No, I mean it, sure, that's very sensitive of you, but I have my own money, Don. I'd prefer to pay for the ticket.'

'Fine, Angel,' he said.

'How many days?'

'You said you had six days. I booked for that.' He smiled at her.

'God, I love you, Don Richardson,' she said.

The airport was crowded with families, couples, lovers, groups of girls on package tours. None of them were remotely as happy as Ella. She had six days here. Like a honeymoon.

She almost hugged herself at the airport as they came out among the other passengers into the sunshine towards all the hoteliers and travel agents waving banners and shouting out names.

Don had booked a car in advance.

'Sit here, Angel. I'll go and do the boring bit,' he urged. So Ella sat minding their cases and Don's briefcase. She admired him as he walked relaxed and easy to the car desk, his jacket over his arm.

She thought she saw him paying in cash. He seemed to have a fistful of notes. But that was unlikely. Maybe he was just changing money. He was coming back to her, smiling.

'Enjoy your vacation, Señor Brady,' the man at the car desk called to him.

'I put your name on the rented car too. He obviously knows who is the important one here,' Don said with his arm around Ella's shoulder.

She was childishly pleased. 'I've never driven on the wrong side of the road,' she began.

'A bright girl like you, of course you can do it,' he teased.

'It's very good of you, Don.'

'Not a bit of it. Anyway, nice for you to have the car if I have to do a little work. Come on now, let's go find it and we'll toss a coin for who drives.'

'I think we've tossed it and you won,' she said, laughing and taking him by the arm.

It was a very luxurious hotel. They had a huge balcony, where room service delivered their meal, lit candles for them, and gave Ella a great big white orchid, which she put in her hair. 'I'm so happy here,' she said.

'Tomorrow I have to trek off and meet people, do things, set up things. Will you be all right on your own?'

'Of course I will. I'll just lie out here and read. And get sun-tanned. And maybe trip up and down to the pool.'

'Good girl. I'll be back by seven at the latest.' He smiled lazily at her over his Spanish brandy.

'Will you take the car?' she asked innocently.

She saw his eyes narrow momentarily. 'I might, Angel, I might not. I'll see, okay?'

'Sure. I didn't want you to tire yourself out, that's all.'

He relaxed.

Next morning she watched from the balcony as he went off on his list of meetings. A woman picked him up in the forecourt of the hotel. A woman who looked very like his wife Margery.

The day seemed endless. There were just so many times you could swim up and down a pool. The thriller she had bought at Dublin airport didn't hold her attention. She wasn't hungry enough for the hotel buffet.

She took a taxi into town to the harbour and had a glass of wine, some cheese and olives as she looked at the boats bobbing up and down and the tourists walking up and down. She would not ask him. It could have been anyone. She would not call Margery Richardson's house back in Killiney. What would it prove if she were not there? Either you trusted someone or you did not. It was as simple as that. And she must have been mistaken, he would have told her if Margery were in Spain. But suppose just for a moment that Margery were here. After all, she was still involved in her father's business. She had a right to be here. The marriage was over. How often had he told her this? He had taken her on this magical holiday because he loved her and wanted to be with her ... Wouldn't Ella be very silly to make a big scene about it? However much it cost her, she would say nothing.

It was very hard not to ask innocent questions that could sound like an interrogation. So when he returned in time for a swim in the sunset, Ella asked nothing. He was very loving. She had been insane to imagine that he had met up with his ex-wife or estranged wife or whatever she was. Nobody who loved her the way Don did, so passionately, could have spent the day with another woman. Then he said he had to do a bit of work, check that he had all the notes of today's work in his computer, and make the backup disk. She sat and watched him dreamily.

'Order up some supper, Angel. I'll be through in half an hour,' he said.

She ordered asparagus and a plate of grilled prawns to follow.

'Was it a tiring day?' she asked.

She had considered the remark for a long time. There was surely no way he could take offence at that.

He looked at her and took her hand. 'It was, Angel, very tiring. People are very greedy, you know. A lot of my clients want the sun, moon and stars, and then some more. They think they own me.'

'You don't need them that badly, do you?'

'We do, really, Angel. Ricky always says that they are the most demanding, the ex-pats, they have nothing to do all day except play golf, swim and read their portfolios.'

'Why can't they come back to Dublin to see you?' she asked innocently.

'Why do you think?' His face was hard.

She realised that a lot of them were tax exiles; some of them might have even more pressing need to stay away.

'Sorry,' she said.

He got up and went over to kneel beside her. 'No, I'm the one that's sorry. One of these guys just insists I spend a couple of nights in his *hacienda*, as he calls it . . . He won't let me stay all alone in a hotel.'

'No!' She was shocked.

'Yes, I'm afraid I have to. What do I tell Ricky? That I won't go out to a huge place with two swimming pools, billiard room, and the works . . .'

'He can't eat into your private time, Don . . .'

'He doesn't see it as private time. Please don't make a scene, Ella. I'm so upset myself already, I couldn't bear it if you . . .'

'No, of course I won't.'

'Thank you.' He kissed her on the forehead. Then she saw him moving towards the big carved chest of drawers.

'Not tonight, Don?'

'He insists. I'm so very sorry. You know how little I want it. This was meant to be our time.' He said it with his hands spread out in mystification.

She must be very careful not to upset him, but she was so annoyed she could barely speak. Imagine her sitting here like a fool in a big posh hotel, while Don played billiards and swam with some tax dodger, or worse. To please his father-in-law.

'Don't be silent on me, Angel.'

'No, of course not. Let's get you packed. The sooner you're gone the sooner you're back.'

He looked very relieved. A row averted.

She watched him pack. Don Richardson, the fastidious man who was going away for three days, took one shirt, one change of underwear. And his laptop computer.

She told him she would be just fine and that she would dress up and cruise the swimming pool and find a new companion. She would have forgotten his name when he got back.

'Don't forget me, Angel. I am the great love of your life. As you are of mine. One of the reasons I'm doing all this nonsense is so that we can be free to spend long years together, in places like this where I can throw the laptop out into the sea and we never have to go and be nice to boring old clients who are semi-crooks. Do you believe me?'

Ella did. Why else would he have taken her out to Spain if he didn't love her?

It was a long two and a half days, but she kept busy. She went on a bus tour of the area. They passed a cluster of very wealthy homes.

'They all have two swimming pools and billiard rooms and mountain views from one side and sea views from the other,' the guide said proudly. 'Mainly English and Irish people, who come very often here,' he added.

It could be the very place where Don was playing billiards to please his father-in-law, Ella thought. She noted what it was called: *Playa de los Angeles.* Place or beach of the Angels. How ironic it would be if he had to leave his own Angel for a place with the same name.

'Did you find a new love?' Don asked when he came back, two and a half days later.

'No, did you?' she laughed.

'No, but I'm weary. Can our vacation begin now, Angel?'

So she knew there would be no chat about the client who'd insisted on taking up all his time and wrecking their holiday.

Don spent a lot of time at the laptop, more than she would have liked. When she woke he was tapping away. Often, after they made love in the evening, he slipped from the bed and seemed to come to life again at the little screen. That's today's world, she told herself. He is doing it so that we can have all these years together when the time comes.

'Will we go through separately?' Ella asked at Dublin airport.
'Why?' Don was mystified.
'Well, in case anyone sees us,' Ella said.
'Like who?'
'Like Margery,' she said.
'But how could she see us? Isn't she still in Spain?' he asked, confused.
So she had been right. Margery had been in Spain after all.

'Ella, it's your mother,' Don called out.
Usually he didn't answer the phone in her flat, but he had been waiting for an urgent call and had given the number.
'Thanks, Don. Hi, Mother.'
'Oh, Don is there, I gather.' Her mother sounded both doubtful and disapproving.
'Yes, we were just about to go out to a reception together. He said he'd pick me up. Well, what's new?'
'When will you be on your own?'
'I beg your pardon?'
'Can I talk to you when you are alone?'
'Talk away, Mother.'
'Call me back when you are free to talk.' She hung up.
'Shit,' Ella said.
'Something wrong?' Don raised his eyes from the computer.
'No, just a mad mother. You don't ever talk about yours.'
'Nothing to say. She's quiet, lives her own life. Lets other people live their own lives.'
'How admirable of her!' Ella began dialling her mother. 'Listen, Don's gone out to get his car. What did you want to say?'
'Have you seen tonight's evening paper?' her mother asked in clipped tones.
Ella pretended she needed to get some milk and coffee. She went around to the convenience store. The evening paper had a big gossip column spread over two pages, and specialised in lots of photographs. 'Who is the blonde on Don Richardson's arm as he comes back from Spain? The tycoon from the troubled R and R

firm doesn't look as if he is suffering any of the anxieties that their customers report. R and R need not mean Rice and Richardson, maybe Rest and Relaxation.' There was a picture of Ella and Don laughing happily together at Dublin airport.

Ella felt the energy drain out of her as she leaned against the doorway of the shop. She read the whole paragraph again.

She was there in full view of the whole of Dublin described as a blonde in the same tone as you might say she was a tramp. What would people say or think?

But more frightening than any of that, what did it mean that Rice and Richardson was a troubled firm? Could they seriously be in any financial difficulty? Could Don be in danger? The newspapers always exaggerated about things but surely it was dangerous to imply that a company was in trouble unless it were true? The newspaper could well be sued.

When she got back to the flat, Don was still bent over the computer. She laid the newspaper on the table and went into the kitchen. She needed tea or coffee, something to stop her trembling.

'Anything you'd like, Don?' she called, forcing her voice to sound normal.

'Oh, peace of mind would be nice,' he said with a hollow little laugh.

'Two of those on toast then!' she said, trying to laugh. But she wasn't laughing at all.

He left the computer and came across to the table where she put a large whiskey and the paper folded in front of him so that he could see the picture and caption.

'This is what caused the alarm bells with your mother, I suppose?' he said.

'You've seen it?' she said, shocked.

'Yeah, Ricky got an early copy.'

'Why didn't you tell me?'

'I told you before, Angel. Let me worry about the work side of things.'

'But this isn't about the work side of things,' she said, bewildered.

'What else is it about, Ella? Once clients read that other clients have reported difficulties, there'll be a run on the place. Ricky and I have to get our strategy right.'

She looked at him, dumbfounded.

'What is it, Ella?'

'The picture, the picture of you and me.'

'That's not important.'

'What?'

'I mean, compared to all the rest that could be going down.'

'But your wife, your father-in-law, my parents, everyone ...' Her voice was shaky.

'Listen, Angel, believe me, that's the least of our worries.' His face was white and strained. He looked really ill and it alarmed her. So, it was true. Something was wrong. What was happening? But Don was so on top of everything.

'Don, you are going to be able to sort all this out, aren't you?'

'Oh, yes. There's always plan B.' He gave a mirthless little laugh.

'What's plan B?'

'It's an expression. If this plan isn't working we have to turn to another. It's just a phrase.'

'Do you have a plan B?' she asked.

'There are loads of plans, but I didn't want to have to change to one of them. I like things the way they are.' He looked around the room almost wistfully.

Ella felt herself shudder for no reason.

He downed his drink and became all businesslike. 'I have to go out to Killiney.'

'I thought you said she was in Spain.'

'I go out there for a lot of other reasons than to see my ex-wife, as I tell you over and over, Angel.'

'Will you be coming back tonight, Don?'

'No, but I tell you, I'll take you to a big treat lunch tomorrow in Quentins.'

'We can't, not after the picture of us ...' She indicated the evening paper.

'Nonsense. Everyone will have forgotten that – yesterday's news. Once they know their money's safe, they won't mind how many blondes parade through airports with Ricky and myself.' He saw her face. 'Joke, Angel.'

'Sure.' She saw he was packing his few things in a suitcase. 'Getting rid of the evidence?' she said, and wished she hadn't.

'Should be ready for whatever hits the fan.' He smiled. 'Please, Angel, I'm stressed out enough as it is. Tomorrow, Quentins, one o'clock. I'll tell you everything then.'

He was rushed and fussed. Calm, cool Don Richardson, who

always moved languorously, wasn't moving like that now. Twice he put down his briefcase, his coat, his overnight bag, the evening paper. Twice he picked them all up again. She must not allow him to leave thinking she was in a sulk.

'Come over here and kiss me goodnight then, if I'm not to have the pleasure, the great pleasure, of you tonight.' She ran her hands all over him and he began to respond.

But he pulled away. 'No, Ella angel, that's not fair, that's using weapons that haven't been invented yet . . . Let me get out of here before we end up in the sack.'

'Nothing wrong with that,' she said into his ear. But he escaped her clutches and ran out of the door.

Then suddenly with a shock she saw his briefcase. He had left his laptop. Did that mean he was stressed or what? He never parted from it for a moment. But at least it meant he was coming back. She had been so nervous when she saw him packing his things and looking wistfully around the room.

Ella wasn't hungry. She put away the food she had been about to cook. She called her mother and said that it was idiotic to get into a tizzy about what a stupid paper wrote. And that it was just a picture of friends who had met at the airport or on the plane or whatever.

'Or on a holiday in Spain,' her mother said.

'Or that,' Ella said.

'Your father and I wondered.'

'It's a mistake to wonder too much,' Ella said.

'Don't be offensive, Ella.'

'I'm sorry, Mother. I'm just worried about something else, as it happens.'

'Is he still there? In your flat?' her mother whispered.

'No, Mother, I'm all on my own. Come round and check.'

'I only want what's best for you. We both do.'

'We all want what's best. That's the problem,' Ella said with a great sigh and hung up.

Then she phoned Deirdre. It was an answering machine. 'It's Ella, Dee. Be very glad you're not at home. I was going to groan and grumble and complain for a bit at you, but, well, now I can't. You must have seen the paper. It's not as bad as it looks. Don is very confident about it all, and I'll know much more after tomorrow lunchtime so I'll tell you everything then. Do you remember when we thought that life was a bit tame and dull? Wasn't it nice then?'

She hung up and sat at the table for a long time. She knew she wouldn't sleep, but she had better go to bed and try.

At three she got up despairing, and made tea. At four she opened the laptop computer. She typed out the word 'Angel' that he had said was the password. It didn't come to life as it had when he typed it. It just said Password Invalid. She closed the machine and waited until dawn. Then she dressed carefully and went to the school. She supposed that she must have taught her students normally, on some kind of autopilot. But she couldn't remember a word she had said. Then it was lunchtime, and she drove to Quentins.

Chapter Four

Mrs Brennan ushered her to a table for two. 'Will you have a drink while you're waiting, Ms Brady?'

'No, thanks. I have to teach this afternoon. Better not be breathing fumes over them. One glass of wine with lunch will be my limit.'

Brenda Brennan laughed. 'They're not all as wise as you are, Ms Brady. They often go back to run big companies or indeed the country after considerably more than one glass of wine, I tell you.'

'You'll have to write your memoirs,' Ella said.

'No, I want to go on serving meals for a long time. No point in closing us down.' She moved on to other tables, always a pleasant word here and there, never staying too long anywhere. She was amazingly elegant, Ella thought, and gracious. No wonder the place was so successful.

Brenda Brennan could make generalised remarks, but she would never say anything specifically indiscreet. Brenda would have realised that Ella was meeting Don Richardson, known family man. She might even have seen the photo in yesterday's paper. But she would give no hint. Of course, she had an easy life, Ella thought enviously. She was married to the man she loved, the chef Patrick Brennan. Lucky Brenda, she had no nerve-racking lunch ahead of her.

Ella wondered if she should order a brandy, but decided against it. Whatever he said, Ella would take it. She would not be like she was last night, whimpering and talking about herself and her picture in the paper. Clearly he had his problems. She could have kicked herself for behaving so badly when he needed her most.

At one-fifteen he wasn't there. It was very unlike him. At one-thirty she began to worry. Quentins was not the kind of place that hurried you or told you that the kitchen would be closing. But at twenty minutes before two, Ella went to the ladies' room. Brenda Brennan hated mobile phones at the table and she had to try and phone him.

There was no reply from his mobile. And no message recording service. This was very unusual. She would order something to eat. Or should she call the school first? Or should she telephone the house in Killiney? Or the office of Rice and Richardson? 'Don't fuss, Ella,' she spoke to herself aloud. She decided she would order food, something cold for both of them, and then when he eventually arrived there would be something to eat.

As she returned to her table, she noticed that Brenda had ordered her things moved to a private booth. Her book and glass of mineral water were there, waiting for her. Also, what looked like a small brandy.

Ella looked around her in surprise. Mon, the waitress, was nearby.

'Here you are, Ella. Much more cosy set-up if you're meeting a fellow.' Mon had a huge smile and two jaunty little bunches of hair which stuck out at angles from her head.

'Yes, but . . .'

'Listen, compared to most that come in here, Ella, you don't have anything to worry about. That fellow's mad about you, we often say it behind your back, so why not to your face?' Mon was eager and reassuring.

'Did Don ring and ask to change the table?' Ella asked Mon.

'No idea.' Mon was cheerful. 'Mrs Brennan said do it double quick, so it's done.'

Ella felt a great sense of alarm. Whatever he wanted to tell her must be terrible if it had to be told in a secluded booth. Then she noticed Brenda Brennan slipping in opposite her. She carried an early copy of the evening paper for today.

'Ella,' she said urgently.

What had happened to all the 'Ms Brady' bit of an hour ago? 'What is it?' She was full of fear.

'One or two customers recognised you. I thought best you be in here.'

She opened the paper, and there it was again – the picture of Ella laughing up at Don at the airport. But why had they printed it a second time?

'When he comes in, he'll explain.'

'He's not coming in, Ella. It was on the news at one-thirty. We heard it in the kitchen. He's gone to Spain. He left on the first plane this morning.'

'No!' Ella cried. 'No, he can't have gone away.'

'He has, apparently. He was out there setting it all up. He has his wife and children there already, his father-in-law went yesterday through London . . .'

'How do they know . . .?'

Brenda's voice was just a whisper. 'When all the clients went around to the office today to check on their assets, they couldn't get in. The place was locked up. They called the Guards and the Fraud Squad . . . and apparently he was on the eight a.m. plane.'

'This is not happening.'

'I took the liberty of getting you a Cognac.'

'Thank you,' she said automatically but she didn't reach for it.

'And I could call the school for you if you gave me the number and told me who to call.'

'That's kind of you, Mrs Brennan, but I actually don't believe any of this. Don is coming in. He keeps his word.'

'It's important how you behave now, for your own sake. You don't want to be running into a rake of journalists and photographers.'

'Why would I?'

'This idiotic paper said he had a love nest with you in Spain. Gives your name and where you work.'

'Well, see!' Ella was triumphant. 'They know what you don't, that he'd never leave without me, never.' Her voice was getting high, shrill, and very near hysteria.

Brenda caught her by the wrist. 'The news programme on the radio knows what this crowd in the newspaper didn't know. They spoke to neighbours in Killiney about the house being closed up. They spoke to Irish people living in Spain, who were all very tight-lipped, as you might imagine.'

'He couldn't, he couldn't.' Ella shook her head.

Brenda released the girl's wrist. 'There's an explanation. He'll get in touch, but the main thing is to get you out of here before someone sneaks a call to a journalist.'

'They wouldn't!'

'They would. Don't go home and don't go to your school.'

'Where will I go?' She looked pitiful.

'Go upstairs to our rooms. We live over the shop. Drink that down, write out the name and number for your school, and then go straight over to that green door there near the entrance to the kitchen . . .'

'How will you know what to say to the school?'

'I'll know,' Brenda said. She didn't add that it would hardly be necessary to say anything. They would all have read the paper and heard the lunchtime news. They would not be expecting Miss Brady back to classes this afternoon.

Ella was surprised to see the big, handsome brass bed with the frill-edged pillows and rose-pink coverlet. It looked too luxurious, too sensual, for this couple, somehow. She took her shoes off and lay down for a moment to get her head straight. But the sleepless night and the shock worked more than she believed they would. She fell into a deep sleep and dreamed that she and Don were carrying a picnic up a hill, but everything was in a tablecloth and getting jumbled together. In the dream, she kept asking why did they have to do it this way, and Don kept saying, 'Trust me, Angel, this is the way,' and all the time there was a rattling of broken china.

She woke suddenly to the sound of a cup and saucer being placed beside her by Brenda Brennan. It was almost six o'clock. There was no picnic. She couldn't trust Don Richardson any more. Was there the slightest possibility that he might be back in her flat waiting for her? She began to get out of bed.

Brenda said she was going to have a shower. Perhaps Ella might like to look at the six o'clock news on television. 'I'll be in the bathroom just next door if you need me,' Brenda called.

Ella turned on the TV and found the news. She watched without thinking until the story came on. It was worse than she thought. Don had gone. That much was certain. And he had been out in Spain last week setting it all up. There were interviews with people who had lost their life savings. A man with a red face who had given money to Don Richardson every month so that he could buy a little retirement home in Spain, because his wife had a bad chest and needed good weather. 'We are never going to see Spain now,' said the man, twisting his hands to show how upset he was.

There was a tall, pale woman who looked as if she were too frail to stand and talk to a man with a microphone. 'I can't believe it. He was so charming, so persuasive. I believe he will be back to explain everything. They tell me I don't own any apartment in that block. But I must. He showed me pictures of it.'

Mike Martin, a man she knew, a friend of Don's and described by the newsreader as a financial expert, came on next. Ella had had a drink with him several times. He knew all about her. Don had said he was a bit of a smart aleck, always in something for what he could get out of it, but not the worst. Mike looked horrified by it all and said that it couldn't have come as a greater shock. Don and Ricky were such a pair of characters, of course, and everyone who flies near the sun gets their wings burned now and then.

But then he went on: 'It looks as if they must have known for about six months. But I still can't believe it. Don Richardson is such a decent fellow, he'd help anyone, you know, fellows on the street, people he met in bars. He was always generous with advice. Other guys in his line of business would say: "If you want my advice, come into the office and consult me." But never Don. I can't imagine him spending months plotting this runaway life, knowing he's leaving people in the lurch. He cared about people. I know he did.'

Ella watched, open-mouthed.

The interviewer asked: 'And will he miss people, friends, a lifestyle that he had in Dublin, do you think?'

'Well, of course, when all was said and done he was a family man, he loved his wife and boys, they went everywhere with him.'

'Wasn't there a rumour that he had this blonde girlfriend, a teacher, who was photographed with him?'

'No. You better believe one thing,' Mike Martin said. 'I may not know a lot about Don, and I sure as hell didn't know what he's been up to in the last six months in terms of his clients . . . but one thing shines out. He never looked at another woman. Come on, now. If you were married to Margery Rice, would you?'

And then they cut to a picture of Margery Rice presenting prizes at a youth charity, very tiny and immaculately groomed, watched by her husband with pride.

Ella put the cup down.

Brenda came back into the room in her slip and put on a fresh black dress and arranged a lace collar in position.

'He knows about me and Don,' she said. 'I've met him many times.'

'Well, isn't it just as well he kept his mouth shut?' Brenda said.

'No, it's not, it's better people know the truth. Don loves me. He told me so last night.'

'Listen to me very carefully, Ella. I have to go down and serve a room full of people who will be talking about nothing else. I will have a polite, inscrutable smile on my face. I will say it's hard to know and difficult to guess and a dozen other meaningless things. But I know one thing. Only you must survive this, you must call your parents, tell them you're all right, decide what to do about your job and then go and find some of your friends, your own friends, not his. He only has business friends.'

'You don't like him, do you?'

'No, I don't. My very close friends have lost their savings. Thanks to Mr Charming.'

'He'll give them back,' Ella cried.

'No, he won't. Fortunately it's not very much. She and her fellow don't have very much, but they were saving hard and Mr Richardson told them how to double their money. They believed him.'

'He often said people were greedy,' Ella said.

'Not these two, if you knew them. But that's neither here nor there. Survive, Ella, and rejoice that he may have loved you – well, at least enough not to let you or your family lose any of your savings in his schemes.'

'No.' She stood up. Her legs felt weak.

'What is it, Ella?'

'It's just my father. He's always going on about ideas Don gave him, hints here, a word there ... he wouldn't have been so foolish ...'

'When were you talking to your parents?'

'Yesterday, but they said nothing. They were going on about my picture in the paper. If there was anything to say they'd have said it then.'

'Nobody knew the extent of the scandal then. People only began to know it this morning.'

They looked at each other in alarm.

'Ring them, Ella.'

'He couldn't ... he didn't.'

'You heard what they said on the television ...'

Brenda Brennan pointed to the white phone beside the bed.

Ella dialled. Her mother answered. She was in tears. 'Where *were* you, Ella? Your father thought you'd gone to Spain with him. Where are you?'

'Is Dad all right?'

'Of course he's not all right, Ella. I have the doctor here with him. He's ruined.'

'Tell me, tell me, what did he lose?'

'Oh, Ella, everything. But it's not what we lost that matters, it's what the firm lost. What his clients lost. He may have to go to gaol.'

That was when Ella fainted.

Mrs Brady hadn't hung up. That was something. At least Brenda could keep her there for long enough to get her address. She held Ella's head downwards so that more blood would flow towards the brain.

'I have to get home to them,' Ella said over and over.

'You will, don't worry.'

'Your restaurant – won't you be needed downstairs?'

'Head *down*,' Brenda insisted.

Then she summoned Patrick's younger brother, Blouse. 'You know where Tara Road is?'

'I do. I often deliver vegetables to Colm's restaurant if he's short.'

'In about fifteen minutes, when she's up to it, drive her there, will you, Blouse?'

'Where are the car keys?' he asked.

Brenda turned out the contents of Ella's handbag. The keys were all on one ring.

It had a cherub on it.

'Angel,' said Ella weakly.

'Yes, we have the keys.' Brenda crammed everything back into the handbag, pausing only a fraction of a second to glance at a picture of Don Richardson smiling at the girl who had loved him. Ella's eyes were open and she was watching. Otherwise, Brenda would have torn it into a dozen pieces.

Ella gave Blouse directions to her parents' house. When they arrived, Ella's mother ran to the car. 'I suppose you're one of his friends,' she said when Blouse helped Ella from the car.

'I'm not really anyone's friend, Madam. I'm Brenda's brother-in-law. She asked me to drive this lady home.'

'From where, exactly?'

'From Quentins Restaurant,' he said proudly.

'Leave him, Mam. He's got nothing to do with anything.'

'What do we know what has to do with anything?' Her mother looked as if somebody had given her a beating.

'Where's Dad?'

'In the sitting room. He won't go to bed. He won't take any sedation. He says he has to be alert if the office rings him.'

'And have they rung him?'

'Not since lunchtime. Not since we learned that Don has left the country. There's no point in anyone ringing anyone now, Ella. It's all gone. All gone.'

'I can't tell you how sorry I am,' she said.

'Well, I'll be off now, then,' Blouse Brennan said.

'Thank you very much, and will you thank your sister?'

'Sister-in-law,' he corrected.

'Yes, well, say I'm very grateful.'

'It's nothing,' he said.

'How will you get back?' Ella's mother realised that he had left the car keys on the table.

'Which end of Tara Road is shorter to the bus?' he asked cheerfully. He was so unconcerned, he lived in a world where you drove people home in their own cars and took a bus back to a kitchen or scullery or wherever he worked. A world where people weren't greedy and didn't win and lose huge sums of money over business deals. He would never know anyone who lied and lied and lied like Don Richardson had lied. Even to people who loved him. Particularly to people who loved him. But Ella was too tired to care any more. All she wanted was to reassure her father that the world hadn't come to an end. She wanted to look him in the face and tell him that it would be all right. It was just that with every passing second, it seemed so unlikely that this was true.

He looked like an old man, a paper-thin old man whose skeleton was covered with a very fine parchment. When he smiled it was like a death mask. 'I didn't know, Dad. I didn't have any idea,' she said.

'It's not your fault, Ella.'

'It is. I introduced him to you. I made you think he was my friend. I thought he loved me, Dad. He told me last night that he loved me. You see, I was sure he did.'

She knelt beside him. Her mother watched from the door with tears on her face.

'Dad, I'm young and I'm strong, and if I have to work day and night to make sure that you and Mother are all right, I will never take a day's holiday until I know I've done all that can be done.'

'Child, don't upset yourself.' His voice was very hesitant, as if he were having trouble breathing.

'I'm not a child, Dad, and I will be upset, very upset till the day I die that this should happen, because I made such a stupid, stupid error of judgement. But you know, Dad, even at this late stage, there *could* be an explanation. Perhaps it was all his father-in-law's doing.'

'Please, Ella. Everyone trusts people when they love them,' her mother said.

Her mother? Instead of bawling her out, she actually seemed to understand.

'No, I couldn't be like ordinary people, normal people like you and Dad, who found someone decent to love. I had to find a criminal, someone who ruins people and steals their livelihood and their savings.'

'I don't mind losing the savings, Ella, that was just greed. I wanted to make a profit so that we could buy you a little house.'

'A what? But I don't want a little house.'

'But we knew you weren't ever going to come and live here, so we wanted you to have a small place with character, and what with property being so dear, you'd never get that on a teacher's salary . . .'

'Father, what did you lose? Tell me.'

'But I don't *mind* about what we lost. It's the office. He had been so helpful, you know, always seemed to be in the know.'

'Yes, he was in the know, all right.'

'And those first bits of advice that I gave people went down so well . . . I took risks, Ella. I can't blame anyone but myself . . . it's just, it's just . . .'

'Just what, Dad?'

'Just that two weeks ago, he said it would be easiest and quickest if I gave him the money direct to invest for a few of my clients. I'd never done it before. You know the laws and rules there are about that . . . but Don made it all sound so normal, somehow. He said he was going out to Spain. He could invest it there and then save time, cut a few corners. Why not? That's what he said, and you know I did think ... why not?'

'I know, Dad. Who are you telling?' She stroked his hand. But her mind was far, far away. It was in Spain. The bastard. He had conned her father out of money which he had spent in that hotel. Don had spent the money that he pretended to be investing for her father's clients in shoring up his love nest for himself, wife and kiddies. While the daughter of the victim lay in the hotel swimming pool, waiting for him. Was there anything in the whole history of faithless love as sick and pathetic?

'Dad, you won't really have to go to gaol?'

'I will certainly have to go to court,' he said.

'But wasn't Don a legitimate adviser? You know, with a licence and everything ... surely *you* can't be held responsible?'

'All that would have helped if my clients were his clients, but they weren't. I only took his advice, his tips, his hints, as hearsay.'

'Dad, your bosses, they know ...'

'They know me for what I am, a weak, foolish old man,' he said, and then for the very first time she began to cry.

She would recover. She knew that sometime in the future she might get over it and over him. But her father never would. That's why Don could never be forgiven.

Everything passes, even scandalous stories like the disappearance of Ricky Rice and Don Richardson, and soon the front pages had other stories to tell. There was an official inquiry announced, of course, and people became much more cautious about investing anything anywhere. There had been much speculation about whether the family was really in Spain or had gone further afield. After all, there were extradition laws in Europe now. People could not hide in one member state from the law they had broken in another. Perhaps they were in Africa or South America.

Ella had been questioned by detectives. Did Mr Richardson say anything about any plans to relocate in Spain when he and Ella had been on holiday there? Ella told them grimly that she knew of no such plans. The pain in her face seemed to convince them. She was as much a victim as many others had been.

Then the interest died down. In the media, if not for those whose hearts had been broken. The man with the red face, who had put all his money in a retirement villa for his wife, didn't forget. Nor did the pale woman who thought she had made a wonderful investment and owned an apartment in the south of Spain. The friends of Brenda Brennan, who had saved money for a wedding party, decided to laugh and make the best of it. They were people of middle years. Maybe fate was telling them they would have been foolish to have had a big celebration. Possibly a plate of sandwiches would do them fine.

Tim Brady took early retirement from his firm and spent his days filling out forms and dossiers about how and why he had given advice based on the casual snippets of information he had heard from a man he hardly knew. Barbara Brady offered to take early retirement from her firm of lawyers saying that she didn't want to embarrass them by staying on. Delicately, they managed to convince her that nobody knew who she was and it didn't matter anyway, and possibly theirs was a household that might need a little money coming in.

And Ella? Each day seemed to be forty-eight hours long. And no day seemed different from any other day nor any night from the one which followed.

It was just that the nights were worse.

Sleep would vanish. She would get up and pace around her room looking up at the shelf where she had hidden his briefcase and the laptop it contained. A hundred times she had wanted to take it to the Fraud Squad, say she had found it. They might be able to track down some of the money and rescue people like her father, like Brenda's friend Nora whose wedding savings were gone, like the man with the red face buying a villa, so he thought, for his wife who had a bad chest, like the pale woman on the television interview who said she knew she owned the flat because Don had shown her a picture of it.

But she couldn't do it.

He had trusted her, he never left that briefcase behind him, she used to joke that it was chained to his arm. She had delayed him by kissing him when he was leaving her flat in a rush that day but he hadn't worried or panicked. He hadn't called her or got anyone else to. He knew she would keep it safe for him.

And, in spite of all the evidence, she knew he would be coming back for her.

Anyway it was all down to Ricky Rice, he ran the whole show. Everyone knew that, people just did his bidding. Indeed, the very fact that Don had left the computer with her was some kind of message. Why hadn't she thought of that before?

Of course he would just come walking back into her life to tell her that it had been sorted. A love like theirs wasn't the ordinary kind of affair that people thought it was.

He was just sorting things out.

At night it seemed clear and certain.

She just had to wait for it to happen.

It was during the days that it seemed unlikely. There was no message from Spain, no call on the mobile, no text message. And then one day there was the request for a meeting by the Fraud Squad. Did Ella have anything pertinent to their enquiries? Like a list of files?

Ella looked the two men straight in the eye and said no, she had no files and no knowledge of anything that would help them.

'He didn't give you anything to look after for him, Madam? Any records, that sort of thing?'

She wasn't quite sure why she said no. Strictly speaking it was true. He hadn't asked her to look after anything for him. But of course she was lying to them and she knew it. Why? she wondered. Why had she wrapped Don's laptop in a great amount of padding and put it deep in her suitcases of clothes that were on the way back to Tara Road? If they had a search warrant they would have found the little machine and she would have been in real trouble. But in a mad way she felt she owed it to him not to hand over something he had left in her care. And of course he knew she had it, so he might well get in touch with her about it.

It was a very unreal time. She would have been lost without her friends. Deirdre had been there day and night whenever she was needed. Sometimes they said nothing, they just listened to music. Sometimes they played gin rummy. Deirdre helped her to pack up all her things in the flat and move them back to Tara Road. Ella wanted to burn the sheets on the bed. Deirdre said this was no time for dramatic gestures; she would take them to the laundry and then give them to a charity shop.

It was Deirdre who explained to the landlord that Ella would not be in a position to pay any more rent, and could they cut the agreement short? Deirdre often made sure she was there in the evening, about suppertime, so that the family would have to give the appearance of normality and sit down and have something to eat.

Sometimes Deirdre asked her, 'Do you still love him?'

Always Ella answered, 'I don't know.'

Deirdre asked would she take him back suppose he did ask her? Ella took the question very seriously. 'I think not, and when I look at my father's face, I think surely I'd never be able to look at Don again. But then I keep hoping there's some other explanation for the whole thing, which of course there isn't. So, crazy as it sounds, I must have some feelings for him still.'

And Deirdre would nod and consider it too. Deirdre had insisted on only one thing: that she go in to the school and face them immediately. So Ella went to see the school principal.

'I'll leave whenever you want me to,' she said.

'We don't want you to.'

'But where's the bit about us giving a good example to the little flock?'

'The little flock would buy and sell us all, Ella, you know it, I know it.'

'I can't stay, Mrs Ennis, not after this scandal.'

'What did you do? You were taken in by a man. You won't be the first or the last to have that happen to you, let me tell you. You're a good teacher. Please don't go.'

'The parents?'

'The parents will gossip for a couple of weeks and the kids will make jokes, then it will be forgotten.'

'I don't know if I can face it.'

'What's to face? You have to look at people whatever job you do. And presumably you have to earn a living.'

'Oh, I do, Mrs Ennis, I do.'

'Then earn it here. Go on just to the end of the school year anyway. See how you feel then.'

'I might want to get out of teaching entirely, you know, try something different.'

'If you do, then do it, but not in mid-year. You owe us this, and you owe it to yourself not to run away, like he did.'

'You've been very understanding. Imagine an Irish convent school allowing a scarlet woman to stay on.'

'You're not very scarlet, Ella, just a bit pink-eyed at the moment. Get back into those classrooms. The one thing we can all say about teaching is that it's demanding enough to take your mind off other things.'

'Thank you, Mrs Ennis.'

'Ella, he won't get away with it totally, you know. Even if he doesn't get a gaol sentence. He'll get some sort of punishment.'

Ella shrugged. 'Whatever.'

'He will. He can't swan around here any more, go to golf clubs, yacht clubs, be recognised in restaurants.'

'They've all those things in Spain, too.'

'Not the same at all. Anyway, none of my business. Hang in there for the rest of the year, will you, and then we'll talk again.'

'You're very kind, very understanding.'

'Well, we've all been there, Ella, and just between us, the late Mr Ennis, as he is often respectfully called, is not late, he's just out of the frame. He had a different view of his future which involved my savings account and a girl young enough to be his daughter, so of course I understand.'

For days afterwards, Ella wondered whether she had imagined this conversation. It seemed highly unreal as did everything else these days. It was as if she were watching all these conversations on a stage rather than taking part in them.

First Sandy phoned. She still worked with Nick in Firefly Films.

'I just rang to say that if you were looking for extra work, there's always a bit of night work going here.'

'Thanks, Sandy, that's very nice of you. Nick okay with this?'

'Yeah, but you know the way he is. He didn't want to ask you in case you thought he was patronising you or patting you on the head or something.'

'I wouldn't think that.'

'Men are complicated.'

'Tell me about it, Sandy.'

'What'll I tell Nick?'

'Tell him I'd love it, anything at all.'

And Brenda Brennan offered her work when Ella had telephoned to thank her for all the kindness. 'If you want any weekend work here in Quentins, just ask. I know it's only a few euros when what you need is thousands, but it might be a start.'

'Half the city wants to work in Quentins, you can't let me waltz in there ahead of the rest.'

'There's a bit of solidarity among women, Ella. You got a punch in the face and now you need a hand up as well. You'll find a lot of people will offer one.'

'Ella Brady?'

'Yes?' She always sounded jumpy and nervy on the telephone

now. It was a bad habit and she must get out of it.

'This is Ria Lynch from down the road.'

'Oh yes, indeed.'

There had been a time when this woman, rather than Ella, had been the subject of gossip all over Tara Road. Her husband had left her, and in a very short time Ria had taken up with Colm, who owned the successful suburban restaurant. The place had buzzed for a while, but now they were as settled and staid as any regular married couple. What could she be calling about?

'I heard you were badly hit by Don Richardson, and I want to give you some advice. I thought I'd talk to you rather than your parents.'

'Yes?' Ella had been a little cold. Unasked-for advice wasn't too welcome these days.

'Don't let your father sell the house to raise money. Change it into four flats; they were flats already – you're halfway there. You'll get a fortune for renting them. Then take your garden shed, make it bigger and live in it for a couple of years.'

'Live in the shed?' Ella wondered if the woman was deranged.

'Look, it's enormous. All it needs is a couple of thousand spent on it, put in plumbing, and it can be made into two bedrooms, and a living-room with a kitchenette.'

'We don't have a couple of thousand.'

'You would have in weeks if you let your beautiful house. I'll take you and show you Colm's old house if you like. It's a gold mine. Everyone wants to live in this road these days, and there's so much money about.'

'Why are you telling me this, Ria?' Ella had hardly ever talked properly to this woman before.

'Because we've all been through this – bankruptcy, a fellow not being what he said he was.'

Ella wondered if this was true. Had half the country been cheated and duped?

One night she dreamed that he had sent her a text message on her mobile phone. Just two words: Sorry Angel. It was such a real dream Ella had to get up in the middle of the night and check her phone. There was nothing there but a message from Nick.

'I really need your help for a competition . . . Say yes.'

She phoned him next morning. He brought a sandwich up to the school and they had lunch in her car. His enthusiasm was as boyish as ever. There was going to be a film festival on a theme. Some aspect of Dublin life which would illustrate all the changes there had been in the city over the years.

'What kind of change do you mean? Architecture or something?'

'No, I don't think everyone will go for that,' Nick said.

'Well, what then? The growth in Irish self-confidence?'

'Yes, but we can't just make a film saying everyone's becoming more confident. Lord, just look at those confident faces passing by ... there has to be something that binds them together, some theme.'

'And if we found one, what do we do next?'

'Go to New York and sell it to this fellow there who has a foundation. The King Foundation, to help young people in the arts. If we made this film, Ella, and won a prize at the Festival, we'd be made. Made, I tell you. Something that gives a picture of Dublin changing ... Can you think of anything that sort of sums it all up?'

'Sorry to ask, Nick, but would there be money in it? You know we're cleaned out.'

'I sort of heard,' he said, looking away.

'So is there?'

'Yes, there would be, if we got the right idea.'

'And when would it need to be done?'

'We need to be ready to pitch in three months' time.'

'That would work out all right. I could work during the day, once we get school holidays from here in two weeks from tomorrow.'

'Do you have any ideas at all?' he asked.

She was silent for a moment. 'Quentins,' she said eventually.

'What do you mean?'

'Do a documentary about the restaurant, the changes in people's aspirations, their hopes and dreams, since it was founded about forty years ago.'

'It's never been there that long.'

'Well, it was a totally different kind of café in the sixties and early seventies, until Brenda and Patrick took it over. It was really only watery soup and beans on toast before then, you know.'

'I didn't know that.'

'Well, that's what people wanted then. And look how different it all is nowadays. You could tell the stories of the kind of people

76

who come there . . . how it's all changed since the days when it was full of people with suitcases tied with string come in for tea and a couple of fried eggs before they took the emigrant ship.'

'It was never like that, surely?'

'It was, Nick. They have pictures of it all up in their bedroom, a whole history waiting to be told.'

He didn't ask how she had been in the Brennans' bedroom. Nick was very restful sometimes. But he didn't buy the idea. 'It would just be a plug for them. It would be like a commercial for the restaurant.'

'They don't need it. Aren't they full all the time? No, it wouldn't be done like that . . . it could be a series of interviews with people remembering different times . . . you know . . . oh, all kinds of things – the way First Communions have changed, stag party dinners, corporate entertaining. It sure tells the story of a changing economy better than anything I know.'

He was interested now. 'Other restaurants are going to be full of grizzles and complaints about why we didn't pick them.'

'Deal with that when it happens, Nick.'

He looked at her admiringly. 'You're very bright, Ella,' he said.

'Where did it get me?' she asked.

'You asked about money,' he said, changing the subject. 'Well, this is what I suggest. If you help me develop this and sell it to Derry King, I'll pay you a proper wage for five weeks. Suppose I said eight hundred euros a week?'

'That's four thousand euros. Fantastic,' she said, delighted.

'What do you need it for so badly?'

'To do up the garden shed for my mother and father, because thanks to my lover, they are going to have to leave their own house.'

He laughed first and then stopped. 'You're bloody serious,' Nick said, shocked.

'Yes, I am.'

'I can give it to you now, tomorrow.'

'No, you can't, Nick.'

'I can. Let's say I can get my hands on it easier than you can.'

'You're not to go into debt.'

'No, but we've got to get the Bradys a henhouse or whatever to live in.' He grinned at her.

Wouldn't it have been much easier if she had loved Nick, Ella thought.

They made an appointment with the Brennans the next day. Nick and Sandy and Ella sat in the kitchen of Quentins at five o'clock and told them about the project. Brenda and Patrick were doubtful at first. They listed their reservations. It would be too much upheaval, it would get in the way of their main business, which was to provide food. They didn't need the publicity. Perhaps some of the customers might not like to be interviewed.

Slowly they were worn down. Soon they began to think of the positive side of it. In a way, it would be some kind of permanent proof of what they had done. It would be exciting to be considered part of the history of Ireland. Customers who didn't want to be interviewed need not be approached. They had huge amounts of memorabilia. Both of them were magpies who collected things and refused to throw them away. And then the most compelling reason of all ... Quentin would surely love it.

'Quentin?' Ella said. 'You mean, there really is a living person called Quentin?'

'Oh yes, indeed there is,' said Patrick Brennan the chef.

'Yes, he would,' Brenda said slowly. 'It could be a sort of monument to him.'

'Could you tell us some of the stories about the place?' Ella asked, and as she turned on the tape recorder she realised that for the past hour and a half she had not thought about Don Richardson once. The pain that was like something sticking into her ribs was not nearly so sharp. Still there, of course, but not like it had been earlier.

Quentin's Story

Quentin Barry had always wished that he had been called Sean or Brian. It was hard to be called Quentin at a Christian Brothers school in the 1970s. But that was the name they had wanted, his beautiful mother Sara Barry had wanted, she who had always lived in a dream world far more elegant than the one she really lived in.

And it was what his hard-working father Derek wanted too. Derek, who was a partner in Bob O'Neill's accountancy firm. He had always seen the day when his son's name would be on the notepaper too. That had been very important to him. Bob O'Neill had no son to succeed him. If people saw the name Quentin Barry on the office paper as well as Derek's, they would know who was important.

Since his earliest days, Quentin knew that he was going to work in his father's firm. It was never questioned. He even knew which room he would work in. It was across the corridor from his father's. At present, it was a storeroom and his father was keeping it that way until it was time for Quentin to take over.

The other lads at the Brothers didn't know what jobs, if any, they would get when they left school. A few of them might go to university. Some might go to England or America. There would, of course, be a couple of vocations to the priesthood or the Brothers.

Quentin used to pretend that he too had a choice in it all. He said that he might be a pilot or a car mechanic. These were things that sounded normal and masculine. Not like his name, not precious, like his lifestyle as an only child with a mother who looked like a film star and talked very fancy when she drove by school to collect her son in a cream-coloured car.

Sometimes Quentin felt able to tell his mother about his doubts about his future career. 'You know, Mother, I might not be a good accountant like Dad is,' he would begin nervously.

'Quentin, my sweet one, you are twelve years old!' she would say. 'Don't get involved in the awful world of business until you have to.'

He loved to help in the home, choosing fabrics for the sitting-room, making table decorations for dinner parties.

His father frowned on this kind of activity. 'Don't have the lad doing girly things like that,' he would say.

'The lad, as you call him, likes to help, which is a blessing since all you do is sit down, put your elbows on the table, and eat and drink what's put in front of you.'

Quentin wondered did other people's parents bicker as much as his did. Probably. It wasn't something they talked much about at school. He knew one thing, which was that the other boys' mothers did not talk to them like his mother did.

Sara Barry always called him her Sweet One, and the Light of her Life. Or something else very fancy. Other boys' mothers called them great galumphing clods and useless good-for-nothings. It was very different. And although his mother loved him to bits, she was always saying it, she never took him seriously about not wanting to be an accountant. 'But my sweet boy, you are only twelve.'

Or thirteen or fourteen. By the time he was sixteen, he knew he had to say something.

'I do not think I'm cut out for accountancy, Dad.'

'No one's cut out for it, boy. We have to work at it.'

'I won't be any good at it, truly.'

'Of course you will, when you're involved. Just concentrate on getting your exams like a good lad.'

'I'm way behind at Maths, and honestly, I'm not going to get any good exam results in anything. Isn't it better to be prepared for that now rather than it coming as an awful shock?'

'Do you study, do your homework?' His father's frown was mighty.

'Well, yes, I do, but ...'

'There you are. It's just nerves. You're too like your mother, highly strung, not a good thing for a man to be.'

Quentin failed his exams quite spectacularly.

The atmosphere at home was very hostile. It made it worse that his parents blamed each other much more than they blamed him.

'You upset him with all that pressure that he has to be a dull boring accountant and fill your shoes,' Sara Barry hissed.

'You fill him up with nonsense, mollycoddling him and taking him shopping with you like a poodle,' Derek Barry countered.

'You don't care about Quentin, all you care about is having two Barrys in that plodding office to annoy Bob O'Neill,' Sara snapped.

'And what do you care about, Sara? You only care that the dull plodding office, as you call it, makes enough money for you to buy ever more clothes in Haywards.'

Quentin hated hearing them shout over him. He agreed to repeat the year and have extra tuition. Derek Barry was glad that he had never mentioned any actual timings to Bob O'Neill.

One of the Brothers up at the school was a gentle man with a faraway look. Brother Rooney was always to be found in the school gardens, digging here, planting there. He used to teach a long time ago, but he said he wasn't good at it, he would drift away and tell the boys stories.

'That would have been nice,' Quentin said.

'It wasn't really, Quentin, it was no use to them. I was meant to be putting facts into their heads, getting them exams. So I sort of drifted out to the garden, which was where I wanted to be in the first place, and I'm as happy as Larry now.'

'Aren't you lucky, Brother Rooney? I don't want to be an accountant at all!'

'Then don't be, Quentin, be what you want.'

'I wish I could.'

'What do you like? What are you good at?'

'Nothing much. I like food. I love beautiful things and I like helping people enjoy themselves.'

'You could work in a restaurant.'

'With *my* parents, Brother Rooney? Can you see it?'

'Well, it's good, honest work, and they'd get used to it in time. They'd have to.'

'And what about the bit where God says, "Honour thy Father and thy Mother"?' Quentin smiled at the older Brother.

'It only says honour them, it doesn't say lie down like a doormat and go along with any of their cracked schemes.' The old man with the gardener's hands and the faded blue eyes looked as if he was on very safe ground.

'Is that what you did, Brother Rooney?'

'I did it twice, boy, first to get into the Order. My parents wanted me to work on the buildings in London and bring in big money, but I wanted peace, not more noise and bustle. They were very put out, but I never raised my voice to them, and it worked. Eventually. And then when I was in here I had to fight again to get out of the classroom and into the garden. I explained over and over that I couldn't hold the children's attention, couldn't make them understand things, but I'd love to make the garden bloom, that I could serve God best that way, and that worked. Eventually.'

'I wonder how long is eventually.' Quentin sounded wistful.

'You'd be wise to start at once, Quentin,' said Brother Rooney, picking up his hoe and getting at some of the hard-to-reach weeds at the back of the flowerbed.

'Eventually is now, Father, Mother,' Quentin said that evening at supper.

'What's the boy talking about?' His father rattled the paper.

'Derek, have the courtesy at least to listen to your son.'

'Not when he's talking rubbish. What does that mean, Quentin? Is it something you got from one of your loutish friends up in the place we thought was going to make a man of you and give you an education? Nicely fooled we were, too.' Derek Barry snorted.

'No, Father, I don't have many friends as you may notice. I'm not interested in football or drinking or going to the disco, so I'm mainly on my own. I was talking to Brother Rooney, who does the gardens up in the school.'

'Well, you might have tried talking to one of the more educated Brothers, one who would tell us what on earth we are to do with you, my darling.' This time it was Quentin's mother's turn to look sad and impatient with him.

'You see, I'll never be an accountant. I'll never get the qualifications to get me taken on to study as one. We will all understand and accept that eventually. So why don't we accept it now?'

'And you'll do what with your life, exactly?' his father asked.

'I'll get a job, Father, go out and get a job like everyone else.'

'And what about the place in my office I was keeping for you?' His father had lines of disappointment almost etched into his face.

'Father, I'm sorry, but it was only a dream, your dream. We'll all understand that eventually. Can we not understand it now?'

'Oh, stop repeating that gardener's mumbo-jumbo.'

'I can't bear telling Hannah Mitchell. She's so proud of her son going to do law like his father.' Sara Barry's pretty face pouted. Ladies' lunches didn't look so good from this viewpoint.

'What kind of job?' Derek Barry said.

And Quentin knew that Brother Rooney had advised him well. Eventually was now.

He worked first in a seaside café south of Dublin, then an Italian restaurant in the city. Then he got a kitchen and bar job in one of the big hotels. This meant antisocial hours, so he moved out of his parents' home and got a bed-sitter. His father didn't seem to notice or care. And his mother was vague and confused about it all.

And eventually he went for an interview in Haywards store where they needed someone in their restaurant. He was interviewed by Harold Hayward, one of the many cousins who worked in the family firm. This was much smarter than the other places he had worked. More like home, in fact, where he had loved helping his mother with her dinner parties.

And this is exactly what Quentin Barry did, imitate his own mother's stylish presentation. Soon there were heavy linen napkins, good bone china, and the best of silverware all on display.

He suggested special afternoon teas, with warm scones dripping in butter, served with little bowls of clotted cream and berries to spread on top ...

He presided over it all as if he loved being there and as if it were his own little kingdom which he had created.

His mother was not best pleased. Quite a lot of the ladies she lunched with went to Haywards. None of *their* sons worked at tables.

'You could tell them I'm serving my time until I open my own place,' Quentin suggested.

'I could, I suppose,' his mother said doubtfully.

He was shocked. He had been making a joke, and she took it seriously. What was so awful about doing a job he liked? Good, honest work. Sitting around over coffee afterwards, discussing how to make the place even better. His beautiful mother did not call him the Light of her Life or Sweet One these days. Possibly he had given all that up when he had passed on being an accountant.

From time to time, Quentin went to see Brother Rooney back at his old school. He brought the man a packet of cigarettes and they would sit on a carved wooden seat or in the greenhouse. The old man with the pale, watery blue eyes would point out proudly some of the changes there had been since Quentin's last visit. The dramatic difference it had made cutting that hedge right back; there were magical things under it that no one had ever seen and now they were flowering away once they had been given the light.

'Did you miss girls when you came here?' Quentin asked him one day.

'Don't they have girls now?' The school had become co-educational in the last couple of years. It had been a big change.

'No, I meant girlfriends. Did you miss that side of things?'

'No, not at all,' Brother Rooney said. 'Funny, but it never bothered me at all. I never had a girlfriend, couldn't take to it.'

'Would you have preferred fellows, do you think?' Quentin knew the old man wouldn't be offended.

'Divil a bit of it, neither one nor the other, a kind of a eunuch, I suppose. But you know, Quentin, that's not as big a loss as people might think.'

'I suppose it's a positive benefit, if you're in a religious order and taken a vow of chastity,' Quentin smiled at him.

'No, I didn't mean that at all. I meant like if you're not taken up by desire for people then you can see beauty more around you. I see all kinds of colours and textures in flowers and trees that I don't think other fellows see at all.' He seemed pleased with himself over the way attributes had been handed out. Some got this, some got that.

'You're one of the happiest people I know, Brother Rooney.'

'And if you won't be offended and take it the wrong way, I think you're quite like me, Quentin. You see beauty in things too, and you have great enthusiasms. It does my heart good to hear you talking about that restaurant you run.'

'Oh, I don't run it, Brother. I only work there.'

'Well, you sound as if you did, and that's a great thing.'

'Will you come in and see me there one day?'

'I'd feel out of place in a fancy restaurant like that. They'd be looking at my nails and everything.'

'They would not. Come in and see me one day.'

84

But Quentin knew that Brother Rooney would not make the journey from the garden where he lived and would probably die without ever visiting him. He wondered, was the old Brother right about Quentin being like him? A eunuch, interested in neither men nor women? It could very possibly be true. Anyway, there was no time to think about it today. The restaurant was full.

The legendary afternoon teas were a huge success; tiny warmed scones with a serving of cream and raspberry jam were disappearing rapidly from trolleys. There was hardly room for all the customers.

'Move that old tramp on, Quentin, will you?' Harold Hayward the manager said with a wave at a shabby man in the corner.

'He's not a tramp. He's just a bit untidy,' Quentin protested. Perhaps Brother Rooney had been right and this was not the place for a man with grimy hands.

'Move him on anyway. He's only had a pot of tea in the last hour and there's a line forming at the door.'

Quentin went to the table. The man looked up at him from a sheaf of papers. A near-empty teapot sat on the table. Harold the manager had been right. This was not a customer from whom they would make much money this afternoon. But it didn't seem a reason to move him on.

Quentin smiled apologetically at the man, who was in his sixties. 'I'm sorry to inconvenience you, sir, but as you can see, people are standing in a long queue waiting for tables.'

'Are you asking me to get out?' He had bushy eyebrows, a red weather-beaten face and a slightly Australian accent.

'Certainly not! I just wondered, would you mind if I helped you move your papers so that we could let other people share your table?'

'He asked you to move me on, didn't he?' The old man jerked his head at where Harold Hayward stood watching.

'Now we have room for those two ladies who both have walking sticks. They will appreciate it. May I bring them over?' Quentin was charm itself. He replaced the teapot with a fresh one at no extra charge.

The old man outstayed three sets of people who were brought to his table. At the end of the day he asked Quentin if he was part of the Hayward family himself.

'Alas, no,' he smiled apologetically. 'Just a labourer in the field, as they say.'

'Why do you say "alas"? They can't be any great shakes as a family, judging by the face of the guy who looks as if he swallowed four lemons.'

Harold Hayward did indeed look a bit sour.

'Oh, I suppose I meant it would have made life much easier for me if I could have joined the family firm. My father is an accountant and he had my name on a door in his place, but I couldn't face it. At least Harold's family are pleased with him.'

The old man came in regularly after that and he always sat at one of Quentin's tables. His name was Toby, shortened to Tobe. He had travelled the world, he said, and seen wonderful things. 'Have you travelled?' he asked Quentin.

'No. My problem was that since I decided not to go in with my father, I was so determined to make a living, I never gave myself time to go anywhere. I'd love to see the colours in Provence or in Tuscany, and I'd love to go to North Africa. One day, maybe,' he smiled sadly.

'Don't leave it too late, Quentin.'

'Eventually should be now,' Quentin said, thinking of old Brother Rooney.

'There was never a truer word said.' Tobe nodded his head vigorously.

There was no doubt that he looked a lot shabbier than the rest of the clientele. Sometimes Quentin would tell him there was this miracle stain remover he had discovered, and when Harold Hayward was not looking, he would attack a particularly noticeable stain on Tobe's chest. Once he handed him a comb and another time he gave him elastic bands to hold back his frayed cuffs. He didn't know why he did this, probably because he wanted to prove Harold Hayward wrong in his attitude. Also, he knew he wasn't offending Tobe, who was totally unaware that he looked rather eccentric and was perfectly agreeable to being brought courteously more into the mainstream.

And work was becoming Quentin's life. He still had few friends apart from the pleasant and casual relationships with those he worked with and served.

His kindness did not go unnoticed. Even his fellow staff were aware of how well he got on with the customers.

'You're very warm to people,' Brenda Brennan said to him one day.

She was one of their part-time staff, but a superior girl, cool and elegant, calm in a crisis and always perfectly capable of dealing with whatever the day might pitch at them.

He wished she would take a permanent job there but she told him that she and her husband had dreams of owning their own place.

'That was a nice gesture,' she said to him when she had seen him give the odd refill to Tobe without charging.

'Lord, Brenda, it's only hot water and a teabag,' Quentin said. 'He's happy here watching people come and go. I like his company. You should hear him talk about those orange and purple sunrises they have out in Australia.'

'I wonder what sent him out there all those years ago,' Brenda said.

'Probably his family.' Quentin was thoughtful. 'He never talks about them and it's our families who usually upset us most.'

His own father and mother barely spoke to each other now. On the few occasions when he went there to try and cook a lunch, the atmosphere was intolerable. Tobe may have gone through something like that years ago. Quentin wondered where he ate when he did eat. He obviously couldn't afford the prices in Haywards.

One night by accident he found out. There was such a bad mood in his family home, with his mother retiring to bed and his father sighing and saying he would go to his club, that Quentin had left quietly.

He didn't think that either of them were really aware that he had left. He went to a café called Mick's on a corner where he often bought chips on his way home from the cinema, but had never sat down to have a meal.

Beans on toast, fried eggs and chips, two sausages and a spoon of mashed potatoes and peas. That was the choice at Mick's. The place smelled of cooking fat, nobody wiped down the tables, the lino on the floor was torn and yet something about the place itself was enchanting. It was very handy to get at on a corner of a busy street but a little oasis when you went into its cobbled courtyard and closed the door. It was as if the world slowed down there.

Quentin saw Brenda the waitress and her husband Patrick, a serious guy, deep in conversation over their beans and toast. Then he saw Tobe with his plate of sausages, egg and chips.

Tobe waved him over. 'If you're not meeting anyone . . .?'

'No, indeed, I'd be happy to have your company.' Quentin sat down with the older man and they talked about this and that.

Neither asking the other what they were doing there. 'See you tomorrow at Haywards,' Tobe said.

He paused for ten seconds to greet Brenda and her husband, enough to show them he had noticed them but not enough to intrude on what looked like a very private conversation.

So the weeks went by, and every now and then they met in Mick's for eggs and beans, and Quentin said what he would do with this place if it was his and he had a backer, and Tobe said that his visit was nearing its end and he was going back to Australia.

Quentin told him how his parents would be so much better in two small separate establishments, but that neither of them would budge. Tobe told Quentin that for forty years in Australia he had wondered about his Irish family. Now that he had discovered them he would waste no more time, not one second, wondering about them, they simply weren't worth it.

'You can't have spent much time with them, Tobe. Weren't you in Haywards all day and at Mick's Café all night?'

'I saw them all right, and I didn't like what I saw. Have you made your plans to travel, Quentin?'

'Yes, I have got as far as enquiring the price of off-peak travel, it's still very dear. But Tobe, are you changing the subject away from your family? I'll probably never see you again after next week when you go back. I'll go mad wondering what you said to your family and they to you. Can't you tell me?'

'Not yet. I have something to think through. But I'll tell you next week, in Mick's. Would Thursday be all right, do you think?'

At Mick's on Thursday Tobe looked different, more together somehow. 'Come on, Quentin, my treat. We'll lash out and have beans *and* egg *and* sausages.'

It was hard to put a finger on it, but it was as if Tobe had suddenly taken charge. 'It's been a great pleasure meeting you. It made my visit to Dublin worthwhile and helped to clear my thoughts. Will you come and see me in Australia in a few years' time?'

'Look, Tobe, I'm having difficulty getting the money to go to Italy or Marrakesh, for heaven's sake. How could I get to Australia? Even if I do want to see the purple and orange sunrises.'

'You'll be able to afford it,' Tobe said, quite calmly, as if he knew it would happen.

'Oh, I wish,' Quentin said, pushing his hair back from his face. And then Tobe told him the story.

Beginning with his name, which was Toby Hayward.

He was the cousin who didn't fit in, the remittance man who got an allowance as long as he stayed out of the country and far away. He had come back to see the Haywards, but since they didn't know him, he thought he would observe them a bit first. He had seen nothing in their store that he liked, nothing except Quentin. Tobe had done well in Australia, better than any of the Haywards had ever known. It wasn't their business, so he hadn't told them.

And now that he had seen haughty Harold in the restaurant, and arrogant George Hayward in the furniture department, sour and prissy Lucy Hayward in the silver department, he realised they were not people he wanted to be involved with.

Quentin, on the other hand, a boy with a dream who wanted to run a restaurant. Now that was something different. That was what he could pay back to Ireland, the land where he had been born. Quentin would come to a solicitor tomorrow morning with him and then be in a position to buy Mick's Café that afternoon.

'This doesn't happen in real life,' Quentin said.

'But you believe me, don't you? You believe I have the money and I'm giving it to you. I'm not out of the funny farm or anything.'

'Yes, of course I believe you want to do this, and I know I would do the same myself if it were me, so I understand. But it won't work, Tobe.'

'Why not?'

'Your family?'

'Don't know I'm home. I'm just the shabby old person they move from section to section of their store.'

'They might feel they have a prior claim ... family money.'

'No, I made this money. I worked and invested, and I worked day and night and invested more.'

'Maybe you should give it to a charity.'

'I've given plenty to charity. I'm just giving you enough to buy this place.'

'Maybe Mick won't sell.' Quentin was afraid to let himself believe it would happen.

'How much do you think would be a fair price, Quentin?'

Quentin told him.

'Give him half as much again, he'll sell, he'll run out of the place.'

'And then?'

'And then you'll call in sick to Haywards tomorrow and we get the money organised.'

'This doesn't happen,' Quentin said for the second time.

'Mick, could you come over here for a minute, mate?' Tobe called.

And Mick, who was tired and wanted nothing more than to be able to take his wife and handicapped daughter down to the country to live, was summoned to the table to hear the news that would change his life.

Brenda's Decision

Brenda and her friend Nora had been inseparable during catering college. They made plans for life, which varied a bit depending on what was happening. Sometimes they thought they would go to Paris together and learn from a French chef. Then they might set up a thirty-bedroom hotel in the countryside, which would have a waiting list of six months for people trying to come and stay.

In reality, of course, it was slightly different. Shifts here and there and a lot of waitressing. Too many people after the same jobs, plenty of young men and women with experience. Nora and Brenda found it hard going at the start.

So they went to London, where two things of great significance happened. Nora met an Italian man called Mario who said he loved her more than he loved life itself. And Nora certainly loved him as much, if not more.

Brenda at the time caught a heavy cold, which turned into pneumonia, and as a result lost her hearing for a time. She regarded this deafness as a terrible blow. She, who could almost hear the grass grow, before her illness.

'I was never sympathetic enough to deaf people,' she wept to the busy doctor who gave her leaflets on lip-reading classes and told her to stop this self-pity, her hearing would return in time.

So Brenda went to the classes, mainly much older people, men and women struggling with hearing aids.

She learned how to practise on a VCR machine. You watched

the news with the volume turned down over and over until you could guess what they were saying, and then you turned it up very high to check if you were right.

Miss Hill, the teacher, loved Brenda as she was so eager to learn. Brenda learned to study people's faces as they spoke, trying to make sense of what she couldn't hear. She understood that the hard letters to hear were the ones in the middle of a word. Most people could read the word 'pay' or 'pan', for example, but it was much harder to see a hidden consonant like an l or an r in the middle of a word. 'Pray' or 'plan' were much more difficult to work out. You had to do that from the meaning of the sentence.

Brenda had taken to it all so much, she hardly realised when her normal hearing returned. By this stage she could read conversations across a room.

Nora and Mario were very impressed. 'If all else fails, we can put you in a circus,' Nora cried, delighted.

'And I will sell tickets outside,' Mario promised.

But they all knew this wouldn't happen. Mario was going back shortly to Sicily to marry his fiancée, the girl Gabriella who lived next door to him back there.

Nora knew this too, but she just would not accept it. She was not going to stay in London without Mario, or go back to Ireland to cry over him there. She would follow him to Sicily and all it would bring.

Brenda was lonely in London when her friend had gone. She was bewildered by a love so great that it could withstand such humiliation. In her letters, Nora wrote of how she lived in a bed-sitting-room in the village that looked down on Mario's hotel. How she saw his wedding and the children's christenings and was slowly becoming part of the life of the place.

Brenda could never have loved like that. Sometimes she wondered if she would ever love at all. She came back to Dublin, but it was the same there. Nobody filled her days and nights with passion like Mario had been able to do for Nora O'Donoghue. Everyone said that Brenda was cool and calm in a crisis, a great reliable person to have around if someone spilled the gravy or dropped a tray. Brenda wondered was she going to be like that all her life, look calm and unflappable? Never in love like the couples she served at table, never upset and aching like the colleagues she consoled in kitchens when their love affairs were shaky. Never to marry even as two of her younger sisters had married, with huge drama and great expenditure of nerves. Brenda had been there, cups of tea, aspirins and calm advice at the ready.

She didn't know why she went to the dance that night. Possibly to have something to write to Nora about. It was for past pupils of their catering college. Maybe she hoped she might hear of some job opportunities.

She wore the new dress she had bought for her sister's wedding. It was very dressy, cream lace with a rose-pink jacket. It looked well with her dark hair. She thought that she got many admiring looks, but perhaps she was only imagining it.

Across the room she suddenly saw Pillowcase. Now she couldn't remember why she and Nora had called him that, an over-serious fellow, head in his books, barely any time to socialise. She heard he had gone to some high-flying place in Scotland, that he had been with a pastry cook in France. What was he doing back here? And even more important, what was his name? Paddy ... Pat?

She looked over at him. As clearly as if the words were written like subtitles, she read his lips and heard him say to the man he was with, 'Will you look at that. It's Brenda O'Hara from our year in college. Isn't she a very fine looking girl? I haven't seen her in years. Very classy, altogether.' He seemed full of admiration.

The man he was with, a loudmouth whom Brenda knew around town, said, 'Oh, you'll get nowhere there. Real ice maiden, let me tell you.'

'Well, I'll go over and say hallo. She can't take offence at that.' He walked towards her.

Sometimes she felt a little guilty at having advance knowledge because of her extra hearing due to the lip-reading. Why hadn't the other eejit said his name, so that at least she'd know that much?

Pillowcase approached her with a broad smile. He had smartened himself up. He looked taller, or else he didn't crouch over so much.

'Patrick Brennan,' he said as he shook her hand.

'Brenda O'Hara, delighted to see you again.' She must beat the silly nickname out of her mind.

'Don't I remember you and Nora O'Donoghue very well, and is she here tonight as well?'

'Sometime when you have an hour, remind me to tell you what happened to Nora,' Brenda laughed.

'I have an hour and more now, Brenda,' he said.

Would she have seen the admiration in his face anyhow, or was it because she had lip-read his praise of her that Brenda turned her charm on Patrick Brennan?

Whatever it was, she saw him most evenings for the next two weeks. He seemed pleased that she still lived with her family. 'I'd have thought a glamour girl like you would have gone off with a rich man long ago,' he teased.

'No, no, I'm an ice maiden, didn't they tell you that?' she teased him back.

'I think I heard it said.' He shuffled awkwardly.

She wrote about him to Nora.

He's still very serious about work. He'd rather do nothing than work for a place that he doesn't think is worth it. He says I'm wasting myself doing waitress shifts here, there and anywhere. He'll do construction work or delivering cases of wine rather than work in a kitchen which would give him a bad name. But I don't agree. It's all work. You're learning all the time and anyway, he's a man who doesn't even have a flat of his own. He sleeps on people's sofas or floors. He doesn't notice.

He told her about the small farm in the country where he grew up; how his younger brother, who wasn't exactly simple-minded but not far off it, lived there still. She told him about the corner shop where her father had worked so hard to make a living. They went to the cinema and sometimes she paid if Patrick had no money. They went to Mick's Café for old times' sake.

One lunchtime as she unpacked their sandwiches to eat by the Grand Canal, she said to him firmly that she had her own plans as to how they would spend the evening.

'I live at home, Patrick. For over a month now I've been going out every single night with you.'

'Yes?' He looked anxious.

'So I'd like to let them see you, know the kind of person I'm meeting.'

'Sure.'

'No, you don't understand. It's not for them to inspect you. It's not a gun to your head. It's common courtesy.'

'No, I agree entirely. I thought you were going to say you were tired of going out with me. When we have a daughter won't we feel the very same way about her, want to know her friends?'

94

'What?' said Brenda.

'When we have a daughter. It's not the same with sons.'

'But what are you saying, exactly?'

He looked at her, bewildered. 'When we're married. We will have children, won't we?' He was genuinely concerned.

'Patrick, excuse me. Did I miss something here? Did you ask me to marry you? Did I say yes? It's quite a big thing. I should have remembered it, I know I should.'

He held her hand. 'You will, won't you?' he begged.

'I don't know, Patrick. I really don't know yet.'

'What else would you do?' he said, alarmed.

'Well, a number of things. I might marry no one. Or I might marry someone else as yet un-met. Or I might marry you in the fullness of time when we know that we love each other.'

'But don't we know now?'

'No, we don't. We haven't talked about it at all.'

'We haven't stopped talking about what we'll do,' he said.

'But that's work, Patrick, what jobs we'll get.'

'No, it's about what kind of life we'll live. I thought it was about our life together.'

'This is nonsense, Patrick.' She stood up, upset. 'You can't take us for granted like that. We're not even lovers.' She was very indignant.

'It's not for want of trying,' he protested.

'Not on the sofa of some ghastly flat with half of Dublin about to walk through the door with cans of Guinness any minute.'

'So what do you want, Brenda? A night in a b. & b. and for me to go down on one knee? Is that it?'

'No.' She was hurt and angry. 'Not that at all. It sounds ludicrous. I *do* like you, Patrick, you fool. Why else was I inviting you home? But I wanted love and passion and desire and all those things too. Not a casual munching on a sandwich and talking about our daughter as if it were all planned.'

'I'm sorry I did it wrong,' he said.

'If I thought you loved me and would take any kind of job like I do while saving for a home, and if you talked more rather than having glum silences about your future. And if you asked me properly and . . . well, if you desired me . . . I can't think of a better word, then I would strongly think of marrying you, and sooner rather than later. But it's useless now, because if you do all those

95

things it's only my having written the script and my having fed you the lines.'

'So I can't come to supper? Is this what you're saying?' he asked.

'No, you clown, come to supper,' she said, and went away fast before he could see the tears in her eyes.

That night she reassured her mother that there was nothing in it. 'He's just a friend, Mam, a quiet friend without much to say for himself. Can't anyone of your sex-mad older generation realise that people in their twenties can be friends these days?'

At supper, Patrick Brennan brought flowers to her mother and sat down to have chicken and ham pie. And from the moment he came in the door, he never stopped talking. He praised the lightness of the pastry and flavour of the sauce. He admired the cushion covers which Mrs O'Hara had embroidered. He begged to see the wedding albums. He asked Mr O'Hara where he got fresh vegetables and told him of a cheaper place. And when they were all worn out trying to get a word in edgeways, he told them all, her two younger sisters included, that he loved Brenda but up to now had no prospects and no hope of being able to make a home for her. But suddenly on the canal bank he had got enlightenment and he realised it was a matter of any old job in catering until they had a home and could go and build their dream.

The O'Haras were astonished at him. Brenda was dumb-founded. When he left, they said he was a very nice fellow indeed, gabby though, very over-talkative, hyper almost. Hadn't Brenda said he was quiet?

'I got it wrong,' Brenda said humbly.

In weeks he had found them a job together, Patrick as chef and Brenda as front-of-house manager.

'You despise this kind of place,' she said.

'What does it matter, Brenda? A month's salary and we'll have our bed-sitter,' he said.

'We can have it now, from my savings,' she said.

They found one that day, and they practised passion and desire that night and found it fine.

They were married very shortly after that, a simple wedding with just cake and wine. It was a beautiful cake made and iced by Patrick and much photographed.

There was a series of jobs, none of them really satisfactory, none of them giving scope to what they thought they could do. But they had no money, no one to back them, to set them up in a place where they could make their mark.

And as time went by there was no sign of the daughter they had spoken of, or the son. But they were still young and perhaps it was better that they didn't have to worry yet about raising a family.

They worked in a place which only served food smothered in batter. In another where there was after-hours drinking and people wanted omelettes way into the night. They tried to take over an office canteen but were given so little money, it was impossible to present decent food. Finally, they were in a place where they realised that tax avoidance and cutting corners were going to have it closed down. This last place began to break their hearts. Particularly since the management was supercilious and snobbish and made the guests feel uneasy.

'We'll have to leave here,' Brenda said. 'If you saw how they humiliate people in the dining-room.'

'Don't let's go until we have somewhere else,' Patrick begged.

The very next night Brenda saw the nice boy Quentin Barry, whom she often met when doing extra afternoon shifts at Haywards. He was with his mother and had chosen a quiet table far across the room from her.

It was a quiet night. She had served her tables. Quietly she took off her shoes as she stood behind a serving table with its long tablecloths hiding her indiscretion from the restaurant. Her shoes were tight and high and she had been on her feet since 8 a.m. It was bliss to be in her stockinged feet.

She looked across at the mother and son talking. Very alike in blonde and handsome looks, but not in manner. Mrs Barry was fussy and very self-conscious. Quentin was gentle and a listener. But not tonight. He was telling his mother about something that seemed to astonish her.

Automatically, Brenda tuned in. She didn't have any sense of eavesdropping, to her this was as if they were speaking at the top of their voices.

'You only get peanuts, working as a waiter,' Sara Barry was saying.

'I got enough working there to keep myself for several years.' Quentin was quiet.

'Yes, but you can't *buy* a place, Quentin. Be serious, sweetheart. You're not the kind of person who can buy a place and make a restaurant out of it.'

'It's not very smart now. In fact, Mick's Café, well, it's very down at heel, but if I get the right people . . .'

'No, darling, listen to me. You know nothing of business. You'd be bankrupt in a month . . .'

'I'll get people who would know, people who were trained, who would do it right.'

'You'd tire of it every day. The anxiety . . .'

'I wouldn't be there. I'd be travelling.'

'I feel quite weak, Quentin,' Sara said.

'No, Mother. Don't feel weak. I just wanted you to know how happy I am. I haven't been happy for a very long time. You used to tell me I was the love and the light of your life. I thought you'd be pleased to know I am so happy.'

Brenda then for the first time realised she was in a private conversation and looked away. She put on her shoes, walked to the kitchen on unsteady feet.

'Patrick,' she said, 'could you pour me a small brandy?'

'You look as if you've seen a ghost.'

'I've seen our future,' she said.

And in a matter of days it was sorted out.

It would be their future to turn Mick's Café into the restaurant they had always dreamed of.

'What will you call it?' they asked Quentin.

'If you don't think it's too arrogant, I think my own name,' he said shyly. 'And now can I ask you one thing, how did you hear I was buying Mick's place? I know he didn't tell anyone, and I didn't tell anyone. So it's a mystery,' he smiled.

Brenda paused. 'I don't put it on my CV. It's not a nice quality. But I lip-read. I heard you telling your mother.' She looked down.

'It's a good quality to have when you run a restaurant,' Quentin said. 'I bet we'll be glad of it through the years.'

Blouse Brennan

No one could remember why he was called Blouse Brennan. No one except his big brother Patrick.

Blouse was a bit slow at school, but he was very willing so they didn't make fun of him. The Brothers liked him, Blouse was always there to do a message, run down town and get them a pack of cigarettes, and the shopkeepers never minded giving them to Blouse though he was well underage, because you'd know they weren't for himself.

The other boys decided that Blouse was not to be tormented because of his brother Patrick. Patrick was built like a tank and you'd be a foolish lad to take him on. So Blouse lived a fairly peaceful life for a guy who couldn't play games properly, who stumbled over his shoes and couldn't remember more than two lines of poetry no matter how long he studied.

When Patrick left school to serve his time in a hotel, Blouse worried. 'They might beat me when you're gone next term,' he said fearfully.

'They won't.' Patrick was a man of few words.

'But you won't be there, Patrick.'

'I'll come in once a week until they understand,' Patrick said. And true to his word, he was there on the first day of term walking idly around the schoolyard, giving a cuff here, a push there to establish a presence. Anyone who had even contemplated picking on Blouse Brennan had a severe change of mind.

Patrick Brennan would be back.

Patrick came home every weekend and always took his brother out for a run. The boy could talk to him in a way he didn't talk at home. Their parents were elderly and distant. Too absorbed in making a living from the smallholding with its few animals and its rocky soil.

'Why do they call me Blouse, do you know, Patrick?'

'Sure, they have to call you something, they call me Pillowcase at work.' Patrick was shruggy about it all.

'I've no idea how it all came about,' Blouse said sadly.

Patrick knew that it had all started when the lad had been heard calling his shirt his blouse years back and some of the kids picked up on the name.

For some reason it had stuck. Even the Brothers called him that, and half the people in the town. His mother and father called him Sonny so hardly anyone knew that he had been baptised Joseph Matthew Brennan.

Patrick worked very hard in the hotel business. He rose from scullery helper to kitchen hand, he did stints as a porter and at the front desk, and went to do a catering course where he eventually met a girl called Brenda and brought her photograph home for inspection.

'She's got a lovely smile,' said Blouse.

'She looks healthy enough,' his father admitted grudgingly.

'Not a girl to settle in the land, I'd say,' his mother complained.

'Well, that's also for the best then, since Brenda and I haven't a notion of running this place, Blouse will be in charge here in the fullness of time.'

Patrick spoke very definitely.

The parents, as was their custom, said nothing at all.

And that was the day Blouse got his great bout of confidence. He was fourteen years old, but one day he would be a landowner. That made him superior to nearly everyone else in his class at school. He made the mistake of telling Horse Harris who was a bully, and Horse mocked him and pushed him around. 'Squire Blouse', he kept calling him.

Patrick made one appearance in the schoolyard and rearranged the nose of Horse Harris. Nothing more was said, the word 'Squire' was never mentioned again.

*

One day Patrick bought Blouse a pint and said that when he and Brenda married, he would like Blouse to be their best man.

'Imagine, you a married man with a home of your own,' Blouse said.

'You're always welcome to come and see us, stay the night, even a weekend.'

'I know, but I wouldn't have much call going to Dublin. What would a fellow called Blouse be doing in a big city?' he asked.

Patrick brought Brenda home for a visit.

Very good-looking, Blouse thought, and confident. Not like people round here. She was very polite to his mother and father, helped with the washing up, and didn't mind the big hairy dog pawing her smart skirt.

She explained to Blouse and Patrick's mother that the wedding would be performed by her uncle who was a priest, and she reassured their father that it would be a very small affair, only twenty people at the most. They were going to have a beautiful wedding cake and bottles of wine.

Wouldn't people think it off not to have plates of cold chicken and ham? Blouse's mother wanted to know.

Apparently not in Dublin, where people were as odd as two left shoes.

There was a lot of groaning and grumbling when the day came. Blouse drove his parents to the railway station and Patrick met them in Dublin. Blouse wondered how anyone could live in a place as full of noise and strangers as Dublin, but he said nothing, just smiled at everyone and shook hands when it seemed the right thing to do.

He thought the meal was extraordinary all right, no bit of dinner, but the cake was a miracle. Imagine, his own big brother had iced it and done all those curly bits himself and the pink writing too with the names and the date.

He was taking his parents home on the five o'clock train. There had been no question of an overnight in Dublin. It would have been too much for them.

Brenda, his new sister-in-law, had been very kind. 'When we get a place with more room than just the floor, Blouse, you'll come and stay with us. We'd like that and we'll show you Dublin.'

'I'll do that one day, maybe even drive the whole way in the van,' Blouse said proudly.

It would be something to think about, look forward to.

Something to say around the village. 'My sister-in-law in Dublin wants me to go and stay.'

His father got a pain in his chest and died three months after Patrick's wedding. His mother seemed to think it was just one more low in life, like the hens not laying properly or the blight in the apple trees. Blouse looked after her the best he could. And time went on the way it always had.

There weren't any girlfriends because Blouse said he wasn't really at ease with girls. He never understood what they were laughing at, and if he laughed too they stopped laughing. But he wasn't lonely. He even went to Dublin to see his brother and sister-in-law. He drove the van the whole way.

Brenda and Patrick worried about how Blouse would cope with the traffic, but it wasn't necessary. He arrived at the house without a bother.

'I meant to tell you about the quays being one way,' Patrick said.

'That wasn't a problem,' Blouse said. He sat eagerly like a child waiting to be entertained.

They talked to him easily and told him how they were hoping to get a job running a really classy restaurant for a man called Quentin Barry.

'It has all been due to Brenda,' Patrick said proudly. She had managed to find them this opportunity just at the right time.

Quentin Barry had come into some money, bought Mick's Café and wanted to set up a restaurant. He needed a chef and manager.

If this were to happen!

If they got this place going properly they were made, because the man would hardly be back at all, they could put their own stamp on the restaurant.

Blouse wasn't a drinker, but he had a glass of champagne with them to celebrate. When he got home, his mother said that Horse Harris had been around to talk business about the farm.

'What did Horse want to know?' Blouse was worried. Horse had never been good news. Apparently he had talked business with his mother. That was all she would say. Blouse wondered should he tell Patrick all about it, but no, they were too busy and excited. They had got the job working for this man Quentin who was going to let them set up their own class of a place. It wouldn't be fair, boring them with matters like Horse Harris coming to the farm and Mam's refusal to talk about it all.

Brenda wrote a note every week as regular as clockwork, and Patrick wrote a few lines at the end.

'I don't know what it is that has her writing all that nonsense every week, and putting a stamp on it,' Mrs Brennan said. 'Too little to do, that's her problem.'

But Blouse liked it. He told Horse one day that he got a letter every week from Dublin.

'Don't bother your barney replying to those two, they're after the place, that's all,' Horse had said scathingly.

Blouse went to take his mother her mug of tea and found her dead. He knelt down beside her bed and said a prayer, then he got the doctor, the priest and Shay Harris, the undertaker. When he had everything organised he phoned Patrick and Brenda.

There were a respectable number of people there.

'You're very much liked here, Blouse,' Patrick said to him.

'Aw, sure, they all liked Mam and Dad,' Blouse said.

Shay Harris asked if Patrick was going to take his things with him when he was going back to Dublin.

'What things?' Patrick asked.

And they learned that Shay's brother Horse had bought the little farm. His money was in the bank safe and sound, it was all legal and documented. Blouse would have to leave in a month.

Patrick was incensed but, oddly, Brenda didn't agree. 'He'd be far too lonely here on his own, Patrick. He would become a recluse. Tell him to come and live with us in Dublin.'

'Blouse would be lost in Dublin,' said Patrick.

Blouse couldn't believe it all. 'I'm too stupid to live anywhere,' he said sadly. 'I should have told you about Horse coming round here, but I was afraid you'd think I wanted you to come down and hit him for me again.'

'My days of belting people are over, Blouse,' Patrick said.

'You'll come and be near us,' Brenda said. 'You'll have your own money from the sale of the farm, so when you want to find a place for yourself you can, and you'd be a great help to us.'

'What could I do? I only dig fields and mind sheep and collect eggs from under the hens.'

'Couldn't you do that for us in Dublin too?' Brenda suggested.

Patrick looked at her, bewildered.

'Well, maybe not the sheep, but we could get an allotment.'

'A what?'

'Allotment. You know, Blouse. They must have them in country towns too. Big bits of waste ground and everyone rents a patch and grows their own things on it, digs and plants and harvests.'

'And who would it belong to?' Blouse was confused.

'Well, whoever owns the bit of ground, I suppose. I'll bring you and show you. They have little sheds and huts to put your shovels and forks in and big fences of wire to grow things up against, and what you grow you keep.'

Even his brother Patrick seemed to think it was a good idea. 'We could put that on the menu ... organic vegetables, fresh free-range eggs,' he said.

'But where would I live?' Blouse began.

'There are plenty of places letting rooms near here. I'll ask around and find out,' Patrick said.

'And you could eventually come and live with us, of course,' said Brenda. 'There's a warren of old rooms in the back and upstairs. They're in the most desperate state at the moment but it will all look fine in time. We've done our room upstairs so when we have time to get the rubble cleared out, we'll paint one of them for you. You could help choose the paint and all.'

His mother had never asked him what colour room he'd like. Blouse had always wanted yellow walls and a white ceiling. He had seen a room like that in a magazine and thought it would be very cheerful with a tartan bedspread. And now he was going to have one of his own.

'I'd love to see the place and have a vision of it,' he said.

There was something about the way he said 'vision' that made Brenda and Patrick feel choked up.

They had a million other things to do which were higher priority than finding Blouse somewhere to stay but that's not the way it seemed now.

'Come on and we'll take you to see where you might live,' Brenda said.

Once they arrived at the shambles that was going to be their beloved restaurant they found themselves leading Blouse off to the storehouses, outhouses and falling-down rooms that formed the back of Quentins.

Blouse found a room that suited him well. He was not one to sit down and talk about things. 'Will I start on it now, do you think, Brenda?' he asked with his big, innocent smile.

She seemed to have tears in her eyes when she said that would be great, but he might have imagined it.

He got a wheelbarrow and got rid of the rubble. Blouse wanted the room to be nice and empty when they brought up all the furniture from home, from the little farm that Horse Harris had bought. They would bring the bed he had slept in all his life and the grandfather clock.

'Maybe I'll clear out a few other rooms for you,' Blouse offered. 'We have a lot of furniture coming up from home, and if in the future you could offer the staff living accommodation you might get them cheaper.'

They looked at him in amazement. It was all coming together. Thanks to Blouse. And it was arranged much more speedily than anyone could have believed.

Patrick managed to call and see Horse Harris before they left the town with every stick of furniture on board a huge rented van.

'Glad there are no hard feelings,' Horse said with the horrible smile of a man who knew he had beaten the slightly simple Blouse Brennan and his smart-arse brother.

'None at all, Horse,' said Patrick, giving him a handshake that could have broken every finger in Horse's hand and a twist of the wrist that could have and did twist the muscle.

Horse had no grounds to complain.

Blouse worked hard on the allotment. He drove there every day in the old van that had belonged to his parents. He learned about new vegetables that had never been part of his life back home. He had two dozen Rhode Island Reds who laid big fresh eggs and he was planning to get two dozen more.

Some evenings he helped behind the scenes in the restaurant. Blouse never minded what he was asked to do. Take out the rubbish, stack the dish-washing machines. He moved out of Patrick's house and got himself a little place near the allotment so that he could keep an eye on the hens. He had a lock on their coop at night, but it was nice to be near them.

A young, businesslike woman called on him one day. She said she was Mary O'Brien, and she had been given his address by Mrs Brennan in Quentins. She was anxious to do an article in a magazine about keeping hens and growing vegetables and she wondered if she could discuss the finer points with him.

They sat and talked, and he stroked the feathers of the hens as he spoke, and he picked out seedlings to show her how they should be planted.

Mary said she hadn't enjoyed herself so much for ages, and now could he show her where to get the bus back to the office?

'Don't you have a car?' Blouse thought she was a smart kind of person who would definitely be driving an office car and changing it every eighteen months.

'I'm afraid to drive. I've tried lessons, but I always panic,' she admitted.

'Ah no, it's very simple,' Blouse explained. 'When you panic you just indicate and pull in, that's what I always did for years and I drive now like as if I had wings.' He gave her a lift back in his battered van, and pretended he was anxious now and then.

'I don't like the look of that big bus bearing down on me. I see a place on my side so I'll indicate and move in until we catch our breath and then we can go.'

Mary O'Brien looked at him with amazement. 'Would you teach me to drive?' she begged.

'Oh, no, I'm not qualified. I'm only an eejit. You have to go to a professional, they wouldn't want a half-wit like me to be taking away their living.'

She shook his hand and said she'd send a photographer out to his allotment. 'You're no eejit, don't put yourself down. I really hope I'll see you again,' she said.

Blouse felt terrific. He knew she meant it. 'If you got a nice driving teacher, maybe he'd let me sit at the back of the car as a kind of support,' he said.

'I think that wouldn't be a problem,' said Mary O'Brien.

They were loath to part.

'You'll be famous after this article, Blouse Brennan. Self-sufficiency guru, they'll call you. Well, I'll call you that anyway, and then other people will.'

'Imagine,' he said.

'Oh, by the way, about your name ... your brother said your real name was ...'

'I'm happy with Blouse,' he said quickly.

'I think you're right. If I had a name like that, I'd keep it,' Mary O'Brien said wistfully.

'I'll give you a ring when the photographer has been and gone,' said Blouse Brennan, who had never had his picture taken professionally and never telephoned a girl before in his life.

Longings

Brenda had been very sure that she would conceive quickly. Her mother had given birth to five daughters and there were hints that there would have been many more had not great abstinence been practised. Two of her sisters had what were called honeymoon babies, and apart from her friend Nora out in Italy, everyone else that she knew had children. In fact, there were times when she feared that pregnancy might come too early and leave her unable to cope. In those years she had thought about it from time to time. But now, with the eighteen-hour days they often worked at the setting up of Quentins, in those early, exhausting months dealing with builders, planning the layout of the kitchens and the dining area, the setting up of suppliers, it was the furthest thing from their minds.

When it got a little calmer, after the opening of the restaurant when Quentin had gone away with an easy heart to Morocco to leave them totally in charge, Brenda began to think about it all again. They had been many years married now, both of them apparently fit and strong.

'About us having children?' she began one evening when they were sitting with mugs of tea in the kitchen they had insisted on having in their upstairs flat. Even though they would live over one of the best kitchens in Dublin, they didn't want to go down there if they needed a scrambled egg.

She saw Patrick's eyes light up and he reached for her hand. 'Brenda, no?' There was such hope in his voice and face.

'No, sadly no.' She tried to keep her own voice light and not to dwell on the sense of loss she had just noticed.

He got up to try and hide his face. 'Sorry, I just thought when you said about us having children,' he muttered away from her.

She sat still. 'I know. I want it as much as you do, Patrick. So don't you think we should talk?'

'I didn't think that's how you got children, by talking,' he said in a slightly mutinous way. He didn't usually have a tone like that. She decided to ignore it.

'No, I agree with you, but we do a fair amount of what does get children as well and it's not working, so I wondered, should we go and get ourselves looked at, if you know what I mean?'

'I know what you mean,' Patrick Brennan said. 'And I'm not crazy about the sound of it.'

'Me neither, a lot of legs in stirrups and things,' Brenda said. 'But if it works, then it will have been worth it.'

'When you think of what you read in the papers, half the country seems to get pregnant after one drunken fumble on a Friday night,' Patrick grumbled.

'So will I make an appointment for us with Dr Flynn?' Brenda asked.

'Does he see us both together, do you think?' Patrick wondered.

'Probably for a chat, I'd say, and then he sends us off for tests.'

They both thought about the whole undertaking ahead with no pleasure at all. They didn't book the appointment that week, because it was the week the inspectors were coming to check the ventilation. Nor the next because there was the huge excitement that Blouse Brennan and Mary O'Brien announced they would marry. Nor the week after, as there were several intense social visits with the O'Brien family, who had to be convinced that a man called Blouse was the right match for their daughter.

And then there were the meetings with Quentin's accountants, with the bank, and with lawyers. Even the meeting with the sign painter, who was coming to put their name up, took far longer than it should have. It was in heavy gold paint on very dark rich green: a huge Q in front and a hanging sign with the name on the side. They looked at it in disbelief. The whole word ran into one; the painter had put no apostrophe after the name.

'But we showed you, Brian, look at the drawings, we agreed.'

'I know, it's a mystery all right.' Brian scratched his head.

'Brian, we could have had really good painters like the Kennedy

Brothers and instead we took you to give you a start, and what happens? We're the laughing stock of Dublin, that's what. We can't spell the name of our own place. That's what people will say.'

Brian saw the two upset faces looking up at the sign. 'I'll give it to you for nothing. Can't be fairer than that, can I?' he asked.

They asked Quentin on his weekly phone call.

'I was never one for punctuation. I'd prefer it the way your painter did it,' he said.

So week after week went by without Brenda and Patrick Brennan thinking they had the luxury of an hour or two to visit the doctor about something which was not after all a serious illness.

And often at night, after their long, busy days, they reached for each other in their big double bed with the white lace curtains around it. If they thought that maybe the whole matter would right itself before they needed to discuss it with Dr Flynn, neither of them said anything about it at all.

Blouse and Mary had a small wedding and a week's honeymoon on an organic farm in Scotland. They came home full of further ideas of what they could grow. Blouse was a married man now. No more living in a shed up beside the allotment. No, indeed. They had transformed the small room at the back of Quentins, taking in other storerooms, and made the whole thing into a perfect little apartment.

Mary got herself a regular column in a newspaper where she became highly respected as an adviser on growing your own vegetables in a small space. She even appeared on television programmes as an expert on the subject, her wonderful red curls bobbing and her eyes dancing as she spoke of her husband Blouse, without any self-consciousness about the name but with huge pride in the man.

Blouse grew more confident every day and no day did he seem more happy and self-assured than the day he told Patrick and Brenda that they were expecting a child. Four months married, and now this great news.

They managed to show their enthusiasm and hide their jealousy until they were alone that night in their bedroom. They tried to be generous but it was hard. The sense of unfairness was all around them. Although they sat side by side there was a huge gulf between them. Their shoulders didn't even touch.

'It will be all right,' Brenda said.

'Of course it will,' Patrick said.

'I'll ring Dr Flynn tomorrow,' she promised. 'To wave his magic wand.'

When they got into bed, she put her arm around him. At bad times they were a great consolation to each other. So often making love had washed away the cares and anxieties of the day.

But not tonight.

'I'm tired, love,' he said, and turned on one side away from her.

Brenda lay awake all night looking at the walls covered with pictures and memories. Even though her limbs were aching with fatigue, she couldn't find any sleep.

Dr Flynn was pleasant and technical and made them feel that he was not sounding overly intimate when he asked questions about whether full penetrative intercourse had taken place. He then sent them both to a hospital for a series of tests and asked them to come back in six weeks.

It was a strange time in their lives. They made love only twice and a third time, when it had seemed likely, Patrick said there was no point as it was the wrong time of the month for Brenda, nothing would come of it.

And during all this time, Mary patted her small bump proudly and Blouse talked about the responsibilities of fatherhood ahead of him.

Every woman Brenda met seemed to be talking about children, for good or evil. Either they were such darlings and so wonderful that the women couldn't bear to go out to work and leave them. Or else they were as troublesome as weasels, snarling and ungrateful, and if their mothers could get rid of them legally they would.

And Brenda listened and smiled.

The only person who understood was her friend Nora, miles and miles away in Sicily. Nora who could never tell the village that she loved Mario, even though many of them may have suspected. Sometimes people then said to Signora, which was what they called her, not Nora, that she was lucky to be childless, not to have the problems they had. But Nora would sit at her window and watch Mario playing in the square with his boys. How she yearned for a little dark curly-haired baby of his to hold in her arms. She longed with such an ache that she nearly convinced herself he might leave Gabriella and his other children and stay with her if she were to produce a baby for him.

But fortunately she had never tested the theory.

Brenda wrote to Nora as she could write to no one close. She wrote one night as Patrick slept on deeply on his side of the bed:

He doesn't love me as me any more. He will only consider touching me when I am meant to be most fertile. The tests showed that there is nothing preventing us conceiving. I ovulate normally. Patrick's sperm count is normal. They keep telling us we're not ready for fertility drugs yet. Patrick just keeps wondering how old do we have to get? I don't know any more, Nora, I really don't. You keep hearing of people having eleven embryos with fertility drugs. Then Mary and Blouse will have their baby next week. And I have to be glad and delighted and thrilled. I feel so mean-spirited not to be.

Patrick didn't want to talk about it. 'What do you mean, how do I *feel* about Blouse being able to father a child when I'm not? How do you think I feel?' he snapped.

'I didn't put it that way.' Tears of hurt sprang in Brenda's eyes.

'It's what you meant, though, Brenda. The fool of the family is able to get his girl pregnant but you can't say the same for the elder brother.'

'I will not have you speak of Blouse that way, Patrick. You never did before. You never let anyone else do so. He told me you used to go to his schoolyard and fight battles with anyone who made such a remark, and now you're doing it yourself.'

He felt ashamed, she could see it, his head hung down. 'I'm sorry. I don't know what came into me.'

'What came into you is what's in me too, a longing, a longing to have a child of our own, no wonder it unbalances us, Patrick.'

'You're not unbalanced about it. You're very calm,' he said.

'No, that's my way of coping, pretend everything's normal and it may become normal.'

'I'm sorry, Brenda. It's hard on you too. I'm not trying to excuse myself for anything. It's just sometimes when I'm as tired as a dog at the end of a day I wonder what it's all for.'

'All what?'

'All the hard work. What are we doing it for, exactly?'

Brenda thought they were doing it for themselves, for each

other, for the shared dream. But she knew she must speak very carefully. 'I know, I feel the same,' she said slowly.

'You do?' He seemed surprised.

'Well, of course I do, Patrick. What do you think I feel?'

'It's just that last month you said ... when we realised once more that it hadn't happened ... you said maybe, just maybe, it was all for the best for the moment.'

'What would you have preferred, that I would have opened my mouth and howled out from the bathroom in front of everyone, the suppliers, the customers, Blouse and Mary, anyone else passing through, that yet again we had failed to make a child? Should I have sobbed and upset everyone? You tell me, so that I'll do it right next month.'

He put his arms around her and she cried into his chest for about fifteen minutes before her shoulders stopped shaking. Then he held her away from him and he looked at her tear-stained face. 'Come on, now, put on your face for both of us, brave Brenda Brennan,' he said, and kissed her for the first time in a long time.

Mary and Blouse had a little boy. They called him Brendan Patrick. He was perfect.

Brenda went in to see him every day. His little fingers tightened over hers. He smiled sleepily up at her. He would stop crying when she held him. She was good with children. One day she would have one of her own.

She rang Dr Flynn and said yes to any fertility drugs available, including experimental ones. He urged caution and waiting. She said there wasn't any question of that any more.

She kept the smile of welcome and delight about little Brendan Patrick nailed to her face. She was sure that nobody saw in her face the yearning, the longing for her own child. Then one day her lip-reading skills showed her a conversation between Blouse and Mary.

'Isn't it great that Brenda loves him so much?' Blouse was saying.

'Yes, but I think we shouldn't boast about him so much,' Mary said.

'Boast? Doesn't she admire him and talk about him just like us?' Blouse was astonished.

'It's just that she might have wanted one of her own,' said little Mary O'Brien with the red curls and the perfect new baby.

*

There were reasons why the drugs didn't seem to suit. High blood pressure, allergies, contra-indications. In vitro fertilisation had a very long waiting list. Brenda never really understood what each problem was because the shroud of disappointment was so great, and the hard lines of Patrick's face more firmly etched.

Dr Flynn tried to explain it to them. He got the feeling he was talking to two brick walls. He talked about resuming and keeping up the active happy sex life they had told him they had before. He mentioned adoption tentatively. Very often this was a wonderful thing, not only in itself but it had the additional side effect of leaving the parents more relaxed and therefore having a successful conception.

They said nothing.

Dr Flynn said that adoption wasn't as easy as it used to be, too many people chasing after a small pool of babies. The days were gone when single girls gave up their babies to orphanages or for adoption. Very much healthier attitude, of course, but not helpful when you were looking for a child.

And of course there was the age factor, nobody over forty was really in with a chance of adopting, so it would have to be speedy if they wanted to try and apply.

To the outside world, nothing had changed, but for the great team that had been Brenda and Patrick Brennan, something had. Only those very close to them guessed that there was anything wrong at all. Blouse and Mary thought the couple were very overworked, that they didn't seem to laugh as much as they had in earlier times. Brenda's mother noticed nothing except that any time she was unwise enough to enquire about the patter of tiny feet, she got a very short answer.

Quentin Barry noticed in his weekly phone call that the same spark wasn't there in Brenda.

He put it down to strain and rules and regulations and anxiety. 'Don't kill yourselves,' he wrote kindly. 'I know that we won't be trading at a profit for quite a long time. My accountant barks much more loudly than he bites. Together we will have something marvellous, don't lose your passion and fire over this.'

If Patrick and Brenda had both read his instructions about not losing fire and passion with a wry laugh they said nothing to each other. They had been serving food and changing everything restlessly for months now.

There were so many teething troubles. Who would have known

. . . that parking would be such a nightmare. That taxi firms would be so likely to let them down. That the fish catch would be so unreliable at times. That well-known people would have used-up credit cards. That people would steal ashtrays and linen napkins. They learned, slowly and sometimes bitterly. This was the first time they had run their own place. Or Quentin's place. He had told them to think of it as theirs.

But when Brenda saw Patrick sighing, she remembered how he had asked, 'What's it all for? What am I doing all this for?' Her heart was heavy.

By the time the end of their first year approached, Brenda had lost a great deal of weight and looked very tired. Mary, Blouse's wife, who looked blooming in motherhood, was also, it appeared, able to hold down a series of jobs as well. Through her contacts she had arranged huge publicity for the first anniversary party.

Three nights before the event, when every catastrophe that *could* have happened *had* happened, Patrick and Brenda were still in the restaurant kitchen at 3 a.m. They had lived through a day when a car had reversed into one of their windows, leaving broken glass and a whistling wind until the whole thing could be boarded up and made to appear like a bomb site. Then there had been a gas leak, a shelf containing a lot of valuable produce collapsing, and a lavatory in the ladies' room overflowing. Somebody had sent back the fish because it tasted 'funny' and everyone else felt uneasy about their portions, which had tasted fine up to then. One of the waiters had left because he said, frankly, the place was a shambles and would never take off as a top-class place to work.

'What are we doing it for?' Patrick asked again.

'Sorry, Patrick?'

'You heard me. What's it *for*? I'm bloody exhausted. You're like skin and bone. You've aged twenty years. We were mad to try to do all this. Crazy, that's what we were . . .'

'Would it have been worth it if we had a child or even the prospect of one, do you think? Would it have made sense out of a day from hell like today?'

'You know it would.'

'No, I don't. We would have been just as tired, even more so.'

'You know what I mean. There would have been some sort of purpose to it all. Something at the end.'

'And there's nothing now, no purpose in anything, is this what you're saying?'

'You're picking a row, Brenda. It's far too late.'

'You're right. Why don't you go on up to bed?'

'Aren't you coming?'

'In a while. Please go on up.'

Patrick dragged himself to the door and climbed the stairs.

Brenda looked around the place where she had soldiered since 7 a.m. Twenty hours. She walked thoughtfully over to a mirror they had put strategically for staff to give themselves a quick glance before going into the dining-room. Skin and bone, he had said. Aged twenty years, he had said.

She wrote a short note to Patrick.

I'm sorry, but I don't feel like sharing a bed with you tonight. Not if you think I'm old and sad and wretched-looking. Not if you see no hope, no purpose in anything. I'm going to a friend for the night, or what's left of it. But whatever I am, I am a pro. I'll be back tomorrow, 12 noon for the photo call Mary has arranged, and for my lunchtime shift. I don't feel the need to say anything about this to anyone, so you needn't either.

Brenda

She left it on the table beside where he slept in a deep sleep, arm thrown across to her side of the bed as he had done for years. She took her coat, a change of clothes and some washing things, and let herself out into the early morning of Dublin City.

She took a taxi to Tara Road where Colm ran a restaurant. He was a recovering alcoholic, a man who slept lightly. He too lived over the premises. They had always joked about being rivals, but his restaurant in its green suburb catered to an entirely different clientele from Quentins' city-centre trade.

She rang the bell and he answered in a wide-awake voice. 'Brenda Brennan? The very person.'

'Colm, could I have a bed for the night, what's left of it?'

'Sure. Will you have tea and toast or do you want to sleep straight away?'

'Tea and toast will be fine,' she said.

He never asked her what it was about and she went to bed half an hour later in Colm's spare room, where she slept until 10 a.m.

'Do I look skin and bone and twenty years older, Colm?' she asked at a breakfast of melon, champagne and orange juice, and a freshly baked pastry.

'No, and only an overtired husband in a blind panic over his restaurant would have said that. Are you going back to him?'

'Of course I am. I'm a professional.'

'And you love him?' he pleaded.

'Maybe.'

'No, definitely,' he said.

'Anyway, Colm, could you get me a taxi, and know you are the truest friend anyone ever had?'

The taxi came in five minutes. Eleven minutes into the journey the taxi was hit by a large truck. It came from the side where Brenda was seated. The blow to her head knocked her unconscious at once. She knew nothing at all after the impact.

Brenda had never been late for anything. Patrick began to be seriously worried. She had said she would be back. He knew that she would. He wondered what friend she had gone to see. He wished that he hadn't been so sharp-tempered. Why could he not have given her a hug and said that when the world settled down they would talk? Brenda was never moody. She wouldn't make a scene like this on such a very important day.

When she hadn't turned up for the photo call, he became seriously alarmed. He had tried to reassure everyone else, insisted that Blouse and Mary be included in the pictures as well as the newly recruited staff. He said there were a million last-minute things that each of them had to see to.

They served a lunch short-handed, every moment he expected to see her come in to the kitchen and slip her coat off. But lunch was over, and there was still no sign.

The afternoon didn't bring her, either. He was now getting really worried. By six o'clock he was ready to call the Guards. They were not helpful. A domestic incident at 4 a.m.! They were sympathetic, but they had better things to do with their time. Most missing people came home, they said. Try her friends, they suggested.

He had no idea who to call. He slapped the food on to plates for the dinner with no idea what he was serving.

She would *not* have left him like this.

In hospital, they searched for any identification which would tell them who the dark-haired woman was. All they had was a set of keys and some bank notes in her pockets, a change of clothes in an overnight bag. No hint at all about whom they might contact.

During dinner Patrick went upstairs again. He saw Brenda's handbag on the floor beside the dressing table. She had gone away without anything. It wasn't possible that she had gone away to kill herself. He didn't want to involve Blouse and Mary. Blouse was so simple and innocent. But by eleven o'clock that night he had to tell them.

He was sitting crying in the kitchen and they demanded to know why.

'We'll call the hospitals,' Mary said.

They took six of the major places and tried two each.

Blouse found her on his first go.

'Long, straight, dark hair usually tied up in what is called a French pleat,' he said, proud of having got it all together.

Patrick wondered if he would have been able to give such a good description. He grabbed the phone. 'Is she alive?' he sobbed. 'Thank God. Thank God.'

She had come round for a moment, spoken in a garbled way of Patrick and Quentin but they had no idea what she meant. They were letting her sleep now.

Blouse got out of the van. Patrick sat inside holding his head. Had he really said to this wonderful, strong, loyal woman that there was no hope, no purpose in anything? Could he have driven her out in to the night because she couldn't bear to lie beside him? The only thing that mattered was Brenda, he knew it somewhere inside. Why could he not have admitted it, and said it to her? Please, please God, may there be years and years ahead when he could tell her.

He sat by her bed all night and stroked her thin, pale cheek. He half-remembered people telling him about the accident and the taxi and the truck. She had been on her way home to him and this had happened.

Then at dawn she woke and he laid his head on her chest and sobbed as if his heart would break.

There was no concussion, very little bruising, just great shock. She had been lucky. The taxi driver had been lucky. Everyone was all right.

'I think I'll make it for the party after all,' she said.

'You're everything in the world to me, Brenda. You're enough, do you hear what I'm saying? You're more than enough. I love you so much, we have huge hope, a huge future together, you and I.'

Everyone was there that night at the anniversary party of Quentins, which was as glittery a do as Dublin had seen for a long time, and they would always remember one particular moment.

It was when Patrick Brennan took his wife's hand in his and held it very tight. He looked around the crowd and lowered his voice slightly.

'Brenda and I have a wonderful baby to rejoice over with you tonight. The baby is one year old and we have all of you here to celebrate the fact we have a restaurant which survived a year and where we hope to make friends and strangers alike welcome and happy with us. It's not as wonderful as a real christening with a real baby, but for us it's everything that a real christening is, with a sense of fulfilment and hope and a future ahead of us all. So will you drink to our baby, Quentins, and wish us all well in the adventures that the rest of life will bring to everyone in this room?'

Even hard-bitten media people and professional first nighters were silent as Patrick Brennan kissed his thin, elegant wife Brenda. As the years went on, people said that Brenda Brennan never cried, they must have imagined it. But those who were there knew that they hadn't imagined it. And it wasn't only the Brennans who had cried. Everyone in the room seemed to have been affected, too.

PART II

Chapter Five

There were so many stories about Quentins, it was hard to sort out which they could use and which to throw away. Setting up a movie seemed to cost a great deal of money. They pored over their budget with anxious faces. Sandy had some money in a savings account which she willingly put into the fund. Nick mortgaged his flat and raised a reasonable sum. But, of course, if they were going to make a film that would win prizes and awards, they would have to have high production values and it would mean asking for serious finance from the King Foundation. They had received their application form and took great care over filling it in.

'I'll have to work much harder than you two because I have nothing to invest,' Ella said. 'So today I brought us a bottle of champagne that a customer gave me in Colm's last night. Imagine, he said he didn't want to insult me with money! If he only knew how ready I was to be insulted with money.'

They laughed as they got great tumblers and poured it out. They toasted Firefly Films, Quentins, and the King Foundation in New York.

When they had finished the bottle of champagne, Nick had said they must be realistic. They were looking for something that was way out of their league. 'It's not Mickey Mouse money this time,' he said, frowning.

Sandy tried to make light of it. She hated to see Nick frown.

'Don't knock Mickey Mouse. He made a lot of money for Walt Disney in his time,' she said.

He grinned feebly. 'Sandy, I'm only saying aloud what we're all thinking. Maybe we can come up with another terrific idea. Ella got us this far. All we need is another leap now.'

Ella saw the shadow pass over Sandy's face. 'I didn't get us very far. It was Sandy who wrote out the whole proposal that won the pitch. And in addition, as soon as this champagne's finished I'm going to have to leave you and look for more paid work with other people. I hate to do it, but you know the scene.'

'Are your parents in the shed yet?' Nick asked.

'Yes, we all are, but we actually call it the Annexe, to make ourselves feel better.'

'Is it very cramped?' Sandy wanted to know.

'Not too bad, amazingly. Colm knew some builder in the early days, and they do each other favours. Anyway, this fellow built us a grand place with lots of windows in the roof so at least there's plenty of light coming in and there's a whole bank of storage lock-ups so that my mother can keep things for when we get out of debt again. I even put my things in there.'

'And will you? Ever get out of debt?' Nick was blunt.

'I don't know. I wouldn't think so, but it's a start, and my father's calmed down again. For a while I thought he was going to be in a mental home. People know he's doing his utmost to pay them back and that's a help. And two of the flats are already occupied in what we now call the Main House; two more ready by the end of next week. That's not a bad recovery.' She forced her voice to sound cheerful.

Sandy and Nick nodded with respect. Compared to what the Bradys were going through, their own problems were small. They would find the money for their project, or they wouldn't – at least they didn't owe real money to anyone.

'What work are you going to do?' Nick asked.

'Deirdre's got me a part-time job up in her lab. I've got two nights a week waitressing in Colm's, two nights a week for Scarlet Feather – you know, your pals Tom and Cathy – weekends in Quentins and, wait for it, two hours a week teaching a pair of twins maths and basic science. They're something else, those two. They keep asking me am I part of the New Poor. I don't know where they heard the expression, but they love it.'

'Doesn't sound as if there's much time for a social life,' Nick said.

'Oh, Nick, I've had as much social life in the last two years as any girl needs,' she laughed wryly.

'Was it as long as that?' He seemed disappointed that her affair had gone on for such a time.

'Give or take a bit,' she said. 'In my case, mainly give, but who's counting?'

Afterwards Sandy asked her very confidentially, 'Do you think Nick likes me at all, Ella, or am I just wasting my time?'

'Oh, I think he likes you a great deal, Sandy. But I beg of you, don't listen to me, what do I know about men and what they like and don't like? Nothing, that's what I know.'

Deirdre said that Nuala was coming over next week. 'Great, let's get a bottle of wine each and entertain her,' Ella said. 'But wait, it will have to be after midnight or between four and six Wednesday and Saturday.'

'Oh, God, I can't wait till you're back in teaching and have normal hours again.'

'I'm not going back,' Ella said.

'Of course you are.'

'I can't afford to,' Ella said simply. 'Why don't we say we'll have a picnic in Stephen's Green? Nuala would like that, then I can get back to Quentins at six.'

'I'll check it out,' Deirdre said.

'Bad news, Ella. I'm going to give it to you straight. Nuala doesn't want to meet you in Stephen's Green.'

'Okay, where does she suggest?'

'This is the hard bit. She doesn't want to meet you at all.'

'I don't believe you.'

'It's what the lady says.'

'Has she gone soft in the head or something?'

'It's to do with Don. Her husband and his brothers lost a lot of money because of Mr Richardson. Apparently she's feeling a bit sore about it.'

'Well, I'm sure she is, and so are a lot of other innocent people, but why doesn't she want to meet *me*? I haven't got her bloody money.' Ella was hurt and angry.

'Oh, I don't know, some garbled thing about you having a fine time out in Spanish hotels with Frank's money.'

'Isn't she a weak slob? Couldn't I do the same to her, moan and groan and say that it was at her awful in-laws' party that I met Don and ruined my life?'

'Leave it, Ella. She's not worth it.'

'But you're still going to meet her?'

'Not if you don't want me to.'

'Oh, meet her, for God's sake. What do I care?'

'Ella, come on now!'

'No, I don't care. What does one more small-minded, petty self-seeker matter?'

'She used to be our pal.'

'She's forgotten that pretty quickly.'

'I'll tell you what she says,' Deirdre sighed.

'If you must.'

'I'll take her to Quentins, some time you're not working there.'

'Yeah, make sure I'm not working when she's there. I've a neat way with very hot soup straight into someone's lap,' said Ella.

It was Ella's weekly lunchtime lesson with Simon and Maud. They lived with their grandparents in St Jarlath's Crescent. They were bright enough, but had missed out on some mathematics teaching. They were some kind of cousins of Cathy Scarlet. Ella had learned never to ask for too much detail. But then, she had never met children like Simon and Maud before. They insisted on telling her their whole life story and that they were really related to Cathy's ex-husband, the lawyer Neil Mitchell, but that through a lot of adventures and eventually court orders, they were now living with Cathy's mother and father, Muttie and Lizzie.

They had a dog called Hooves, who had a limp. They had a brother who was on the run from the police in several countries. They had their own passports, which they had needed because they'd been to Chicago to dance at a christening party. On the plane, they had been allowed up to the flight deck. In Chicago they had . . .

'Sure, but I think we'd better get down to the algebra before I hear any more.'

'Are we boring you?' Simon asked very earnestly. 'People say we go on a bit.'

'No, you're not boring at all,' Ella said truthfully. 'It's just that I am being paid proper money to teach you, and I don't want to cheat your grandparents or whatever.'

'Strictly speaking, they're not *our* grandparents,' Simon began.

'So I brought this book. It's simpler than the one you have at school, but I thought if we went through it first, then when it was all a bit clearer, we could look at your book.'

'And can we have real conversation with you when we've understood it?' Maud asked.

'Certainly,' Ella said, flattered.

'It's just that we were told not to be asking you questions about your sad life, but we wanted to know all the same,' Simon explained.

Ella put her hand up to her face to hide the smile. 'I'll give you blow-by-blow details if you can get your heads round these equations,' she promised.

'You're not going to spend the whole lunch looking at me as if I'm some kind of criminal?' Nuala said.

Deirdre shrugged. 'No, because I'm sure you have some very good reason for behaving like a prize arsehole.'

'Deirdre, please, there's no call for that kind of language.'

'There's every call. Ella's had enough worries. She was looking forward to seeing you, and you as good as spat in her face.'

'But, Dee, she knew what she was doing, going on luxury holidays all on Frank's money and his family's investments. You have no idea the mess that Don Richardson left behind him.'

'She spent one long weekend with him, her half-term from school, she bought her own ticket, you fool.'

'I heard . . .'

'You heard what you wanted to hear, Nuala. I know what went on, including the fact that the man she met at your party lied to her, betrayed her, humiliated her, left her father without a name, house or reputation to call his own. I don't care what you know or think you know. Let's look at the facts: Ella is working sixteen hours a day to make up what the bastard took from her parents . . . and she doesn't even have the comfort of having a picnic lunch with someone she once thought was a friend.'

There was a great silence.

'Why did *you* come then, if this is the way you feel?' Nuala said in a very small voice.

'To tell it to you straight.'

'Please tell her I'm very sorry. I didn't think it through.'

'No, I'll tell her nothing, you know her phone number. Tell her yourself.'

Nuala began to take her phone out of her handbag.

'Not here, it's not allowed,' Deirdre said.

Nuala went to the ladies' room. Brenda Brennan asked was everything all right.

'Yes, Mrs Brennan.'

'Correct me if I'm wrong, but isn't that the young lady who got proposed to here in this restaurant?'

'The very one.'

'And did it all ... er ... work out ... all right and everything?' Brenda Brennan could sense the tension.

'Yes, I suppose it did, he's a greedy money-mad pig of a man, but he's reasonably faithful to her and she seems content enough. The only problem in paradise is that they were burned badly by Don Richardson, of course.'

'They're not alone there.'

'No, but she had the nerve to imply that Ella had gained something out of it all.'

'Everyone knows that's not the way things were. I thought she and Ella were friends?'

'So did Ella,' Deirdre said.

'Well, thank heavens Ella has at least one good friend in you.'

'And in you, Mrs Brennan. She's very grateful to you.'

'She's working too hard, that's my only worry. She's white as a sheet. Patrick and I worry about her health, and whether she'll be able to carry on. She's taken on far too much for any one woman.'

They saw Nuala coming to the table and Brenda nodded and left to talk to another customer.

'She had her mobile on answer,' Nuala said.

'Yes, well, she'll be working, trying to pay back what that bastard stole from her father and his clients. Working while we have lunch here in Quentins.'

'Don't make me feel worse, Deirdre. Life isn't actually a bed of roses with me either, you know.'

'It never is, Nuala,' Deirdre sighed. 'Come on, let's have the pasta starter and the seared tuna for main course, and you can tell me what Frank's been up to now.'

'How on earth did you know he's been up to something?' Nuala was stricken.

'Your face, Nuala. It's written all over it. You have suspicions, isn't that it? You think he's looking at some woman over there in London in a certain way.'

'Oh, Dee, you can read minds,' Nuala said.

'There's probably nothing in it at all.' Deirdre began giving the speech that Nuala wanted to hear. 'After a few years, all couples go through this. It's only we, the old maids, who get to hear about it. They don't tell other wives.'

'But it's been going on a bit.' Nuala was doubtful.

'It could have been going on a bit just in your mind, you know. Frank is like his brothers, charming to everyone. It could be a matter of nothing,' Deirdre said.

Nuala's eyes were shining. 'That's exactly what Frank says. He says it's all in my mind.'

'Well then, there you are,' said Deirdre wearily.

There was a very positive letter from the King Foundation. The application had been read and had been moved on to a shortlist. There were various other technical details to attend to, and criteria to meet, but in general they had met all the main requirements and they were on to the next level. The letter was signed 'Derry and Kimberly King'. Nicky and Sandy wished that Ella were there to share it with them, but she was giving private tuition to these extraordinary twins. They would celebrate with her later. Meanwhile, they held hands and rejoiced at having got so far.

'If we do get it made and it goes to festivals and we get known and have plenty of money, what would you do with it?' Sandy asked suddenly.

'What would *we* do with it, you mean?'

'No, I mean you, actually.'

He looked at her, dumbfounded. 'We'd get better premises, wouldn't we? New equipment. Take on someone full-time, have a honeymoon of some kind, get a really good, glossy brochure out. Isn't that what you'd do?'

'Yes,' she said, her cheeks getting pinker. He had actually said honeymoon.

'You'd do all that too?' Nick teased her.

'I would, yes.' She didn't look at him.

'But there's one thing, Sandy. We can't have a honeymoon without getting married first.'

'I know,' she said.

'So are you going to ask me to marry you?' he went on.

'Doesn't the man do that?' Poor Sandy was still not sure if he was teasing her or proposing.

'Not always. The better decision-maker usually does it. You're the better decision-maker in our company.'

'And should I wait until we got rich, do you think?' Her anxiety was so obvious now he couldn't bear to let it go on any longer.

'I'd love if we got married, rich or poor,' he said.

'Oh, Nick.' Her smile was so broad, he picked up a Polaroid camera. 'I want to show this to our grandchildren some day, tell them what you looked like the day you proposed.'

The phone rang just then. It was Mike Martin, a friend of Don Richardson's in the past, he had put some work their way. Nick was surprised to hear from him.

'It's not a job, alas, those are thin on the ground these days with the climate we have now.'

'That's for sure,' Nick agreed sadly.

'It's more of a personal favour. You know Ella Brady, I believe.'

'Yes.' Nick was cautious.

'Well, you remember a friend of hers. Someone who no longer lives in this land – who went to Spain?'

'Do you mean Don Richardson?' Nick asked baldly.

'Yes. Well, I was trying to be more discreet.'

'I have no need to be discreet. That was his name. This isn't a police state. We can say people's names, surely?'

'No, but the guns are out for him, Nick. You know that.'

'The guns may well be out for him, but they are hardly tapping my phone about him.' Nick felt very annoyed with this man.

'Did you lose money, Nick? I know for a fact that Don is doing his level best.'

'I'm sure he is, his very level best. No, I didn't lose anything, but I have great friends who were ruined.'

'And believe me, they will be recompensed, compensated.'

'That's not what we read in the papers.'

'What do journalists know? And it's actually about that I'm calling. Is this a convenient time?'

'Yes. You interrupted a marriage proposal, but it can be continued when we've finished talking.' Nick leaned over and stroked Sandy's face.

'I never know whether to take you seriously or not.'

'I know, it's a worry.'

Nick let a silence fall.

'Anyway, our friend hasn't been able to contact Ella.'

'I think Don probably knows Ella's phone number.'

'It's not as simple as that.'

'It probably is, or he could send a letter, a postcard, an e-mail.'

'I'm going to cut to the chase, Nick. You're not being as co-operative and understanding about the problem as we'd hoped.'

'We?'

'Um ... Don and I.'

'You're with him as you speak?'

'That's neither here nor there. What I was going to do ...'

'... was cut to the chase. I heard you.'

'There's this briefcase with a laptop computer.'

'I'll bet there is.'

'Which Mr Richardson inadvertently left in Ms Brady's apartment ...'

'That must have been a day or two ago.'

'I beg your pardon?'

'Don Richardson ran out of here four months ago. He must have missed his briefcase before now.'

'Now is when he's looking for it, Nick.'

'Well, he can come home and pick it up, can't he?'

'He can't find Ella. She's not in that apartment. She's not in the house in Tara Road.'

'And I imagine he knows why. They had to sell everything, give up everything, because of him.'

'I don't think he sees it that way ...'

'You do surprise me!'

'I'd like to give you a phone number. Please give it to Ms Brady and ask her to call Mr Richardson.'

'I wouldn't hold your breath, Mr Martin.'

'I'll dictate the number, and I'm sure you'll be responsible enough to pass it on.'

'I'll take lessons in responsibility from your pal Don, will I?'

'Have you a pen or pencil?'

'Yes, but what's to stop me giving this to the newspapers, the authorities, or some of the people he robbed blind?'

'I'm sure you'll do the right thing, Nick,' said Mike Martin, and read out a number. Then they both hung up.

'What was that all about?' Sandy asked, round-eyed.

'About a tactless oaf who interrupted you when you were about to kneel down in front of me ... wait, wait ... and meet me kneeling down in front of you, and we were going to ask each other the most important question of our lives.'

'And that guy in Spain?'

'Can wait his turn like everyone else,' said Nick, kneeling down on the floor.

Barbara and Tim Brady were having a late lunch in the little bit of garden they had kept for themselves beside their Annexe. Through the bamboo hedge they could see the Main House, where they had lived until three months ago. All of it now let at astronomical rents. Oddly, they didn't miss it nearly as much as they had thought they would.

Looking back on it now, they realised it had been too big for them. And lonely, too. Somehow, since they had come here, it was much more companionable, and they saw so much more of Ella as she dashed in and out and grabbed cups of tea. Her friend Deirdre called a lot, which was nice. They still had a great deal of anxiety and the nightmare about the debts they owed and the people in Tim's office who had lost money. But all in all, it was a happier time, a better quality of life. They hardly dared to admit it to anyone except each other. And they were able to talk to each other these days. Which was another change for the better.

Chapter Six

'It's not too hard, when you put your mind to it,' Simon said.

'That's what I've always found,' Ella agreed.

'But of course, there's no real point to it,' Maud said.

'I don't know. There's a sort of a point, like it's a principle, a formula. When you know how to do it once, you can always apply it again.'

'But when would you ever want to apply it again?' Maud wondered thoughtfully.

'For exams, I suppose,' Simon said. 'Do we really need to do that whole page of problems before next week?'

'Yes, you do if I'm to be sure you've understood it and move on to the next thing.'

'Nobody else at school has to do a page of problems,' Maud said with a slightly downturned mouth.

'I know, Maud. Aren't you lucky that they're paying extra for you to learn more?' Ella said.

Maud was debating this when Ella's phone rang. It was Nuala. She was in tears. She was so sorry, she was such a fool, she had quite rightly had the head bitten off her by Deirdre. She'd love to talk to Ella. That is, if Ella would ever forgive her.

'Sure, I'll forgive you,' Ella said. 'That bastard upsets everyone, makes them behave out of character, that's all.'

Maud and Simon exchanged glances.

'But Nuala, I have to go. I'm at work at the moment.'

'Dee says you never stop.'

'No, I'm fine. I'm entering the social phase of work now. Isn't that right, Maud and Simon?' she said to the children.

They looked at her, startled.

'What on earth does that mean?' Nuala asked with a giggle.

'It means that Simon and Maud are going to put away their books, get me a huge mug of tea, and I'm going to tell them all about my very unhappy life,' Ella said.

'You sound absolutely unhinged, Ella, but I'm so glad you forgive me. You can behave however you like. I'll call you tonight.'

'Not between six and midnight,' Ella said cheerfully and hung up her phone.

She had just got to telling the twins the bit of her very unhappy life where she hadn't been chosen for the hockey team.

'It doesn't sound *terribly* unhappy,' Maud complained.

'No real, awful things,' Simon added.

'If you wanted to be on the First Eleven, and should have been, then that's pretty terrible,' Ella protested.

Her phone rang again. This time it was Nick. She listened and her face got red and then white again. The twins watched her with interest. 'The bastard,' she said eventually. 'The class-A bastard.' She took down a number on the back of her notebook. 'Thanks, Nick, I'll get back to you on this.' Her voice was slightly shaky, but a promise was a promise.

Those children had got their heads around quadratic equations. Now she had to tell them the story of an unhappy life. 'So the day of the school's hockey final approached . . .' she began.

'Could you tell us about the bastard, please?' Maud asked politely. 'It sounds much more interesting.'

All evening she thought about that slimy Mike Martin, out there in Spain with Don, after telling the television cameras that he couldn't understand the disappearance, the flight, the whole thing. He had told the nation that Don Richardson adored his wife, the lovely Margery Rice. Now he was contacting Ella, the mistress, and looking for a computer.

The only thing this proved was that there was something in the laptop that they didn't want found. Now that was interesting. Very interesting. And also a little frightening. It was only a matter of time before they found where she lived. Someone would tell Mike Martin that they lived in the garden shed on Tara Road. And then surely he would come to collect the computer that belonged to the great Don Richardson, and presumably must contain some of his secrets. Ella had assumed that Don must have deleted every file in it, and that was the reason why his password, 'Angel', didn't work.

It was packed with her things in storage at the Annexe in Tara Road. She hadn't thought about it in weeks. She wouldn't think about it now, she was working too hard. And also because she did not want to believe that it had not been left there purposely. And so he would not be coming back for it himself. Ever.

'God, Ella, you look dreadful,' Nick said when they met down by the Liffey for coffee.

'Thanks, Nick, and I always think you look very handsome, too,' she said.

'No, you look as if you've been on a ten-day binge. You've got huge dark circles under your eyes.'

'Yes, Nick. Sorry, Nick. Now tell me, is there any good news on the search for investors?'

'There's other news first ... Sandy and I are going to get married,' he said sheepishly.

She flung her arms around him. 'I'm so pleased. You'll be very happy, both of you.'

'Why do you say that?'

'Because you're such friends. That's a huge start.'

'Weren't you and Don friends?'

'No, as it happened, it didn't seem to matter at the time, but looking back on it, of course that was the huge gap in it all.'

'What are you going to do about his bloody computer?'

'I gave it away,' she said, looking straight at him.

'No, you didn't, Ella.'

'Why should I keep it?'

He looked at her, his head on one side. 'I know you, for heaven's sake. You didn't give it away. Who would you give it to, for one thing?'

'I don't have it.' She looked mutinous.

'You *do*, Ella. You're talking to me, your friend. I know you have it and you must give it to the Fraud Squad as quick as possible and don't have these goons coming after you. Give it in, be done with it, I beg you.' His face was troubled.

'There's nothing in it, anyway.'

'So what's the problem then?'

'It's not something you do, informing, sneaking, getting people into trouble.'

Nick looked at her in disbelief. 'Listen to yourself speak for a moment. What has *he* done, Ella? Think for a moment. Just because you loved him doesn't make you remotely his sort of person. We're just not the kind of people who do everything under the table and run like rats when it all goes up in flames.'

'Okay, Nick, don't go on.'

'I have to go on. You seem to have lost your marbles on this one, Ella. You did not give it away. If you had, he wouldn't be looking for it all over the place.'

'There's nothing on it.'

'There must be some information in there. Why do you think he's set Mike Martin on to you? Saying give us a number to phone. Or else.'

'He didn't say "Or else", did he?'

'No, but it was in Martin's tone.'

'What do you think I should do, Nick?'

'If you won't give it to the police then go away,' he said.

'I can't go away. You know that. This isn't the time for a holiday. My head would explode.'

'It wouldn't be a holiday. It would be work, paid work.'

'Where?'

'New York City! We've had more good news. The King Foundation says we've got to the next level. We're on the shortlist.'

'Nick, that's great. Why didn't you tell me?'

'There were bigger things to talk about. But this is great, and one of us has to go, so it's perfect timing. Go on, Ella. It would solve everything.'

'I can't leave all my jobs.'

'We've asked round. They'll all let you go. Tom and Cathy, Quentins, Colm's and Deirdre's laboratory. The only parties having any problems with this are Maud and Simon, who have learned whatever it is you asked them to and fear they might have forgotten it when you come back.'

'You asked them without telling me . . . you dared to do this on my behalf?' Ella was incensed.

'We had to prove to you that you could go, before we bought the ticket.'

'Ticket?' she said.

'Yes, yes. You need a plane ticket to get to New York. Go, Ella.'

'Make the call,' she said suddenly. 'I'll go out and look at the river.'

'I'll tell him you are away and it will be true,' Nick said.

Mike Martin answered the phone.

'I went to find her,' Nick said slowly.

'And?'

'And she's not here, apparently.'

'Not here? What does that mean?'

'What it says. She's gone away. No one knew where.'

'Who did you ask?'

'Her various employers. You can check with them.'

'She'd be wise not to play around with Don.'

'Oh, I'm sure she knows that now, but at the time she probably thought it was a good idea and that he meant what he said and that sort of thing.'

'You're a smart-arse, aren't you, Nick?'

'No, I'm relatively simple, but I was pleased that Ella is away, as it happens, and hope that she's strong enough to face you all when she gets home.' He hung up, shaking.

Ella came back from the river.

'They believe you've gone, Ella, so now let me brief you properly on Derry King.'

'On what?'

'A very rich guy indeed. He set up a foundation to help artists and film-makers. More strong black coffee. All the hopes and the entire current assets of Firefly Films are going into this trip.'

'You can't do this to me, Nick.' Ella was alarmed.

'We have to. It's our only hope.'

'I'm fragile. You said yourself I look like shit.'

'You have two and a half days before you meet him. You could paint your face or something.'

Her parents were pleased with the news. 'It will get you out in the real world again,' her mother said.

'Lord, I don't think staying in a Manhattan hotel and trying to get a man to invest in a tiny Irish company is exactly what you'd call the real world,' Ella said.

'It's a change,' her father said.

'There's one thing I have to tell you. Otherwise I can't go. You know that man, Mike Martin? He's often on television.'

'I know him,' her father said.

'Well, he's a friend of Don's, apparently, and Don is looking for a laptop machine he left in my flat. So Mike Martin might just possibly come and ask you about it. Suppose he does come and enquire. Can I ask you to say you have no idea where I am, but you know I took a laptop with me? I hate the lies, more lies, but it's nearly true. I am taking it with me, and you won't know where I am every hour of the day.' She looked from one to the other pleadingly.

'That's fine. We'll say it just like that,' her mother said.

'You never tell us your movements, that's what we'll say,' her father agreed.

'And you won't let them browbeat you or anything?' She was looking at her parents fondly.

'Browbeat ... what a marvellous word. I wonder what it means.' Her father was smiling a less papery smile than he had some months back.

'Let's look it up, Dad.' She went for the dictionary. It wasn't all that helpful. It meant to bear down on someone sternly, to bully them.

'We knew that already,' he said.

'It's from Old English, "bru",' Ella read.

'A lot of help that is,' her mother laughed.

They were much more like a happy family out there in the shed than they had ever been before.

Ella called in briefly to the twins in Muttie and Lizzie's house.

'Hallo, Ella. We heard you weren't coming. We were just talking about you.' Simon sounded pleased.

'You were?' Ella was apprehensive.

'The man who rang and said you're not coming for two weeks, was that the bastard?'

'No, no it wasn't at all. It was Nick, a very nice man.'

'Is he part of your future?'

'No, Simon, he's not, as it happens.' Ella had a nearly irresistible urge to say that Nick was part of her distant past, the first man she had slept with, in fact. But not with those two, never wise to let them have any real information at all.

'I'll tell Maud. She's making fudge in the kitchen.'

'Simon, I'll be posting a letter in the mail to you. We were meant to be doing some geometry this week . . .'

'But we don't have to work if you're not here, surely?'

'You don't *have* to, but wouldn't it be nice if when I got back you had both studied this nice, easy explanation that I've written out for you about circles?'

'Oh, they're too hard. We couldn't understand those at all. One thing was the radius and then they called it the diameter and then they called it the circumference . . . no, that's too hard on our own.'

'Not if you read it in the simple way I explain it, it isn't.'

'It *is*, Ella.'

'But you're going to do it. And you're going to know acute angles and obtuse angles. Believe me, you are.'

Simon had a conference with his sister in the kitchen. 'Maud wants to know, do you get paid for this?'

'Yes, your grandparents give me money.'

'They're not exactly our grandparents.'

'So when this letter arrives . . . you are both to take it seriously too.'

'Why can't you send it by e-mail, it would be quicker?' Simon countered.

'I can't do that.'

'Don't you have a computer?' He was scornful.

'Yes, I do, actually. But the password is jammed, I can't get into it.'

'I could do that in a minute,' Simon said. 'Do you have it with you in your bag?'

'Yes.' Ella wasn't sure.

'Simon is terrific at computers,' Maud said reassuringly.

'It's just that it's not mine. It's a friend's. He asked me to open it for him.'

'Well then, Simon, help her pull it from the briefcase.'

'What do you think the password is?'

'I thought it was "Angel". I saw him type it in,' she said. Her heart was thumping. Was she really insane enough to share this with these two children?

'No, it's not Angel.' Simon had tried it expertly. 'It often is something just like that.'

'Cherubs,' Maud said. 'Feathers? Wings?'

'Don't think so,' Ella said.

'Is he in America?' Simon asked.

'No. Why?'

'It could be something like Los Angeles.'

She remembered the blue and white tiles on the white walls of the resort of Playa de los Angeles. Playground of the rich, criminal or famous. The hiding place full of billiard rooms and swimming pools. *That* must be where Don lived. That could be the password. She wrote it down with a trembling hand.

Simon entered it and the screen sprang to life. List after list of initials and numbers, column after column of them.

'It wasn't hard,' Simon said loftily.

'No, no indeed.' She closed it down. 'Thank you both very much. I'll bring you a present from . . .'

'From where?' Maud asked.

'From where she's getting her head stuck together,' Simon explained.

It was midnight. She would be leaving Dublin at noon the next day. She was sitting drinking coffee in Deirdre's flat. Ella needed her wits about her. Deirdre and Nuala were drinking a great deal of wine and laughing a lot. It was as if there had never been any coldness. But they had agreed not to tell Nuala about New York, just that Ella was heading off somewhere to get her head together.

Ella was trying on Deirdre's clothes. 'I think I'll take this red jacket, and the black dress, definitely,' she said.

'Yes, I'll be walking to work in my knickers,' Deirdre said. 'Take the red and black scarf too, while you're at it.'

'Imagine going off to wherever you want to.' Nuala sounded envious. 'It's years since I've been able to do that.'

If the others thought that Nuala's husband Frank was always able to do just that, they didn't say it.

She hadn't slept at all by the time she got on the plane. Her only expense at the airport was a fairly heavy duty makeup. And something the assistant recommended, which was an under-eye concealer.

On the plane she studied the brief that Sandy and Nick had prepared for her. There was an entire folder of clippings, photographs and a biography of the man she was going to meet. She looked at the pictures first. Pleasant enough face, square-shaped, his hair short, thick and coarse, like a brush with bristles.

In most pictures he appeared to be peering, almost squinting, at something, causing very exaggerated smile lines at his eyes. His nose was quite snub, but his chin was strong. It was hard to see if he was tall or small. He dressed formally. He was rarely photographed without collar and tie even at a young film-makers' gathering, where everyone else was much more casual. Either he had many tuxedos or he got the same one cleaned regularly, since he always looked smart at the many functions where he was captured. There were no pictures of his home surroundings.

She wondered how old he was, and began to check up. He was born forty-three years ago in New York, the son of an Irish father and a Canadian mother. The eldest of three sons, he described himself as self-educated. Yet some of his citations included honorary degrees from universities, so he must have done a good job educating himself. She read how he had worked in many different aspects of the stationery trade and eventually set up a company specialising in office equipment. It had become a market leader, with branches all over the United States. She read many company profiles, trying to analyse its success and its award-winning status. Nobody seemed to be able to pinpoint the exact reason it had gone on when so many had fallen by the wayside. Any more than anyone had been able to define Derry King, the Chief Executive Officer and Chairman. He was described as hard-working and easy-going, and said to be determined but not ruthless.

Ella got the feeling that he had been courteous to those who interviewed him, but not greatly forthcoming. He gave no details about what he did for breakfast or how he spent his leisure time. He gave hardly any information about his taste in books, music or theatre, saying apologetically that he had worked so hard in his youth that he had never known the luxury of losing himself in music, drama or literature.

But he did love the visual arts. When he was nine, he had a very inspiring teacher at school who told the children that they could all paint and all find beauty inside and around them if only they looked. This had been a great surprise to the young Derry King. He said that he never claimed to have any artistic talent himself, but it had certainly opened his eyes to the beauty around him, which is why he sponsored so many art competitions among the young in the inner cities.

One of the many jobs he took in order to pay his school fees was that of cleaning and tidying up in a cinema. It meant he saw many movies free. It had left him with a love of the film world all his life. No, he had never been tempted to sink his considerable fortune into a studio or a production company, but had tried instead to encourage young people in various aspects of film-making.

When asked about his typical day, Derry King gave no little human glimpses of himself reading the stocks and shares over a plate of fruit or visiting a personal trainer, or any minimal insight into his family life at home. Either he did not know how to manage publicity or else he knew how to manage it very well. Ella wasn't sure.

He emerged as a philanthropic benefactor who gave to charities across the board. Always he was interested in causes that helped young people, and advanced funds to those who had not been given an easy start in life. You had to read very hard between the lines to work out what he was like and so far he sounded quite staid, Ella thought.

But that didn't matter. She was coming to New York, on Nick and Sandy's hard-earned money, to be entertained and fascinated by this guy. It was her job to make him interested in their project. To sell it as well as she possibly could. There was not a great deal of publicity about his foundation. It was as if he didn't want to be thanked in public for doing good. She could have done with more information.

It was in many ways a bald file. No pictures of him in a penthouse suite or in a Malibu Beach home. On a ranch at weekends. There was mention of a wife, Mrs Kimberly King, a leggy number, very possibly a trophy wife. In one interview he said they had no children. In another he said that both his parents were now dead. Nowhere did he say anything about his Irish ancestry. Twice in the clippings he mentioned happy childhood vacations in Alberta, Canada.

She looked long and hard at his picture again.

A man of forty-three, the same age as Don Richardson, who had worked hard all his life. She learned little from his picture. But then she had learned little of Don after two years of loving him. This Derry King looked much older than Don. Perhaps his life had been harder. He might not have had all the perks and pleasures that Don had. And, indeed, probably continued to have.

Chapter Seven

The hotel was a small, inexpensive but chic place off Fifth Avenue in midtown Manhattan, far from the boarding house in Queens where she and Deirdre had stayed that time so many years ago when they had come to New York. It was a place owned by someone's brother who was meant to give them a great deal but there had been a great misunderstanding. He had thought they were coming out to his place to give him the trade, not the other way round looking for a bargain. She had been so young then, Ella thought. Imagine them getting upset by that! If she had known what upset was really like!

Anyway, no point in brooding. She must enjoy the days in the hotel to the full. She had said she didn't really need to spend all this time in New York, but they had insisted. Nick and Sandy had said it was essential that she should be on the spot and available, in case Derry King needed to rethink something through with her.

Deirdre had said that it took everyone at least fourteen days to get a head together, especially since Ella's head had been so battered and then tried to cure itself by overwork. Brenda Brennan said that she should make the most of it. New York City in autumn was everyone's dream. She must not think of running back. Her father and mother said she must write down some of the things she saw, they'd love to hear all about it when she came back. She realised that they were all afraid for her. They were afraid of Don Richardson and what he might do when he came back.

Ella shared a taxi into town with a small, plump Dublin woman who knew every angle there was in the world. She was a dealer, she said proudly, had travelled over with four empty suitcases. She was going to buy stuff in bargain basements for the next four days, fantastic stuff you didn't see at home at all, slippers with pink fur on them, black underwear with red feathers. She'd sell it all at three times what she paid. She did it every year. She could not understand to save her life why there weren't more people in on it. It was the easiest money she'd ever made, and believe her, she had made money in many different ways.

She asked Ella what line she was in herself.

'I'm trying to raise money to make a film,' Ella said.

The woman said her name was Harriet, and that if ever Ella was lonely, give her a ring at her hotel and they'd go out for a few drinks.

Ella tried to cover her amazement that Harriet named a very expensive, five-star hotel. There must be good money in importing exotic lingerie. Or was it smuggling? The lines were getting more and more blurred. If you could afford a hotel like that, why were you bringing over four empty suitcases to buy cheap gear? Why were you sharing a taxi with someone into town? Then again, maybe that kind of economy was exactly *why* Harriet could afford the five-star hotel she was staying in.

She settled into her own hotel and had a long bath. Deirdre had given her a very expensive oil, 'to put you in a good mood'. Its scent seemed to seep into every part of her body and all around the room. Ella didn't really believe that these unguents and lotions did any good, but she did feel a lot better. And maybe looked a little less drawn.

Then she called the hotel beauty salon to make an appointment for the next morning. She had promised Nick and Sandy that she would have her hair done before she met Derry King. On behalf of the company they said she had to do this. They didn't want her frightening him away before the negotiations started. And then she found herself wandering around the room, pacing like an animal in a cage. To her amazement, she felt restless and edgy. In need of company, any company. It might be midnight back home, but it was only 7 p.m. here. Outside her windows, a New York evening was just getting under way. If only Deirdre were here. They would have great fun. Or Nick and Sandy, she enjoyed their company. If they were here now, with a bottle of inexpensive wine that Sandy would have found in some liquor shop, they could sit and plan their strategy.

Or anyone else she liked. Brenda Brennan from Quentins, for example. She was surprisingly good fun when you got to know her.

She looked over at the laptop. No, she would keep her promise to herself. Don't look into all it contained until she had dealt with Derry King. There would be plenty of time later. And now at last she knew how to unlock its secrets. She really owed young Simon for that.

Deirdre called around to the Bradys for solidarity. 'It will do her no end of good, this trip,' she said.

'I'm very anxious, Deirdre, our daughter to be running away from someone like as if we were all in gangland! Couldn't she have given the laptop to the Guards and be done with it?'

'She will do that when she comes back, I'm sure of that,' Deirdre murmured. 'She'll do the right thing. It will just take her a little time.'

'Deirdre, I've been phoning you all night.'

'I was out, Nuala. But now I'm home. What is it?'

'Listen, Frank got a message from Don.'

'He never did.'

'Yes, late this afternoon. I've been trying to find you.'

'And what did he have to say to Frank?'

'Apparently a lot of it was completely wrongly reported.'

'Yes, I'm sure.'

'No, really, he explained it was all taken out of proportion.'

'Is this why you rang me, Nuala?'

'Well, yes and no. You see, Frank was wondering whether Don might contact Ella?'

'Why in the name of God would Frank think that?'

'Well, I said that she went off somewhere today and she didn't tell any of us where she was going.'

'So?'

'So Frank thought she might still be carrying a torch for Don.'

'Carrying a torch!' Deirdre screamed with laughter. 'A torch, no less. What a ludicrous thing to say. Is Frank losing his marbles?

If she was carrying a torch anywhere near him, she would gouge his eyes out with it. She hates him, Nuala, you know that.'

'Love and hate aren't all that far apart,' Nuala said prissily.

'I don't think so in this case, and did Frank get this idea out of the air or did you sow it in his mind?'

'No, I didn't sow it in his mind, but after he was talking to Don, he seemed to think it was a possibility.'

'And he's all buddy-buddy with Don now?'

'I told you, there was a misunderstanding. Don has sent a sum of money to a PO box, one of Frank's brothers picked it up.'

'So Frank has forgiven him.'

'He's listening to him anyway.'

'And what does he hear?'

'That Don wants to make it up to Ella. He'd like to know where she is.'

'Well, I have no idea. She went to clear her head and I don't want to talk about it any more.'

Deirdre sent up a silent prayer of thanks that they had told Nuala nothing. Suppose they had innocently said where Ella was going? One of Don's henchmen could have been waiting for her in the New York hotel this very minute.

Nick and Sandy were just going to bed when Deirdre rang. 'I know it's silly, but I'm just sitting here on my own worrying. She *is* all right, isn't she? It's just that Don's getting Frank and his desperate brothers to use Nuala to get to Ella. He even paid them the money they lost.'

'Do you think we should tell her?' Nick asked.

'I don't know. Part of me thinks we should, but then it's your pitch. I don't want her to go to pieces on you out there.'

'The job's not as important as her being all right. Look, I'll discuss it with Sandy and then we'll give her a call.'

'Think about it, Nick. If she's on her own out there, it might be worse for her to know.'

'Go to bed, Deirdre. Don Richardson can't ruin every night's sleep in the Western world.'

They called Ella's hotel, but she was not in her room. Nor was she in the hotel dining-room. 'It's one in the morning,' Sandy said disapprovingly.

'It's only eight p.m. there. We're not her mother and father.'
'Still, who does she know there? Where can she be?'

Ella was at a party in Harriet's suite, drinking cocktails and meeting some of Harriet's contacts. They were mainly women in their fifties, scouts that she had sent out looking for supplies. Some of them were younger and wearing a lot of jewellery and expensive jackets. Harriet had not been at all surprised that she phoned and had welcomed Ella warmly. Everyone was interested for a moment when she was introduced as a movie-maker, but they lost interest when they heard it was a documentary.

Harriet's contacts had brought her samples. Ella examined yellow negligees with rhinestones, scarlet thongs and black panties with pink lace rosebuds on them. Had Ireland changed a great deal? Or did everyone else at home wear underwear like this and Ella was the only one left out?

'You can buy anything you need at cost,' Harriet said to her kindly.

'Thanks, Harriet. I don't have much of a sex life going at the moment. I think I'll pass, if you don't mind.'

'Fine-looking girl like you, you do surprise me,' Harriet said.

Some of the contacts seemed to suggest that owning a proper wardrobe of what was on display was the surefire way of restoring a good sex life fairly speedily.

Ella had eaten nothing and was beginning to feel a little light-headed. 'Well, if I thought they'd help sell my film idea to Derry King,' she said, pretending to consider one of the little corsets.

'Not *the* Derry King!' said one of the contacts.

'You've heard of him?'

'There was a big piece about him in the paper today . . . but what was in it?'

None of them could remember.

'I hope he hasn't gone bankrupt,' Ella said. That would be all they'd need. But it appeared that it had something to do with rescuing a dog shelter. Derry King had not only given the place the funds it needed, but he had marched with the protesters personally and raised their profile considerably. 'A dog lover, I see,' Ella noted. It hadn't mentioned that in any of the files. 'Then I'll buy that jewelled dog collar for him,' she said.

'It's a bit flash, Ella. I mean, it's only five dollars. It's for guys to give their girls who have silly bow-wows.' Harriet didn't want to steer her wrong.

'No, what's more, I'll buy two. I know a dog called Hooves back in Dublin who'd absolutely love it.'

She had three more cocktails, went back to her own hotel, and fell into sleep without even listening to her voice-mail on the telephone.

This was meant to be her day off. Her whole day to relax and get ready for tomorrow to meet the great Derry King, investor and apparently a dog lover. And now she had the most unmerciful hangover. Slowly she got herself into the day. The woman at the beauty salon suggested a facial. It was very expensive, but what the hell? She would pay Firefly Films back one day. That's what she was going to spend the rest of her life doing anyway, it seemed. Paying people back.

'Sorry, Nick, I was out last night. I forgot to check my messages,' she said when she found the winking light and called him back.

'Great, Ella. You're really on top of things over there,' he said.

'No, I'm fine. I have such hair and such skin you just wouldn't believe it.'

'Terrific.'

'What were you on about anyway?'

He told her briefly about it all, how they were all a little bit worried in case Nuala might just have got any of it right.

'Not very likely, based on previous performance.' She was brisk.

'Don't be flip, Ella. We're your friends, okay?'

'Sure, sorry, it's just that I'm a bit frail. Nuala's half-wit take on everything doesn't seem real from here.'

'Why are you frail?'

'Hung over. Mixed cocktails.'

'Jesus, Sandy, she's been spending our money on cocktails.'

'No, they were free. I met this woman on the plane ...'

'I don't want to hear about it ... listen, Ella. It could be serious. He's paid off Frank and his brothers simply because he's married to a friend of yours and hopes she knows where you are.'

'No, he doesn't want to contact me,' she said.

'Why do you say that? Hasn't he got Mike Martin and Frank sending out feelers?'

'If Don really wanted to talk to me, he'd find me.'

'And would you talk to him?' Nick asked fearfully. He had a

sinking feeling why Ella had kept the laptop. She wanted Don to get in touch with her.

'Probably.' She sounded very far away.

'But you can't. Not without someone else being there.'

'This is costing you a fortune, Nick. Thanks for being involved, I mean it, and thank Sandy and Dee for me. But I'm fine.'

'You're okay, really?'

'Really I am. And I can't wait to meet Derry King. I bought him a jewelled dog collar, by the way.'

'I ask myself over and over if we did the right thing, sending you to New York,' Nick said.

Harriet rang to know had she survived.

'Yes, just about. Sorry for laying into your booze so heavily.'

'Not at all. It's just that . . . I don't know, those dog collars are a bit tacky. You know, if you really do want to impress him that might not be the right way to go.'

'Thanks, Harriet. I'm meeting him tomorrow. I'll see how it goes.'

'Anyway, who am I, talking to someone like you . . . you're well able to look after yourself.'

'I wish.'

'I recognised you as that money broker's girl, the one they thought he had run off with.'

'Oh, you did.' Ella's voice was dull. She often wondered if people recognised her. Now that the months had gone by very few remembered her, but of course she had to meet someone who did.

'Only because a mate of mine, a real nice woman, Nora O'Donoghue, she lost her wedding money to him.'

'I know Nora. She works in the kitchen of Quentins sometimes. She's very nice.'

'She lodged with my sister once in Mountainview and she's getting married to this teacher. Apparently he was giving Latin lessons to Richardson's sons . . . anyway, they lost their savings . . . that's why I'd remember.'

'A lot of people lost their savings, my own parents did,' Ella said.

'And no one knows where he is?'

'Well, we think he's in Spain. He must have been setting up a different name and home when I was with him. It all seems so long ago.'

'You know, I half-wondered when I saw you if he was out here. New York would be a good place to hide, and maybe you were coming out to meet him. And I said to myself it might be dangerous for you.'

Ella felt a sudden shiver of fear. It was probably the hangover, she told herself firmly. But two people within five minutes of each other warning her on the telephone was hard to take.

'No, truly, Harriet. He's long gone out of my life.'

'So good luck with the film anyway, and remember what I said. Think carefully about the dog collar.'

'Good luck, Harriet, and thanks for everything.'

'There'll be other fellows, there always are.'

'Oh, I'm sure of it. It's just that I'm not ready for one yet.'

'They turn up when you least expect them.'

'Did someone turn up for you, Harriet?'

'The nicest fellow that ever wore shoe leather. Married to a right bitch. She pushed him too far one day and he came over to me with a suitcase. That's ten years ago.'

'And why isn't he here with you?'

'He's terrified of planes and big cities.'

'And what'll he do while you're here?'

'He'll cook grand things like chicken pies and spaghetti sauces and label them and put them in the freezer. And he'll talk to his pigeons, and he'll go and have a pint with his son, and he'll be at the airport in a van to lift me and the bags home.'

'Good luck to you,' Ella said.

'And to you, Ella, and you know that no one blames you for that bastard. But I'd love it all to come out about your family and everything . . .'

'One day,' Ella promised as she looked over at the laptop computer on her desk.

It was such a lovely day. No blustery wind to blow her new hair-do away, so she went for a long walk down Fifth Avenue.

New York was full of energy. Ella felt a new spring in her step as she walked. She called into St Patrick's Cathedral and longed to have enough faith to pray to God and ask for the meeting with Derry King to go well. But it wouldn't be fair. And it wouldn't work anyway because God knew that she didn't really believe.

So instead she told God that if He still happened to be listening to sinners, and there were no strings attached, she'd like to remind

Him that thousands of films got made every year and it wouldn't upset anyone if theirs was one of them next year.

She looked at florist displays. She read the menus on windows. She admired the uniforms of doormen. She strolled through the atriums of office blocks. She watched the office workers coming out into the street to smoke or grab sandwiches in a deli. She wondered what it would be like to work in this huge, exciting city where nobody seemed to know anyone like people did in Dublin, where you were always nodding at people and saluting each other.

A tall man passed by and looked at her appreciatively. Ella felt alarmed. Suppose Harriet had been right about New York being a good place to hide. Possibly Don *was* in this city. She might meet him at the end of this block, at the next traffic lights. But she must not give in to silly fears. This is the way madness and weakness lay.

'You've got to have courage,' she said aloud suddenly.

'Right on, lady,' said a man at a news-stand who was the only one who had heard her.

Ella hugged herself. She liked New York, she was as safe here as anywhere. She would walk until she was too tired to walk a step further, and then she would take a taxi back to her hotel.

She slept for fourteen hours and got up feeling better than she had felt for ages.

'I thought you'd be older,' Derry King said as he shook hands with her in the foyer of the hotel.

'I thought you'd be older too,' Ella said with spirit. 'But here we are, babes in a big business world, so can I offer you coffee?'

He smiled.

He had a good smile for a square-built man with a very heavily lined face. She knew to the day how old he was, and yet he didn't look it. Forty-three-year-old New Yorkers wore their years better than most Dubliners of the same age.

'I'll drink coffee, sure. Do you want us to talk here, or should we talk in your suite?'

'We are a small outfit, Mr King. I have a bedroom, not a suite. I think we'd be much happier here.'

'And I'd be happier if you called me Derry. I prefer the first-name thing.'

'Fine, Derry. I brought you a present,' she said.

'You did?' He was surprised.

'I heard you loved dogs, so I got you a nice dog collar.' She produced it from her handbag.

'It's horrific! Where on earth did you get it?' he laughed.

'It's not horrific. It cost me five dollars from a dealer who comes to New York every year to buy really tasteful gifts for the Christmas market back home,' Ella said defensively.

'You and I are going to get on fine, Ella Brady,' he said, and her churning stomach settled down.

He was right. They would get on fine.

Chapter Eight

'Do you think she's seriously going to give him a dog collar?' Sandy asked Nick.

'Nothing would surprise me,' he said gloomily.

'Of course, it may work out very well. He may fall in love with her.'

'Jesus, I hope he doesn't. He has a wife called Kimberly who owns half the business.'

'Does Ella know that?' Sandy sounded fearful now.

'Oh, definitely, she's read the file. But the presence of a wife didn't exactly stop her before, if you know what I mean.'

The man who came to ask the Bradys about renting a flat in Tara Road was very polite. He admired their garden residence, as he called it, and said he loved a place with photographs. It made a house into a home.

'Is that your daughter, and isn't she a very handsome girl?' he asked, looking at a picture of Ella.

'That's right,' Barbara said.

Ella had told her to be cautious and she would be, but this well-dressed man couldn't be in any way sinister. He was so courteous and he wanted an apartment for a colleague who was coming over from the UK in a few months' time.

'Does she live with you?' He was still looking at the picture of Ella.

'Oh yes, in and out.'

'And is she here at the moment?'

'No, she's gone off ... the way they do at that age.'

'Has she gone abroad, do you think?'

Ella's mother was frightened now. This was no courteous man looking for an apartment for a colleague. It was someone looking for Ella.

'Do young people ever tell you where they're going these days?' She laughed nervously.

'Oh, I know, but doesn't she have to work? I think you said she was a teacher.'

They hadn't said Ella was a teacher.

'She does a bit of this and a bit of that ... it's easier to get time off.'

'Maybe she went out to the sun, to Greece or Spain?' the man suggested. 'Lots of people go out there in September.'

Barbara Brady directed her firmest gaze on her husband. 'She didn't say anything about going to the Continent to me, did she mention it to you, Tim?'

'Not a word,' he said. 'Somewhere down in Kerry or West Cork, she said. It could be that she's got herself an extra little job. She ran into a spot of bad luck earlier in the year, and she's desperately trying to gather some money together.'

'So anyway, to go back to the flat ...' Barbara began.

But the man had lost interest in the flat in Tara Road.

'We're back here for a few days. Will you have lunch with me, Deirdre?'

'No, Nuala, thanks, but I can't.'

'You didn't even wait to hear which day,' Nuala complained.

'I can't any day. There's a crisis at work. We're all on short lunch hours,' Deirdre lied.

'Are you annoyed with me about something, Dee?'

'No, I'm annoyed about having to eat into my lunch break. Why would I be annoyed with you, for God's sake?'

'You seemed pissed off when I asked you where Ella was. It's just that I have to know. Frank keeps going on at me. He says it's the one thing I might be expected to know and I don't even deliver on that.'

'Real charmer Frank turned out to be,' Deirdre said unsympathetically.

'No, they're frightened. His brothers too, all of them.'

'I thought they got their money back in a brown paper bag?'
'That was just a little to show that they *could* get it back if ...'
'If what?'
'I suppose, if they played ball ...'
'And handed Ella over, is that it?'
'I don't think it's quite like that.'
'So it's just as well that neither of us knows where she is, then, isn't it, Nuala?' Deirdre was brisk.
'You know, Dee.'
'I wish I did.'
'Advise me. Help me, *please*.' Nuala was desperate.
'I don't suppose it's the kind of thing you'd get the Guards in on,' Deirdre said.
'Not really. Frank and his brothers always steer clear of police and lawyers,' said Nuala.

Patrick and Brenda Brennan were going to bed. It had been a long, busy night. 'I ask myself, do we need this documentary? Every table was full tonight,' Patrick said.
'I know, I've thought that too. We'd have to consider expanding.' Brenda was frowning.
'Which would change it all.' Patrick frowned too.
'Still, it's not meant to be just an advertisement,' Brenda cheered up. 'It's more like a history of Dublin, isn't it, as seen through the changes in one place.'
'Now you're beginning to sound just like young Ella Brady,' he said, yawning.
'I wonder how she's getting on out there,' Brenda said as she sat at her dressing table and took off her makeup.
She couldn't hear what Patrick said, since he was under the duvet and mumbling into the pillow.
'I do hope she's all right. She's been through a really terrible summer,' Brenda said to herself as she creamed away the last traces of the stylish makeup that always took ten years off her age.

Derry King was right. They did get on well together. Ella told him no lies, and exaggerated no aspect of Firefly Films.
'What's in it for me?' he had asked early on, and she had tried to tell him as truthfully as she could. He would be part of something fresh and new, made with high production values, which could

well win prizes at film festivals, that would be shown on television in many lands.

'How is it new and fresh?' he wanted to know.

'It's not going to be full of shamrockery,' she said and he had laughed.

'What's that?'

'Oh, you know, the how-are-things-in-Gloccamora, top-of-the-morning approach. There's nobody doing leprechaun duty on this movie.'

He was interested. 'Warts and all, then?'

'Well, yes ... we'd want to make fun of everything pretentious,' she said.

'Give me an example.'

'Patrick's very funny about the way Irish people often pretend they know things when they don't, like they don't want to look foolish. He says that you should never drink the second cheapest wine on the menu. It could be any kind of old rubbish, because it's the one people go for so they don't look cheap or shabby by buying the very cheapest on the list.'

Derry was smiling at her. 'And he'll say all this?'

'Certainly.'

'Not afraid of losing his clientele?'

'No, he'll walk a fine line. You'll like him when you come over. I'm actually amazed you were never in Quentins when you were in Ireland before,' Ella said.

'I was never in Ireland,' Derry said flatly.

'I'm sorry?'

'I was never there,' he said, and though his smile did not leave his face, his eyes looked hard. 'And I never intend to go.'

Cathy Scarlet and Tom Feather had only lost a small sum when Rice and Richardson had gone to the wall. Compared to others, they had been very lucky. Only an outstanding bill for 700 euros: One catered function unpaid for.

It was the one afternoon a week when Maud and Simon were in to polish what were called Tom and Cathy's 'treasures', and to discuss in detail the forthcoming baby. What would it be called? Where would it live? Would it be grown up when Tom and Cathy finally got around to getting married? Could they teach the baby to do step-dancing?

It was almost a relief when the bell rang in the front office and they could escape the children's questions for a few minutes. It was someone enquiring about brochures and price lists. He was a well-dressed man who didn't seem to have any precise idea about what he wanted. There was something about the vagueness of his request that made them suspicious.

'I believe you know Ella Brady,' he said, out of the blue.

'Yes,' Tom said, giving nothing away.

'Slightly,' said Cathy, making sure that she was even more distant. They knew where Ella was, but that it had to be kept a secret.

'Would you have any idea where she is now?' he asked politely.

'None at all, I'm afraid,' Tom said.

'Not a clue,' Cathy said.

'Now, that's a pity . . . I've been asked to give you some money for a debt that was overlooked. Inadvertently, of course. Around seven hundred euros, I think.'

Tom and Cathy looked at each other, astounded. 'You're from Rice and Richardson?' Cathy said, stunned.

'No, alas, I'm not, but let's say I'm a friend of one of the people involved, and he felt bad that there had been this misunderstanding and shortfall.'

'I'm sure he did,' Cathy said.

The man opened his wallet. 'He asked me to get it to you personally. He's not a man who likes to leave bills unpaid.' The man paused as he laid the seven notes on the small table. 'And he'd be very grateful if you could ask Ella to call him at this number.'

'Well, this is great to get the money,' Tom said. 'But we don't have any idea where Ella is.'

'So if one depends on the other,' Cathy began, 'then we shouldn't take the money.'

'No, keep it. It might remind you of where she is.'

'We know where she is,' came a clear voice. Tom and Cathy looked in horror at Maud.

Was there a possibility that Ella might have been so foolish as to mention anything to those children?

'Go back to the kitchen, Maud, *please*,' Cathy begged.

'You don't know anything about Ella's whereabouts,' Tom said.

Simon was stung by the unfairness of this. 'We do know,' he said mutinously.

'And where is that, exactly?' the man was interested.

'She's gone to hospital,' Simon said triumphantly.

'She's having a piece of her head put back on,' Maud added. 'It will take two weeks, altogether.'

The man looked at Tom and Cathy as if for confirmation. They both shrugged.

'Could be, I suppose,' Cathy said.

'Quite possible,' Tom agreed.

The man turned and left without saying a word. As he went down the cobbled lane they saw him pause and take out his mobile phone.

'I guess he's calling Spain,' Cathy said.

'Is that where the hospital is?' Simon said. 'I thought it might be in America, from something Ella said.'

Tom let his breath out slowly. 'And why didn't you share that view with the gentleman when he was here?'

'I wasn't sure. It's just she said something about spending her last dollar on something but it could have been just an expression.'

'It could,' Cathy said, holding Tom's hand in relief.

'Will you be mating again when the baby is born?' Maud asked.

'Probably. If we have the energy,' Cathy said.

'Does it take a lot of energy?' Simon was interested.

'Back to the kitchen, everybody,' Tom suggested.

From the corner of the road, the man phoned Don Richardson. 'I'm not having much luck, Don. Nothing from the film-makers, her parents, that restaurant; and nothing from the caterers.'

He listened for a while and then nodded. 'All right. Plan C then, as you say.'

Ella looked at Derry King open-mouthed. 'You're never going to Ireland!' she said, astonished.

'Not if I can help it, no.'

'Then what are you doing, talking about making a movie there?'

'I'm not making it, you are.' He spread out his hands to show how simple his argument was.

'But what have we been talking about if you don't ... if you never intend ... I'm sorry, Derry. I don't understand.' She looked hurt and annoyed.

'I don't have to *love* Ireland to invest in a movie about it. Anyway, from what I see it's not a hymn of praise to the place ... it's showing up all its weaknesses, all this new money, greed, so-called style.'

'We didn't say that ...'

'Well, that's what it came over like, people imitating Europeans.'

'But we *are* Europeans!' Ella cried.

'No, you said it was warts and all ... just a minute ago.'

'Derry, there's something very wrong here.' She looked down at her notes. 'I've been talking to you in this coffee shop for hours and I must have been giving you completely the wrong message.'

'I have, for personal reasons of my own, no love for Ireland,' he said. 'The legacy of my father is not one that would make me go and look for my roots. I was interested in this project because I thought you were sending them up.'

'But you have the initial notes from Nick.'

'He said it would be frank and groundbreaking. That's why I'm here ... to learn how.'

'And what have you learned so far?' Ella felt a cold lump of disappointment in her chest.

'I've learned that we have stayed too long in this coffee shop. We should have a break now, then I'll send a car for you and take you to a meal. All this talk about food has made me hungry.'

She was afraid to let him out of her sight. 'They have a restaurant here ...' she began.

'No, they don't, not a real restaurant. Car will be here for you at seven. Okay?'

'One thing before you go.'

'Sure, fire away.'

'I'll be talking to Nick. Will I say it was all a misunderstanding, the whole thing?'

'Why would you say that?'

'From what you said, I thought that it had been.'

'Hey, we're only into talks about talks so far. The real talks are way down the road.'

'But I couldn't betray this restaurant, none of us could. I mean, we'd have to cancel the project if that's what you wanted.'

'I understand, and I respect you. Seven p.m.'

It was an awkward telephone conversation. 'I'm not getting the whole picture,' Nick said.

'Neither am I, to be honest. Could I leave it that we're in talks about talks?'

'Not really, Ella. We've invested all we can in this; we're both in a bit of a panic.'

'That makes three of us, or possibly four. Derry could be in a bit of a panic as well. It turns out that he hated his father and he hates Ireland.'

'I don't believe you.'

'That's what he told me. Will I ring you when I get back? It will be about three or four a.m. your time.'

'Don't bother, Ella. Leave it till tomorrow.'

Ella wore Deirdre's black dress and red jacket. She had taken a large handbag, which was big enough to hold papers and photographs without looking like a briefcase. A chauffeur collected her.

'What restaurant are we going to?' Ella asked chattily.

The chauffeur pronounced the name of the place with awe, and as if it were the only possible place to go if you were the guest of Mr King.

He was waiting at the table. He wore a dinner jacket. In a way he looked quite as formal as he did in the photographs in those clippings she had read so carefully on the flight over to New York. Yet those interviews and articles told very little about him. They gave no hint of his enthusiasm and willingness to work at something until it was achieved. They didn't speak of how his face lit up when he thought they were getting somewhere. He was a very keen businessman, out of her league.

Suddenly Ella felt a wave of inadequacy. 'I hope I'm dressed enough,' she said.

'You look very nice,' he said.

'Your wife was not able to join us tonight?'

'Not for many nights,' he smiled.

'Sorry, that's another thing I got wrong,' she apologised.

'No, you looked up your files perfectly correctly. You just didn't get to the bit where it says "Marriage Dissolved".'

'Was that a long time ago?' Ella tried to be as cool as he was being.

'Oh, ten years, I'd say, but it's hard to remember because we meet every week at the foundation, you see.'

'Does that work? Well, obviously it does because otherwise you wouldn't both be able to do it.'

'It does work, remarkably well as it happens, and Kimberly is remarried and goes out a lot at night. I don't, so we rarely meet in the evenings. But we met this afternoon. She was most interested in the project, and she will join us tomorrow.'

'There will be a tomorrow, then?' Ella was almost tearful in her gratitude.

'Of course there will, Ella. Now look at this menu and tell me. Do your pals in Quentins match up to this place?'

'I wish they could see me now. I wish everyone could see me now.' She looked confident and happy for the first time since she had come to New York.

Kimberly looked as if she were twenty-two, but Ella knew she must be almost forty. With a perfect, glossy hairstyle that had to be freshly done at a salon every day, a perfect smile with even white teeth, a pale, peach-coloured designer outfit and high black heels, she was dazzling. She was also as smart as anyone Ella had ever met. She was totally on top of the project, and realised what Firefly Films was trying to do. She told them of other movies they had underwritten, one about a young songwriter who had believed so mightily in her own career that she overcame all the rejections and obstacles en route. Another was about a woman who arranged a social club for mentally handicapped children to give their parents a break, but was closed down by the authorities because she did not have the necessary official qualifications. There was another about the stress of being police wives, and another about a woman who had kept a cat for thirteen years in a No Pets Allowed condominium without anyone finding out.

Ella couldn't find any common thread amongst them. Derry and Kimberly seemed pleased. They didn't want to be predictable. Tomorrow they would get down to the nitty-gritty, Kimberly said, and plan out a tour for Derry to make when he got to Ireland.

Ella looked up, startled. 'But I didn't think you were going to Ireland, Derry?'

'Of course he is. That's only nonsense,' Kimberly said.

'No way, Kim, forget it.' Derry smiled lazily.

'Would you come instead, Kimberly?' Ella pleaded.

'Yes, Kim, you'd love it.' He was teasing her.

'Derry knows I am not going to stir from New York and leave my very young and suggestible husband to all the temptations of this city.'

'Oh, Lorenzo wouldn't stray,' Derry said. 'Not in a million years.'

'His name is Larry, Ella, which Derry very well knows, and he is not being left alone to test out any theory.'

Ella looked back at Derry. He didn't seem at all annoyed.

'It will all be sorted out eventually. Kim likes to play games. Always her little weakness.' He spoke without malice, affectionately in fact.

'Lord, someone has to play games around this place,' she laughed, ruffling his hair.

'Now less of this wasting time doing a re-run of an old argument.'

'Derry has to go to Ireland sooner or later. He will leave when he's ready. Why don't you tell us your stories, Ella? Tell us all about these people who will make up the movie.'

It was time now, time to convince them that this restaurant was filled with people's lives. She took out her notes and began to tell the stories.

The Short Fuse

Martin went back to sleep after he had switched off his alarm. He dreamed a troubled, complicated dream about having the wrong change and being refused service. He woke shaking with irritation about it all and became even more annoyed when he realised it was seven o'clock and that he would now be twenty minutes late for work. Today of all days. He tried to hurry and naturally that made him slower than ever. He got into a shower that was too hot and had to leap out again, knocking down the contents of a shelf. He lost a button off his best shirt, spilled the orange juice in the fridge. He remembered that he had intended to drop clothes off at the dry cleaners, now there would be no time. This meant that he would not have a freshly cleaned suit for tomorrow. It was the day to put out the rubbish and he had literally no time. He ran out and realised it was raining, went back for an umbrella, and heard the phone ring. Before eight o'clock in the morning, it must be urgent. He answered it and discovered to his great irritation that it was his son.

'Hi, Dad, it's Jody. Just wanted to make sure you hadn't forgotten.'

Why did the boy think that he might have forgotten a lunch arrangement made over a month ago?

'It's just that you're always so very busy. It could have slipped your mind.'

'No, Joseph, believe me, busy people don't forget things like longstanding arrangements. I'm afraid that the luxury of forgetting is only for those who are not busy, don't have anything important to do. Those who have nothing important in their lives.'

Why did he do it? Anger the boy further, widen the gulf between them still more. Delay himself still further. And now Joseph was twittering on about the menu, saying his father must choose whatever he wanted to eat. 'Yes, yes, I think that's what one usually does in restaurants,' Martin snapped.

But Jody heard no coolness in his father's tone. 'I just wanted to make sure you knew you didn't have to keep to the fixed menu or anything,' he tried to explain.

'Joseph, I have to go.' Martin hung up. Outside in the wet street, everyone else had managed to put out rubbish. Other people had got up in time and gone to their dreary little jobs and yet he, Martin, hadn't managed it. Martin, who ran the biggest advertising agency in the city, a man known all over the country. Today they were making a pitch for the biggest corporate client ever. Something they had been preparing for three months and now that the day was here, he had to have this tedious anxiety dream and go back to sleep. There were other things that had to be done today too. Kit Morris, his secretary, must be smartened up. She was too old for the job, her face didn't fit and she wasn't up to speed on all the new technology. Perhaps he should put off talking to her until much later in the day. The thing about Kit was that she never watched the clock, she worked very hard. She had been with him a long time. Probably had no other life outside.

On any day of the week it wasn't going to be easy telling her that she didn't give the image he wanted by appearing in a shapeless skirt and long cardigan. But today was a tense day and it wasn't going to be an early night, either. They were having a reception for their American partners at 5 p.m. with dinner to follow. The timing could not have been worse. If they didn't get the new corporate account, they would not feel at all like entertaining the Americans.

Martin sighed as he hastened along the slippery pavement. This of all days to have to meet Joseph for lunch. But the boy had been adamant. It was the anniversary of Rose's death. His wife had been dead for fifteen years. Martin had thrown himself into work since it happened. But tragedies affect people in different ways. Joseph had dropped out of school only weeks after the funeral. It had been impossible to talk to the boy about anything since then.

Martin arrived wet, out of breath and bad-tempered at his office.

'They're waiting for you,' Kit said cheerfully.

'Please, Kit, don't come at me with profound wisdom. Not today.'

Kit was not at all put out. 'It's all right, Martin. I've given them coffee and your apologies. I told them you'd had a power breakfast you couldn't cancel. Actually it might work to your advantage.' She smiled at him reassuringly.

Martin squared his shoulders and began his morning.

He wasn't to know it, but other people's mornings were difficult too. His son Jody had paced and paced around a small bed-sitting-room rehearsing over and over the speech he would make at lunchtime in Quentins Restaurant. Would it come out as he intended it to? The more often he said it, the less likely it seemed.

In the restaurant, under the watchful eye of Brenda Brennan, the Breton waiter Yan was polishing the cutlery on each table with a soft cloth and having a bad morning. There had been a letter from home with vague mentions of his father going to Concarneau to have tests in the hospital. Nobody said what the tests were for. Should he go home and find out? It would be useless to telephone, they would only tell him not to waste his hard-earned money.

Kit Morris was not having a good day either. It didn't help that Martin was behaving like a spoiled child. She had her own problems. Like how the future was going to work out for her elderly mother. She was no longer able to cope on her own. It would be coming to live with Kit or going in to a home. There were no other options, her married brothers had made that clear. Kit needed some time to think it through. She had been going to ask Martin for a few days' leave. But today was not the day to ask him.

Martin sat at his table in Quentins, drumming his fingers. One of his colleagues had driven him there. The man had patronisingly urged Martin to have a good relaxed lunch, noting that he was on a fairly short fuse today. So now he was fifteen minutes early and of course that boy would be late as he always was. Martin went over the meeting in his mind. The people had been very cagey, they had not said yes or no to the pitch that had been made. They would let him know later in the day. Most things had gone well.

What he needed was a good stiff drink. The waiter, foreign of course, didn't manage to catch his eye. The boy did look over once, but his eyes were vacant, so Martin clicked his fingers to attract his attention. Something happened to the boy's face then. A veneer of coldness came over it. It was so deliberate that Martin could not believe his eyes. The young pup was not even going to acknowledge him. This was not good enough, it simply was not. This was a top-class restaurant with standards. He clicked his fingers again and the boy's face was like stone. Martin felt a nerve beginning to tic in his forehead. He stood up and was just about to approach Brenda Brennan to complain in the most forceful of tones when there was a sudden power cut. Every light in the place went out. In a dark, heavily curtained restaurant on a wet, overcast day, it was astonishing the effect it caused. The place seemed to be in complete darkness. For a moment, Martin thought that he had been having a blackout and was greatly relieved to hear fellow diners gasp, laugh and make remarks about the incident.

Holding the table for support, he eased himself back into his seat. Brenda had organised her troops with candles on every table within minutes. She moved amongst them all, assuring everyone that they cooked by gas as well as electricity. So there would be no problem and she insisted that everyone have a drink on the house by way of an apology.

'That's if you can get anyone who will serve you one,' Martin grumbled.

'I beg your pardon, sir?' Brenda Brennan was startled.

'Well, that Latin Lover over there seems to have been stricken with deafness and blindness even at a time when the lights *were* on,' Martin said.

'Yan is one of our best waiters, so you do surprise me, but let me please serve you, sir. What would you like?'

He saw her speaking to Yan while the boy tried to explain something. He was being very definite about whatever it was he was saying. Martin couldn't hear, but he saw Brenda seem to console him and place her hand on his arm. And then she was back with exemplary speed with his vodka and he tried to relax. Eventually the waiter approached to leave him the menus. Martin had not yet succeeded in relaxing.

'Oh, I see you've noticed me at last,' he said.

'I'm sorry, sir,' he said.

'Don't even try to tell me that you didn't see me,' Martin began.

'No, sir, I did see you. I am sorry for not coming over.'

'And why didn't you?'

'You made this sound with your fingers.' Yan did that click.

'Yes, because I wanted to get you to see me.'

'I trained with a *maître d'hôtel* who said we must develop a diplomatic blindness if such a thing happened, and not to serve the person. Ever. But Mrs Brennan, she has just explained this is not the policy here, so I apologise.'

'Things like that might work in France . . .' Martin began.

'I am from Brittany, sir,' Yan said. His face looked pale and anxious. Possibly Brenda had threatened to sack him. The boy did not look well.

'Are you all right?' Martin asked unexpectedly.

'Thank you for asking me. Just I'm a little worried in case my father might be ill and if I should be beside him.'

'Are you close to your father?' Martin asked.

'No, he is far away in Brittany,' Yan explained.

'I meant, can you talk to him, do you like each other?'

'No father can really talk to his son, no son can really talk to his father, only the very lucky ones. But I care very much, yes.'

At that moment, Martin saw his own son being shown to the table. The familiar surge of annoyance filled him. Joseph . . . or Jody as he insisted on calling himself . . . wore a torn anorak and grey faded sweater underneath. He looked so shabby, so out of place, yet his smile was confident and happy.

'Dad, I'm so sorry I'm late. The buses were full because of the rain, and I was so anxious to get here because . . .'

'It's all right, Joseph. Give the waiter your order for a drink. It's free because the electricity has failed.'

'Has it?' Jody looked around in amazement. He said, 'I didn't even notice.'

Martin looked very impatient. The boy was showing himself to be almost an imbecile.

'Please, Joseph, get some grip on reality,' he began.

'But Dad, I was so excited coming to see you to tell you the great news, great, great news.'

'You've got a job?' his father asked.

'I've always had a job, Dad,' Jody said.

'If you call sweeping up leaves a job.'

'It's gardening, Dad, but that's not the point. The point is that . . .' Jody stopped, hardly able to speak for the magnitude of what he was going to say. 'The point is, Dad, I spent two whole mornings wondering how to tell you and now I wonder why, why was I rehearsing it?'

'Rehearsing what?'

'I saw you, Dad, as I came across the room, talking to the waiter ...'

Jody indicated Yan, who had not left but was looking from one to the other as if he were at a tennis match. 'And you looked so kind and concerned, like an ordinary person not a great business-man ... so I said to myself, why do I have to wait until it's a good time to tell you? We are going to have a baby, Jenny and I ... we are so excited, I can't tell you how pleased and happy we are. Imagine, a son or daughter of our own. A new person!'

The hint of tears was in his eyes, the eagerness that had never died. The optimism that even his father's cool dismissive attitude had never managed to quench shone out of him.

At that very moment Brenda came over with an envelope for Martin. 'Your secretary delivered it by hand. She said she knew you would not like to be disturbed by the telephone.'

Kit had chosen this moment of all moments to bother him with some office business. He barely looked at it but tried instead to think of a response to his son. Before Martin could speak, Yan had taken Jody's hand. '*Mes félicitations* ... I mean, my congratula-tions, what a wonderful piece of news. You must be happy, you and your wife.'

'Jenny and I aren't married ... we never saw the need ...' Jody began.

'No, no ... in French it is the same word, wife and woman.'

'So it is,' Jody said, but his eyes were on his father. 'Do you want to open your message from the office, Dad? It might be important,' he said humbly.

Martin was almost too choked to speak. 'Nothing is as important as this,' he stammered eventually. 'I'm so very pleased for you both, and for me, and maybe ... maybe ...' his voice broke, '... maybe there's even a way your mother might know.'

'Of course she does,' Jody beamed.

Yan stood back as if he expected the two men to stand up and embrace ... and with one movement they did. Something they had never done before. Almost embarrassed, they sat down and looked at each other.

'Now, please, Dad, open the message. It's making me nervous,' Jody said.

Kit had written to say that they had got the corporate contract and she had taken the liberty of ordering champagne to celebrate with the American partners. 'Everyone is so pleased, Martin,' Kit wrote. 'You've made this place much more like a family than a workplace. Well done from all of us.'

Martin felt almost weak as he read these words.

What had he been *thinking* of to want to change Kit?

She was utterly essential to the office the way she was.

Thank God he had said nothing to her, it would have been unforgivable.

Jody talked on about names and plans and how he would look after the baby as much as Jenny would.

'I wish I had done that with you,' Martin said slowly.

'I asked Mother about that, but she said you had far too short a fuse for minding a child,' said Jody, who didn't seem to have an ounce of resentment in his body.

'When I say goodbye to the people in the boardroom this evening, can I come around to you and Jenny to celebrate?'

Jody looked at him in amazement. His father had never been to his flat. Perhaps the short fuse wasn't as important for grand-fathers.

Serious Celebration

When Maggie Nolan did so well in her Leaving Certificate, her father said it was something that called for a Serious Celebration. The Nolan family were going out to have dinner in a hotel.

This had never happened before. They had never even been in an ordinary restaurant, let alone a hotel restaurant. Other people went to the Chinese or the Italian – the country was becoming cosmopolitan. Well, some of it was.

But not the Nolans.

There was never the money to spare. There was so much to pay for and so many calls on their time. Mrs Nolan's mam lived with them, for one thing, and Mr Nolan's dad had to have his dinner cooked for him and taken over to his flat every day.

Mr Nolan worked in charge of the bacon counter at one of those old-fashioned grocery stores that people said were on the way out. He was very happy and well-respected there but, of course, if the store really were on the way out, it would be hard for Mr Nolan to get another job.

Mrs Nolan worked as a cleaner in the hospital. She was very popular with the nurses and with the patients, but the hours were long and tiring, her veins were bad, and she hoped she would be able to continue working until all the children had been accounted for.

Maggie was the eldest of five. The others were all boys who wanted to play for English soccer teams. They had no interest in their studies and were utterly amazed that their big sister had got enough marks in exams to make people talk seriously about her going to university. They were even more amazed that their father was going to take them to the big posh hotel where nobody they knew had even been inside the door.

But he kept saying Maggie's marks would mean nothing unless there was a Serious Celebration.

'Will it be just the three of you – Mam, Dad and Maggie?' they wanted to know.

'A family celebration,' he insisted.

'Will Grandma come?' they asked.

Grandma Kelly was inclined to take her teeth out in public. The money would not extend to Grandma, it was explained firmly. Grandpa Nolan said that he wouldn't cross the door of such a place on principle. He said this before anyone had invited him, without explaining what the exact principle was.

But that still meant seven people going to a preposterously expensive hotel.

'We can't do it – it's ludicrous, Mam,' Maggie said. Her mother looked tired after a long day pushing a heavy, awkward cleaning trolley around the wards.

'Listen, child, we are so proud of you, and what has your father been in there slicing bacon for, year after year, if he can't take his family to a posh place when the eldest turns out to be a genius?' Maggie's mother's eyes were bright as they shone in her weary face.

So this stopped the discussion. There could be no more protesting.

Maggie went to her room.

She was eighteen. She knew that the celebration dinner would cost a fortune, maybe two weeks of her father's wages. He would have to borrow from the Credit Union at work. Maggie would have much preferred them to have had chicken and chips and for her father to have given her fifty pounds towards books for university.

But she listened to her mother. This Serious Celebration at the best restaurant in Dublin would give some meaning to a lot of lives. Not only her father's – her mother, too, would like to walk around the ward mentioning casually what was on the menu at the dinner party last night.

Her two difficult grandparents would rejoice as much as if they had been there. Her four younger brothers would think it was a great adventure. And if they could perhaps be persuaded not to peel the potatoes with their nails . . .

Mr Nolan made the reservation.

'Did they need a deposit?' Maggie's mother wondered.

'Indeed they did not. They asked for a phone number and I gave them the bacon counter extension,' he said proudly.

The boys became very annoyed about the amount of washing and scrubbing and clean shirts involved in it all. Maggie's mother said that she had told the matron where she was going and the matron had kindly lent her a stole. Maggie's father had told the general manager where he was going and the general manager had insisted that he would phone ahead and offer them a cocktail before dinner with his compliments.

And eventually the evening arrived.

Maggie had not thought a great deal about it because there was so much else to think of, like the fees for university and how to fit in her studies with all the hours that she would have to work earning the money. The night out in the posh restaurant, the Serious Celebration, was only one more crisis along the line. Since the Nolans didn't have a car they took two buses to get there. Mr Nolan had the money in an envelope in his inside pocket. He patted it proudly half a dozen times on the journey. Maggie felt an urge to cry every time she saw this but she kept cheerful and said over and over that she couldn't believe they were all going to this restaurant. Her friends would be so envious, she said over and over. And she was rewarded by her mother hitching her borrowed stole higher, and her father saying that the general manager was altogether too good to arrange the cocktails.

They arrived at the door and the place seemed enormous and intimidating, nobody wanted to be the first up the steps.

They felt nervous and out of place once in the restaurant. Mr Nolan wondered, should they have the cocktails in the lounge or at the table? Maggie, who thought that the boys might do less damage if corralled into just one destination, was in favour of the dining-room, but her mother thought that Mr Nolan might like to see the lounge as well.

There was endless confusion when Mr Nolan mentioned the general manager's name. There had been no message about cocktails. Apparently nobody had phoned ahead with any such order.

'Just as well, Da, we'd have all been on our ear if we had them,' Maggie said, and tried not to watch the waiter wince as he overheard her remark.

They decided to study the menu and bypass the cocktails.

The menu was in French.

'Can you translate it for us, please?' Maggie said to the scornful waiter.

She was maddened with grief that the Serious Celebration was somehow going to be dimmed.

The waiter translated, under duress; Maggie remembered what everything was. She decided that her father was going to have the steak, her mother the chicken, and that she and the boys would have well-done lamb chops. Nobody would have any starters, she said, but they would all have dessert, she promised the sneering waiter.

The boys were so shocked and overawed by it all that for once in their wild lives they agreed with her.

She had never felt so angry and upset in her whole life. The look on her parents' faces was like a knife sticking into her. They were embarrassed and ashamed – after all their borrowing and planning it had not been a good idea.

'This is something I will always remember, Mam, Dad,' Maggie said truthfully. She would remember it every day of her life, when she was a high-flying lawyer, when she was confident enough to know every dish on the menu and to be known with admiration by every one of the hotel staff here.

'Maybe it wasn't quite . . .' Dad began.

Maggie felt faint, quite literally, as if she were going to fall over. He had wanted so much for this outing to be a success for her. The more she protested, the worse it was going to get, and the more pathetic she would make him seem.

A waitress was setting up the table with the appropriate cutlery. An elegant, groomed woman, aged around thirty, she wore a white lace collar and she was probably as horrible, snobbish and dismissive as the rest of them. Maggie burned with rage at it all.

But this woman somehow managed to catch her eye with a look of understanding. This woman seemed to know it was a special occasion.

'My name is Brenda Brennan, and I'll be serving at your table. Might I enquire if this is a special family celebration?' she asked.

'My eldest – you wouldn't believe, Miss, the marks she got.'

Poor Da was bursting with eagerness to tell someone, anyone, what it was all about.

'Well, I'll tell this to Chef. He just loves to hear that we have academic people in. Usually it's only people on expense accounts,' the woman called Brenda said.

Maggie wanted to get up and hug her. But she knew that she must not do that – there was a role to be played.

'Thank you so much. When you're qualified and on your way, Chef Patrick and I will have our own restaurant,' the woman called Brenda said.

Maggie's father's face was glowing red with pleasure.

'You will leave us your name, won't you, sir, so that we can keep you on our lists?' she asked.

The scornful waiter was surprised when Patrick, the tall, dark and moody chef, said he was doing a special dessert, free, for everyone in the Nolan party.

He piped the name 'Maggie' on it in chocolate and asked for it to be brought out and photographed. He posed beside it, wearing his chef's hat, with his arms around the family.

The supercilious waiter sniffed. Imagine making a fuss of riff-raff like these people ...

The Nolans went home on the bus with half the cake. It had been a seriously good celebration.

Maggie looked out of her window that night and thought of the length of time it would take her father to pay it all back.

By the time she was a qualified lawyer and received her Parchment as a solicitor, four years had passed. And a lot of things had happened.

Her father's company had sold out, as had been predicted, but he had been taken on by the new buyers and he wore a straw hat and striped apron at the bacon counter, which pleased him a lot.

Maggie's mother had had a successful operation on her varicose veins and felt like a new woman. She had been made supervisor of cleaning. One of Maggie's brothers had, in fact, gone to train with a big English soccer team, though the others were going nowhere fast.

Her grandmother went to a day centre now; things for old people had vastly improved. She loved it there, where she could terrorise everyone happily all day.

Maggie's grandfather, who when he was seventy couldn't cook

his own lunch, met when he was seventy-two a tough woman who taught him to cook everything, married him and turned round his life.

Maggie won the Gold Medal in Law and was in a position to choose from any law firm in the country.

She knew her father wanted to take her back to the dull, snobbish restaurant, which had by now become totally *passé*. She couldn't tell him that the place had fallen from grace and that no one went there now.

She didn't need to tell him.

Once Maggie's Gold Medal was announced in the papers, an invitation arrived at her father's house. Brenda and Patrick Brennan, who were now managing the magnificent Quentins Restaurant, hoped the family would join them for a Serious Celebration. They wrote to say that their luck had turned on the night they met the Nolans. It was only fitting that they all mark this in a special way.

Maggie's father was a generous man. He had no idea that Quentins was the last word these days.

'Well, I'd like to have got you the best, Maggie, but seeing as these people did well, it would seem to be ungracious not to go, don't you think?'

'You've never been ungracious, Da.'

'And you know it's not just to have a free dinner? I have the money saved to go back to that smart place,' he said, anxious there should be no misunderstandings.

They went to Quentins by bus, but they would go home by taxi – this was going to be Mam's treat. Maggie's brothers were not overawed this time. They were four years older for one thing; but the place didn't try to put them down.

Maggie recognised the woman. Everyone was greeting her, trying to catch her eye. Brenda Brennan was warm to everyone but dallied at no table; she was always on the move.

'We can never thank you enough for this,' Brenda began.

'And do you run this place yourself, Miss? I must say, it's very respectable-looking,' Da interrupted.

Brenda said she did run it, and that Chef Patrick this time had a cake with a gold medal on it for Maggie.

It was ten times as good a meal as the one they had had four years ago, they all agreed.

Mam's taxi arrived to take them home and they were getting their coats.

'Why did you do it for us, Mrs Brennan?' Maggie asked quietly as they were leaving. 'All that business about pretending that your luck changed the night we met you ...'

'But that was true,' Brenda said. 'That was the night we realised we could not go on working for a place like that, no matter how good it looked on a CV. Supercilious, snobbish people, no welcome, no warmth, no love of food ...'

'How do you remember it was the night we were there?' Maggie wanted to know.

'You were real people, honest people having a celebration. They treated you like dirt. We couldn't bear it. We talked about you for a long time that night. The evening seemed to sum up how degrading it was to work for a place that treated its visitors so badly. And as it happened I came across some information the next night, sort of heard, you might say, that they were looking for people to run Quentins. And because of your family we somehow found the courage. We gave in our notice – and, as you see, it worked out rather well.'

Maggie knew Mrs Brennan wasn't an emotional person. Not someone you might hug. But Maggie still put a hug in her eyes. And saw it had been received. The woman swallowed and spoke slowly.

'In fact, Maggie, as you must realise, I'm very much understating it – it's a habit you get into at work. It all worked out better than we could have dreamed. It's we who owe you – that's why you were our guests tonight and you must come again.'

'When my parents are twenty-five years married, maybe?' Maggie said with a smile.

Brenda Brennan agreed. 'That, or when your brother gets picked to play soccer for Ireland. My brother-in-law out in the kitchen recognised him – he wants his autograph. Would it be all right if he asked your brother for it, do you think?'

'I think it would make this into the most Serious Celebration this family has ever known,' Maggie said.

Change of Heart

Drew had never been to Ireland in his life. And had never even considered going there until the company announced that the sales conference would be held in Dublin. Moira said it would just be a piss-up, an excuse to waste even more money than usual. 'The company is paying for it all,' Drew protested.

'Not for everything,' Moira said. She knew that there would be pints and outings and items that no company would pay for.

Drew and Moira had been going out together for three years. A lot of things were agreed between them but nothing was settled. They loved each other, that was agreed, and they would marry and have two children one day, that was agreed. But when this would happen was not settled.

Moira wanted them to get a house, which meant having a deposit. Drew wanted them both to move into his flat which was cheaper than Moira's. Moira wanted them to have a big wedding with all their friends and relations. Drew wanted them to have six people at the Register Office with pints and sandwiches afterwards.

Moira thought you only had one crack at life and you should give it your all, like putting away a certain amount of money each week. Drew thought you had only one crack at life and you should enjoy yourself first time round.

Moira realised that there was no way Drew would not go to a sales conference in Dublin which he insisted on thinking of as a

175

freebie outing but she knew would cost money. Drew realised that he was going to have to come to some decision about all this very soon. He had given up the Friday night out with the lads, and he had given up the thought of ever having a decent new jacket. Now it looked as if he were going to have to give up the notion of having any extras while he was on this great trip.

When he kissed her goodbye before the conference, they both knew that something would have to be settled by the time this meeting was over. They were nervous because they didn't dare to say it to each other. It was too big, too important, in their lives.

When they got to Dublin they stayed in a big, modern hotel. The first night, Drew told his colleagues that he was way behind with his figures. He'd love to come out with them on the town but seriously now, they'd have to forgive him this time. They accused him of being over-eager and ambitious. He was going to be a tycoon, they said, a captain of industry.

Drew grinned weakly. He was trying to save the twenty pounds he would have spent in the pubs and more, much more, if they had gone on to a nightclub. He saw there were tea-making facilities in the hotel, so he would have tea and biscuits and look at what was on television. He might even do what he had said and look over his sales figures, examine some trends.

If only he got a promotion, then he and Moira would not have to set aside an amount that meant they literally had nothing to spend on fun any more. He yearned to talk to her, hear her say something loving, to remind himself why all this self-denial was necessary. But as they had to pay for their own calls, phoning Scotland would have been a huge extravagance.

The Irish Lottery was on. That's what he needed, win that and come back a millionaire. But it was too late. If only he had bought a ticket on the way in from the airport. He saw later that there had been six lucky winners. He could have been one of them with never a financial worry again. But it hadn't happened.

Drew began to feel unreasonably irritated with those six lucky winners. What had they done after all, except have the time to buy a lottery ticket? But he tried to get this very useless and destructive envy out of his system. He reminded himself that people made their own luck and created their own chances. He had read enough of this in management books to believe it might even be true.

The next chance he got he would take. There were many

chances that he could take now, this very minute. He would just learn the names of all the senior people who would be addressing them tomorrow and study the little biographies that were among the papers they were all meant to look at.

Maybe he might look brighter than he was. Possibly someone could pick Drew for a promotion. It happened all the time.

Next day, he did seem to be brighter than the others, mainly because he had been asleep some four hours before any of them. And he hadn't discovered how much better Guinness tasted when drunk by the River Liffey in great quantities. So this was possibly why he was among twenty of the group chosen to go to dinner at Quentins.

Drew found out that not only was the company paying, but they would all go there and back in taxis, so this was another huge saving.

Quentins was certainly very elegant. You had to ring at the door to get in. They had a notice saying that they did this, as they liked to welcome their guests. Drew decided they probably also liked to keep out unsuitable people. He must remember the details of it all to tell Moira.

Moira worked as a waitress and would love to move to a classier place. She would even press her face to the windows of smart restaurants at home to get the feel of smart places. She would love to be walking in by his side tonight, to a place like this.

Would it ever happen? Or would he put so much in his savings that there would be nothing left for him ever to have a treat like a night out in Quentins or somewhere of its class?

Some of the lads he had been at school with were into great schemes for making money. One of them had a big line in issuing fake certificates for old motor cars.

Drew would have been able to do this and square it with his conscience. People spent far too much time and bureaucracy on cars anyway. But of course Moira wouldn't hear of it. Only Crims did that she said. Moira and her family had a great fear of criminals and what they called the Crim mentality.

Sometimes it would have been much easier not to love Moira, she was so unbending in her ways. Not flexible like other girls he had known. And she didn't understand how hard it was to go on a trip like this and be thought tight-fisted. She would say something stupid about the bosses watching him and how impressed they'd be.

That wasn't the way it happened in the real world. The boss class often spent more than anyone else.

Still here he was now on a real fancy night out and he was going to enjoy it. Maybe they might give away little boxes of Irish chocolates and bits of Irish glass as well, then he'd have a present for Moira and for his mother's birthday.

Drew thought to himself that it would be nice not to have to be so obsessed with money and the price of things. Not to be looking at the floor endlessly in case someone had dropped a wad of notes. Would he give it in to the authorities if he found one? Oh how he would not!

When they were all in the restaurant they were shown to two round tables for ten. The young waiters and waitresses were Europeans from different lands, all smartly dressed in their dark trousers and white shirts.

Around them moved an elegant woman, Mrs Brennan, apparently, who put everyone at their ease, translating the names of dishes casually as if they had all easily known them already. She had a way of explaining how they were made as if it were peculiar to the restaurant. She even said in a conspiratorial whisper to Drew and his end of the table that they must be very highly thought of indeed, since the best of wines had been ordered and no effort was to be spared.

His mind wandered back to the unfairness of life. Why could some people have this lifestyle all the time, and for others like himself must it be a one time only that he would describe to Moira at second hand.

He didn't even need a whole sixth of the lottery. Just a few hundred pounds would be fine.

He dragged himself back to the conversation the others were having. It was about a girl with big sad eyes sitting at the next table. The table was set for two but she was alone.

Some of his mates thought she might be persuaded to join them. Drew had his doubts. Quentins didn't look like a place where you could pick up a bird at a nearby table. And she looked tearful. Quite possibly having drunk a little too much. Much wiser to leave her where she was. 'Aw, don't mind Drew, he's in love,' someone said.

He was, he knew it, but unless he had some more money soon,

he might not be and that was very frightening. Drew decided to think about something else.

Nobody was talking to Mr Ball, the Head of Department, an anxious uncommunicative man with no small talk whatsoever. But it was either talk to Mr Ball or think about Moira. And the same Moira had often said that everyone was interesting if only you could find their subject.

'Are you a golfer, Mr Ball?' Drew asked desperately.

'Oh no, Drew, never saw the sense of it, actually,' Mr Ball said, closing the door to any more talk of that.

Drew wasn't giving up. 'But you look so fit, Mr Ball, I thought you must do some sport and I know I once asked you, did you play football, and you said no.'

Mr Ball looked left of him and right of him and then he told Drew in endless detail about his visits to the gym. There was no point in going once or twice a week, he said. You had to go five days a week. Fortunately, this hotel here in Dublin had a reasonable workout room. Had Drew seen it? No? Well, Mr Ball would show him round it tomorrow.

'I'm sorry to drone on about money, Mr Ball, but is that gym you go to back home expensive?'

Mr Ball mentioned the annual figure and saw the look on Drew's face.

'Of course, when you get to the next level in the firm, if you're promoted, the company will pay for your subscription. It's in their interest to have fit personnel,' he said. In truth, he had never thought of Drew as on the fast track.

'And tell me about your programme, Mr Ball,' Drew said in desperation, nailing on to his face a smile of interest as he heard about muscles and movements and routines. He nodded and shook his head as he heard of machines that did all they promised and those that did not. He got an ache in his face but Mr Ball thought that Drew was fascinated. Drew saw that Mr Ball was loath to leave the conversation and only had to do so out of a sense of duty.

Drew joined his own colleagues again. They were still talking about the girl and speculating abut whether she might be an available companion for the evening.

'Get sense,' Drew advised them. 'She'd be no fun at all. Look at her, she's crying. Didn't any of you notice?'

At that moment, Mrs Brennan the manageress woman had

arranged that the customer with tears in her eyes be helped to the door gently and discreetly by one of the young waiters. The taxi had already been phoned for by the restaurant. Possibly she was someone who ate here regularly and maybe drank a little too much. Someone worth looking after. It was all done with great dignity, Drew noticed. Then he saw the wallet on the floor.

He leaned back and put it into his pocket. Nobody had seen. He went to the gentlemen's cloakroom. Inside the cubicle he opened it. A big, black, soft leather wallet. It had credit cards, receipts, tickets for a theatre and a letter.

It also had plenty of cash.

Silly girl, drunk on her own, leaving without checking. She could have lost it in the taxi. Or on the pavement while getting into the taxi. Or getting out of the taxi.

He would take the cash and tomorrow he would mail the wallet back to the restaurant anonymously.

He never knew when he decided to read the letter. He wasn't a criminal, just someone taking a chance. She was called Judy and she wrote to some guy saying she was sorry to plead and beg with him to have this last dinner with her, but she had so many things to tell him – how much she loved him and how nothing else mattered. And she had to tell him that she was pregnant, but she would be noble about it and never tell his wife.

And Judy would not ask him for child support. She wanted nothing from him, except the memory of their love and the hope of their child in the future. She would have this last dinner, leave early and hand him this letter and then go out of his life. She wanted only that he would know how much he had been loved.

Drew sat there and thought about love and deception and how some people had it really very, very difficult indeed.

He left the men's room and went straight to Mrs Brennan.

'I found this under a table,' he said.

'Yes, I sort of noticed you did,' she said.

She wasn't disapproving or anything.

'Did you know anything about the . . . um . . . the situation?' he asked.

'A little. It was not a happy one, but I don't think I want to go into any of that . . .'

'It's just, I'm from miles away. I'll never be here again. I wondered should anyone tell him she's pregnant?'

If Mrs Brennan was startled that he revealed this to her, admitting that he had read a private letter, she made no criticism.

'I don't think that will change anything at all one way or the other,' she said reflectively.

'But shouldn't a man know that he was going to be a father? She intended giving it to him tonight but he didn't show up.'

'He's quite good at not showing up, it never stops the ladies.' She shook her head at the folly of people and their relationships.

'So he'll never know?' Drew was astounded.

'Or maybe care,' Brenda said.

'That's hard to believe,' he said.

'For a nice young man like you and a decent, hard-working woman like me it is, but not for people like the no-show tonight.'

'I'm not a nice young man,' Drew said. 'But it's all there, every penny of it.'

'I'm sure it is,' Brenda Brennan said with a smile.

'Why are you sure?' He was puzzled. She was serene and she was non-judgemental.

'Because if it wasn't all there, then you'd just have kicked it under the table when you had a change of heart,' she said simply.

'A change of heart!' he said, surprised at her accuracy.

'Sure, that's what it was. Can I offer you a dinner here some evening, another time, you and a friend?' she suggested.

'It would mean getting back here all the way from Scotland,' Drew said.

The others were all getting up to leave now, and asking about nightclubs.

'Not for me, alas,' Drew said. 'Too old and staid. I'm heading off in my Head of Department's taxi for an early night.'

'I've a feeling it will stand to you,' Brenda Brennan said.

Drew saw her talking to Mr Ball, but he knew that she wasn't telling tales, that he had almost stolen a wallet.

He only discovered next day what she *had* been saying.

That he was a remarkable young man, who had not only rescued a wallet for another customer and handed it in, but who had been caring enough to be concerned over the woman's distress.

Mr Ball felt the very same about Drew. A boy who might have been overlooked before.

But once he had discovered Drew's interest in the gym and his obvious sense of disappointment that he couldn't afford to join one, Mr Ball, too, had a change of heart. He would recommend the boy's promotion the moment they got back to Scotland.

Brown Paper Cover

Mon often wished that she was back in Sydney, Australia. On a day like today, she could go out to the beach and lie there with her friends. In Ireland it was what they thought of as summer, but truly it was not a day for the sand. She would be blown to death by the wind, heartbroken by the small tidal ripple instead of the rollers she knew and loved back home, frozen by the ice-cold water if she ever dared get into it.

Still, she hadn't come to Ireland looking for a life of surf. She had come as part of a great world tour. Oddly, there had not been all that much of a tour. It was meant to start with a week in Rome, and then a week in Dublin and six weeks hitchhiking around the rest of Ireland, then a dozen other lands before going back to the rest of her life. But something strange had happened – after the week in Rome she had arrived in Dublin totally broke.

It wasn't exactly that her money had been stolen or lost or anything. It was just that she had managed to spend in one week almost all her two years' savings on a man called Antonio. It was hard to realise quite how, but this had somehow happened.

And so, on her first day in Ireland, she needed a job.

There was an advertisement in the newspaper that she read on her way in from Dublin airport and she had phoned for an interview, got the job in Quentins. Somehow the time had passed.

'You've fallen in love, that's why you're still there,' her mother accused her by e-mail. But it wasn't true.

'There must be a crazy scene with those Irishmen,' her friends wrote. But that wasn't true either.

What had happened was that Mon, or Monica Green (as she was never called), had settled in. She had worked in eleven different jobs since she left college, but for some reason she could never understand, Quentins was the first place she really called home. Patrick Brennan, the chef who taught her how to cook when things weren't too busy, his younger brother, called Blouse for some reason, who was a little less than intelligent but certainly not a fool. Patrick's cool, unflustered wife Brenda, who seemed to know everyone in Dublin. She felt as if she was some kind of a younger sister, part of the family. Mon was part of this team and she liked it. No need to move on. For the moment.

'We'll have to find you a fellow,' Brenda Brennan said unexpectedly to Mon one morning.

'Why?' Mon was genuinely surprised.

It wasn't the way Brenda usually talked. She must have a reason for saying it. And indeed she had.

'You're very good, the customers like you, Mon, you'll go on somewhere else unless you get caught up in some complicated messy romance like they all do.'

Brenda smiled as she spoke, as if she alone knew the ways of the mad world they lived in.

'Any advice and help always welcome,' Mon said.

'Someone once said to me that I should keep my heart open as well as my eyes. It worked.'

Mon gasped – immaculate, ice maiden Brenda telling her this. Maybe she was right. But after that amazingly foolish and romantic adventure with Antonio in Rome, Mon was being cautious. Perhaps she had swung too much to the other side. Maybe she should keep her heart more open. Or a fraction more open anyway.

Mon went through the restaurant before lunch as she did every day, checking that everything was in place on every single table. Mr Harris from the bank next door came in, to eat his lunch alone as he did three days a week. Dull man with nothing to say. His head always in a book, usually with a brown paper cover. Once Mon had laughingly asked him if it was pornography and his eyes had been cold. She made no more jokes. Her cheerful Aussie humour had been very unsuccessful.

'Miss Green,' he nodded at her.

'Mr Harris,' Mon nodded back.

But Brenda had insisted on unfailing politeness and charm, even to those who did not return it. So Mon nailed on her smile as she handed him the menu.

'Chef has done a really beautiful monkfish today, Mr Harris. I think you'd like it.'

It was hard to know what the man would or would not like. He seemed to eat without noticing. None of them liked serving him.

About thirty-five, fortyish. Must have some big job in the bank, since he could afford to eat in Quentins so often. Never a guest or companion, never a newspaper or magazine, never a smile to left or right of him. Just studying books covered in brown paper.

Mr Harris said he would try the monkfish and as Mon leaned over to pour him a glass of water, she accidentally knocked against his book, which fell to the ground and the cover came off.

It wasn't pornography, but it was something equally surprising. Pop psychology. A book offering twenty ways to a woman's heart. A Never Known to Fail guide to making any woman love you.

Mr Harris and Mon Green looked aghast at each other and the book revealed in all its humiliating pathos.

Someone had to say something.

'Does it work, do you think?' Mon asked as she handed it back to him.

Mr Harris had a face like thunder. 'Why do you ask?' he wondered.

'Well, over a year back, when I was in Rome, I met this guy, Antonio, and well, I'd have read anything to get him, and they have that kind of guide for women too, to get to fellows' hearts, and you see, I couldn't find the bookstores that sold English books and then it was too late ...'

She knew that she was burbling on and on, but she couldn't stop.

'Too late?' Mr Harris looked interested. 'How did you know it was too late?'

'Well, Antonio had gone, and all my money. You see, I was going to invest in a sandwich bar with him ...'

'He took your money?' Mr Harris was horrified.

'Yes, well, that wasn't the worst bit ... actually none of it was too bad, but I'd sure like to have known the Way to his Heart,' Mon admitted.

Mr Harris was looking at Mon as if he had never seen her before. 'You mean, women actually read these books too?'

'You bet they do. Maybe the person you fancy is reading one wherever she's having lunch today.'

'I don't think so.' Mr Harris shook his head sadly.

'Mr Harris, would you like to have a drink with me about six o'clock this evening and we could sort of pool what we think we know about the opposite sex?' Mon heard herself say.

Brenda Brennan was, of course, passing the table at that moment. She slowed down slightly so that she could hear Mr Harris saying that nothing would give him more pleasure, and where would Miss Green suggest?

And for weeks they went out and sought manuals on how to be appealing to the opposite sex, which mainly involved being thoughtful and considerate and tactile.

Everyone knew that they fancied each other long before Mr Harris and Miss Green did. Their faces lit up when they saw each other. The six o'clock drinks turned into dinners, and theatre visits. And when the annual Bank Dinner Dance came round, Mon was surprised that everyone in the restaurant knew that she was going to go as his guest.

They thought for a considerable time that they were only exchanging helpful books with brown paper covers. But it turned out, of course, that they didn't need these books at all. Mr Harris and Miss Green had well found the way to each other's hearts long before either of them realised it.

The Special Sale

The January Sales started earlier every year. Most of the big stores opened the very day after Christmas. A lot of people protested and said it was ruining family life. But secretly they were often relieved. Family life could often be overrated. Patrick Brennan said they should cash in on it, serve a comforting lunch to take the weight off the weary shoppers' feet.

'And what about the weary staff's feet?' Brenda asked. But she knew that he was right. People would love it. It would take the effort out of shopping if people knew that they could hand their parcels in to Quentins' big roomy cloakroom and sit down to a lunch where cold turkey would make no appearance.

'We won't force anyone to work unless they want to. We wouldn't need the full team.'

Patrick's brother Blouse and his wife Mary would help. There was no way they could open their organic vegetable shop that day. On the day after Christmas people wanted to buy digital cameras, copper saucepans or designer shoes. They did not want Blouse and Mary Brennan's parsnips, guaranteed free from pesticides.

They put a discreet little notice on each table in the restaurant advertising a Special Sale Lunch with a limited but interesting menu on 26 December. Early booking was essential. The menu was not, strictly speaking, limited, since they planned to serve Patrick's legendary steak and kidney pies, rack of lamb and a fiery Bouillabaisse.

Yvonne booked a table for four as soon as she heard about it. It was the ideal choice for her boss Frank. He could take his three children to lunch there as a treat, something totally different on this, the first Christmas that he would spend away from his home. Frank's difficult wife, Anna, who had laid down so many ground rules and made things so awkward, would not object to this. It was quite extraordinary, Yvonne thought, that Anna, who had left Frank for another man, was still calling the shots. She still lived in the family home, and she had the children for Christmas. Frank was altogether too easy-going. He said that there was no point in upsetting little Daisy, Rose and Ivy still further. The whole thing wasn't their fault. He seemed to imply that it was nobody's fault. Anna had suddenly fallen in love with this other man, Harry, and there was nothing anyone could do about it. Everyone at the office was furious with him. Some even went so far as to say that if he were as passive as this then perhaps Anna had a case for leaving him.

But Yvonne knew better. Frank was a loving husband and father who put in long hours in computer sales so that his family could have a holiday abroad, a new carpet, add decking in the garden. Yvonne knew how he worried about these expenses. She saw him sigh and frown when he thought that no one was looking.

Yvonne was always looking at Frank, but he never saw. Why should he see her? The small, dumpy assistant in the sales department. Yvonne lived with her handicapped mother. Yvonne, who had no style or love of her own. A million miles from the tall, blonde Anna, who only had to smile and everyone did what she said.

She told her mother about it.

'And will you go too?' her mother asked eagerly.

Sometimes Yvonne despaired. She would love to have had a great lunch on the day after Christmas in a smart, buzzy restaurant with Frank and his three children. Love it more than anything, but it would have been entirely inappropriate and intrusive. The only part she could play was to call his attention to the lunch and make the reservation for him.

'Oh, no, Mother,' Yvonne said. 'That wouldn't do at all.'

'You must go out yourself over Christmas, Yvonne,' she said. 'I'm fine here on my own with my thoughts and my television.'

'I know, Mother, but there's really not all that many places I want to go.' Yvonne looked into the flames and thought about being thirty-six, the same age as Anna. Even Mother, who was in a wheelchair, had once had a life and a love and a child. Wasn't it odd the way the world turned out for people? Frank reported that Anna had been highly approving of the lunch-in-Quentins idea. She had even praised him for thinking of it.

'I'm afraid I didn't say it was your idea,' he apologised. She wanted to lean over and stroke the side of his face. But she restrained herself. He would have been horrified and embarrassed and eventually the nice, easy friendship they had would have disappeared.

Christmas Day was cold and windy in the city centre. Brenda Brennan cooked a turkey for Patrick, Blouse and Mary. And the new baby Brendan. Mon and her fiancé were with them.

Yan the Breton waiter telephoned to send them greetings and to say that his father was now fully recovered and home from hospital. Mon's family called from Australia to say they had been sunburned at the beach and to know if Mon's Mr Harris was still on for the wedding. Or had he seen sense?

Mr Harris, flushed with port, told them all that he just adored Mon and he didn't care who knew it. They ate in the kitchen of Quentins and played Country and Western music all day long.

'I hope we'll all think it's worth opening tomorrow,' Patrick said.

They reassured him. 'Isn't the place going to be full, and we don't get that every Tuesday,' Brenda said, ever practical. Blouse said he loved the thought of being a waiter for the day, all dressed up and people thinking he was the real thing.

'You *are* the real thing,' they all said to Blouse at the same time. They talked about the bookings they had taken. Blouse had taken one from a woman in a wheelchair who had never been there before. She had been very anxious for a table where she and her companion could be seen by everyone. Brenda had booked a table for a young man who was going to propose to his girlfriend and wondered could they have champagne on ice ready. And if it were not needed he would let them know. They all agreed that there was no other job quite as interesting as watching the human race at feeding time.

Christmas Day was cold and windy outside the big house where Anna and Frank's three little girls opened their presents. Harry stood watching.

'It's a bit rough on Frank that he's not here to see it,' he murmured to Anna.

Her blue eyes were sad. 'We have to start as we mean to go on,' she said, 'and he does get them all day tomorrow.'

Frank didn't notice the weather as he sat in his sister's home playing with her children instead of with his own. Trying all the while to avoid everyone's pity for him and their rage at Anna.

Yvonne and her mother sat together as they had for many a year. Yvonne's mother was resplendent in the fine wool stole with a soft lilac colour which had been Yvonne's gift. Yvonne was sitting speechless, looking at the invitation for two to lunch at Quentins the following day, which had been her mother's gift to her. There was no way she could return or refuse to accept a present like this. She would have to go through with it.

Frank called for the girls at ten-thirty. Anna looked beautiful as she always did. Harry looked a bit embarrassed, not sure how to play it. The girls were excited, they dragged him over to the Christmas tree to see what Santa Claus had brought. All of the gifts were exactly what they had been hoping for. And Mummy had given them each a new velvet dress.

'What time would you like me to deliver everyone home?' he asked mildly.

Anna gave a tinkling laugh. 'Frank, honestly, you don't have to ask, you are their father. We aren't the kind of people who have court rulings. Keep them all day until they're tired. Right, girls?'

Right, they said, pleased that there was no row. Daisy was nearly nine and almost grown up, so when the others weren't listening she whispered some of her theories about Santa Claus to her father. Frank listened thoughtfully and said it was hard to know all right and we should all keep an open mind on things.

'Do you mind about Harry being here, Dad?' she said.

'No, darling, not if it makes your mother happy.' He tried to read her face, but wasn't sure if he had given the right answer or not.

The shops were crowded. It was hard for six-, seven- and eight-year-olds to make decisions. The little legs were tired when they got to Quentins, the first guests.

'You're welcome,' the waiter said. 'Can I take your parcels for you, ladies?' Daisy, Rose and Ivy giggled at being called ladies.

'How will you know which are ours?' Ivy asked.

'You'll give me your names and I'll write them down,' he said.

'What's your name?' Daisy asked.

'Blouse Brennan,' the man said.

'Why?' Ivy asked.

'When I was a young fellow I called my shirt my blouse. I forgot all about it, but no one else did.'

'Well, a shirt *is* a sort of blouse,' said Daisy.

'That's what I always thought,' Blouse said, pleased.

Frank looked at his eldest daughter with pride. The restaurant filled up, mainly families, the odd twosome. Even though he felt a deep sense of loneliness not to be part of a proper family, Frank thought from time to time that he got envious glances with his three beautiful daughters. Alert and smiling and interested in everyone.

'Look at that couple kissing,' Rose said as a bottle of champagne was opened at a nearby table.

'Does that woman have any legs?' Daisy said in her bell-like voice.

The woman in the wheelchair turned round with a smile. 'I do, dear, but they're not any use to me, so the waiter wheeled me in up the ramp. He was very helpful.'

'I saw you come in. That was Blouse that wheeled you in.'

'Blouse, is it? A very nice young man,' the old lady nodded.

Finally her companion looked up from staring at the floor. It was Yvonne from work.

Frank was amazed and pleased. 'So you decided to come yourself, too,' he said happily. 'Isn't it great! I must introduce you to my daughters.' He brought them over to Yvonne's table where they all stood in everyone's way until Blouse Brennan suggested that he merge the two parties to save on space.

Yvonne's face was scarlet. 'I can't tell you how sorry I am, Frank. This was all my mother's idea,' she hissed at him.

'But I can't tell you how delighted I am ...' he began.

They could hear the children talking to Yvonne's mother, asking her how her legs had decayed, and did she bother wearing stockings, and what would happen if the restaurant went on fire? 'Blouse would push me down the ramp,' Yvonne's mother said.

'Indeed I would, Madam,' he said as he tied Ivy's table napkin around her neck, the way the French do.

'What lovely dresses you have.' The old woman felt the coloured velvet frocks.

'They're from our mother. She doesn't live with Dad any more, you see, so that's why she's not here.' Daisy seemed to have a mission to explain today.

'So you must remember it all to tell her. She'll want to know what you did because she loves you so much, like your father does. He must love you a lot to think of taking you to a very high-class restaurant like this.'

'Is it high class?' Rose was interested.

'The highest there is.' Yvonne's mother was firm on this.

'It's a pity they're not both here together,' Daisy sighed.

'Oh, I don't know . . . you can have better times separately. Like Yvonne's father and I. We loved her to bits, but we changed in loving each other, and she was always happy with both of us, weren't you, Yvonne?'

'Yes, I was, indeed,' Yvonne said, astounded.

'So her dad loved someone else eventually, and I loved someone else, but it didn't take away one bit from loving Yvonne. *Isn't that right?*' she barked at her daughter.

'Oh, absolutely right, Mother. Like as if your heart got bigger or something and there was more love in it,' Yvonne said, wild-eyed at the whole thing.

Frank patted her knee and stroked her hand. 'Yvonne, I wish you knew how much this means . . .' he began.

But Yvonne was listening to what her mother might be up to now. It was reasonably harmless. She was asking her new best friend Blouse Brennan for some bread that they could throw to the ducks in St Stephen's Green.

'Can we come too?' Rose asked.

'Please,' Frank begged. '*Please.*' And it was arranged. There would be time later, much later, when she would tell him that her mother and father had never separated, and he had died fifteen years ago and her mother had never looked at another man. This was not the time to do it. The Special Sale Lunch was nearly over, the rain had stopped and it was time to go and feed the ducks.

PART III

Chapter Nine

Ella looked up when the stories were told. As far as she could see, they had gone well. At least she had managed to hold their interest. She must leave them now and give them a chance to talk about it all. She moved swiftly. No, no, she would get herself a taxi, she pleaded. It was part of the excitement of being in New York. Please let them not see her out, she would much prefer them to stay and discuss what she had told them.

And then she escaped. Down in the lift, out of the quiet building into the amazingly noisy traffic. And then she got to her little hotel, which was beginning to seem like home, and up to her room.

Now she could do what she had been putting off until she got her work settled. She sat down and opened up Don Richardson's computer.

It got dark in New York as she trawled through the computer. Bank account numbers in the Isle of Man, in the Cayman Islands, in Switzerland. None of it made any sense, since the names were in some kind of code.

She recognised property agreements there, but none in Don's name or in his father-in-law's. Then she saw the file with her own name and her heart leaped. Maybe he *had* made an investment for her as he had once told her he would. Something to provide for her after his time. She gulped in case he really had done that. He must have loved her at one stage. But it didn't seem likely. It wasn't Ella Brady. This Brady family, a family of five, a man, his son, the son's wife and two children, and they were living in Playa de los Angeles. There were letters about them to banks and from banks. Whoever they were, these Bradys had plenty of money. And a lot of it deposited very recently. By far the largest sum had been the week that she had been in Spain with Don. When he had been away from the hotel. When his wife Margery Rice, mother of his two children, was there. Suddenly she realised that not only had he taken everything else she had but he had also taken her name.

There were so many things she could do. She could find the number of the Fraud Squad in Dublin and tell them the machine was ready for collection. She could contact an Irish television station. She could telephone Don now; the Brady family had a phone number and were listed in his machine. She could tell him that if he restored all that her father had lost, she would hand him back the computer, no questions asked. She could contact one of the various insurance companies involved and offer to give it to them. She realised that this was a decision she had to make entirely on her own. Everyone's judgement would be partisan. They would want to do what they thought was best for her or for them or for somebody. Why did she not give it straight to the police? That was what a normal citizen would do.

She opened the mini bar in her room and took out a miniature Jack Daniel's and drank it from a tooth mug. It made nothing clearer. It did nothing to sharpen the blurred edges. If you had loved someone, slept with him, shared everything with him for month after month, you didn't hand over the files without a backward glance. There was some kind of mad nobility about it ... Even if *he* behaved like a bastard, she was not going to. This was just one more test of her loyalty.

There was a way she wanted to show him that not everyone sold out their friends and lovers. She didn't want to talk to Deirdre about it, or Nick or Sandy or anyone. She had to make up her own mind what to do. In some crazy way she wanted to talk to Don. Well, that was an option too. Mad as it sounded. There were so many things she wanted answers to. Like had he always known he was going to call himself Brady or was it because of her? Like how could he have planned everything so meticulously and then left the machine in her flat? Did he intend to or was it an oversight?

And if he had always loved Margery, why had they lived such totally separate lives? And did he have any guilt, or could he live with it all, saying it was just showbiz? In some insane way, she could imagine the conversation. But she would not have it from here. She had been alarmed to know that he was now looking for the machine and sending messengers around the place trying to track her down. It had been a bit frightening.

But she hadn't felt frightened before. In fact, having the laptop made her feel in some odd way more secure. And as long as she had this computer in her possession, he might get in touch. She realised now that this was why she had never let it go. It was her last link with him. For four months it had been a sort of comfort to her to know that it was there physically. Some solid reminder of all they had.

But things were suddenly very different now. She could no longer tell herself that Don knew nothing of all that had been going on. That he had been swept along somehow in his father-in-law's plans. That there was going to be a perfectly innocent explanation.

Having opened the lid of the laptop, she could no longer tell herself this. It was beginning to dawn on her that Don Richardson was deeply involved. For the very first time she realised that she might indeed be in real danger and she had no idea what to do. She was so tired she couldn't think.

She would do nothing tonight. There was no need. After all, the briefcase containing the computer had been in her possession for over four months. If she had been going to turn him in, he could well assume that she would have done it by now. He must think that she had never got into it and had decided not to hand it over to those who would be able to learn what it contained. He should be feeling safe and secure now, so why on earth was he suddenly getting jittery and sending her messages about it? Maybe he really wanted to see her.

A man went up the lane behind Tara Road and put a letter into what they called the Annexe of what used to be the Bradys' house. It was not in an envelope, just folded in half. It had been sent by e-mail and printed out, but with no name or identifying marks at the top.

Barbara and Tim Brady didn't hear it coming through the letterbox, because they were asleep. They didn't see it until the next morning at eight o'clock, when Barbara was going out to work. And she did not read it then because the hall was dark and she was running for the bus. She let herself out by the wooden door into the lane behind the house. The garden didn't belong to them any more. It never would again.

In New York, Ella was in bed. Not asleep but resting. No pressure, no hurry, she told herself over and over.

She had to be at Derry and Kimberly's office tomorrow at nine. She must sleep well.

There was a system on the hotel telephone where you could switch it to automatic voice-mail. She switched it over. That meant if someone called in the night it wouldn't wake you. Not that she was expecting a call, but she had to be alert tomorrow, no matter what happened. No pressure, no hurry. He doesn't know you've opened it.

She had a long, warm bath, went to bed, and fell asleep with a television chat show blaring away.

So she missed the series of phone calls that began at about ten minutes after 3 a.m. New York time, just after everyone in Ireland had come to grips with the 8 a.m. news there. She didn't look at the little winking light until she was dressed and ready to leave the room. Hoping it wasn't a message from either Derry or Kimberly about the meeting, Ella dialled the number to retrieve the messages.

She sat in horror on the edge of her bed as she heard Nick and Deirdre and her father tell her what had happened.

These were the only households who knew where she was staying. Nothing they said made any sense. It was like words that were all jumbled, strung together, not proper sentences.

Only one more person knew her address and that was her new friend Harriet, the dealer who had sold her the dog collar. She had called also. Because Harriet's voice was less shocked, less horrified and sympathetic than the others, it was the only message that Ella understood.

'Listen, Ella. In case nobody's told you, he's killed himself out in Spain. He was scum. He wouldn't even stay and face what a mess he'd got everyone into. Probably half the country's already told you, but just in case I wanted you to be warned, just in case. You're worth twenty of him, so don't weep over him, Ella. He's not worth it.'

When she got her breath back, she played the first three messages again. Now she understood what they were saying. It had to be true. They couldn't all have imagined it. Who should she phone first? Ella didn't want to talk to any of them.

She looked across at the computer. It really didn't matter any more. He had taken a boat out to jagged rocks and ended his life. She wondered had he choked or suffocated to death, or had his body been dashed against rocks? Had he any last-minute regrets and tried to survive? Don dead. Because of other people's money? Because of failure? Because he couldn't get his hands on that briefcase. *Why* hadn't she given it back to him? She hadn't even known what to do with it herself. If she had called him and said he could have it, then he would still be alive. She would call up the Irish newspapers on the Internet and see what they said. Before she talked to anyone, she needed to know more.

Don Richardson's handsome face looked out of every newspaper in Ireland and even some in England. He was described as a disgraced financier. The newspapers congratulated themselves for having correctly speculated that he had been in hiding in Spain. It was reported that his small boat had foundered on rocks at a particularly dangerous Spanish headland. A place where nobody took any kind of craft. Certainly, an experienced boatman like Don Richardson would have been aware of its perils. His body had not been found. The tides in this area could have carried it far out to the Atlantic.

He had parked his car on a nearby pier and left several envelopes on the front seat. The contents had not been made public, but it was understood that the letters were in the nature of an apology and an attempted explanation. Sympathy and concern had already been expressed by many of the business community in Ireland. Shock and disbelief had been registered by those of his family and former friends when they had been contacted. Of his immediate family there was no information. Some papers thought that they were co-operating with the authorities. Others said there had been no trace of them. One newspaper, in an article called 'Darling Margery', claimed that one of his letters had been to his wife, urging her to bring up the children in dignity. But since that newspaper was also one which in the past believed it had interviewed extraterrestrials and women who had been born with four legs, it was not given a lot of credence.

She telephoned her father first, but his phone was engaged. So she called Deirdre on her mobile.

'I know there are ways it's sad for you,' Dee said, 'as well as being a terrible shock, but honestly there are ways it's for the best.'

'That someone should kill himself, that's somehow the best?'

'I'm thinking of you, Ella. That's all I'm doing. You can get on with your life now.'

'I'm getting on with my life fine. I've been doing that since he walked out on me months ago. It's he who's not getting on with his life. Can't breathe or talk or know what day it is today.'

'I'm not making light of it. I thought in a way it kind of ended all the stress . . . somehow.' Deirdre was backtracking now. She had most definitely said the wrong thing.

'What stress did I have that has ended? I still know he never loved me. I still have to work to pay off the debts he left my family with. What's better about his being at the bottom of the ocean?'

'I'm so sorry, Ella, so very sorry,' Deirdre said.

'I know you are, Dee. Just don't go round thinking it's all for the best, will you?'

Deirdre made a quick call to Nick. 'She's probably trying to get through to you now. Whatever you do, walk on eggshells. She doesn't see it all as the great relief that we do. I opened my big mouth and felt a right eejit.'

'Thanks, Dee. I'll warn Sandy.'

'Heavy on the sympathy, that's where I fell down,' Deirdre said ruefully.

'You're a good friend. She'll know that.'

'I hope.'

'Hi, Nick.'

'Ella, poor, poor Ella.'

'Why am I poor Ella, Nick? He never loved me. He stole everyone's money. I was just saying to Dee, nothing's changed. That's all the same as it was. He's dead, that's all. I just wanted to talk to you about this meeting today.'

'You're going to it?' He was astounded.

'Well, of course I am, isn't that what I'm here for?'

'But maybe not today, Ella. I could call them and explain.'

'This is my job, my pitch. Don't dare interfere. The thing I wanted to talk to you about was these clearances they talk about so much here. Our usual form which people sign agreeing to let us use the interview . . . that's enough, isn't it?'

'Those forms are fine. You can reassure them I checked all that out,' said Nick, who decided that women were so unpredictable there was no point in trying to understand them any more.

'Dad?'

'Oh, Ella, thank God you rang.'

'You're not to get upset, Dad. He was a grown man. He knew what he was doing, he must have.'

'No, it's not that.'

'And people say you should remember the good, there was some good, Dad. I had a bit of a time trying to drag it up but I have, so ...'

'Ella, stop. Let me speak.' His voice was like a cry.

She paused.

'He sent you a letter.'

'What?'

'A letter was delivered here last night by hand.'

'No, Dad, it can't be from him ... he was drowned out in Spain. How could he have ...'

'It was an e-mail, put through the door by someone when we were asleep.'

'But how do you know it's from him?'

'It was open, not in an envelope.'

'It's not from Don. Dad, there's a mistake.'

'I don't know what to do, Ella. I've told your mother. She didn't read it on her way out ... she said I could take it to her office and she would fax it to you.'

'Is it long, Dad?'

'No, it's quite short.'

'So could you read it to me?'

'But perhaps you wouldn't want me to ...'

'You've read it already, Dad, and you've read it to Mother. Just once more. Please.'

She could hear him putting on his glasses and rustling the paper. It probably took a couple of seconds. It seemed like infinity.

'"Dearest Angel,"' he read. '"By the time you get this it will all be over. Maybe you won't care at all. You refused to get in touch with me through the many, many messages that I sent you, so perhaps you never cared. But I can't believe that. I can't believe those hours and hours of love meant nothing to you. So I want to say a special goodbye and a great thank you for making my life so happy, and to tell you three things.

'"There was room in my heart for you all, you and my family. I couldn't leave them when the crisis hit. I was always trying to come back for you, too, but you wouldn't listen. The briefcase doesn't matter now. I won't be there to face what it reveals. If you have the generosity to throw it away on the grounds that I trusted it to you and that you would like to show me some trust too, then that would be great. But it's up to you. And lastly, I really liked your father and I know he lost clients' money because of my advice. I arranged some bank drafts, things that can be easily cashed. It's to say sorry to him and to you. This is the number of the deposit box. I wish I could give everything back to everybody. But then I wish a lot of things, mainly that I had years ahead with you, Angel Ella. You made me feel young and happy, you made my heart sing. Please know I loved you. Don."' Her father's voice trembled as he came to the end. There was a silence.

'Thank you, Dad.'

'I wish you weren't so many miles away, Ella. We wish you were at home.'

'I'm better off working hard, Dad. Believe me, I'm fine, and tell Mother, won't you?'

'He did love you, Ella.'

'Of course he did, Dad.'

She sat for a while and looked at her reflection in the mirror. None of this was happening. She would wake up soon back at a time before she had even met Don Richardson. When conversations like she was having this morning were totally impossible. But meantime she had to get on with what the rest of the day was going to throw at her.

She went down to the lobby and asked for a taxi to Derry and Kimberly's office. She was shown into their boardroom, where they sat close together at the far end of a table. They jumped up when she arrived.

'Ella!' Kimberly said as if surprised.

'You're here?' Derry was definitely surprised.

'We did say nine o'clock, didn't we?' Now Ella felt suddenly anxious. Maybe the shock had wiped everything out. They reassured her, that was what they had said. There was something odd about the way they looked at her, as if they hadn't expected her to make it. Had Nick disobeyed her and told them? No, he wouldn't dare.

She sat at the table and Kimberly poured coffee for them all.

'Have you been on to Dublin ... um ... this morning?' Derry began.

'We were just wondering if you'd been able to talk to anyone back there,' Kimberly asked.

They did know something. But how?

Ella was determined not to weaken or to put her head down on the shiny table and cry her heart out to these people about her dead love. The man who had written her a letter and e-mailed it some hours before he killed himself.

'I spoke to Nick,' she said brightly. 'He said to tell you that those clearance forms are standard.' She looked from one to the other. They didn't seem to be listening to her. 'So if that's all right, then ...' She waited for them to get on with the meeting.

'You know, if you don't feel like working or concentrating today, then that's fine, there are many other days.' Derry's eyes were very kind and he actually patted her hand in a gesture you don't see outside the movies.

Kimberly was offering the same kind of sympathetic reassurance. 'No need to force yourself,' she pleaded. 'It can be done when you're feeling more up to it.'

'You know,' Ella said slowly. 'Someone told you about me and Don and what happened.'

'We always knew about you and Don from the outset,' Derry said simply. 'We just read what happened to him this morning.'

'How did you know?' She felt cold.

'Same way as you knew I liked dogs. We looked up the files.'

'That's different. You're a public person. There's no file on me,' Ella said with spirit.

'There's plenty of information. We're not going to take up with a tiny outfit like Firefly Films, make a movie about a place we never heard of called Quentins, unless we have someone on the ground to advise us.'

'And who did you ask to advise you?'

'A lawyer. Nice guy. He marked our card, everything you said all checked out. This is about four months ago, remember, so you were a bit in the news.'

'And he bothers with tittle-tattle like that!' Ella was stung.

'To be fair to him, I think he was just letting us see everything that was on the table about everything. It has never had the slightest relevance to anything, only today we wondered ...' Derry's voice trailed away.

'You know Don seems to have been thorough to the end,' Kimberly said.

Ella wondered how they could work together so amicably after a long spell of marriage. Once there must have been a time when they had both wished for years ahead together ... and, what were Don's words, when they had felt young and happy and made each other's hearts sing.

Ella tried to lift her coffee cup but her hand was shaking so she put it down again. She *must* pull herself together, banish the sound of his voice. She must. But at this point she could almost hear Don saying, 'I want to say a special goodbye, a special goodbye, special goodbye...' It was booming through her head.

She gripped the sides of the table very hard, but she felt herself falling down. Right down into a great black pit with the voice still there in her ears. When she saw shapes they were vague shapes first, then they turned into legs. They were legs of chairs, and Kimberly's amazing, shapely ankles in their high dark shoes, and also legs in brown trousers, and eventually she saw Derry King's face only inches from her own. The square, lined face that gave nothing away. Except now it was worried and full of concern.

'She's coming round, Kim,' he said with relief.

'Keep her head down. You're meant to let the blood flow to the head.' Kimberly was authoritative.

'We'll have to lift her back on to a chair then, to get her head down.'

Gently they did that, and she actually did feel something happening to her head as if everything really was sliding back into place.

'What happened?' she began, but by the time she asked the question she knew the answer. She had fainted. She struggled to sit up, but she could feel Derry's hand on her neck and she could hear his voice speaking urgently.

'You're just fine. Keep your head down. Breathe deeply, you'll be okay in ten seconds.'

Ella counted to ten and then sat up. They were both looking at her anxiously. She managed a weak grin. 'Textbook lesson on how not to present your case,' she said feebly.

'We've all the time in the world. Stop fussing,' Derry said.

'You've had a shock,' Kimberly said.

'But I was fine and suddenly everything tilted.'

'Could you be pregnant?' Kimberly asked.

Derry seemed startled by her question, but Ella wasn't at all put out by it. 'No, when you consider all the disasters that have happened ... and there have been many ... that's not one of them.'

'Maybe you had no breakfast?' Derry wondered.

'I can't really remember if I had or not, but that wouldn't be it.'

'Your colour is coming back a little,' Kimberly said. 'Have a glass of water.'

'You're both so kind.' She sipped the water.

'Would you like us to contact a doctor for you?'

'No, Derry, thank you. It was just a silly faint. Just nerves, I imagine. At all this. And how much depends on me.'

'You're not nervous, Ella. We were saying that about you just as you came in. You have no real film-making experience, yet you're very confident and calm ...' Kimberly was admiring.

'I hope I didn't pretend to have more experience than I do ...' Ella began.

'No, indeed, you've been very open and frank, but you didn't come over as nervous to us,' Derry said.

'I was fine yesterday,' she said without meaning to.

They looked at each other as if unsure what to say. 'And now?'

'And now, if you'll forgive me for collapsing on your floor ... I'll try not to do it again ... now I'll try to get back to where we were.' Ella's eyes were very bright.

'We don't have to ...'

'But we do have to, Derry, or I have to. This is my chance. There will be others who will get their time. Others who won't waste it by fainting on the carpet ... so I must tell you.'

'Slowly, Ella, catch your breath,' Kimberly laughed gently.

Ella's face was agitated. 'No, there's no time for me to go slowly. I've talked to Nick about those release and disclaimer forms you spoke of. He's on top of all that. Apparently they have the same legal standing as here. And I have my notes all here, all ready when you are.' She opened her file with shaking hands. She could see them watching as she tried to pull the right piece of paper out. It was protruding from the others but it still wouldn't come out properly. It seemed to take for ever.

Eventually Derry leaned over gently and took it out for her. He placed it on the table. 'It's all right, Ella,' he said. His voice was very gentle.

So was Kimberly's voice when she said, 'Ella, you've got it, you've convinced us.'

'What?' She was confused.

'It's all right,' Derry said. 'No more pitching, we're going to give you the grant. All we do now is talk about how we make the film.'

She looked at them wildly. In the middle of all this terrible nightmare, one thing had turned out as she had hardly dared to hope. 'Seriously?' she checked as if they might only be teasing her.

'Very seriously,' he said with a smile.

It was the smile that did it. She put her head down on the table and cried until they all thought her heart would break.

Chapter Ten

Ella could barely remember how she got back to her hotel. She knew Derry and Kimberly stood together smiling at her from the foyer as the yellow cab pulled out into the New York traffic. Somewhere she heard a bell ring. Or a clock strike. It was only ten o'clock in the morning. She got to her room and called Firefly Films.

'How did it go?' She could hear the raw anxiety in Sandy's voice.

'It's over, Sandy,' she said. 'It's finished. Would you believe it?'

There was a silence and then she heard Sandy speak to Nick. 'Okay, Nick, she did her very best but it didn't work. She says it's over. Nick, she gave it all she could.'

Kind, good Sandy, so loyal and supportive. Trying to say something to take the bleak look off the face of the man she loved.

'*No*, Sandy . . . *no* . . . We got it, they're giving it to us. We won, we won the grant.'

Ella could hear the gasp and then the phone was handed over. 'Is this possible?' Nick's voice was shaking.

'Open up the e-mail in half an hour. They're sending you a confirmation, Nick.'

'I don't believe you were able to go out and pitch today with everything . . . with all you had to cope with. You're a hero, Ella, a bloody hero. How did you do it?'

'Don't ask too much about it. Let's just thank the Lord or someone that it worked out.'

'What did you say to them, Ella? Tell us, we want to know every word, every heartbeat.'

'You don't want to know.'

'But we do. We've been sitting here rigidly for the last hour and a bit ... now she's going in. Now she's saying this, now that.'

'Yes.'

'Ella, *please*, we're only here in a panic, you're there on the spot. You've done it! Tell us!'

'I fainted on the floor first, and then they lifted me back into the chair, and then when I was starting the pitch proper they said we'd got it and I cried for what seemed like an hour but may only have been fifteen minutes ...'

'She's totally unhinged,' Nick explained to Sandy. 'Probably drunk as well. We're going to get nothing out of her until she calms down.'

'Brenda?'

'Is that you, Ella? Everything all right?'

'Yes, fine ... I just rang ...'

'I'm so sorry about Don. It must have been a terrible shock to you.'

'Yes, it was.'

'And of course people who do something as terrible as that don't really know what they're doing ...'

'No, he knew exactly what he was doing, but that's not what I'm ringing about ...'

'Are you in ... well, where you went?'

'Yes, I'm in New York. It doesn't matter anyone knowing now. He can't send anyone after me. Actually of course he never would have.'

'No, of course not,' Brenda murmured reassuringly.

'It's just that we've got the funding. We can go ahead with the project now,' she said proudly.

Brenda seemed astounded that she could speak of such things. 'Well, now. That's wonderful. Well done. And thank God you got it over before you had all this other thing to upset you.'

'Well, in fact, I didn't. I did it this morning, just after I heard about Don. I told you I'd call the moment I knew.'

'You are remarkable, Ella. That's all I can say.'

'No, I'm only hanging in by a thread, if you must know.'

'None of us knows what's in people's minds.'

'No, I'm okay, because I do know what was in his mind. He loved me. He really did. You know, he wrote me a letter just before he died. Imagine, Brenda!'

'That's ... that's ... extraordinary,' Brenda stammered.

'It's amazing,' Ella said and hung up.

'I think she's having a nervous breakdown,' Brenda said in a low voice.

'Well, she's certainly right about the documentary,' Patrick replied. 'Sandy was in half an hour ago to get me to sign some forms. It's all going ahead.'

'But she couldn't suddenly think that guy could have loved her,' Brenda said. 'She spent over four months getting over him. She can't possibly believe he had a change of heart two minutes before he killed himself. It seems too simple, too easy. And not a word about what happened to Margery and the children, not to mention Ricky Rice.'

'I sound more like my old father every day, but it's not over by a long chalk,' Patrick said.

'Deirdre, she got us the funding,' Nick said. 'She'd have called you from New York but it's too expensive.'

'Proper order,' said Deirdre. 'If you're going to be tycoons, first step: you must become as tight as ticks with money.'

'Very funny. Anyway, she may be home earlier than we thought. There's no need for her to be in hiding any more if the guy is dead.'

'*If* he's dead,' Deirdre said.

Tim and Barbara Brady got a three-minute call from Ella. 'I can't speak long, but the *great* news is that the movie is up and running.'

'Well done, Ella,' her mother cried.

Ella's father sat there in his chair. It had not been a good day. The death of Don Richardson had drawn a final line under the hopes that some of his clients might have nourished about ever seeing any of their money again. Several had been in touch with him. They had not been easy conversations. He watched his wife's pleasure as she told him with delight how Ella had managed to make the King Foundation underwrite the project. And now that Don was no longer a threat, she was going to come straight home. Rather than hiding out in New York.

'Why aren't you cheerful, Tim? It's wonderful news,' Barbara complained.

'It's great news,' he said, forcing a smile on his face. Quite a few of the people he had talked to today had expressed the view that Don Richardson might have faked his suicide. By the following morning, the newspapers had begun to express the same doubts. They reprinted stories of those who had folded their clothes, left farewell notes on beaches and had turned up in different countries with different passports years later. But then, the Richardson family was already in a different country at the time of the drowning. There were a lot of things that didn't quite fit together, causing a great deal of vague and uninformed speculation in the various feature articles of the newspapers.

What had happened to his family? The wife, sons and father-in-law whom he was meant to adore? They had not come out of hiding to mourn his death. Why had Don Richardson left his wallet and documents to be readily found in a car that he had only rented that morning? What had happened to the missing money? He must have used an alias for the past four months. Were his family still living in this disguise? And if the family still had the embezzled funds, then what did Don Richardson's suicide actually achieve? It hadn't restored any livelihood to those who had lost it.

The press carried on for a few more days. The mystery of the months spent in Spain. The possible lifestyle the Richardsons might have lived on what was once called the Costa del Crime. The whereabouts of the grieving family. As always, Spanish authorities said they were co-operating closely with the Irish law forces to track them down. Efforts to find the family had been intensified among British and Irish expatriates in the area of the drowning tragedy. They had led to nothing. Nobody had ever heard of this family. There had been no trace of any of them since that morning four months ago when they had arrived in Spain using their own passports, and simply never been seen again.

And gradually, as other things happened, the story and speculation about Don Richardson disappeared from the papers. And public opinion began to revert to the thinking that he really had drowned. Brenda noticed from hearing people talk in the restaurant that the pendulum had swung back to where it was before. There had been no sightings of Don back in Dublin. And surely, if he had staged his own suicide, it would have been to get away from the mindless anonymity of being in a Spanish resort, back to where he had been king of everything. To Dublin, where he was a somebody. Don the great risk-taker would have known enough people who would have hidden him. And yet there had not been a whisper.

Ella was in control again. She was alert and interested when Derry had introduced her to some of his financial people, the section where Firefly Films would direct their final budgets. She concentrated hard so that she would be able to put a face to each name.

Kimberly suggested she see some films already made on similar themes, and got her in touch with a viewing theatre. It was all very simple, if you had an introduction through the Kings. Ella realised more each day how important they must be and was glad she had not really understood this at the outset.

Most evenings she ate in a restaurant with Derry. He chose all kinds of different places for her, and seemed pleased with her company. He said he hated to eat alone in restaurants and usually wound up with take-out and ate at home, so she was saving him from indigestion. They talked easily. She never asked him why a man so wealthy, so single and obviously very eligible, managed to escape the New York prowling ladies. She told him tales about her childhood, and though she mentioned that they lived in what had been a garden shed next to their old house, she never said why.

Derry told her tales of holidays in Alberta when he was a child; the three children went to their Canadian grandparents for the whole summer. Five years they had done that, it had always been magical. He never said why his mother had not gone with them, and she never asked.

She told him about Deirdre who had been her friend since she was ten and how Nick and Sandy were going to get married. She said she missed teaching, but that she had needed to leave herself free to make money this summer.

He seemed to think that this was a perfectly normal thing to do. He himself had left school at fifteen and had worked in a variety of jobs. When he was twenty, he realised he'd need qualifications if he were to try to give his brothers any kind of start in life. So he got a job as a cleaner/janitor in a college and arranged his hours so that he could do business studies as well. It hadn't been easy, of course, mopping the floors and clearing the litter bins when other kids were going out to ball games or bowling alleys. But then nobody had it easy all the time, and he got a few good night-watchman stints too, which of course made it very easy for him to study. So he had done well in his examinations and won scholarships. And he had got his brothers into college as well.

So Ella didn't ask questions. She told how she would have loved brothers and sisters, but Deirdre had said that they were vastly overrated and that rabbits were a much better idea.

He had laughed. 'She sounds like a character, this Deirdre.'

'Oh, you'll meet her in Dublin.'

'I'm not going to Dublin, Ella,' he said.

'Sorry, I forgot.'

Ella had decided not to push it. And maybe it would be much better if he didn't come. They would be freer to get on with things.

He very rarely talked about his work as the head of a hugely successful office supplies company, one of the biggest in the United States. He said it was a team effort, that he had been lucky to identify a need at the right time, something that wouldn't change every few hours as computer software seemed to do. Kimberly had been brilliant on the marketing side, and almost everyone had been there from Day One, so in many ways it ran itself without his having to be there every day. That's what gave him so much time to deal with the Foundation, which was what he really enjoyed.

Yes, of course he had to be ruthless sometimes at work, make decisions that he hated in his heart. When he had to close down a division of his company he made sure the employees were retrained or given early retirement. He was indeed easy company. Kimberly must have met someone very special in Larry if she were able to walk out on Derry King.

Every night when she came back from her dinner with Derry King, Ella sat down at the computer and looked up the Irish papers of the day. She read with horror how there had been a thought that Don was not really dead. If only this were true. If only it were possible. She would go to any part of the earth to tell him she loved him. That she understood why he had to do what he had done. But she knew that he was dead. He had written to her to say goodbye.

Then she would read about Margery and the children. And where they could be in hiding. Only Ella knew where they were. In Playa de los Angeles, using her name. Calling themselves Brady.

It was strange to think that she could lift a telephone and give their address to the authorities. But she would never do that. Don deserved better than a girlfriend who would blow everything. He had looked after those who needed to be looked after. His children and their mother and their grandfather.

And Ella. He had sent her those bank drafts, which she could cash and get her father out of trouble. Oh, if only he were alive, even for an afternoon, she would tell him how glad she was that he had loved her after all.

The emptiness of the last four months had been filled by something strange like a curious sense of peace.

And eventually the formalities were all done. Ella had booked the Thursday night plane home. 'I'm going to miss our suppers,' Derry said.

'Me, too, but you won't come to Ireland and continue them, so what can we do?' she said.

'So if tonight's going to be the last night, then let's make it in my place,' he said.

'That would be great.' Ella was pleased. She wanted to see his duplex apartment that she had read about long before she met him. Full of paintings by young people. Many of them now valuable since the artists had been on the way up. Some of them by people who had never made it. But Derry King bought what he liked, not what he thought would appreciate in value.

Kimberly too seemed sorry she was leaving and asked her for a last lunch.

'You even get to meet Larry,' Kimberly promised. 'And that's not given to every looker that comes across my path.'

'Oh, I'm not a looker,' Ella laughed. She meant it, too. Since she had come to New York she realised how unglamorous she looked, so shabby and ungroomed.

'Oh, you are a looker, Ella Brady,' said Kimberly, and she meant it, too. So much so that Larry was only going to join them for a cocktail.

He was handsome with longish dark hair and a designer suit, sunglasses which he took off at once, very assured and confident. Slightly showy, with large gestures, holding Kimberly away from him so that he and everyone could admire her grey silk outfit. Then a long, admiring look at Ella and a light stroke of her long blonde hair.

'Perfect,' he said as if he had been asked for an opinion by a judging panel. 'Just perfect.' And then to the waiter: 'Am I not a lucky guy, having cocktails with not one but two beautiful women?'

'Very lucky gentleman,' said the Chinese waiter, who had taken in the whole situation at a glance and knew that the lady in grey silk would be the one with the credit card.

Larry spent thirty over-excited minutes with them. He told them about various dramas and screaming matches back at the showrooms. How this buyer had threatened to burn the place down unless she got her order and that designer had said he was leaving for the Islands before he had finished his spring collection.

'Which islands?' Ella asked with interest.

'Oh, who knows, who cares, Ella. He won't go there, it's only a cry for attention,' Larry explained.

He asked nothing about Kimberly's morning, which had been spent meeting their advertising agency. He asked nothing about what Ella was doing, with her long blonde hair and Irish accent, in New York. But he was very excited about a reception they were going to later. It was an art exhibition and it was so far uptown they were thinking Albany. But they *had* to go, and Kimberly must leave time to go home and change, and if she was tempted to eat pasta carbonara for lunch, then she must remember the zipper of the new dress was notoriously sticky and had to be fastened so maybe she might think twice about carbonara!

And he was gone, with a flurry of goodbyes, secure in the knowledge that everyone in the bar saw him go.

'Isn't he something else?' Kimberly said proudly.

Ella struggled to agree.

'Very different from Derry, as you can see,' Kimberly said.

'Oh, indeed, yes, totally.'

Ella had just been thinking that and wondering what kind of madness had made Kimberly King attracted to Larry. Maybe being a part of the fashion world appealed to her. But to give up Derry King, with his crinkly smile and his ability to understand what you were thinking before you said it . . . for this guy. A man who looked at himself in mirrors, for God's sake. It was beyond comprehension.

'Larry makes me feel young again, you see.' Kimberly answered the question Ella had not asked aloud.

'He's full of excitement, isn't he, and totally gorgeous looking.'

Ella hoped there was enough enthusiasm in her voice to match the look of adoration there had been in Kimberly's eyes when she spoke to Larry.

'He certainly keeps me on my toes. I had indeed been thinking of pasta before he reminded me of the new dress.' Kimberly gave a little giggle and picked up the menu to choose the salad with no dressing which she ordered instead.

'I'll have the same,' Ella said.

'No, you like your food, have what you like,' Kimberly pleaded.

'I'm having dinner with Derry tonight. I'll have plenty then,' Ella explained.

'Where's he taking you?' Kimberly had a huge interest in good restaurants, although she had rarely eaten three hundred calories worth of food in any of them.

'At his place. I'm looking forward to seeing it.'

'Well, be prepared for a two-hour tour of child art first. He's kept all kinds of rubbish as well as the valuable stuff. Oh, and remind him to call the take-out early on. Often he leaves it too late.'

'You and he are wonderful together. Kind of jokey, but no bitterness.'

'What's to be bitter about? Derry's a great guy. He gave me half of everything. That's how I set up the business with Larry. And he's so practical, he said there was no use trying to hang on to me if I wanted to go. I would have done that for him too, if he had been the one to fall in love with someone else. It's crazy to try and kick life into something that's over.'

Ella thought of Margery Rice. Suppose she had thought like that? Would everything have been different? She could have had half of what Don had. More. She would have let him go. Don would not have taken all those risks. He would have been alive today. And he and Ella would have been together. For one moment Ella almost told Kimberly the whole story.

She was a good listener. Her perfect face was alert and interested but not eager. If Ella wanted to talk, she would have had a sympathetic audience. For a moment she was tempted. But then she decided against it. It was her last day in New York. Tomorrow she would go back to Ireland and whatever was going to happen now. All the decisions that had to be made. About the bank drafts in a safe deposit account. About the knowledge of where Don's family lived. It would take a lot of working out. An emotional lunch was not what she needed just now.

'I'll never be able to thank you both for such solidarity. It was exactly what I needed.' She was closing the door very politely.

Kimberly understood. 'Sure, well, we were there if you needed us, still are.'

'I know one thing I did want to talk to you about, if it's not indiscreet. Is Derry really dead-set against going to Ireland? It would be marvellous for us if he came.'

'Utterly. His father was a wife-beater and a drunk and an all-round bad guy. And Derry simply blames it on his being Irish.'

'So it's really deep. I won't try any more.'

'I wish you would try. It's exactly what he needs, to go there, to get the monkey off his back or whatever the expression is.'

'You think it would help?'

'It might make him normal. That's his problem, you see, these demons he has about Ireland. It was part of our difficulties, part of everything for him. He had to damn a whole country because of his father.'

'But why did he choose an Irish project to support?'

'He thought it was going to send the place up, make it all look very foolish.'

'But he doesn't now. I explained all that at the first meeting.'

'He's honourable enough to go along with something once he's into it, in order to be fair. He wouldn't raise your hopes, get you over here, and then because of his prejudices pull the plug. But you asked why he chose it in the first place, and I told you. He thought it was going to be a hatchet job.'

'He seems so calm and in control.'

'And he *is* calm and in control. He looked after his whole family. He raised his brothers, they adore him. He wanted to get his mom a nice home back in Canada where she grew up, couldn't understand that she had lived so long in New York that she is a New Yorker now.'

'So she didn't go?' Ella asked.

'No, she had all her friends in the neighbourhood, she even had some happy memories of her husband. Derry couldn't see any of that. His father is his one blind spot. He can't go into an Irish pub, hear Irish music, says they glorify drink and violence. He's never going to change unless he got back there to Ireland and saw they were all as normal as anyone else. Just getting on with their lives.'

'Have you been to Ireland, Kimberly?' Ella asked suddenly.

'Why do you ask?'

'Just the way you said that made me think you had.'

'You're right. When we were first having our problems I went there. I even went to see his relations. Perfectly ordinary people. I didn't tell them about Derry, just asked around a bit. He has two cousins who started as house painters, run their own business now. They are so like him in many ways. But he'll never get to know them.'

'Did you tell him?'

'Tried to, but no use. Then I met Larry, so I had other things on my mind.'

'How long have you and Larry been married?' Ella asked.

'Eighteen months. I hope it lasts.' She laughed a very brittle laugh.

'You are very hard on yourself, Kimberly. He adores you. Anyone can see that.'

'Aha, I wish I had your faith and optimism.'

'Oh, but he does. You saw him. And so does Derry. He looks at you as if he still loves you a lot.'

'No, Derry doesn't love me. He's my great friend. He looks out for me. He keeps a quiet eye on some of Larry's worst extravagances. He doesn't think I know. And I care for him too, as a friend. Were you and this Don Richardson friends?'

'What?'

'I know you loved him, but were you friends?'

'No, no, he went away and left me. He wasn't a friend in that sense. But he still loved me, he wrote to me to tell me that the night before ... the night before it happened.'

Kimberly looked as if she were struggling to find something to say. Ella rescued her. 'It's all right. Everything changed then. I can do anything now that I know he really loved me.'

'I can see by your face that's true,' Kimberly said truthfully. Ella's face did look serene and calm. Whatever this guy had said to her, she believed it and it was doing her good.

The tour of the artwork was leisurely. They walked, glass of wine in hand, while Derry King explained about the young people and their sense of vision. Some of the artists were from inner-city schemes, where their brothers and neighbours were mainly into gangs and drugs, yet they saw beauty in everyday life.

And Derry King didn't send out for a take-away, either. Instead, he took Ella into his state-of-the-art kitchen and said he was going to make a stir-fry in a wok. He had asked the butcher to cut up the meat into tiny strips, the vegetables were chopped and prepared too. 'It's probably not so much making it, more assembling it,' he said apologetically.

'Oh, no. I'd definitely consider it was making it,' Ella reassured him. 'You went to the butcher's yourself, and you don't have a fleet of staff serving it.'

'Did you expect that?' Derry still had the habit she had noticed the first time she met him of asking simple, direct questions that made you reveal much more about yourself than you intended to.

'Well, I suppose I know you're very wealthy. This is an extremely classy building. I suppose I thought people opening your door for you and cooking your meals might go with the territory,' she admitted.

'Is that what you'd have?'

'No! I'd hate it. If I had a place like this, I'd well look after it on my own, no matter how much money I earned.' She stared around it admiringly.

'I do have a team that comes in three times a week when I'm not here. They clean and iron, and I have to admit that today I called them and asked them to do the vegetables. Was that cheating?' He had a very infectious smile.

'I bet they're mad about you,' she teased.

'Oh, I doubt it. One more job in a long day of hauling cleaning stuff around Manhattan.'

'You're probably their only client who has that much sympathy for them.'

'I have admiration for them too. They saw a niche in the market and went for it.'

'Did you find them, or did Kimberly?'

'I did. Kim liked to have someone live in. It was a different kind of life, kind of place entirely.'

'So you and she didn't live here then?'

'Lord, no. Kim thinks this isn't a home. She thinks it's a school project room. No, her place, and indeed our place when we were together, was a matter of one drawing room opening into another

'... perfect for entertaining. I don't do much of that ... as you can see ... so all this suits me better.'

And then it was as if he had very politely pulled down a shutter. It was as if he were saying, This is as far as you are going to go today, Ella Brady, no more personal questions ...

She took the message on board. She told him about her plans for the next day. She had a small sum of money kept aside to buy gifts if her mission had been successful, and now it was, so she would go shopping.

'Women love that,' he said, almost wistfully. 'I can't get a kick out of it myself, clothes are just to keep you warm and decent.'

'Oh, I won't be shopping for clothes. I'm talking about trinkets. You know the kind of thing ... joke clapper board for Nick and Sandy to show they're really in the big time now, some big paper sunflowers for my mother, a football hat for my father, a frilly nightie for Deirdre, a book of table decorations for Thanksgiving for Brenda and Patrick in Quentins. Oh, I've got another dog collar for Simon and Maud, like the one I gave you that horrified you so much.'

'It did *not* horrify me. It touched me to the heart,' he protested.

'Now, Derry, I want to leave this country while still continuing to respect your honesty,' Ella laughed.

'Then look at this.' He opened his wallet and took out a Polaroid of a lopsided puppy with a hopeless grin wearing the twinkling, bejewelled collar.

'You actually did put it on an animal! Aren't you just marvellous!' she cried.

'That's not an animal, that's no ordinary dog. I'll have you know you're looking at Fennel.'

'Well doesn't Fennel look just fine in his new collar!'

'He loves it, apparently. They tell me at the kennels he won't have it taken off. He pines until they put it back on. Maybe you know more about dogs than I do.'

'He lives at a kennel?'

'He has to live somewhere. He can't live here. He followed me home one night. I couldn't leave him.'

'Maybe he belongs to somebody.'

'Fennel never belonged to anybody. He was born in some alley. His mother may have been killed. He lived by his wits until he found me. He's a survivor, Fennel. He found one of the few men in New York who would look him in the eye and then pay for him to live in luxury for the rest of his life. I take him for walks in the park. We get some very odd looks, thanks to that collar ... but what do I know? Maybe the other dogs are drop-dead envious.'

'You're a very kind man, Derry King,' Ella said.

'And you're a kind girl, Ella Brady, going off to stores getting gifts for all your friends when your heart is broken,' he said.

Then everything changed a little, as if they had been old friends for ever.

She helped him to make the salad and told him about Don quite calmly, from the very first day she had met him, right down to the letter that had been delivered to her parents' house.

He asked questions that never seemed intrusive, but which carried the story along. 'Did he seem sad when you were in Spain together?'

'Yes, he did, sometimes. I didn't realise that it was worry because he was preparing a hiding place. I thought it was because he wanted it to go on for ever ... the two of us there.'

'Perhaps it *was* that,' Derry suggested.

And then, later, she was telling him about the numbing shock of reading in the newspapers that he had left people without their life savings. Story after story unfolding of loss and deceit.

'What was the very worst bit?' Derry asked.

'At the start, the worst bit was the papers talking about him and his wife, this close couple which I knew they were not. That hurt a lot. But the very worst bit was my father trying to be brave. My poor, decent, hard-working father, who would never cheat anyone in his life, ending his career in disgrace because *my* boyfriend gave him some false leads. It was bad enough for him to know that I was having an affair with a married man, that alone was enough to upset him and my mother. But the other. That was unbearable. I literally could not bear to think about it, which was why Nick and everyone got me involved in this project, so that I wouldn't have to think any more.'

'And look what you did with it!' He was admiring.

'Ah, that was due to everyone else, and now finally to you helping me. But what thanks do you get? A dog collar for Fennel. And here I am, sitting blubbing away about it, hour after hour.'

'No, you're not. In fact, you're remarkably calm.'

'I am because he loved me. I know that now. For some months I thought that maybe I had only imagined it. Invented the whole thing for myself.'

'But he's dead, Ella. You'll never see him again. Isn't that very bleak for you?'

'It's a waste, a desperate waste. But it's what happened and we have to get on with life.'

'And when you get back ...'

'I'll be so busy with the Quentins project, I promise ...' she smiled at him.

'No, I don't mean that. You will have four major decisions to make about all this and quite soon.'

'Four decisions?' She was surprised that he was so precise.

'One ... whether you'll cash the bank drafts for your father. Two ... whether you'll hand over the laptop to the authorities. Three ... if you *do* give it over, will you erase the information about where his wife and family live? Four ... if you *don't* hand it over, what will you do with it, throw it away or hang on to it?'

'No wonder you did well in business, Derry. You have a very sharp mind. You can get down to the bones of something in seconds.'

'Yes, but those are, as you say, just the bones. You have many other things to think about. It seems that you have good friends. They'll help you.'

'I'll keep you informed, Derry.'

'You don't need to. There's something sacred about confidences, part of that is you need never follow up unless you want to.'

'That's true, but part of a confidence, if it is to be sacred, means that the listener must give as well as the talker.'

'What do you mean?'

'I've told you my whole heart and life story,' she said.

'You know mine.' He tried to be light.

'I don't, really. What is so terrible out there that you can't face visiting the country where your father was born? He's dead and as you said to me about Don, you'll never see him again.'

'We're not talking the same planet here, Ella.'

'I know it's not bleak for you and a waste, like it is for me. For you it's probably a good thing, because you can only hate him and what he did in retrospect. But he had to be born somewhere, and he happened to be born in my country, and that, whether you like it or not, makes you part-Irish.'

'You don't understand.'

'Well, *tell* me then.'

And slowly he told her. The life of disappointment that this big square man had lived. The blame that he sent in every direction. Towards his native country for not giving him a living back in the early 1960s. To his new country for not giving him streets paved with gold as he had been led to expect. Towards his gentle, hard-working Canadian wife because she looked wistfully backwards to the peace and tranquillity of her country home. Towards his three sons who were never good enough for him, and then too good for him. Derry told the stories of the beatings and how his mother would neither leave him nor report him. His mother believed that if you said 'for better or worse', then it was easy to stay when it was better, the only testing ground was when it was worse. And that was when you really *did* have to stay.

His face was sad and twisted when he spoke of her. 'She preferred to stay in that run-down place, that place where he disappeared for days, where he had burned her with a saucepan of hot soup.'

'Maybe she was just afraid to go back to her own small town in Canada.'

'She'd have had nothing to fear there. She would have had peace, respect, roots ... far away from all he had put her through.'

It was clear to Ella that this woman must have had some happy times with her husband. It had not all been misery. There must have been times of hope ... hope that they would turn a corner. She wished that she had Derry's clear mind, that somehow she could reduce it all to four main points. But it was more complicated than that. It was a lifetime of hatred and regret.

'So I have no wish to set foot in Jim Kennedy's birthplace and see all the great sights he talked about when he was drunk.'

'Jim Kennedy?' she asked.

'My father. You don't think I kept his name, do you? He gave me nothing else. Why should I take his name? I changed it when I was old enough. And amazingly you are old enough to change your name quite early in life. I've called myself Derry King since I was fifteen. Since the day I went out to work.'

'We were asking Ella what you'd call the baby when it gets born,' Maud said to Cathy Scarlet.

'Were you, now? And did she know?' Cathy smiled.

'She said we were trying to get her mind off all the equations,' Simon said.

'And was she right?'

'Sort of, but we were wondering. We've thought of some great names ourselves.'

'I'm sure you have, but it's an oddly personal thing, Simon. Tom and I will think nearer the time.'

'You'd want to think soon,' Maud said reprovingly. 'You never know the day or the hour.'

'Well, we know vaguely the day and the hour, and it's not for another two months,' Cathy said. 'But the day and the hour that Ella is coming here again for a lesson is in two days' time, so I hope you've done all those problems she left you.'

'Her head got mended very quickly,' Simon grumbled.

'I don't think it was broken at all, to tell you the truth,' Maud agreed with him.

Cathy wondered whether to tell them to go easy on her when she came back. The girl had had terrible news while she was away. But that wasn't the kind of information anyone would ever put in Maud and Simon's direction. Ella would be worse off if the twins had been warned to treat her gently.

Ella's mother couldn't sleep. And she couldn't talk to Tim about it, either. Only the three of them knew the contents of the letter. Ella had said nothing on the telephone about Don's offer to give back what he had taken. Tim said he couldn't take those bank drafts to clear up his own and his clients' debts. It wouldn't be fair. There were too many other demands on the assets of Rice and Richardson. But if Ella cashed them and gave him the money, then he would *have* to take it. Barbara Brady prayed that she would manage to keep out of it, as her husband had pleaded that she should. It was just so hard looking at his frailty and realising that it was in Ella's power to sort all that out.

'I wish he'd come over with her, could you credit him having an allergy to coming near the place,' Nick complained.

'Ella says she has pages of notes,' Sandy consoled him.

'And the whole thing about your man has died down,' Nick said thoughtfully.

'He was never *my* man, thank God,' Sandy said.

They sat easily together in the huge apartment, looking out at the lights of New York. Their conversation was as intense as either of them had ever known, yet there were no tears or signs of upset. At no stage did they reach out to console each other. At no stage did they feel they had to backtrack on what they said, explain or apologise.

'I got us green figs as dessert ... would you like those?' Derry said.

'Love them, thank you,' Ella said.

They had drunk very little wine. She noticed that he rarely had more than one glass throughout an evening. The reaction to his father must have been very deep-seated.

'Cream with them?' he called from the kitchen.

'Please.'

She thought suddenly of Kimberly's handsome Larry telling her not to eat a fattening pasta. Possibly Derry had never served figs and cream to his beautiful wife. She wondered, had he been able to talk to her like they had talked together tonight? But she could ask him anything.

'Did Kimberly help you over any of this?'

'Immensely,' he said. 'You can see how good she is with people, and how smart. She said it was holding me back as a person, and she's right, of course. She even went to Ireland to find my roots for me, but I handed them back to her. I prefer the hate, you see. I don't want Jim Kennedy to be an ordinary, decent man who took to the hard stuff. I did all I did, and denied myself so much, just because he was a monster.'

She listened to him and was silent for a moment. 'I see – you don't want him to be normal, with normal relatives who work hard like you do. You don't want him to have an ordinary background. You want him to have come straight out of the pit of hell, all steaming and hissing.'

'Something like that,' he agreed ruefully.

They finished the figs.

'It's really your story we should be telling in a movie, isn't it,' she said with a smile.

'Oh, no, they don't make movies like that. They make them where the son goes home and everyone loves him and drinks themselves senseless and dances jigs. Then the guy goes to his father's birthplace and weeps and begs his dead father to forgive him for not talking to him more. That's what would sell.'

'I wish you were coming back to Dublin tomorrow with me, in many ways. Not for you but for me,' Ella said suddenly.

'You do? Why do you say that?' He was gentle as he always was, interested but not invasive.

'It's funny. I've only known you for just over a week, and yet I feel very safe talking to you. When I step off the plane in Ireland, I'm back in a land where anything could happen, anything *did* happen. I have to go to a city where I know Don Richardson will never walk or breathe again. That's hard. All these decisions you identified ... I have to make them but I may do it all wrong. It would be much easier if you were there. That's all I'm saying, I suppose.'

'Very well,' he said.

'What?'

'I'll come with you,' Derry King said simply.

'You can't, not just like that?'

'But you just asked me to.' He seemed surprised.

'Yes, but why?'

'If you have to face all that and get through it, then surely I can face a few old memories,' he said.

And he took away the plate that had held her figs and cream before it fell on the floor.

Chapter Eleven

It had never occurred to Ella that Derry King's office would have booked him first class to Dublin and neither of them discovered this until they were at Kennedy airport in New York. 'Dumb of them not to check,' he said, and went to change.

'No, please, you *must* have your comfortable seat,' Ella begged him. It was quite bad enough that he was coming to Ireland on a whim without him turning up with backache and stiff legs from travelling at the back of the bus.

But he wouldn't hear of it. 'It's only a few short hours. It would be highly antisocial and, alas, first class is full, or we'd upgrade you,' he said.

Ella began to panic. What would she talk to him about for six hours, knowing all the time that he could have stretched his legs out in comfort and watched a movie of his choice?

They heard the over-hearty laughter of a group on the other side of the departure lounge. They were rather red-faced and might have had a couple of cocktails to speed them on their trip. Ella listened to them carefully and then identified American, rather than Irish, accents.

'Yours, I think,' she said to Derry.

'What do you mean?'

'You have me so sensitive and quivering now about the Irish being loud and drunk that I'm very relieved to say that those people over there aren't my lot, they're actually yours.'

'Oh dear, that's a pity. I thought that we might keep score and tick them off,' he mocked her.

He was easy company on the plane as he had been everywhere else. Talking some of the time, reading a magazine or even sleeping a little. When the trolley passed along the aisle selling duty-free goods, the stewardess asked, 'Do you want to wake your husband in case he wants to make any purchases?'

Ella didn't correct her about the relationship. 'No, he doesn't want any, nor do I, thank you.'

She would have bought Deirdre a bottle of duty-free gin, under normal circumstances. But these were far from normal times.

Why had she said she would like him to come to Dublin? Now she had to look after him, make sure he liked the place. Confirm that he had done the right thing in lending the Foundation's name and support to this venture. She had to draw him into her life, introduce him to her friends and family. Yes, it would certainly take her mind off Dublin now being a city without Don, but she wanted some time on her own to think about that too. Time to mourn him, without having to plunge into all this. And to decide what to do.

But to be fair, he hadn't asked her to make any arrangements for him. His office had booked his hotel, and a limousine would meet them at the airport. He said that he realised she would have to get back to work. He knew she would not be free to dine with him every night because she would possibly be working in the very restaurants where he might want to go and eat. In Quentins itself, and in Colm's restaurant up in Tara Road. It would be very different from the life of a lady that she had been leading in New York.

She looked at him as he slept. This was a man who had worked all his life. He would understand she had a living to earn.

She fell asleep herself. And dreamed a troubled dream, where Don Richardson was waiting for her at the airport, saying that he had come back from the next world for twenty-four hours to give her a message, but he had now forgotten what it was. In her dream, Ella had clutched the computer harder and harder.

She woke just before they were making their approach to Dublin in the pink Irish dawn. She heard the stewardess asking Derry King to make sure his wife's seatbelt was fastened, and he had not bothered to correct the relationship either.

She realised that there would be no Don at the airport or

anywhere ever again. She bit her lip to hide what she feared might be a look of upset on her face. If he noticed, Derry said nothing. He just looked out of the window at all the green. It was hard to read his expression.

Then the plane landed, and there was no time to discuss anything.

She had never come into the city any way except the bus. It was curious to see the road from the back of a big black Mercedes. The chauffeur asked Derry which route he should take. Ella began to protest that she should be dropped at Derry's hotel in St Stephen's Green, and that then she would find her own way home from there.

Derry took no notice. 'Tara Road first, please,' he said simply, and there had been no argument.

Neither of them commented on the city that they were both looking at with new eyes. Ella was glad to see that the weather was good. It was a crisp, late-autumn day. The early-morning rush hour had not yet begun. The streets looked as if they had been cleaned by a recent shower of rain.

He could not find this place repulsive at first glance. He had to see it as a gracious city.

Derry was pleased to see some colour return to her face. She had looked very pale as they had landed. It was a series of hard things for a girl to have had to face over a period of four months. The loss of the man she considered her true love, the financial ruin of her family. And then the second loss of the suicide. Not easy for her to come back, but at least she had friends in this place. She would survive.

They made arrangements for her to pick him up at his hotel that night for an early dinner.

'This is a beautiful street,' he said when they came to Tara Road.

'Yes, but I'm round at the tradesmen's entrance these days,' she said with a bright little smile.

'Not for ever, Ella,' he consoled her.

'Well,' she shrugged.

'Shall I take the car up the lane, Madam?' the chauffeur enquired.

'No, it would get stuck, I'm afraid. Just leave me at the corner, if you don't mind.'

The chauffeur was about to carry her case but she wouldn't hear of it.

'See you tonight at six, Derry.' She ran off before anyone could say more, down the narrow lane behind the big houses of Tara Road to where her parents would be waiting, up already for hours, and peering out the windows of what used to be the garden shed.

Ella couldn't sleep. She tried, but it didn't work. Her mother had gone to work, her father sat at the kitchen table moving papers around him. The huge, paper sunflowers looked cheerful in the window as she had known they would. She looked across at the house where her parents had lived since their marriage until this summer. She remembered Derry King saying that this situation would not be for ever. Maybe a man thought differently, in that he would work and scheme and slave to get it all back. While Ella would lose it all and more on top of it if she only thought she could see Don just once more. She wished she could sleep because she felt a great weariness and sense that life was going to be so empty from now on, it didn't really matter what happened.

In his hotel room, Derry King paced up and down. He had a stiff neck from the plane journey. His eyes felt heavy. In theory, he should be able to sleep. In the past, when he had criss-crossed the United States to go to conventions, meetings, sales conferences, his ability to snatch sleep had been legendary. He would wake refreshed and ready for everything.

But it was different here. These were the streets that Jim Kennedy had walked when he was young. This was the land that had not given him a living or an understanding, the city he had fled to find a better and brighter life. Jim Kennedy would not have been welcome in a hotel of this calibre. He would not have been allowed past the door. But those small bars they had passed on the journey from the airport, places with family names over the door, that would have been his territory. And in the telephone directory there were people who could tell Derry about it all.

But he didn't want to ask and learn. He didn't know what he wanted to do. For years he had steeled himself against useless regrets and time wasting, wishing himself elsewhere. There had been too much maudlin 'if only' in his father's conversations. Derry King would be no part of it. He would spend no time wondering why he had decided to come to this place. Nor wishing that he had stayed where he was and taken Fennel for a three-hour walk every day in Central Park. He was here now and he would make the best of it. And if sleep would not come, then he must go out and walk in that park across from his hotel.

Brenda Brennan's friend Nora was working in the kitchen. She knew that the American was in town. The one who would provide the money to make the film about Quentins.

'Will he sneak in to have a look at the place, do you think?' Signora asked as she expertly cleaned and diced vegetables that Blouse Brennan produced triumphantly in ever-more earth-covered trays.

'No, I think he's too smart for that,' Brenda said thoughtfully. 'He'll have to meet us sooner or later, so he doesn't want to be unmasked as someone having a private peek.'

'That's true, but I bet he has a private peek through the window sometime today, don't you?' Signora said.

'Oh, definitely,' Brenda laughed.

Patrick Brennan looked at them. Women's friendships were amazing. Brenda and Nora O'Donoghue had been so close since they had all met at catering college. Even the years Nora had spent in Sicily didn't seem to have broken it, they wrote each other long letters all that time. It didn't matter that one of them ran the restaurant and the other was scraping vegetables in it. They were still equals. Still like girls, giggling over whether a rich American would come and peek in the window. Patrick wished that men had friendships like that, where there were no secrets, where nothing was hidden.

'Would he be the kind of fellow that would fall for me, do you think?' Deirdre asked in the café at lunchtime.

Ella had begged her to have a quick lunch and they were having a sandwich near Deirdre's work.

'No, I don't think he would. He's too interested in work, more work and art and brooding and more work and homeless dogs to have any time for you,' Ella said.

'Hey, I could be interested in all those things too if I wanted to,' Deirdre protested.

'Well, your powers are extraordinary, Dee. We all know that . . . and what do I know? When you meet him, you might start to sing arias at each other.'

'And will I meet him?'

'Of course you will. I'm just trying to work out where. It can't be Quentins. That has to be formal and work and everything . . . we haven't room to swing a cat at our home these days, otherwise I'd have a Sunday lunch for him to meet my friends . . .'

'I could have a Sunday lunch in my place if you like,' Deirdre offered.

'Would you, Dee? And we could ask Nick and Sandy.' Ella was pleased.

'Your parents could come, and Tom and Cathy,' Deirdre said.

'Oh, Dee, what would I do without you?'

'Nuala is back in town, but I think not, don't you?' Deirdre said.

'I think very much not.' Ella was reflective.

'Sorry for bringing her up,' Deirdre said. 'But you might just run into her or Frank of the one-track mind.'

'Now that Don's dead, do you think he'll shut up about it all, and let him rest in peace?'

'Are you asking me for an honest answer?'

'Of course I am.'

'Then I don't think that people like Frank and his brothers would let anyone rest in peace while they think that someone owes them a sum of money.'

'Oh well, welcome back to the real world, Ella,' she told herself ruefully.

'You never left the real world, Ella! You're terrific to cope with all that's being fired at you. Truly you are.'

'No, you're right, I'll survive.'

'I'm only babbling on because I honestly don't have the words to tell you face to face how sorry I am about what Don did. It's a nightmare for you, and I just want you to understand that I know this.' Deirdre's eyes were full of tears.

'Let's think of what we'll eat on Sunday,' Ella said. She could cope with anything but sympathy just now.

Tom and Cathy were delighted with the invitation to lunch. Something they didn't have to cook and serve themselves. It was heaven. But there was a problem which they had to work around.

'Deirdre, we'd just love to come to lunch, and we'll bring you a really luscious dessert from the freezer,' Tom offered.

'You don't need to do that. I'd love it, but you don't need to . . .'

'We do.'

'Why?' Deirdre was suspicious.

'Because we're going to ask you if we can bring the twins. We're meant to be looking after them that day. Muttie and Lizzie are going on an outing. We said we'd take the kids. They're so mad and awful really we thought if we gave you a roulade *and* a pavlova it might sort of make up.'

'How mad and awful?' Deirdre asked.

'Just desperately curious and inquisitive, really. They ask all kinds of intimate questions without realising it. They might offer to dance, but we can close them down on that.'

'No, we might need it if it's all a bit sticky. Ella says they're great value. Of course they can come and I get two puddings as well.' Deirdre sounded well pleased.

'What's the worst Maud and Simon could say to this rich American guy, do you think?' Cathy asked Tom.

'They're very into mating conversations just now. They could ask him about his sexual habits, I suppose,' Tom suggested.

'Oh, yes, they'll definitely want to know about who he mates with. I was wondering if they want parts in the film or anything, you know how much they like to belong,' said Cathy.

'I'm sure he'll be able to deal with them.' Tom hoped he sounded more certain than he felt.

Ella called in to Firefly Films. They weren't expecting her. They hadn't their response ready.

'It's all so unfair, Ella,' Sandy began.

'People put too much pressure on him,' said Nick, who used to say that there was no pit of hell deep enough for Don Richardson.

'Yes, when Derry King's gone back to New York, I'll cry on your shoulder, believe me I will, but now we have to work out how to make the best of his sudden decision to come here. I'm meeting him tonight to go over our notes.'

She saw their faces lighten. This was exactly what they had hoped for, but they didn't want to appear crass by not acknowledging that the love of her life had first left her and then killed himself. They sat down to plan the campaign.

Nick and Sandy looked at her with admiration as she pushed the hair out of her eyes. She took out an armful of files, some with coloured stickers on them.

'There are so many different ways we could go. In a way it will depend on who talks best. But come on, let's have a look at the stories anyway.'

Starters

Derek Barry was entertaining a couple of wealthy clients to lunch. He didn't actually know them. But Bob O'Neill, his partner, had been most insistent.

They put plenty of work through the books of Barry and O'Neill Accountants, and they were threatening to move elsewhere.

All they needed was some stroking and patting and reassurance. Bob had intended to take them himself, but his plane was delayed in London and he couldn't get back. Derek must hold the fort.

There had been hardly any time to check them out. All he knew was their bank balance. That and the fact that Bob O'Neill, the senior partner in the firm, said that it was a Must Do.

So, Derek sighed and booked a table in Quentins.

That was one advantage of being the father of the restaurant's owner. He always got a table there. He arrived early.

'Where can I put you, Mr Barry?' Brenda Brennan was always outwardly polite, but he felt she didn't like him.

'It doesn't really matter, Brenda. I'm meeting a pair of clients, Bob's, not mine, loads of money, dot-com millionaires or something. Complete nobodies.' He shook his head disapprovingly.

'Well, I hope they'll enjoy their lunch, Mr Barry.'

She was too cool. He didn't like it. She was, after all, an employee of his son Quentin, and so was her husband, that fancy chef Patrick. Derek Barry, small and self-important, sat down at his table, bristling with a sense that he wasn't being treated with enough respect.

The couple were shown to his table. In their late thirties, he decided, big, both of them, far from elegant, cheap, ill-fitting clothes. The woman carried a shabby handbag, the man wore a loud jacket. They looked out of place in this quiet, smart restaurant, decorated for Christmas, but not garishly so. Little Christmas trees with small white lights dotted around.

Still, Bob O'Neill had been adamant. These two were to get the treatment. They paid big fees for the firm's services. Derek Barry was to make sure that they were happy and continued to be so.

'Mr and Mrs Costello, what a pleasure,' he said, standing up. 'I'm Mr Barry.'

'Bob O'Neill's not coming to the dinner?' the woman said, surprised that the table was set only for three.

'Er . . . no. Mr O'Neill sends his best regards but you know the pressure of business . . . he was delayed in London. And as one of the senior partners myself, I thought it was time for us to get to know each other.' Derek hated her calling lunch 'dinner', and in a place like this.

'Well, I'm Jimmy and my wife is Cath,' the man said.

'Ah,' Derek said.

'What's your first name?' Cath asked.

It was ignorant rather than impolite, Derek thought, just a woman with no social graces. He wished he had made the time to find out exactly what kind of business they were in.

He told them his name.

'So you drew the short straw, Derek,' said Jimmy, settling in and looking at the menu.

Flinching at the way his first name was being used so easily, Derek asked nervously what that meant.

'Well, I suppose it means that Bob O'Neill sent you to this dinner to do his dirty work,' Jimmy explained cheerfully.

'Like, so that you'll be blamed when we take our business away from you,' Cath added. 'Do they serve draught beer here? I'd really love a pint.'

Derek Barry felt dizzy. Things were moving out of control. People calling lunch 'dinner' and wanting pints in Quentins. These two people talking casually about moving their business away from the firm.

'Well, well, whatever we must be, we must not be hasty,' he said.

'No haste at all, Derek,' Jimmy said good-naturedly. 'We'll just come back to the office with you after our dinner and collect the papers.'

Derek Barry felt a slow anger begin to burn inside him. Had Bob O'Neill realised how serious the situation with these people was? Probably not. Jimmy and Cath Costello were not the kind of people Bob would have known socially. But he would have known that something was wrong. That was why he had made Derek the fall guy.

Cath was deep in the menu. 'Are we all going to have starters?' she asked, almost childlike in her enthusiasm.

'I don't know what any of them are,' Jimmy said, examining the list.

They were about to lose wealthy clients, and this woman with her tight perm and her nylon scarf twisted around her neck was proving to be far too confident in a restaurant of this standing.

The waitress said her name was Monica, Mon for short, and she was delighted to help. This one was quails' eggs, tiny little things, in a bed of pastry with a gorgeous sauce served on the side. This one was kidneys with a mustard sauce on toasted scone.

'I never had a quail's egg,' said Jimmy. 'But I'd love kidneys in mustard sauce. I'm in a lather of indecision.'

'I'm the same way myself, Jimmy. We'll have two starters, that's what we'll have.'

'I don't really think ...' Derek began. But he stopped. There was something about Cath's expression that he didn't like. It was as if she could see right through him, could read his embarrassment and snobbish feelings about her earthy way of going on.

'Are you going to have starters and mains?' she asked Derek with interest.

He tried not to shudder and show how little he liked every phrase she uttered. These vulgar people were important to his company. Bob had said only this morning that they couldn't afford to lose their business. So Derek knew he must turn on his charm.

'Before I decide what to eat, why don't you let me get some drinks in, Cath and ... er ... Jimmy, and then you'll tell me what it is you actually do.'

'But you know what we do,' Cath said simply. 'You are our accountants. You must know what we do.'

'Well, you see, as you said, it's really Bob O'Neill who deals with you ... very big firm, lots of clients nowadays, many different aspects, the whole problem of expanding ...' He looked at them helplessly.

'Then why did you ask us to dinner?' Jimmy asked, tearing his bread roll apart as if it were a killer fish which he had to demolish first.

'Bob couldn't make it himself this once. So he asked me to stand in at the last moment ...'

'And you never looked us up?' Jimmy said. 'Lord, I wouldn't last one day if I didn't know about the people I was meeting.'

Derek looked miserable. 'I'm sorry, Mr Costello – I'm sorry, Jimmy. You're right. It was a courtesy and I did not have time. I didn't make time. I apologise. Can you tell me about yourselves? Now?'

'What do you want to know, Derek?' Jimmy asked.

Derek wondered what to ask them. 'Do you have children?' he heard himself ask. He wondered why he had said it. Normally he never asked about people's families.

'Do you?' Cath asked in a level voice.

'Yes, just one son. He didn't follow me into the business, as I had hoped he would. I even had a room ready for him, but I'm afraid he didn't take to the accountancy business.'

'Imagine!' Cath said. 'And did he do all right on his own?'

'Very well. This is his restaurant, as it happens.'

'Well, you must be delighted with him,' Cath said, her eyes far away.

'And your children?' Derek asked. 'Did they go into your business with you?' Again he didn't know why he wanted to know. He was not one for the personal question.

'No, we went into it for them, really,' Jimmy said.

There was a silence. Derek knew that he must smile and be charming. Tomorrow he could rail at Bob O'Neill for landing him in all this so very ill-prepared. Today, he had to get these people on his side.

'So? Your actual day-to-day work?' he said, his face nearly splitting with a smile.

'Takes up about sixteen or seventeen hours of the twenty-four,' Cath said, in a matter-of-fact way.

'Starting at six in the morning and ending at ten or eleven with a pint before closing time,' Jimmy explained.

'But surely you don't need to work that hard?' he said, appalled.

'Oh, we do,' Cath said.

'But Bob O'Neill told me that you were very financially secure.' Derek was bewildered. 'Why do you work so hard?'

'To forget,' Cath said simply. 'To take our minds off the children.'

'The children?' He looked from one to the other.

'Bob didn't tell you?' They couldn't believe it.

'No, he told me nothing.' Derek was ashamed.

'We had three children who died in a fire ten years ago. We nearly went mad, but someone told us that if we worked and worked it would make it better.'

Derek looked at them wordlessly.

'So we did just that,' Jimmy said.

'Hour after hour, year after year,' Cath said. 'It wasn't great, of course, but I think it would be worse if we hadn't. We've no way of knowing, but I think I would have been worse if there had been time to think.'

'I suppose it gave you a comfortable lifestyle, anyway,' Derek said. He didn't know how to sympathise. Better to look on the bright side.

They looked at him, speechless.

'What do you actually do for a living?' Derek asked eventually.

'Fund-raise,' Cath said. 'Didn't you know? Doesn't Bob tell you anything at all?'

'I'm beginning to think he doesn't,' Derek said. 'He told me you were very wealthy people.'

'Worth a dinner?' Jimmy said.

'Worth a dinner, yes.' Derek felt ashamed.

'And you didn't even know that we're leaving your firm?' Cath asked.

'No, not until I met you. No. And of course nothing is definite yet ...'

'He's an odd kind of partner then, Derek,' Cath said.

'I don't really know the whole story,' Derek blustered a little.

'We went to your firm because you were respectable and well thought of. If we could put your name on the bottom of our notepaper it gave us a bit of standing. People couldn't think we were just two yobbos ...'

'I'm sure they wouldn't have thought ...' Derek began to protest.

Jimmy interrupted him: 'Of course that's what people would say. Two poor, mad yobbos who can't see straight because of their own tragedy. Why should anyone give us money and believe that we'd spend it right? That's why we needed people like you. Or thought we did.'

'Oh, but you do ...' Derek began again.

'No, we don't. We realised this. You see, we said to Bob that we thought the fees were a bit steep ...' Cath said.

'Not that we thought you should work for free or anything, just because our work is for charity ...' Jimmy said.

'But it turned out that he didn't really care at all about what we were doing. He just looked at a file and said there seemed to be a very healthy profit balance and he didn't know what we were complaining about.' Cath was indignant.

'He said there are sort of fixed rates an hour,' Jimmy said.

'Which there are, of course,' Derek said. 'But I imagine we could discuss ...'

'No, that's not it. You see, he didn't even care that we are a charity,' Cath said.

'Oh, come come come ... of course he does. Of course the firm realised you were a charitable ... organisation, but ...' Derek said with a little laugh.

'You didn't,' she said simply.

It was unanswerable.

Brenda Brennan was at their table supervising the serving of a second starter. She also handed Cath an envelope.

'Mrs Costello, everyone in the kitchen was so impressed when they heard you were both here, they made an immediate collection for your children's fund. Every single person contributed.'

'How did they know we were here?' Jimmy wondered.

'I'm afraid we recognised you from television. Believe me, Mr Barry was very discreet about you. Gave us no information at all about you, concealed your identity even.' Her eyes were hard and cold.

Derek remembered how he had described his guests. He flushed darkly to think about it.

Jimmy got out a postcard and wrote a thank you note to the people in the kitchen. Cathy took a receipt book out of her big,

239

shabby handbag. They counted the money and sent a receipt to the kitchen staff as well.

Two honest people maddened with grief over lost children, people who had now been ignored and patronised by his own accountancy firm. He longed to reach out and touch them and hold their hands, beg them to tell him what had happened the night their children died. He wanted to take out his chequebook and give them a donation that would stun them. He could have told them that not everyone has it easy. Take Derek's own life, for example. His wife had left him for a few years. She came back remote and distant. His son lived abroad and kept in very little contact. He felt he could talk to these odd people about it, and he would see they got not only vastly reduced fees, but that they also got a sponsorship as well.

These thoughts welled up, but Derek was a man used to thinking long and carefully before he spoke, so he said nothing. And he missed the moment where Cath had seen some softness in his eyes, and where Jimmy had thought for a second or two that Derek might not be a bad old skin.

Instead of speaking with his heart, Derek spoke with his accountant's mind.

And, as the three of them left Quentins to go back to the firm where they would pick up their papers and he would face the wrath of Bob O'Neill, Derek saw people from other tables smile at them and even clasp their hands as the Costellos walked with him.

Nobody greeted Derek Barry, partner in the accountancy firm and father of the proprietor of Quentins.

The world had changed, and not for the better.

The Independent Streak

Laura Lynch was forty when her husband left home. There had been no row. He just said it had been an empty, shallow, one-way relationship. She had not grown or developed within the marriage while he had and bettered himself.

Laura had been so dependent, so lacking in get-up-and-go, so he could no longer stay in something that was making neither of them happy. And he left with a much younger colleague, who had no problem at all in getting up and going. He had been coldly and clinically fair in the division of property, and even given her some unasked for advice.

'If I were you, Laura, I would develop an Independent Streak,' he said quite seriously, as if he had not insisted that she be a stay-at-home mother for their children.

And in the twenty years since he left, Laura Lynch did indeed develop an independent streak. She needed one since it was hard work, turning what had been the family home into a guest house. The children were fifteen, fourteen and thirteen at the time of the break-up. All of them much more like their father in personality. Independent to a fault, Laura sometimes thought.

It was never a house of hugs and spontaneous gestures. They showed no need for any emotional exchanges or confidences. So Laura learned to be independent. She learned not to be needy and never to allow herself to feel disappointed and let down over things.

She had hoped that she might meet someone and marry again,

but it did not look likely. She managed her money well, and once she had sold the guest house to buy a small garden flat, she made a sort of social life with friends of her own choosing. There were bridge lessons, and theatre groups, and creative writing classes. No empty evenings to sit brooding and wondering why she heard so little from the two daughters and son and four grandchildren that she loved so much. She must indeed have been a very dull and dependent woman as her ex-husband had said.

Amazing that she had not resented his cold parting words, but had actually heeded them instead.

It was great that Mother had such an independent streak, they told each other. A lot of their friends had the most dreadful problems with clinging mothers, interfering mothers, critical mothers. They were indeed blessed with their own.

The Lynch family often told each other this when they met once a month in Quentins for Saturday lunch. It was a tradition they enjoyed: Harry Lynch and his sisters, Lil and Kate. No spouses, just the three of them, twelve times a year they kept up with each other's lives, unlike many families they knew who just lost touch.

Lil looked forward to these Saturdays. She got her hair done and went to the charity shop. Lil's husband, Bob, was careful about money. He said that anyone with a good eye could pick up the most marvellous stylish bargains there. And he was right, Lil said defensively, as she often did. Her sons had Saturday jobs, their father didn't believe in letting young people idle about.

Kate loved the family lunch, too. Weekends were often lonely for her, since Charlie went back to his wife and children for the weekend to keep stability in the family. Charlie was so wonderful to her brother and sister: he admired Lil's crazy 1980s jackets and always asked about Harry's endless garden work.

Harry enjoyed the lunch meeting. He found Lil's Bob rather trying, telling him how to save money on phone calls, and there was something phoney about Kate's Charlie, who appeared to be running two establishments quite cheerfully. Nice to see his two sisters on their own, and tell them about the new pergola and how well the azaleas had done when repotted. He would talk too about Jan and the girls, who always spent Saturdays at the gym and didn't know where Harry had his lunch or even if he had his lunch.

Brenda Brennan wondered how long they had been coming in,

these Lynches. Must be nearly fifteen years now, or was it more? From time to time she had seen Kate in here with that Charlie, the man about town who usually brought his wife here for anniversaries or birthdays. Still, people made their own arrangements, Brenda shrugged – as she often did about the way her customers lived their lives. She knew that Lil was married to a man who had a very good job.

Bob often brought big groups to Quentins for very pricey meals. He always checked and sometimes queried the bill. Maybe that's why his wife dressed in other people's cast-offs. Harry Lynch was a dull bank clerk, whose eyes only lit up when he talked to her about growing vegetables. It was fairly easy for Brenda to talk about vegetables, since Quentins prided themselves on their homegrown organic produce. But how did people in the bank react, she wondered. But this was not her business.

Her husband said that she got far too involved in people's lives. 'Just serve them, Brenda,' Patrick would plead.

But there was no life in that sort of thing, and anyway, part of Quentins' success was due to the fact that she remembered who people were and all about them. She knew that the Lynch family always chose pasta, so she came armed with information about the really good pesto. Contained pine nuts of course, just in case anyone was allergic, but a very distinctive flavour. They would have one glass of house wine each, and Kate would stay on to read her paper and have a second and third glass on her own. There was not much that escaped Brenda.

'I see that there's a booking for twelve, under the name of Lynch, for Mother's Day. Is that your family?' Brenda asked brightly. The moment she had asked she regretted it. They were bewildered, looking at each other in surprise.

'Mother's Day. No, that's not us. We usually just give Jan a bunch of flowers from the garden,' Harry said.

'My boys wouldn't be able to afford this . . . and Bob, well, he doesn't like big gatherings,' Lil said.

'A lot of these Mother's Days and other things are just purely commercial,' Kate said with her brow darkening. Charlie's wife would undoubtedly get the full works.

Brenda recovered herself. 'You're so right, Kate, it only benefits us and the florists and of course the card manufacturers. Still, we are happy to see it! That's commercialism for you, of course!' She laughed easily and moved back to the kitchen, mopping her brow.

'Sometimes, not all the time, Patrick, but sometimes I think you're right about not getting involved in their lives,' she said ruefully.

'What have you said now?' he laughed affectionately.

'I just thought that the Lynches at table nine might have booked to take their mother out for lunch a week from tomorrow, but the thought had never crossed their little minds.'

'We don't need any more bookings. We couldn't cope with them. We're full.' Patrick was mystified.

'That's not the point. They have a mother, they haven't booked her in anywhere at all.'

'Leave it alone, Brenda,' Patrick said, shaking a spoon at her.

'Do you think she might have meant had we booked for Mother?' Kate asked.

'But we never did anything like that. Mother wouldn't have expected it. Nor wanted it,' Harry said. He would have to do a lot of persuading to get Jan and the girls to go along with such a scheme. Sundays were for long healthy walks, not for sitting down and ingesting calories.

'And even if we were to ask Mother out to lunch, it couldn't be a place like this,' Kate said. Kate had a particular distaste for those kinds of wives and mothers who wanted a silly expensive fuss made over them, just to reinforce their status.

'And she's so independent,' Lil said. 'She's always doing something whenever you want to see her.'

'Yes, I suppose so,' Kate said.

'I see her very often,' Harry protested. 'We have coffee quite a lot, as a matter of fact.'

'Only because she goes to the garden centre on late-night opening to meet you there,' Kate said.

There was a silence. Harry seemed put out. 'At least I do see her, and as Lil said, she has a fiercely independent streak. When do you see her?'

'I often ring her and suggest that we go to the cinema on the spur of the moment. Half the time she's doing something else,' Kate said. She knew that the others would realise that she only rang her mother on the nights when Charlie was unexpectedly unable to meet her.

'It's a long way for her to get into town to meet you,' Lil said.

'So what do you do for her, Lil?' Kate asked, stung.

244

Lil paused to think. 'When we go to the market and get vegetables in bulk, we often drop in. You can only buy things in huge quantities, and this way it works out cheaper for Mother, you know ...' Her voice trailed away.

'She's got loads of friends,' Harry said defensively.

'And would hate waste.' Lil was very definite on this.

'I suppose she would consider it a waste?' Kate had done the unforgivable. She had introduced some doubt about Mother's independent streak, the one solid pillar that had given them all the freedom to get on with their slightly complicated lives without considering the needs of a sixty-year-old woman, whose husband had left her two decades previously.

Lil and Harry were uncomfortable. Kate was sorry she had spoken. Their pleasant lunch was turning to ashes on them and it was all her fault. Kate needed her brother and sister rather more than they needed her. After all, they had the fairly unsatisfactory Bob and Jan, plus, of course, their children. Kate had nothing but the part-time attention of Charlie.

'Look, why don't I phone and ask her out somewhere? That would cover it.'

'We don't want to leave it all to you ...' Lil protested very feebly.

'I mean, perhaps we could ... I mean ...' Harry said very unconvincingly.

'No, honestly, I'll do it. I know that dragon lady, Brenda Brennan, hates mobile phones, but if I whisper, she can't complain.' Kate saved the lunch for them.

Mother thanked her and said it was sweet of Kate, but she and a group of friends had already planned to go out that day. But she really did want to thank Kate. So they looked at each other with relief. The day and the ritual of their monthly lunch was secure again. Silly of Kate to have thought Mother, who was so independent, might be at a loose end.

Laura Lynch sat very still for a while. This was the first time that any of her children had offered to celebrate Mother's Day or acknowledged it in any form other than a small, dutiful card.

How odd that she hadn't even been tempted to accept Kate's offer. But there wasn't a question of it. She would so much prefer the previous engagement.

As part of her Independent Streak, Laura had created an annual outing. It was called the Chickless Mothers. Women like herself, who did not have loving or demonstrative families. Women for whom there would be no breakfast in bed and huge fuss made. They knew the expression 'a motherless chick' – it was in some song. But the opposite held good too. The only rules for the outing were that they enjoy themselves, they did not speak disparagingly of their thoughtless young, nor were they allowed to make defensive speeches excusing them. It had worked very well for the past years, and on each occasion they chose a different restaurant.

This year it would be Quentins.

And the twelve Chickless Mothers would certainly enjoy that.

The Molluscs

P atrick Brennan was very annoyed when the message came. His routine prostate examination required him to return to the district hospital for some more tests.

Probably nothing at all to worry about, he had been told by the cheerful young woman from the hospital – a woman who was maybe fifteen years younger than him and who would never have to have a prostate examination herself anyway. Easy for her to say there was nothing to worry about.

'It's all your fault for making me have this checkup,' he grumbled to Brenda. 'One of the busiest weeks in the year, and I have to be out of the restaurant having bits of me poked at and frightening myself to death.'

Brenda ignored him. She was consulting her big contacts book. She would find someone who could cover for him in the restaurant. Patrick knew this.

'If I died, you could just look up that book and replace me in six months,' he said.

'Why should I wait six months?' Brenda asked, absently. 'We'll ask Cathy Scarlet or Tom Feather. One of them will do it for us.'

Anyone she suggested he would object to, and they both knew it.

'They have their own business to run,' Patrick complained. 'They can't abandon that and come in to run our kitchens because some fool in the hospital couldn't do proper tests on me first time round.'

'We helped them in the past, Patrick, and they'll do it. After all, you're only going to be out for three days.'

'That's what they say.' Patrick's voice was sepulchral.

'Oh, for God's sake, will you stop upsetting yourself. And me, Patrick. You're going to be fine and those two will be delighted to come in. Either of them could cope with anything.'

'Don't tell them what is ... what's wrong with me,' Patrick said.

'No, Patrick, I'll just say it's a mystery illness ... some kind of plague originating in our kitchens. Would that satisfy you?'

He smiled for the first time. And stretched out his hand to her.

'It's just that I was worried, if you get my drift,' he began hesitantly.

She squeezed his hand very hard. 'My drift is the same, Patrick my love, but we're both mad to be worried. Instead we should be delighted that we live in such modern medical times.' Brenda blew her nose. 'Now can I ring these two and get us sorted?' she said, briskly.

'You never said yes? Not this week, when we have so much on?' Cathy Scarlet's mouth was a round 'O' of horror and amazement.

'What was I to say? The poor guy has to go back for more tests. Obviously he thinks he's for the high jump.'

'It's probably just routine.'

'Yes, for you and me it looks like routine because it's happening to someone else. Suppose it were us?' Tom Feather's handsome face was upset.

'I know.' Cathy did know. She would have responded exactly the same way.

'So we do it?' Tom checked.

'Of course we do. I was just having a grumble. But don't forget we have that awful family with their graduation party.'

'I know, but we can use Quentins' kitchen to do some of that work there. Brenda said we can use the place as our own.'

Tom had learned that it was often wiser to tell Cathy the good news and let the bad news creep up on them. So he didn't tell her that Brenda said there was going to be a shellfish banquet organised by a company who were really and truly the People From Hell. That would be faced later.

Blouse Brennan drove his brother to the hospital. 'Should I say we'll manage fine without, or should I say we'll be lost entirely?' he asked, innocently.

Patrick managed a weak smile. 'Say you'll manage fine without me for three days but after that you'd be lost entirely,' he suggested.

'I'll make sure the vegetables are top class,' Blouse said soothingly.

'This is the week when I wish you grew oysters, scallops, clams and mussels in that garden of yours,' Patrick said.

'Molluscs,' Blouse said, proudly.

'That's right.' Patrick was surprised. His young brother had been a slow learner at school and to this day frequently read instructions on a packet by putting his finger under each word. Imagine him knowing a word like mollusc!

'The very thing, Blouse.' Patrick tried to keep the amazement out of his voice.

'I'm interested in them. They have no say in anything, did you know that, Paddy? They're just swept along by the tide and stick to rocks. They never make a decision of any kind. Isn't it a queer sort of life?'

'Well, I suppose it is, but no worse than for a lot of sea creatures,' Patrick said, mystified.

'Aw, no, Paddy, a crustacean has legs after all, or claws, and a lot of them even have a jointed shell. They've got a load of choices where to go. Not like your poor mollusc.'

Patrick Brennan took his small suitcase out of the car and went into the hospital. While he was waiting to check in, he thought about the conversation with Blouse.

He would tell Brenda about it when she came to settle him in for the night.

Brenda admired the way Tom and Cathy got down to business and how well they got on with the waiters. Monica, the Australian girl, Yan, the Breton, and Harry, a new boy from Belfast, listened intently as Tom explained how the dishes would be cooked.

'Stay up at the hospital for longer, Brenda,' Cathy pleaded. 'I can do your front-of-house bit for one night. I've seen you do it often enough. Just go through the bookings with me first and then tell me if there's anything I should know.'

From Brenda's face it looked as if she were going to agree.

After all, there was a very solid team already in place.

Mon was a great sunny waitress. Nothing could go wrong with her tables.

Yan the handsome Breton boy was charm itself.

Even Harry the newcomer was showing signs of being a reliable lad. He had the huge advantage of realising that he didn't know everything and the ability to ask when in doubt.

But even though she was tempted, Brenda said that Patrick would never get better if he thought there was nobody minding the shop. So she waited until the dinner was well under way before she got her coat and left them to return to Patrick. 'Save your strength for the real horrors ahead on Wednesday,' she said as she left.

'What real horrors?' Cathy asked Tom when Brenda had gone to the hospital.

'Oh, you know, just the usual Wednesday people,' poor Tom stammered.

'Tom. You are the worst liar in the world. Tell me what's happening on Wednesday or else I shall take out both of your eyes with the melon baller.'

He told her about the shellfish banquet for this hated public relations company.

'A seafood buffet?' she asked.

'No, specifically shellfish, the guy said. Not salmon, not smoked salmon, not trout. Unless the thing lives in its shell it doesn't get on our table.' Tom tried to make light of it.

'We can't do it,' Cathy said, grimly.

'What do you mean? We have to.'

'Listen, Tom, I've been doing the fish-buying for the last couple of weeks. The catch is very small. There were practically no prawns, the lobster cost a fortune, and the oysters had all gone to France.'

'But they'd have contacts ... I mean, this is Quentins. They wouldn't be Mickey Mouse like us ... they must spend a fortune on fish, for God's sake ...'

'Well, let's pray they do,' Cathy said.

'We've a lot of stuff frozen back at the premises. We could give them that.'

'We can't. We thawed the lot today for the Demon Graduation Party.'

'Oh, God, please, please, nice God, won't you be very good to us and let us lay our hands on some shellfish?' Tom prayed.

*

'Tell me more about this job on Wednesday,' Cathy asked Brenda when Quentins had closed. They sat in the kitchen rubbing their ankles and drinking great mugs of tea.

'Something we should never have taken on. He's the most disgusting man. He fights every bill, upsets the staff ... It has been a bit slow recently, so I thought it would be worthwhile. But I fear we have a few problems.'

'Like?' Cathy said, although she knew the problem only too well.

'Like a grave shortage of shellfish. No joy from the usual sources, I'm afraid. I've been on to them all.'

'He'll have to take salmon like everyone else. We'll tell him, Brenda, he can't expect someone to do a quick miracle these days. Those times are long gone.' Cathy spoke firmly as if to encourage her own flagging spirits.

Brenda looked up. Her face was white and drawn. 'I wish you hadn't said that. I was sort of relying on the thought that there might be a few miracles still hovering around.'

The Tuesday seemed to be ninety hours long for everybody. For Patrick, in hospital, the time crawled. He forced himself not to look at his watch again. They would have to come for him sometime soon.

Back at Scarlet Feather's premises, Tom, busy dressing the lobster for the Graduation Lunch, feared catching sight of the clock in case he would panic at how behind they were. They really needed Cathy today, but she was down at Quentins.

Cathy was purple in the face trying to rescue cream sauce that had unaccountably curdled. Brenda showed the guests to their tables with her usual polite, welcoming smile. Inside she was churning. It was lunchtime – surely the doctors must have seen Patrick by now. And if they had, why hadn't she heard? Her friend among the nurses promised to call as soon as the test results came through. Please, please, may it not be bad news.

Tom phoned when the pressure in Quentins Restaurant was at its height. Sorry, sorry, he knew this was the worst time, but the Graduation Party had hit another low. Could someone, anyone, come over with a big bowl of tomato salad? The Graduate's mother was now losing what remained of her senses and was weeping over something that had never been ordered. Was there a chance? If they only knew what it was like here!

'If you knew what it's like here!' Cathy said. She had the phone clamped against her ear while she mixed more sauce and issued directions to the waiters. Brenda's strained face moved in and out of the dining-room. She didn't need another crisis.

'I'll send Blouse,' Cathy said. 'Give him the address, will you, and get off the phone quickly in case the hospital rings.'

At half-past two, Patrick was told he had the all clear. Could he get back to the restaurant? he asked. Apparently not, still a few formalities to go through. And rest. He must rest. But he could leave tomorrow.

Three minutes later, he was on the phone to Brenda. Cathy handed her a paper towel to wipe the tears from her immaculately made-up face. The staff looked away so as not to catch Mrs Brennan with her guard down.

'Where's Blouse?' she wanted to know.

'Don't ask,' Cathy pleaded. But she wondered where on earth he actually was. It was an hour and a half since he'd left in a taxi. Please may there not have been yet another disaster to drive them mad. Had he found the right house? When she next had two seconds, she would call Tom.

But Tom called first. 'Can you talk?'

'Sure. Great news. Patrick's okay. And he'll be back tomorrow.'

'Good news here, too . . .' Tom began.

'Listen, I'm sorry for interrupting you, but have you any idea where Blouse is?'

'He's here, saving our lives.'

'The tomato salad?' she asked, bewildered.

'No, nobody's eating that, like I told them.'

'So what's he doing, then?' Nothing would surprise Cathy by this stage.

'There are about fourteen horrific children, monsters all of them. Anyway, they were annoying everyone, breaking things, sulking. Blouse has them all down at the bottom of the garden. He's running a herb competition.'

'What?'

'You wouldn't believe it. He has them captivated. They all have little yoghurt pots or cream cartons. And he's talking about lovage and verbena.'

'What about the Graduate's mum?'

'Mrs Dracula is fine. She's my new best friend, as it happens.'

'Oh, tell me about it. You turned on the charm. Maybe you could charm some shells out of the rocks for us for tomorrow here?'

'That not sorted yet?'

'No, but we're on the case.'

From his hospital bed, Patrick Brennan was also on the case. And the news was very bad. Not a prawn or lobster to be found. Patrick rang the PR man.

'Why does it have to be shellfish ... please, just tell me?'

'It's an image, a concept – the whole idea of sticking fast. We've used it in our literature just to attract this client's account. You're not telling me you're going to go back on the agreed menu ...'

'I'm not telling you anything. What are you advertising?'

'It's no business of yours ...'

'What is meant to be sticking to what? What's the concept about? Can't you tell me? We're doing the bloody presentation for you,' Patrick roared.

'All you were asked to do was to provide a shellfish buffet.'

'It's in your interest to tell me,' Patrick lowered his voice impressively.

The PR man eventually gave in and told him it was a new insurance company that stuck with you through thick and thin.

'In that case you don't need shellfish, you eejit. You need molluscs.'

'I need what?'

'Prawns and lobsters don't stick to things, you clown. They walk all over the ocean floor. Your clients would drop you as soon as look at you. What you want is molluscs. Why didn't you tell me before?'

He hung up and called the restaurant. 'I need Blouse urgently,' Patrick begged. He was told he would have to wait in line. 'We have to find him quickly, Cathy. Tomorrow we're doing molluscs.'

'Doing what?'

'Didn't they teach you anything at that catering college? Molluscs. Single shell, double shell. There's thousands of them out there, stuck to rocks. All we have to do is get them to the table.'

'Do you mean things like mussels or whelks or cockles?' Cathy felt dizzy.

'Yes, and everything else ... clams, razor shells, limpets ... Blouse will know where to find them. Where is he, anyway?'

'I'll get him to call you in the hospital, Patrick,' Cathy sighed. The restaurant must be in a poor position if Blouse Brennan was going to be sent off to scrape limpets off rocks.

Tom rang again. 'The party's over but the children won't go home. They wouldn't even come up for the group picture with the Graduate. Blouse has them hypnotised, he's like the Pied Piper. I wouldn't be surprised if they followed him back to Quentins.'

'Yeah, well ask him to break off just long enough to call his brother in the hospital. Patrick wants him to do the Pied Piper thing along the shore tomorrow to collect limpets.'

'Isn't this a totally crazy life?' Tom said, with the tone of a man who would never live any other kind of life.

Cathy felt the same. But with one proviso. She wished mightily that tomorrow night was over. She couldn't see one redeeming feature that would save them. But she had reckoned without Blouse and his newly found self-confidence.

And the next night they all watched, astounded, as the boy they had all considered slow, pointed out, with an elegant cane, the variety of shellfish displayed on what he called the Mollusc Medley. The limpet, the cockle, the whelk and the winkle ... all of them praised for their qualities of constancy. The oyster, the scallop, the mussel likewise. These were loyal invertebrates, Blouse told the group earnestly. Like the insurance company they were here to honour, these magnificent molluscs were noted for their sticking power in a world where, alas, not everything could be relied upon.

Patrick Brennan sighed a very great, long sigh. His early release from the hospital had been justified. The PR man was as delighted as the Graduate's demon mother. The PR company he ran was booking further spectaculars, but only if Blouse could be part of the package.

'He doesn't come cheap, of course,' Patrick heard himself saying. His voice sounded weak. It had taken hours to persuade Blouse not to stress the lonely, futile and pathetic lifestyle of the mollusc. He hadn't been sure if Blouse had grasped it until the very last moment. But there were lots of things he wasn't sure of any more. Like how Blouse had found all those children to help him get buckets of those terrible things to the restaurant. They kept coming in all afternoon and all they needed for payment was an ice-cream.

Best not to question good news, Patrick always believed, like the look of love and huge relief in Brenda's eyes as she reached out her hand and stroked his through the most extraordinary – and successful – evening that Quentins had known so far.

Carissima

When Brenda's great friend Nora had lived all those years in Italy, she had written long, long letters. Always she began with the word 'Carissima' ... It sounded a bit fancy, Brenda thought, a little over the top, but Nora had insisted. She spoke Italian, she dreamed Italian now. To say 'Dear Brenda' would sound flat and dull.

Carissima ... dearest ... was a better way to begin.

And Brenda wrote back faithfully. She charted a changing Ireland for her friend, for Nora who lived in the timeless Sicilian village of Anninziata. Brenda wrote how the waves of emigration were halted, how affluence came gradually to the cities, how the power of the Church seemed to slip away and change into something entirely different.

Brenda wrote that young people from different lands came to find work in Ireland now, girls who found themselves pregnant kept their babies instead of giving them up for adoption, young couples lived together for six months or a year before their marriages.

Things that were unheard of when Brenda and Nora were young.

Nora wrote about her friends in this village. The young couple who rented the pottery shop. Signora Leone. And of course Mario.

Mario, who ran the hotel.

Nora never wrote of Mario's wife Gabriella or their children. But that was all right. Some things were too huge to write about.

Brenda wrote about a lot of things, how she had met this guy they used to call Pillowcase, but was most definitely called Patrick Brennan these days, how they had fallen in love and worked in many restaurants. She told how the good fortune of running Quentins had fallen into their lap and they were rapidly making a great name for themselves. She wrote about the people who came and went, staff, and those like Patrick's brother Blouse, who had stayed and flourished there.

But Brenda only once told the deepest secrets of her soul, their great wish to have children, the long, often humiliating and eventually disappointing road of fertility guidance. That was too hard to write about.

Brenda was very helpful in that she acted as a spy for Nora O'Donoghue by going to see Nora's family. Hard, unforgiving people, who regarded her as a sinner and a fool, someone who had disgraced them by running off after a married man.

They were so uncaring about Nora's life that Brenda urged her friend to forget them. 'They have forgotten you unless it suits them,' she had written to Sicily. 'I beg you, don't listen to any pleas they may have when they are older that you should return and be their nurse.'

'*Carissima*,' Nora had written, 'I will never leave this place while there is a chance that I can see my Mario. I wish they could share my happiness. But perhaps one day they will be able to.'

Nora's Mario died, killed in an accident on the mountain roads which he drove across so fast. The village implied that the Signora Irlandese should now leave and go home.

Brenda would never forget the day Nora had appeared at Quentins, long dress, wild hair, her face mad with grief for the only man she had ever loved. She still called Brenda '*Carissima*'. They were still best friends. The long years apart, well over two decades, had changed nothing between them.

And when Nora found a new love, Aidan, the teacher up in Mountainview School, she and Brenda clutched each other like teenagers. 'I'll dance at your wedding,' Brenda promised.

'Hardly, there is the little problem of his first wife,' Nora had giggled.

'Come on, Nora, drag yourself to the present day ... there *is* divorce since 1995.'

'I managed for well over twenty years without marriage first

257

time round. I can do it again.' Nora wasn't asking for the moon and stars.

'You do what you like, but I'm not giving up on it,' Brenda threatened.

Patrick said that it was amazing they found so much to talk about. He was never jealous of their friendship, but often said that men just didn't have conversations like that about every single aspect of life.

'You are the losers,' Brenda said.

'I agree, that's what I'm saying,' Patrick said unexpectedly.

Nora went every week to the hospital where her elderly father lived in the geriatric ward. Rain or shine she wheeled him in the grounds. Sometimes he smiled at her and seemed pleased, other times he just stared ahead. She told him about any happy things that she remembered about her childhood. Often these were difficult to dredge up. She didn't tell him about Sicily because already it was fading in her mind like a highly coloured photograph left in bright sunlight. So she told him about Aidan Dunne and Mountainview School and the Italian classes. And she talked pleasantly about her sisters Rita and Helen, and her largely silent brothers, even though she hardly saw them at all.

The news that she had moved into a bed-sitting-room with a married Latin teacher had horrified them all over again. Really, Nora seemed to be a scourge sent to lash their backs.

Nora called to see her mother every week. Age had not improved her mother's temper or attitude, but Nora was determined to remain calm. Years of practice had given her a skill at being passive. And it was easy to call in for an hour and listen to her mother's list of complaints if she could go back on the bus to good, kind Aidan, who was so different and saw nothing bad in the world.

The day of her father's funeral was bleak and wet. Brenda and Patrick came but they decided against letting Aidan take part. He might be like a red rag to a bull.

Some of her students from the Italian class came to the church, an odd little group which certainly helped to boost the numbers.

'I'd ask you back, but I don't honestly think that my mother would be able to ...'

No, no, they insisted, they had just wanted to pay their respects. That was all.

Nora's mother found fault with everything. The priest had been too young, too swift, too impersonal. People hadn't worn dark clothes. The hotel they had gone to for coffee, just the family, had been entirely unsuitable.

She brooked no conversation at all about Father. Did not care to hear that he had been a kind man and that it was good that he was at peace. Instead there was a litany of his mistakes which were apparently legion and the main one was his never having taken out a proper insurance policy.

'And now of course you'll all go off to your own homes and leave me alone for the rest of my days,' she said.

Nora waited for the others to speak. One by one they did. They told Mother that she was in fine health, that a woman in her seventies was not old these days. They reminded her that her flat was very convenient for bus stops, shops and the church. They said that they would all come to see her regularly and now that there was no longer a matter of visiting Father, they would take her on different outings.

Their mother sighed as if this was not nearly enough. 'You only come once a month,' she said.

This was news to Nora. It had always been implied that the visits from her sisters and sisters-in-law were much more frequent. It meant then that she, with her weekly visit, was indeed the best of them all.

She noted it without allowing her face to change.

Rita and Helen were quick to explain. They were so *busy* and, honestly, others must remember how hard it was with *families* and running *proper homes*.

The implication was that Nora had all the time in the world and no responsibilities so should play nursemaid and be glad to do so. Nora, who worked harder than any of them, Nora, the only one of them without a car who did the awkward shopping, and visited four times as often as the others did, always bearing something she had cooked for her mother.

It was grossly unfair of them to make her of all people feel guilty. And she had promised Brenda Brennan that she would never weaken. But Nora had also promised herself that she would be polite and courteous to the family, she would not return their hostile, bad-mannered attitude.

So she blinked at them all pleasantly as if she hadn't understood the direction of their conversation. She could see it driving them all insane. Still, what the hell, she was not going to lose her dignity on the day of her father's funeral.

And after all, she had Aidan to go home to after all this. Aidan, who would make her strong tea, play some lovely arias in the background as they talked, and want to know every heartbeat of the day.

Then tomorrow she would meet *Carissima* Brenda and tell her the story again.

She looked at her sisters, brothers and their spouses. Not one of them had a fraction of the happiness she had.

This gave Nora great confidence and strength and made it easy to put up with their taunts and very obvious suggestions that she abandon everything and go and look after her mother full-time.

'I'll come round to see you tomorrow,' Nora promised as she left. She kissed the cold parchment of her mother's cheek.

Did this woman miss the man they had buried today? Did she look back at times when there was passion and love? Maybe there had never been any passion and love.

She shuddered at the thought. She who had found it twice in one lifetime.

She saw Helen and Rita looking at her oddly. She knew that her sisters often talked about her with their sisters-in-law. It didn't matter very much.

'Will you be round at Mother's tomorrow also?' she asked them pleasantly.

Helen shrugged. 'If you're going, Nora, there's not much point in us all crowding in,' she said.

'And anyway I'll be there next week,' Rita snapped.

But she could still hear them reassuring their mother, 'Nora'll be in tomorrow.'

'Aren't you going to be fine tomorrow, Nora will do any jobs for you.'

'Nora has nothing to do, Mam, she'll do all the shopping for you when she comes to see you.'

It would be like this always. But it didn't matter. None of the rest of them had known happiness like Nora had. It was only fair that she should give something back.

'Did you end up paying for their coffee and sandwiches yesterday?' Brenda asked her friend Nora.

'Brenda, *mia Carissima* Brenda, don't you always have the hard word?' Nora laughed.

'That means you did,' Brenda cried triumphantly. 'Those four kept their hands in their pockets and you, who have no money at all, paid.'

'Don't I have plenty of money thanks to good people like you?'

She went on washing and chopping vegetables in Quentins, where she was paid the hourly rate.

'Nora, will you stop and listen to what you're saying? We pay you a pittance here because you insist it will all mount up to take Aidan and yourself to Italy, and then those selfish pigs make you spend your few pounds on their bloody sandwiches. It makes my blood boil.'

'Brenda *Carissima* ... you of all people must not boil. You know they call you the ice maiden, you know you must be cool and calm. To boil would be a great, great mistake.'

Brenda laughed. 'What am I to do with you? I can't make it up for you which might stop me boiling. You won't take what you call charity.'

'Certainly not.'

'Well, swear one thing. Now. Swear here and now that you won't listen when they tell you that she needs a full-time carer and that you are it.'

'They won't!'

'Swear it, Nora.'

'I can't. I don't know the future.'

'I know the future,' said Brenda grimly. 'And I'm very sad that you're not going to swear.'

It happened sooner than even Brenda could have believed. Only weeks after her father's funeral, Nora found herself being told that her mother had failed terribly.

They didn't get in touch with her at home because the little flat she shared with Aidan Dunne was still out-of-bounds territory for her brothers and sisters. Some of the letters were sent to Mountainview School, some care of her mother. Helen directed hers through Quentins Restaurant, which was why Brenda became suspicious.

'Tell me, I demand to know what are they asking you to do now,' she begged.

'You are really a very difficult friend, *Carissima*,' Nora laughed as she polished the silver, another little restaurant job she had managed to wangle to help top up the Italy fund.

'No, I'm so helpful and so good for you. Just tell me what they want.'

'Mother is walking around in the night. It came on her suddenly. She can't bear being on her own, apparently.'

'Your father was in hospital for over three years, she had some time to get used to it.'

'She's old and frail, *Carissima*.'

'She's seventy-five and as fit as a flea.'

They looked at each other angrily.

'Are we having a fight?' Nora asked.

'No, we couldn't have a fight, you and I. You know all my secrets, where all the bodies are buried,' Brenda said ruefully. 'But believe me, I tried to persuade you not to run after Mario, and as it turned out I was wrong. You had the life you wanted. However, I'm not wrong this time and that kind of pressure was nothing to what I'm going to put on you now. Before I have to shake it out of you, what have they asked?'

'That I spend some nights in Mother's place,' Nora sounded mutinous. 'It's not much to ask. I mean ...'

'How many nights?' Brenda's voice was like steel.

'Well, until they get full-time help ...'

'Which they won't ...'

'Oh, they will eventually, *Carissima* ...'

'Don't *Carissima* me, Nora. They've asked you to go in every night, haven't they?'

'For a very short time ...'

'And Aidan?'

'He'll understand. I'd want him to do it if it were one of his parents.'

'Listen. That man had one class-A bitch of a wife already. Don't let him have a second wife who turns out to be as mad as a fruitcake.'

'We owe it, we have so much happiness, and isn't it like a bank? You have to give something out if your account is overflowing.'

'No, Nora, that's not the way it works.'

'It is for me and for Aidan too. I know it will be.'

There was a silence.

Nora spoke again. 'It's not that I don't have the guts to refuse

262

them. I do, plenty of guts. I know my mother disapproves of me, and my brothers and sisters do, but that's not the point.'

Brenda knew with terrible clarity that this was indeed the point. This family wanted to destroy Nora's happiness.

Nora had spent too many years in the hot sun of Southern Italy. It had affected her judgement, softened her mind. It was going to lose her the love of that good man Aidan Dunne.

'Will you promise me one thing . . .' Brenda began.

'I can't make any promises.'

'Just do nothing for a week. Say nothing to anyone for one week. It's not long.'

'What's the point if I'm going to do it anyway?'

'Please. Just to humour me.'

'*Bene Carissima* . . . just to humour you, then.'

Brenda Brennan called a friend who was a matron in a hospital. 'Kitty, can I ask you a very small favour? There's a nice bribe of dinner for two in the restaurant.'

'Who do I have to assassinate?' Kitty Doyle asked eagerly.

'Do you like having me around your flat, Mother?' Nora asked.

'What kind of question is that?'

'I just wondered. You don't smile. You don't laugh with me.'

'What's there to smile and laugh about?'

'I tell you little jokes sometimes.'

'Ah, don't start going soft in the head, Nora. Really now, on top of everything else.'

'On top of what else?'

'You know.'

'Can I bring Aidan to meet you, Mother? I've met all his family.'

'You haven't met his lawful wedded wife, I'd say.'

'I have, actually. I met her up at Mountainview School and I met her up at her house. You know, where Aidan used to live. I painted the Italian room so that she could make it into a dining room when she sold the house.'

Her mother showed not the slightest interest.

'Would you like me to paint the kitchen here for you, Mother?'

'What for?' her mother asked.

'No, let's leave it,' Nora said.

*

'Your mind is a million miles away, Nora,' Aidan said that night. 'Is something worrying you?'

'Not really.'

'Tell me.'

'I'll tell you in a week,' she said.

'There's nothing wrong, Nora? I can't wait a week. Tell me, tell me.'

'No, it's no illness or anything. It's just a problem. I promised I'd wait a week. You sometimes wait before you tell me things. Believe me, it's nothing sad,' she said, her hand on his arm.

'I love you so much, my beautiful Nora,' he said, tears in his eyes. 'And I too will have news for you in a week.'

'I'm not beautiful. I'm old and mad,' Nora said seriously.

'No, you foolish love, you are beautiful,' said Aidan, and he meant it.

Back in her mother's flat, Nora assessed how much she needed to bring with her. Sheets, a couple of rugs that could be easily stored when they were not in use on the sofa.

She would have to have a sponge bag, a change of shoes and some underwear that she could store in the bathroom cupboard. She must get a stronger electric light bulb. Maybe she could do some embroidery at night when Mother was asleep.

It would be so lonely without Aidan, and he would be lonely too. But there was no point in trying to get him under her mother's roof. The protest was too strong.

Brenda had been to see Nora's mother yesterday.

As always, Mrs O'Donoghue sighed and said it was such a pity that Nora hadn't turned out like her friend. Properly married, earning a decent living.

'Very selfish, of course, she and her husband not having a family just so that they could get on in their careers.'

'Perhaps they tried and the Lord didn't send them any children,' said Nora, who knew just how hard they had tried.

Her mother sniffed.

'And I hear Helen was here.'

'She hasn't been here for days,' Nora's mother said.

Hard to know which of them to believe.

Helen had said she was leaving a letter for Nora on the dresser. Nora read it. The usual stuff about how Mother was failing every day, some accommodation must be reached, the rest of them had proper homes and families . . .

There was also another couple of letters. They were about Mother's health. Nora took them down to read. One was a typed letter from a Ms K. Doyle, matron of a large hospital, responding to a request to know about the availability of in-home carers.

Nora's heart soared. She always knew that her sisters must have planned for her mother's care. But it was good to see it proved.

Ms Doyle had offered them several options but suggested first that their mother's health should be properly assessed so that her needs could be established. Then, oddly, there was a photocopy of the letter that Helen must have sent back.

Nora stood there reading.

> *Thank you for your concern. I am at a loss to know exactly who it was that contacted you, possibly my sister Nora who has been abroad a lot and is very unbalanced. She doesn't realise that our mother is a very strong, fit, seventy-five-year-old, well able to look after herself. Like all elderly people left on their own, she sometimes suffers from the need for company. But now that Nora has, we think, returned to Ireland permanently, she might well spend overnights with my mother which would get her out of another unsuitable situation and kill many birds with one stone. So there is no question of us needing any help now or in the foreseeable future.*
>
> *I am sorry that you have been bothered in this regard by my sister, who undoubtedly meant well but who, as you can see, has little grasp of the situation. I am surprised that she asked you to reply to me, but glad that I was able to set you right on this.*
>
> *Nora has always been a great problem to this family. We don't suggest that she live full-time with our mother as Nora has no social skills and is unable to be a companion for anyone. Still, the night-time company should surely benefit both of them.*
>
> *Thank you again for your courteous and helpful letter.*

Nora sat for a long time with the letter in her hand. Surely her sister had not intended her to read it. It must have been sent in error. It *must* have been. Helen would surely not want her to see what she had written. That Nora was unfit, without social skills, that Mother was fit and strong, needing no caring, that the family was trying to rescue Nora from an unsuitable situation.

But if Helen had not left her this letter on the high shelf of the dresser, then who had?

For a long moment Nora thought about her friend Brenda, dear, dear, Brenda *Carissima*, who had been so loyal over the decades, and who had asked her to wait a week. Just one week. But even Brenda couldn't have set this up.

This was a real person ... Ms K. Doyle, her name was on the hospital's letterhead. This was Helen's handwriting. Not even wily, cool Brenda could have accomplished this.

Nora went back home to Aidan.

'My week is up, so I'm telling you that I'm going to spend every single night with you until I die,' she said.

'This was what was worrying you?' Aidan was puzzled.

'Yes, I thought I might have to spend every night on my mother's sofa.'

'We'd have been very uncomfortable on a sofa,' he agreed.

'No, you'd have been grand, you'd have been here,' Nora said, stroking his face.

'I wouldn't have been at all grand without you,' he said softly.

'What was your news for me?' she asked.

'I saw Nell about the divorce. She said fine, but that we're far too old to be getting married at our age, but fine.'

'She is right, of course,' Nora said thoughtfully.

'She is *not* right. We will be married, you and I, with all our friends there to celebrate our good luck and happiness,' said Aidan with spirit.

'Aidan, you're wonderful but we can't think of it, we haven't any money, and I've been saving for it all the time.'

'But I'll have the money.'

'How can you save, Aidan?'

'Well, this man Richardson, whose kids I teach. He's a big financial adviser and he told me what to do with my money. In fact, I don't take my fee at all from him. Now each week he invests it for me and it's well over doubled. Imagine that.'

'Imagine!' She looked at him with great love.

'And now about you. Was this big decision about your mother's sofa easy to make?'

'In the end it took about ten seconds,' Nora said. 'I have to tell just one more person, *Carissima*.'

'Will she be surprised?'

'You have no idea with Brenda Brennan,' Nora said. 'She'll be pleased, but I will go to my grave wondering whether or not she's surprised.'

Homecoming

'Why did you call the place Quentins?' Mon asked one morning at coffee break.

'That's his name, the guy who owns it.' Brenda was surprised that the young Australian girl didn't know this. She was so bright, so quick.

'I thought you two owned it.' Mon was very confused. 'You mean, you could be given the push, just like me?'

'Oh, very unlike you,' Brenda laughed. 'He knows we are reliable. You're still proving it.'

'Does he know about me?' Mon wanted to be part of the team.

'Not too much detail, but yes, he would know that we hired you and we're pleased. Now is that all right?'

'Does he ever come over and see the place?'

'No, hardly ever, once he got us in to run it. Sometimes he sends friends and then lets us know that they thought it was all going fine.'

'He must trust you utterly.'

'Well, we send him the accounts regularly, but you know, I think he hardly reads them,' Brenda said wonderingly. 'And I haven't heard from him in a long time. I think I'll send him a cheery message if there's time today.'

'What makes you think there's going to be time today? There never is any other day.' Mon rinsed her coffee cup and went out to check the faultless dining tables in Quentins Restaurant.

By chance, Quentin's father came in to lunch that day. He had now retired from the accountancy practice where he had always hoped that his son would succeed him. Distanced and confused by the boy's wish to go abroad and paint, he was grimly pleased that the dream of being a great artist had somehow eluded his son.

'Do you hear any news from Morocco?' Brenda asked quietly as she settled the older man at his table.

'You'd hear more than I do,' Quentin's father grunted.

'Absolutely not. He's the employer you dream of. Not a word except a raise at Christmas, no wonder we get arrogant, Patrick and I, and think we own it ourselves.'

'By rights you should own it. Didn't the pair of you make it what it is?'

'No, your son had the dream, the idea. We just helped him carry it out.'

Brenda and Patrick never would have been able to raise the capital to buy the place, but it didn't matter. As long as Quentin lived his peaceful life in the hills of Morocco and let them at it, they had no worries. Sometimes they wondered what would happen if Quentin should die suddenly. Still, every day they worked there, their reputation increased. Brenda and Patrick Brennan would not be long unemployed in Dublin.

'My son gets many compliments for this place, but they should all be addressed to you and your husband,' the old man said gruffly.

'They are, Mr Barry, and you are kind enough to send us a lot of marvellous clients ... so please know we are very grateful.' She moved away gracefully.

Over the years she had learned just how much people like to be recognised, acknowledged, but not monopolised by restaurant staff. She wished that Quentin would come back just for a week, sit at the discreet table in the booth and see how the restaurant that bore his name carried on while he lived and painted in the hot African sun.

She would telephone Quentin now, this very afternoon. She needed to keep him up to speed about the documentary anyway. She had written when it was first suggested and asked his permission but as they had expected he wrote back to say that the matter was entirely in their hands, he knew they would make the right choice.

She reached for the telephone.

❊

He was having his early-evening mint tea served in a glass held by
a metal container. One of the little boys in Fatama's corner shop
brought it along at five-thirty every evening. Like the people who
sent him bowls of vegetables scrubbed clean to make soup, or
baskets of luscious fruit wiped lest an insect or a bruise appear.
They were so good to him. Quentin could have never asked for
kinder people, but he had an urge to go home. Just to see was it
home or another country, a different world? That was the moment
she rang. The cool unhurried voice of Brenda Brennan.

They had just served 120 spectacular lunches, his father had
been in, and one of the staff, Mon, a laughing young waitress could
not believe that they didn't actually own the place themselves, and
that there *was* a Quentin.

'Did you tell her I'd be no good to her?' he laughed as he always
did about his sexuality.

'No, I did not. You are good to her providing her with a great
restaurant to train in. Anyway, she doesn't want you, she's landed
one of our most prestigious customers from the bank next door.'

He didn't ask why Brenda called. She would come to it.

'I was thinking, would you like to come back for a visit,
Quentin? Just sit and observe us secretly. We'd love to show off
for you.'

'You're psychic ... I was just thinking of it.'

They fixed a date. It was for a few weeks ahead.

'I'll leave it to you to tell your father about your plans.' Brenda
was diplomatic.

'Thank you. I'll take my mother to choose a hat one day and I'll
probably call Father the day before I leave. Less is best. Do you
feel that too about families?' Quentin was always polite and never
intrusive. Nobody minded answering any of his direct questions.

'Well, my parents are mainly fine, but then I always had plenty
of sisters to share them with, unlike you. Sort of shared the load.'

'Yes, there was just me, a big disappointment to them both.'

'Your father's in here very regularly, Quentin. He can't be all
that disappointed in you. In fact, he boasts of being your father.'

'Imagine.' There were very bitter tones in his voice.

'Will it just be you?' Brenda asked. Once there had been a
delightful young man, Katar.

'I'll be on my own,' he said.

'I'll make sure Patrick has something from our poor imitation of
Moroccan cuisine when you come,' she promised. 'We do a nice

orange and cinnamon salad with a chicken *tajine*, but it's not quite exotic enough.'

'Probably quite exotic enough for Dublin,' Quentin laughed.

'You have been away for a long time,' she said.

She talked to Patrick about it that night.

'You should have said a couscous,' he complained. 'He'd know we were trying, at least.'

'He's not coming home to examine the food,' Brenda said.

'What for, then?'

'I don't know.' She didn't know. It seemed too odd to say she thought he was coming home to say goodbye.

He came in exactly on time and smiled warmly as he was introduced to the staff. A tall, slight man, forty-something, still handsome, tanned, but tired-looking.

'Where did he get the money to own a place like this?' Mon whispered to Yan.

'I heard it was from some inheritance,' Yan said.

'But who? Not his awful father, for sure.' Mon shook her head. 'Look at his face. He looks like a sort of saint really, doesn't he?'

You couldn't speak softly enough to avoid detection by Brenda Brennan, who could, after all, lip-read. 'Quentin's not exactly a saint,' she said to them pleasantly. 'But he came by the place legally. From an old friend.'

She watched their mouths drop open with the shock of being overheard and smiled to herself. It had been so useful, that little trick, she'd learned so very much over the years. Quentin saw her smile when she came back to the table.

'I'd love to know what you're thinking,' he said gently.

'I might even tell you later. Now I have to get the show on the road.'

Brenda made sure that Quentin had two kinds of bottled water. She sensed he would not drink wine. She ordered a tray of appetisers. Something he could pick from. She had seen enough people come and go to know that he was not going to eat very much. Quentin Barry was a sick man.

He ate in the booth and watched his mother come to lunch with three of her friends. Sara Barry had aged in a way that she would not have enjoyed had she been able to observe it properly. She looked puffy and rather silly. He would have advised her against the light pastel colours and the fussy jewellery.

Quentin's mother had no idea that she was being closely watched from the discreet little booth across the restaurant. All she cared about was that the four women at her table realised just how much she spent on clothes. She talked to them about the wisdom of having an account at Haywards store, it saved so much trouble in the end. You just waved your card and that was that, they were so obliging.

Quentin felt sorry for her. The staff in Haywards would be equally helpful and obliging had she waved a credit card, a cheque-book or a fistful of notes. He had worked there for long enough to know. All those years before his luck had changed. He knew Mr George, Mr Harold and Miss Lucy and how little respect they had for card holders above anyone else.

And he thought back on how his future had been written for him through the generosity of Mr Toby Hayward, who still wrote to him from Australia and who had given him this strange, unexpected start and a chance to own his own restaurant.

It had all been so mysterious. Quentin had been told that his best policy was to ask no deep questions.

Katar had said the restaurant had been given to him by God, some vague Irish god who knew Quentin was unhappy and wanted him to have a business that would eventually give him the funds to go out to Morocco. But then, Katar was the sunniest person Quentin ever knew.

Ever had known.

Impossible to believe that he would never hear that laugh or see those dancing eyes again. He had brought Katar to this very table once. Quentin smiled as he remembered the occasion.

'I would like to run around and tell them all at every table that this is ours, ours. Then I would like there to be a trumpet sound . . . ta-ra, ta-ra . . . and you would stand up and we would all sing . . . "For Quentin, he ees the jolly fine fellow".'

Katar would have liked that, and would have seen nothing silly or inappropriate in it. Only a celebration, like his whole happy life had been. Even the last months of his illness.

'It's so good for me, I have you to look after me, to tell me stories in the dark night. Who will do the same for you?'

'Ah, there are plenty who will.' Quentin had put cold rose water on Katar's hot brow.

'Well, you must go and find them, be ready to ask them, let them know you need help. Not the false braveness, swear to me. I will know, I will be looking at you.'

'I swear, Katar,' Quentin had said. 'No false braveness.'

But oddly, when the time did come, Quentin didn't need any friend. He just looked at the beauty of the hot country he had come to think of as his own. Lying calmly and resting there brought him peace. Life didn't seem so huge and important somehow. You were just part of a process, like mountain ranges and sandstorms and the blossoms that came in springtime. Next week he would be back there and he would wait. It would not be frightening. But first, he had decisions to make here.

About his father and mother there would be few problems. They had already said goodbye to him in a meaningful sense, long, long ago.

'Mother, can I take you out and buy you a hat?' Quentin asked on the phone.

'I'm not going out to some awful souk in Marrakesh.'

'I'm in Dublin, Mother.'

'That's good.' She didn't sound excited or pleased.

'So?'

'So, of course I'd love a hat,' Sara Barry said. She didn't say she would love to see her son, but then she didn't know he was dying.

'Did you know that Quentin's in Dublin?' Sara asked her husband that night.

'No, but he'll call from the airport before he leaves, that's what he usually does.' Derek Barry barely looked up from his newspaper.

'That's because you have nothing to talk to him about,' she criticised.

'Yes, that's true, unlike you who can compare shades of lipstick with him after all.' Derek spoke bitterly.

'See what I mean, ready to pick a fight where none exists.'

'Oh, my fights with Quentin are long over,' Derek Barry sighed.

Quentin had one more decision to make.

The restaurant. The place that bore his name.

He had asked Tobe Hayward his thoughts, but the old man had said quite simply, 'Believe me, when it comes to your time, you will do something worthwhile.'

That's all Tobe Hayward could come up with. But he also reminded him that everything was in Quentin's name.

Quentin had always supposed that he would know what to do when the time came. But he had not known how soon the time would come. How ridiculously early in fact. Still, he felt in his heart that everything was clear now, as Tobe had forecast it would be. He knew what should happen next.

For now he would get to know the staff and to talk to them.

The beautiful Mon who told him every heartbeat of her romance with Mr Clive Harris, and how she didn't give a damn about the Italian who had sweet-talked her out of all her money. He was welcome to it.

He heard from Yan about how his father back in Brittany wanted to put money into a small restaurant there for him. And how Yan didn't know how to tell him he was having too much fun in Ireland to leave.

He discovered that Harry had thought working in Dublin, the heart of the Republic of Ireland, would be a misery that he was prepared to endure in order to get a good training. But in fact he was never happier, and all his friends came down to Dublin for the weekends now. Times had changed, he explained to Quentin.

Quentin got to meet some of Brenda and Patrick's friends. The extraordinary woman who called herself Signora, who chopped vegetables, cleaned brasses, spoke flawless Italian, was going to marry a divorced man at her age, and confided to Quentin that she had the happiest life of any human on the planet.

The man she was going to marry had apparently lost money to some financier. They had been planning to have a wedding party with it but they could well survive without a party. And anyway maybe they were too old for one.

He met Blouse Brennan, brother of Patrick, so proud of his red-haired wife Mary and their little son. Blouse confided that, compared to a lot of the fellows he had been at school with like Horse and Shay Harris, he had done very well. And no one would have expected it at the time.

Quentin met all kinds of people that he never knew existed in the old Ireland. There were Ella Brady and Derry King, who were going to put together a documentary about the place. His restaurant! Quentin made a note to write to Tobe about that.

And their colleagues in Firefly Films, Sandy and Nick. Utterly dedicated to their job.

Were there people like that around when he was young, full of courage and determination? Quentin wondered. There was no one to ask. Brother Rooney wasn't there to visit any more. He had gone to some big garden in the sky.

There were Tom and Cathy, who ran a catering service. Sometimes they did outside catering for the restaurant's clients, so they were in and out of the place a lot. They were expecting a baby, and there was a lot of kissing and hugging and wishing them good luck about that from time to time.

Quentin saw the sad look on Brenda's face one day when they had gone.

'Was that something you would have liked?' he asked gently.

'Oh yes, so much. And Patrick would have been a wonderful father.'

'Still, there have been compensations?' he asked hopefully.

'This restaurant is our baby,' Brenda said, looking around the place very proudly.

He smiled and suddenly she realised that perhaps she had been presumptuous. 'I didn't mean to suggest anything except that we have loved working here,' she said, flustered.

'Did you wonder why I came back, Brenda?' Quentin asked her gently.

'Why shouldn't you come back to see how well it's all going? I told you we wanted to show off.'

Her eyes were too bright. She knew all right.

'I'm dying, Brenda,' he said.

'I brought those dates and nuts over to the booth like you asked me,' Blouse Brennan explained to his brother. 'But Brenda and Quentin were crying, so I decided not to interrupt them,' he said.

'Crying?' Patrick was surprised.

'Yes, Brenda was using the starched napkin to wipe her face.'

'That's serious crying. You were right not to disturb them,' Patrick said. 'Any other dramas out there?'

'I was afraid to look,' Blouse admitted. 'It's safer in the kitchen.' And he went back to the vegetables with Signora, the two of them chopping contentedly and expertly. It was good to be far away from All Human Life, which seemed to be fairly volatile out in the dining room.

'What about your friend, Katar?' Brenda asked, unaware of her tear-stained face.

'He went before me, last year,' Quentin said. 'Thank you for remembering his name.'

'Who would forget him? He was charming and so full of life ... to say something which is foolish, because it's no longer true.'

'He liked it here. We sat at this table and Katar said that if the poor and the sick could only eat great food like this, they would surely get well ... or at any rate, they would die happy.'

They laughed at the memory of the handsome laughing Moroccan boy, unafraid to face death, full of optimistic philosophy to the end.

'Well, that's what you could do, Quentin. Sell this place as a going concern and with the money you get set up a kind of charity ... very high-quality food for those who would not have been able to afford it.'

'I can't sell this from over your heads ... you and Patrick have made it what it is,' Quentin protested.

'We'll get employed, our name is good ...'

'But it's like your baby, you said.'

'There are other babies, Quentin.'

'But Blouse and Signora and everyone ...'

'Will also survive.'

'Isn't there enough in the business to do both ... keep this place going and the other?'

'Of course there could be, do you ever read those accountants' reports? They are always saying you should expand ... but you will want money for medication, for clinics, for whatever ...'

'No, no, I will go back to the house where Katar and I lived, that is best.' And his face looked much more peaceful as they talked about practical things. Blouse brought them dates, honey and nuts. Figures were written down on paper.

'And this film documentary, do you not want to be any part of it?' Brenda asked.

He shook his head gently. He wanted nothing at all to do with it but was happy if it went ahead.

Now he wanted her to listen carefully.

Quentin Barry was selling his enterprise to Brenda and Patrick

Brennan, who would pay him a small, once-only payment, and then a share of their profits would be paid every year to a company called The Kindness of Katar. They would cook gourmet food for those who were terminally ill.

'We'll need a lawyer,' he said. 'I don't want my father's stuffy old friends.'

'I know the very girl. Maggie Nolan. She was partly the cause of our coming here. It would be a nice way of rounding it off.'

He loved the story of Maggie's eager family and wiped his eyes. 'Katar said I cried very easily. If he could see me now,' he said.

At the end of the week, Maggie and her colleagues had been in and out of the private dining booth several times and everything was signed.

Quentin Barry had bought his mother an elegant hat and told her that she had the finest cheekbones in Dublin. He had taken his father for a long walk out by the sea and commented on the elegant boats and the good state of the Irish economy. He held their hands a little longer than usual when he said goodbye, but not so much longer that they might get suspicious.

And when he left the restaurant, he hugged Brenda and Patrick as if he never wanted to get into the taxi. If anyone was close enough, they would have heard him say that he too had a baby and that he was leaving it in good hands.

PART IV

Chapter Twelve

Tim and Barbara Brady had soup and toast for a late lunch, as they did most days. 'She didn't go to bed at all?' Barbara asked.

'Apparently not. She made a few calls on her mobile. Then she went out.'

'And did you talk about anything . . . you know?'

'No, Barbara, I said nothing about anything that was in a private letter for her, one which we were never meant to have read.'

'I'm not sure, it was open . . .'

'Anyway, we didn't discuss anything, nor, as I told you, will I bring the matter up. And she called back to ask us to go to a brunch at Deirdre's on Sunday, so that we can meet the millionaire.'

'Good, that's something,' Barbara said.

'I don't know,' Tim Brady said gloomily. 'I've had it up to here with millionaires, if you must know.'

'Apparently, your friend Ella was in America, and it didn't take her long to pick up a sugar daddy there,' Frank said to his wife Nuala.

'I don't know what you're talking about.'

'And you sure don't know much about your so-called friends. They were spotted getting off the New York flight and into a limo this morning. So can you get on to her sharpish?'

'I can't, Frank.'

'Why not? You're always bleating on about what friends the two of you are.'

'Not since you said I shouldn't be friends with her any more. She didn't take well to that.'

'Call her sometime today, Nuala,' Frank said firmly.

'He's dead, what does it matter now?'

'Today, Nuala.'

Ella was early for their meeting, but Derry was there already waiting for her in the bar. It had only been ten hours, yet it seemed much longer since they had been together.

'I had an odd, restless day, how about you?'

'Odd and restless. That covers it,' he agreed.

'Did you sleep?'

'Not a bit. And you?'

'Not a wink. So I don't think we should go to Quentins tonight. We're both so jet-lagged we might fall asleep the moment we got in the door.'

'So what would you suggest?' He was agreeable to whatever she came up with.

But she felt at a loss. If she still had her own flat, she could have made him supper. 'Do you know, Derry, I haven't any idea,' she said honestly.

'Great pair of movie-makers we are,' he laughed. 'We spent day and night in New York talking about this city of Dublin and how to tell its story, and now that we're here, we don't even know where to begin.'

They both began to laugh with a slightly hysterical tinge to the laughter. They agreed to go to the restaurant in the hotel. But just as they got up to move, a man approached them.

'Ella Brady? I'm Mike Martin. Remember we talked before about the late Don Richardson . . .'

'Yes, I was very sorry to hear of his death.' She kept moving but the man moved with them and Derry steered her to the lift.

The man positioned himself between them and the door, and spoke again. 'I know he tried to get in touch with you before he died.'

'I must go now.' She looked at Derry for help.

Very quickly Derry put his large, square frame between them.

Mike Martin reached around behind Derry. 'Please, Ella . . . it was important to him.'

'Excuse me,' she said, and made for the lift.

Derry was behind her. He turned around to the man who was still trying to catch Ella's arm. 'I think you heard the lady,' he said.

'Don't you obstruct me,' Mike Martin began.

Derry King was very swift. He was into the lift before her and then pulled Ella in with him. She was shaking and he put his arms around her to calm her down as he pressed the number of his floor. It was a bear hug, a brotherly gesture. The kind of hug he could have given to anyone who had been through a shock. It only lasted a few seconds. Then the lift stopped.

In the suite he opened a miniature brandy. 'Medicinal. I'll split it with you,' he said.

She swallowed and stopped trembling.

'Who was that?' he asked.

'A henchman,' she said.

'What a great word! What does it mean?'

'You know,' she said.

'Well, I imagine that it means a timeserver, a sidekick, a supporter. But what's a hench exactly?'

'It's okay, Derry. No need to fuss over me. I'm fine now.' She managed a watery smile.

'No, I'm interested. I'll go look it up.'

'You may find a Gideon's Bible, but I don't think they run to dictionaries,' Ella said.

'I never travel without one.' Derry went to a table where he had unpacked some books and papers. She watched, amazed, as he looked it up.

'Apparently it comes from some Old English word and some Old German word meaning a horse! Horseman! Isn't that absurd?' He was shaking his head with annoyance.

'It's not a very *big* dictionary,' Ella said.

'No, but it's a very good one. I look up ten words every day, always have.'

'Why on earth?'

'If you leave school at fifteen, it gives you a complex,' he said.

'I don't buy that. You went *back* to school, for heaven's sake!'

'Yes, but they never catch up on what you should have been learning earlier.'

'This isn't a real conversation,' she said suddenly.

'No, but it will do until we get over that guy downstairs.'

Ella agreed easily. 'I'm sorry for involving you,' she said in a low voice.

'You didn't,' Derry said.

'He's nothing. He's not important. It's not serious.'

'You know that's not true.'

'Why do you say that, Derry?'

'Because he pushed right up to you in a public space, talking about private things which he's not meant to know about in front of the whole of Dublin. He's come out of hiding, Ella, and he doesn't care who knows it. He shoved me. He was going to grab at you. It's very damn serious and you know it.'

She stared at him.

'And if it's not serious, why did you bring that laptop computer with you in that shoulder bag? I'm not a fool. You were afraid to leave it at home, Ella. So can you just stop telling me that people aren't important, that things aren't serious? Give me some credit for something, will you?' He looked angry and upset.

'All right, I'll tell you. I got a call from Nuala. Remember her in the saga?'

He nodded.

'She said she called to see how I was, but I know her husband and his brothers are very anxious indeed to find me. I'm not sure why. But I got scared and brought the laptop with me. I was hoping you might not notice ... but you have very sharp eyes. And I'm really very grateful to you for getting me out of all that business downstairs.'

'Yes, but what about tomorrow and the day after?' he asked. 'Who'll get you out of it then?'

'I'll have to think, Derry.'

'Do you trust me?'

'You know I do.'

'Then why don't we look at it together?' he said.

'What?'

'You could go phone us up some coffee and sandwiches, and we'll open it up and decide what to do.'

There were tears of relief in her eyes as she reached over to the telephone and called room service.

'*No*, Nuala, I don't know where Ella is tonight,' Deirdre said.

'You must know, you're her friend.'

'And so were you, until you started behaving like some kind of security firm trying to get her to talk to Frank.'

'It's not Frank, it's his brothers,' Nuala whined.

'Well, whoever it is, they have no sense. Ella is in bits over Don being dead and they don't have a word of sympathy for her. They just go on behaving like tracker dogs snuffling round to see does she know anything about Don's business affairs. No wonder she doesn't return your calls or speak to you or anything.'

'She *did* speak to me. She just said she was going out. I assumed it was with you.' Nuala was very plaintive.

'It wasn't, Nuala, so leave her alone, will you?'

'I'm just telling you this, they'll find her.'

'And I'm telling you this too. I don't like your tone. It sounds like a threat.'

'It's not a threat, it's just that I'm worried about Frank's brothers.'

'With every reason, and if you come at me again about them, I'll sing loud and clear about what I got up to with Eric, one of the said brothers, on your wedding day. So think carefully before hounding Ella any more. Do you get my drift?'

Deirdre hung up the telephone and took down the recipe book.

'What's that whole series of numbers there?' Ella asked Derry, pointing to a section of figures as they sat looking at the screen.

'It's like a series of routings. Someone bought a property here, sold it on there, it was sold again, the money invested here, the money taken out and put into something else.' He shrugged as he spoke.

'And could you work out where something went? Suppose you ran this program?'

'Yes, but there's no proof that it would all be in the same name, the same ownership, as it started out with at the beginning, if you see what I mean.'

'And I suppose that ordinary people don't keep records in this very complicated way.' Ella looked at him.

'No, not unless they want to obscure things.'

'And can you tell if it had been going on from the very start?' Her voice was very small.

'It goes back a fair number of years, certainly, since they set up this particular program and way of keeping records.'

'It's not a last-minute panic, then?'

'Afraid not, Ella.'

'I suppose I wanted to think they were clean at the start, but you say they were hiding things all along.'

'Perhaps they were doing it with the knowledge of clients who might have wanted to hide things also.' Derry King struggled to be fair. 'But from the sound of things, the clients were not informed of these routings.'

'I think not. So they always planned it, Don and Ricky Rice.' She shook her head in disbelief.

'About this Ricky Rice ...'

'His father-in-law. He pulled all the strings, made all the decisions. He dragged Don into it all. He was struggling to get out.'

'Sure.'

'No, I know I sound as if I'm defending Don. But Ricky Rice was the brains of it all. He ran it with an iron fist. They all had to make disks of their negotiations each day and mail them to Ricky personally. That's how much control he had.'

'Yeah.'

'What are you saying? You're just answering me in grunts, Derry. What is it?'

'There's no mention of Ricky Rice in here, none at all. That man could walk back in to this country without a fear in the world. His name is on nothing here, nothing at all.'

'What do you mean?'

'There's nothing to tie him in with any of it. The entire thing was engineered by Don Richardson.'

'Any luck finding Ella, Nuala?' Frank said when he came in.

'No.' She was sullen.

'Well, you can thank your stars that someone's prepared to go and look for her. Mike Martin phoned. He's found her, wining and dining in Stephen's Green with an American. Staying with him in the hotel there, even. Didn't take long for her to get over her grieving.'

'Frank, listen to me.'

'No, why should I? You listen to me. My brothers asked you to do a simple thing and you wouldn't do it. You *know* how much we owe them and this was one occasion when you could have done a little digging ...'

'I did do a little digging, and they won't like what I found. Not one bit. And if we don't stop hounding Ella everyone will know. Including Carmel, for God's sake.'

'Know what?' Frank was confused.

'Know what your beautiful brother has been up to . . .'

'You mentioned Carmel.'

'Yes, I mentioned Carmel, because your brother Eric, if you remember, is her loving, faithful husband. She would be most interested in knowing what he was up to on our wedding day. Our own wedding day, I tell you, Frank.'

She saw from his face that the escapade with Deirdre did not come entirely as a bolt from the blue to Frank. 'Oh shit,' he said.

'Precisely. And you knew, you *knew* about it, didn't you? Very funny, all lads together. Well, let's see what Carmel says.'

'You're not going to tell her?' Frank was fearful now. Carmel was the most fearsome of the sisters-in-law.

'I hadn't intended to, but believe me, Deirdre will if anyone goes near Ella.'

'It will implicate Deirdre too, of course,' Frank began to bluster.

'She doesn't give a damn if she's implicated or not. And indeed if I thought that this is the kind of thing that *you* go along with, I'd damn well tell Carmel myself.'

'Nuala,' he begged. 'You know I've never looked at another woman in my whole life. You know that, don't you?'

'No, I don't know, but I'm sure your brother will know and will tell me all about it when he has had to face Carmel in full flow,' Nuala said.

Ella tried to take it all in. No mention of Ricky Rice in the company that bore his name. 'Is there something missing, something we just haven't been able to access?'

'I can't see it.'

'But the very name of the company even? Somewhere in there it must show it belonged to Mr Rice.'

'That's all here. Look,' Derry said, scrolling down. 'Three years ago there was a deed transfer. Rice gave it all to Richardson. It was witnessed. It's registered. The entire company belonged to Don Richardson.'

'But why did his father-in-law run away with him, then?' Ella felt her head spinning.

'Maybe it was a set-up. If it all hit the fan, the father-in-law could run with them. If it cleared, well and good, and the father-in-law could walk home free as a bird. An older man, he might have stronger roots in Ireland.'

'And his daughter, didn't she have shares?' Ella could barely speak.

'Not that it shows here.' Derry shook his head.

'So they can all come home now? Now that Don's dead.'

'Well, Lord, Ella. I'm no expert on all this, but it appears to me from reading this for the last two hours that they could. In terms of not being held responsible.'

She was silent.

'They may not want to, of course,' he said hesitantly.

'Derry, I don't feel very well. I don't think I could go back to Tara Road tonight. Would you mind very much if I stayed here?'

'Not at all. I was going to suggest something along the same lines,' he said.

'You were? Good. Then I must ring my parents. Do you mind?'

She spoke in a matter-of-fact voice to her mother. She was going to spend the night in the hotel. There was a lot of work to be done.

'Your mom okay with that?'

'She hasn't been okay with anything I've done for two years, but she didn't make any fuss,' Ella said.

'That was Ella,' Barbara reported. 'She said we were not to wait up for her. She's going to stay the night in the hotel. They have a lot of work to do, apparently.'

'I see,' Ella's father said.

'Don't be like that, Tim.'

'I'm not being like anything. She's a grown-up woman. She's free to do whatever she wants to.' But he sounded tight-lipped.

'All I'm saying is that if you'd been talking to her, you'd have felt the same. This isn't anything like the last time. It's not a romance. I have an intuition about it.'

'I'm sure you're right. Neither of us had much intuition about anything last time round.'

'Should we order more coffee and maybe some dessert? You know, to keep us going while we work things out.'

'Yes, that sounds fine.' Ella sounded vague and distant as if she had forgotten what coffee was. 'What things do we have to work out, exactly?'

Derry walked around the room for a bit, trying to find the

words. For the first time since she met him, he seemed unsure. When he was speaking about his Foundation, about Kimberly, about his work, about his hatred for his father, he had been definite. But now he was searching for a way to say what had to be said.

'Like whether you take the bank drafts for your father. Like whether you should hand this machine in.'

She watched him objectively. A big, square man in his shirtsleeves. Someone so well-known that even Harriet and her friends had heard of him. Tired now, much more tired than he had been earlier. Those lines etched on his face, as if they would never leave.

'What do you think I should do, Derry?' she asked.

'No. No way. It's your call, Ella. I only skimmed the surface, to identify what you have to do.'

'Do I have to do these things now?' She knew she looked piteous, putting off the decision.

'Sooner rather than later, I'd say, since you asked me.' His face was worried.

'Why? It's been going on for months. Why can't we wait a little longer?' She looked at him hopefully.

'Because of that guy down in the bar pushing us around, for one thing. Because of your friend with all the brothers-in-law, for another. Because people know you have this and they want to know what's in it, and to get their hands on what they can.'

'I'm not ready yet to make up my mind,' she said.

'As I said, it's your call.'

He went to the phone and ordered the coffee. She sat there and watched the traffic of Dublin swirl around Stephen's Green.

And then they talked about other things. She told him about her driving test and how she must have been the only person in the world to drive into a motorbike three minutes after she set off. The examiner had said it was entirely the biker's fault and that Ella had been cool and responsible throughout.

Derry said he didn't remember how he learned to drive. Possibly when he was about twelve. It could have been a friend of his father's who taught him. He had often driven his father's van home when the man had passed out.

He asked Ella what else had happened in her odd and restless day. She told him about her lunch with Deirdre, and about the planned lunch party to meet him on Sunday, and the news that the marvellous twins from Hell would be there.

He wondered were there any hints about handling them.

'Tell them nothing about yourself,' Ella warned him.

'I'm good at that,' he admitted.

'You are, too,' she said, smiling at him.

'I'm sorry. Does that make me some kind of a pain?'

'No, not at all. We're all so blabbermouth here … telling everything. You're a refreshing change, keeping yourself to yourself.'

'Ask me anything, Ella, and I'll answer.'

'No, of course I won't.'

'I want you to. I want to be free and open and say what I mean. I've not been that for a long time.'

'Can it be about me and not about you?'

'Anything you like.'

'All right, Derry, if this isn't cheating … What would you do about all this if you were me?' With a sweep of her hand, she pointed to the laptop computer.

He paused, but she didn't rush in. She knew that he was going to answer. Eventually he spoke. 'I'm not you, Ella. But I promised you that I'd answer and therefore I will. I would take the bank drafts for your father, but I know you are not going to do that. And I know without your telling me that he wouldn't take them, either.'

She blinked with amazement at his understanding.

'And about the rest of it, I would hand it over. That's what I, Derry King, would do, but I don't know what you, Ella Brady, should do. If it were my own land and my fellow citizens, I would have to do that. I would think it was illegal to sit on such information and say nothing. But here it could be different. And I know how much you loved this guy, and don't want people's heavy boots walking around in his business. So this is possibly not an option for you at all. And may never be. Now, Ella, is that up-front and blabbermouth or what?'

She looked at him with such gratitude she could hardly speak. 'Thank you, Derry,' she said eventually.

'No, it doesn't hurt to be challenged.'

'You've been a very good friend to me,' Ella said. 'I'd like to do the same for you.'

'Maybe you will,' he said.

'You're right about one thing. I'm not going to take those drafts. There were people who were left much worse off by this whole disaster than we were. And you're right too that my father wouldn't want them, either.'

He nodded.

'But the truth is, I don't know what I'm going to do about all this mess here in the computer. You're right, it will have to be sooner rather than later. But there's something else, just one thing I have to do first.'

He put his head on one side to listen to her.

'Could I talk to you about that tomorrow?' she asked him.

'Whenever, Ella,' he said.

'Thanks, Derry.'

And they sat there as old friends do when they are tired, when there's nothing that has to be said because everything is understood.

They made plans for their Saturday. Derry was to take a bus tour of Dublin. Ella would go to Quentins and get things moving. They would not meet again until they went to Deirdre's apartment, at noon on Sunday.

'What shall I bring?' he asked.

'Wine,' Ella said.

'How much wine?' he wondered.

'Relax. I know this is Ireland, but just one bottle. White or red.'

'Thanks for marking my card,' he said.

'Thanks for giving me a place to sleep,' she said, taking off her shoes.

'Now please. I am a gentleman, in my heart, anyway. Please have the bedroom,' he begged.

'Out of the question, Derry. I sleep on this lovely sofa. Put that rug over me, will you? I'll be out of here before you wake.' She gave him a big, cheerful smile.

'You're a great girl, Ella, and it's a pleasure to be working with you,' he said as he tucked her feet in.

'You're a sort of hero,' she mumbled.

'What?' he asked.

But she was asleep.

At 9 a.m. Derry woke to the phone. It was Kimberly. 'God, you were asleep! I'm just so sorry,' she said. 'I was wakeful, I thought I'd call you.'

'No, I have to get up, it's fine,' he said.

'All I want to know is, did you survive?' she asked.

'I think so. I haven't seen much of the place yet.'

'But no dramas, no scenes, no regrets?' she wanted to know.

'No, none of those things, Kim,' he said.

He looked at the door to the sitting room, which he had left open. Was Ella awake? Listening? He had better go and see. 'Hold on, Kim,' he said, and walked next door. The sofa had a folded rug on it and beside it was her computer. With a note on top.

You are a generous man, Derry King. I will never forget your kindness to me last night. Please, can I leave this machine with you to look after for me? I will have made my decision about what it contains by Sunday night, and I so appreciate your help.

Love, Ella

He went back to the telephone. 'Sorry, Kim. I thought it was room service. No, everything's fine here, as you said to me years ago. It's an ordinary place, not full of dragons, as I thought it might be.' He heard her breathe more easily.

'Thank God, Derry. That's what I wanted so much for you. You deserve it,' she said.

He sat for a while thinking about their conversation. In his whole life he had never lied to her so much. Everything was *not* fine here. He had not been checking room service. There were more dragons in this place than he had encountered for a long time. None of them having anything to do with him but everything to do with Ella Brady.

Chapter Thirteen

'I'm sorry for staying out all night,' Ella said. 'I hope you weren't worried or anything?'

'No, not when you called, of course not,' her father said.

'I meant worried that I was going to start yet another unsuitable affair.' She managed a slight smile.

'No, heavens, no,' he protested.

'Derry's not in the same league at all, totally different. He's all work, no time at all for relationships of any kind. Anyway, you'll meet him tomorrow at Dee's place.'

'And is he enjoying Dublin?' Ella's mother asked.

'Hard to know. He plays it very close to the chest.' Ella's face was thoughtful. She seemed miles away.

'Will you be at home today?'

'No, Mother, I've a lot of things to sort out.' Again she was distant. 'I want you to think about something very seriously,' she said eventually. 'All the money you lost because of Don, it's there, you know, in this safe deposit box, banker's drafts, cash, bearer's bonds, whatever. You've read the letter. You know where it is. I haven't looked, but I know it's there. If you want to take it, I'd be happy for you to do that.'

'Now, Tim,' Barbara said in triumph, 'I *knew* she would feel like this. Your father said not to mention it to you, but I said you'd see sense about it all. After all, it was his last wish that you should be seen all right and not have to work like a dog.'

'Oh, I'm not taking one euro of it, Mother, but you and Father, that's different. It's your choice.'

'And of course, if we don't take it, then it just lies there,' Barbara Brady was almost pleading.

'Or we could give it to others who were defrauded,' Ella said crisply.

'We don't want it,' her father said.

'Tim!'

'Discuss it today. Tell me what you come up with tomorrow. Oh, and there's another thing, Dad. In your talking to people, did you think that Don or Ricky was the brains of the outfit?'

'Ricky Rice, they said, but Don injected all the charm and the sort of razzmatazz into it,' Tim Brady spoke ruefully. A man reduced to living in a wooden house in his own garden because of someone's charm and razzmatazz.

'Would it surprise you to know that Ricky Rice owned nothing, that it was all in Don's name? Ricky is free to come back here any day he wants to and may well do so now that Don is dead.'

'He'd never have the gall. He couldn't face people who've lost money,' Ella's father said.

'If he wasn't a part of it, then why did he flee?' Ella's mother was practical.

'I don't know. I've been thinking about that all night,' Ella said.

'They were always together, he and Don, and he was crazy about his grandchildren. Maybe he couldn't bear to let them go.' Tim Brady tried to work it out.

'But why wasn't his name on things?' Ella wondered.

'There must have been a good reason,' Tim Brady said.

Ella drove down to the Liffey and parked her little car. She walked around the apartment blocks where Don Richardson had had his little hideaway, the place he was meant to be living when he stayed all that time with her. They were small and purpose-built. Not much movement around the place on a Saturday morning. Perhaps people would come out later and buy papers and milk for their coffee. She must enquire what had happened to his little flat here. Who had bought it, who lived a life in those four walls now.

Then she drove back to look at her own flat. The place where she had been so happy with Don. It was rented now by two girls who worked in the television station down the road. Ella had found them in twenty-four hours, once she decided to move. She had slaved to leave the place looking perfect, and even donated some of her own possessions. Like the duvet. She could never sleep under it again.

She parked across the road and looked at the place thoughtfully for a long time. If it had not been for meeting Don Richardson, she might be living there still to this very day. Her garden was shabby. Had she ever noticed that before? She longed to go over and tidy it up a bit, take away some of the autumn leaves and dead stalks of flowers. But what would they say if they had seen her, the women who worked in the television station? They had already thought her eccentric. After all, the time they met her she was famous, her photograph every day in the evening newspaper, usually beside the words 'love nest'. If they were to spot her back months later, kneeling in their garden, then they really would be alarmed.

She drove past the school where she had taught. She had been happy there too, before Don Richardson had been part of her life. The kids had been mainly great. She wondered how the new teacher was getting on. Was she able to cope with loudmouths like that brassy Jacinta, who always answered back and went as far as she could get away with? Still, no point in sighing over them. Kids would learn with whoever was put in front of them. They were very resourceful.

Which reminded her about Maud and Simon, who were coming to lunch tomorrow. She must find out how they were related to Tom or Cathy, whichever it was. They kept saying that Cathy's parents were not really official grandparents, but then they got everything so confused. Dee said she did hear once, but it was all so complicated and far-fetched that you'd be asleep by the time it was explained.

She drove south of Dublin, then through the suburbs and by the sea to Killiney, where Don and Margery had their elegant home. Where his sons had played tennis, where his father-in-law had visited so often it was like his second home. Ella knew the address but she had never seen the place. Today she needed to look at it.

It said Private Road, but there was no gate keeping you out. Just the words and the size of the house would do that, keep you away, unless you had business there. She drove slowly along, noticing the gardeners here, the window-cleaners there, the activity of an autumn Saturday morning in a wealthy area. She saw the big cars parked in the driveways, the women who dressed to go to the supermarkets and shopping centres, the expensive security systems. This was where Margery Rice had lived for years with her father, husband and sons. Yet she must have lived a lot of the time on her own. Her sons had been at school, her father out working, her husband in the arms of Ella Brady. And today Margery was calling herself Mrs Brady and living in Playa de los Angeles, in Spain. Did she want to be back in this splendid house with the immaculate green grass? Had it been sold, or did they rent it out? Would Margery and her father, if they were so blameless about everything, come home and take up where they had left off?

She got out of her car, went to lean on the gate. She had to study this place and see if it told her anything at all about what might have happened.

A woman came out to speak to her. She was about twenty-five, with jeans, untidy hair, and a two-year-old by the hand. 'Can I help you at all?'

'No, I'm just looking at these lovely homes. I used to know people who lived here, the Richardsons.'

'Oh yes, indeed.'

'Did you know them?' Ella asked.

'Only knew *of* them. I'm sort of house-sitting this place. My uncle rented it after they left. He was a great friend of theirs.'

'He must have been very cut up when Don died.'

'Yes, I think he was,' the girl said, rescuing the child who had run away.

'He's sweet, isn't he?' Ella said when the child had been retrieved.

'He's Max. He's a handful. It makes it difficult to go out and work, so that's why it was wonderful to get this place right out of the blue. My name's Sasha, by the way.'

'I'm Ella.'

'Would you like to come in and have a coffee?'

Ella thought for a moment. The name Ella hadn't rung any alarm bells, reminding the young woman of love nests. So why not then? She followed Sasha into Don and Margery's house.

It was fully furnished. There were paintings on the walls by artists she knew Don liked. There were Don's kinds of books. Nothing could have changed. This house was as they had left it the day they disappeared.

'I'd have thought it would be ... you know, more bare.'

'So did I when my uncle approached me. You see, Max doesn't

have any father on the scene, if you know what I mean, and I'm a bit of a family problem one way and another!' She smiled engagingly. She was an attractive person. She showed Ella how she had covered a lot of the good pieces with sheets so that Max wouldn't get his sticky fingers all over them. There was a view of the sea from one side of the house and of the countryside stretching down to the Wicklow Mountains from the other. It was a dream house. No wonder Sasha felt she had fallen on her feet to get to stay there.

'And does your uncle stay here too?'

'He comes and goes, but he travels a lot. Mike's not someone you'd pin down.'

'Mike?'

'That's my uncle's name. Mike Martin. You must know him?'

'I've seen him on television, certainly,' Ella said, looking around her nervously. 'And are you expecting him today, do you think?'

'Oh, he never says, just turns up.'

Ella put down her coffee and said she had to go.

Sasha was disappointed. 'To be honest, I was hoping you'd stay. They're all so old round here, and desperately rich. You're more normal.'

But Ella moved very quickly. Mike Martin was the man who was looking for her and the laptop.

'You didn't say how you knew the family,' Sasha said as she came to see her off.

Ella thought for a moment. Sasha would tell Mike anyway. No point in hiding anything now. 'Actually, I'm a bit of a problem in my family too, Sasha. The reason I knew them was that I was in love with Don Richardson. I was mad about him, and my heart is broken because he's dead. I just wanted to see where he lived when he was alive.'

'Oh my God,' Sasha said.

'So perhaps if you didn't tell your Uncle Mike, it might be better. For all of us.'

Sasha nodded vigorously, and Max held out a face covered in ice-cream for a goodbye kiss.

Nothing would be said about her visit.

For the moment.

Ella had bought a sandwich and a carton of milk. She drove up to Wicklow Gap, where you could sit and see nothing but hills and sheep and rocky paths down to a river in a valley. She always loved it here, and somehow things seemed clearer.

She took the rug out of the car and sat for a long time with her eyes on the quiet scene around her. Sometimes cars passed by and once or twice they parked nearby to look at the view from this vantage point. But nobody bothered her, and she wasn't really aware of them. And eventually the place worked its magic as it always did, and she got back into her car and drove home.

Her parents were anxious to discuss money, but Ella told them there was no need. 'Just listen,' Barbara Brady pleaded. 'Your father won't take it and therefore I have agreed.'

'But not with your heart, Mother.'

'My heart's not important in all this. He's right. There are people worse off than we are, and it wouldn't be fair.'

'I don't have to do anything about it until tomorrow night. You can have more time,' Ella said.

'And what are you going to do tomorrow night?' her mother asked fearfully.

'I'm not quite sure, Mother. That's the truth. I think I know, but I'm not totally certain just yet.'

Deirdre said she'd have everything ready by noon, and that Ella should collect Derry from the hotel and bring him along early so that he didn't have to come in to a room full of strangers.

He was horrified when he saw that Ella was driving. 'Somehow I never thought of myself as trusting my life, what's left of it, to you.'

'I take deep offence at that. You drove me around New York and I put up with that,' she said, avoiding a bus neatly.

'Are there any traffic cops here at all?' he asked through his fingers, hiding his eyes.

'Don't be silly, Derry. It's easy today. You should see a crowded weekday at rush hour. Thing to remember is that no one indicates left and right.'

'Including you?' he asked.

'I don't want to confuse them,' she grinned.

'I'm going to change the habit of a lifetime and have a stiff drink,' he said when they got to Deirdre's.

'Thanks be to God,' Deirdre said. 'Ella said you sipped at one white wine for three hours and I was wondering what we'd do with you, especially when you meet everyone. Maud and Simon came an hour early to set up their puppet show.'

'It's all very different,' said Derry King as he sat down and allowed the panic he had felt over Ella's driving to subside.

Chapter Fourteen

'Ella says you and your wife were very good to her when she was in New York,' Barbara Brady said.

'My former wife Kimberly talks very highly of Ella, and so do I. You have a very bright daughter, Barbara.'

'We love to hear that, any parent does. Do you have children, Mr King?' Ella's father was more formal.

'Oh, call me Derry, please. No, no children. I wish we had. We are an unusual couple in that our separation did not make us enemies. We would have shared children quite amicably. I really do wish Kim well, and she me. I was resisting coming to Ireland for a lot of personal reasons from the past. Kim is delighted that I faced up to it at last.'

'And are *you* delighted?' Ella's father was sharp, observant.

'I'm not sure yet, Tim. It's early days.'

'You and she might get back together one day,' Barbara suggested.

'Oh, no, that's not going to happen. Kimberly has a new husband. They are very happy together.' He spoke simply, as if stating a fact.

Just then Brenda Brennan came in. He recognised her at once from the photographs in the Quentins file he had studied so carefully in New York. They didn't need to be introduced, but talked together easily. She was as he knew already very groomed and in control. But warm as well. She seemed genuinely interested in the things they had talked about, and anxious that his stay in Ireland would be a good one.

'We'll want to keep you here in Dublin all the time, but you'll want to travel, maybe go to the west. It's not a big journey by American standards.'

'A perilous one on these roads, I'd say.'

'Not at all. Grand, big, wide motorways nowadays. You should have seen it back when,' she said proudly. 'Where are your people from, by the way?'

'I have no people.'

'I'm sorry, I misunderstood. I thought Ella said you had an Irish background, as so many Americans coming here do, you see.'

'I do have an Irish background on one side of my family, but no people.'

'So you won't be looking for roots then?'

'No way.' Derry realised he sounded sharp and short. He had better say something that made him seem less abrupt. 'But as it happens, my father's people did come from Dublin.'

'Great. I like to hear of Dubs doing well. My husband is from the country, you see, and he says that they are the lads who succeed abroad.'

'I wouldn't say my father did well.' Derry's eyes were bleak.

Brenda Brennan had had a lifetime of reading faces and moods. 'No? Well, his son doesn't look too much like a loser to me,' she said with a bright smile. She was rewarded. He smiled back. 'Let me introduce you to a couple of people,' she said efficiently. 'These are Ria and Colm. They run a magnificent restaurant on Tara Road, which you must visit while you're here and drop little cards advertising Quentins on each table!'

'As if she needed it!' Ria was small, dark and curly-haired with a huge smile. Her husband was handsome and thoughtful-looking.

Derry saw Ella looking over to see that he was all right. He raised his glass to her. He felt for a moment as if he belonged here in this easy place where no demands were being made on him. He must beware that feeling. It was probably brought on by the strange, strong drink he had taken to recover from Ella's driving. He would have no more. In fact, this moment he would ask for an orange juice.

Beside him, the small, earnest face of a blonde girl aged ten or eleven appeared. 'May I refresh your glass?' she asked.

'That's very good of you ... um, do I know your name?'

'You might have been told about us. I'm Maud Mitchell. My brother Simon and I are providing the entertainment this afternoon.'

'Oh, isn't that splendid. I'm Derry. Derry King.'

'And what do we call you? Simon and I, we're always calling people the wrong thing.'

'Derry,' he said.

'Are you sure? You're much older than we are.'

'Yes, but I want to feel younger than I am, you see.'

Maud accepted this as normal and suggested that he have a grapefruit juice mixed with a tonic. It was meant to be refreshing. Of course, strictly speaking, it was actually two drinks, but since he was the guest of honour, it would probably be all right.

'Am I the guest of honour?' he asked.

'Yes, because we have to check with you about the entertainment. We can't dance because there isn't a proper floor, only an old carpet. We brought a puppet show but Tom and Cathy think it might be too long. We were going to sing, and with you being an American, we were going to sing awful things like "When Irish Eyes are Smiling" and "Come back to Erin", which is what they all loved when we were in Chicago.'

'Are they awful things?'

'Well, they wouldn't sing them here, if you know what I mean. And then we were told you didn't want any of that stuff, you weren't a normal American.'

'No, no, that's true.' Derry was delighted with the child. 'And what would they sing here, do you think, given your choice?'

'Well, "Raglan Road", "Carrickfergus". I'll ask Simon. He's better at judging, but the main thing is that we're not to bore you by singing too long. That's what we do sometimes, go on too long. The puppet play is seven minutes, so if we sang two songs, would that be fair?'

'That would be great,' he said. 'Will you start now?'

'You must have very funny parties in America,' Maud said. 'Of course we can't start now, we have to wait until they're all sitting down with their puddings and cups of coffee.'

'Ella, I'm desperately sorry about the twins monopolising Mr King,' said Cathy. 'I've tried to break them up half a dozen times, but he says he's enchanted with them. He won't talk to anyone else.'

'Don't worry, he really is enjoying them. I've never seen him so happy.'

'It's a great party, Dee,' Ella said.

'Nicky and Sandy are a little disappointed they can't talk to him more – he's spending all his time with those kids.'

'He keeps shunting people away when they try to rescue him,' Ella said. 'I wish I knew what they were talking about.'

'Brenda Brennan can actually lip-read,' Deirdre said. 'I'll ask her later.'

The twins were busy explaining who they were. 'You see Cathy over there with the big stomach? It's a baby actually, but that's not the point.'

'No,' Derry agreed.

'Well, she's the daughter of Muttie and Lizzie, his wife. And we once went to live with Cathy and the husband she had then, who was Neil Mitchell, and he's our cousin. Neil's father and our father are brothers. So that's it!' Maud was triumphant.

'But you live with Muttie?'

'Yes. And his wife Lizzie.'

'Good. But why, exactly?'

'Father and Mother aren't able to have us. They'd like to, but they're not able to so we go and see them on weekends to say hallo. Muttie drives us in his van.'

'And why can't your parents have you?'

'Mother has bad nerves and then Father goes travelling. It's better we stay with Muttie and his wife Lizzie.'

'Nerves?'

'Yes, she gets worried about things and then she drinks lots of vodka and doesn't know where she is any more.'

'And why does she do that? Drink the vodka?' Derry asked.

'It helps her nerves. It's like a magic potion. She forgets whatever was upsetting her. The trouble is that she makes no sense and falls down and everyone gets cross with her,' Maud said.

'But if she stopped, then you could both go and live with her, couldn't you?' Derry was unforgiving about a woman who could leave such marvellous children with strangers.

They explained that they had a brother, but he had done some crime, he was never spoken of, and he didn't come home. One time he used to work in Neil's father's office with Uncle Jock, but he didn't any more and he had gone away. 'Are we talking too much about ourselves?' Maud wondered. 'We haven't asked you any questions so that you could have a bit of talking.'

'Not much to know about me. My father had bad nerves too. He used whiskey as a magic potion to make them better. Lots of it.'

'And did it work?' Maud asked.

'No, not at all. It made him worse.'

'And did your mother go wandering off on travels like our father does?' Simon was so innocent it nearly broke Derry's heart to see children accepting this intolerable state of affairs.

'No, she couldn't. She had to raise her children, and raise us without any money or support.' His face was hard now.

The children noticed. Maud spoke gently. 'But if his nerves were bad, what could anyone do about it?'

'He could have tried to stop drinking. He could have kept a proper tongue in his head to my mother.'

'But he didn't mean all those things,' Simon explained as if to a simpleton. 'When Mother has been drinking she tells Father terrible things like that he has other ladies, and that we are monsters and sneak money from her purse. None of us take any notice.'

'What?' Derry was amazed.

'Well, you *can't* take any notice, they don't mean it. Wouldn't they much prefer to be living a nice, peaceful life like everyone else?'

'And you don't hate them both?'

Simon and Maud looked at him as if he were from another world. 'Hate them? Your mother and father? Nobody could do that. It isn't possible.' They spoke every second sentence.

He was silent for a while. The twins looked at each other. He looked as if he might be going to cry.

'Are you all right, Mr Derry?' Maud said.

'Did we talk too much?' Simon wondered.

Derry King shook his head.

'Do you think we should do the entertainment now?' Simon asked Maud.

'Maybe it mightn't be right for entertainment, Simon, you know the way it sometimes just isn't and everyone expects us to know.'

'I could check with Cathy,' Simon agreed.

'But we don't want to leave him all upset,' Maud said.

Derry still had said nothing. His face was working as he tried to hide his emotions.

'Maybe, Mr Derry, you could go behind the sofa and have a big cry if you want to about your father's nerves and then you'd feel better. Often when we go to see Mother, afterwards we have a big cry to think of all she missed. Would you like to do that?'

'No, but I might have one later,' he stumbled out the words.

'Yes, I bet you will.' She patted him consolingly on the hand in the shared friendship of those who were children of the nervy.

Brenda Brennan, who was lip-reading, reported the conversation to Ella. 'Maud is urging him to go behind the sofa and have a big cry.'

'Jesus, Mary and Joseph. Is he going to?'

'He says he'll have one later.'

'And what's the boy saying?'

'He's wondering whether they should get on with the entertainment,' Brenda reported.

'I think they should start it almost at once, don't you?' said Ella.

Cathy announced that the puppet play, which was about seven minutes long, was called 'The Salmon of Knowledge', but the salmon puppet itself had been damaged in transit and had lost some of his scales, so everyone was to imagine it more scaly. The audience cheered it to the echo, Maud and Simon took several bows. They asked if there were any requests for songs. They were allowed to sing two, they said, looking eagerly around the room, sure of the delighted enthusiasm they would receive.

Derry King couldn't bear them to wait one more second. He heard himself calling for a song. 'Carrickfergus'. He didn't know it at all, he just remembered the name the twins said people liked.

They had true little voices and stood very still, side by side, singing the song of lost love and dreams.

> The seas are deep, love, and I can't swim over
> And neither more have I wings to fly
> I wish I met with a handy boatman
> Who'd ferry over my love and I . . .

Derry felt a very unaccustomed prickling in his nose and eyes. He *hated* this kind of music, glorifying loss and building up a sentimental image of the Old Country. He was not going to let two simple children who had seen no violence in their home make him change his own attitudes. Jim Kennedy was a violent man who had made life hell for everyone around him. There was no way Derry was going to go all soft on him now. There was just some small seed there that made him think he understood why his mother forgave him so often. It must have been some kind of belief, like these children had said, that Jim Kennedy like any other drunk would have preferred a different life, but it had somehow escaped him. Was that in his mother's heart as she insisted on staying in the home that Derry had been urging her to leave?

They were at the last verse now, and generously allowing the audience to join in. Even encouraging them by raising their arms.

> I'm never drunk but I am seldom sober
> A handsome rover from town to town
> Ah, but I'm sick now and my days are over.
> Come all you young men and lay me down.

They all clapped and praised Maud and Simon. The twins were busy trying to decide what their second and last song should be.

'Do you know, that was so terrific, I wonder if you'd consider quitting when you're winning?' Cathy suggested.

It was not a concept that the twins grasped easily. But Maud glanced over at Derry King. He was the guest of honour, the man they had been asked to entertain. She saw what the others had already noticed. That tears were falling unchecked down his face.

'You're right, Cathy. I think we should leave it. Not always, but just this once.'

'Love you, Maud, and you, Simon,' Cathy said.

'Everyone's getting very odd round here,' Simon said, annoyed that they hadn't been able to sing 'Low Lie the Fields of Athenry'.

'You don't have to be quiet just because I cried, and you don't have to drive at five miles an hour because I dared to criticise the mad speed you went at on the way here,' Derry grumbled.

'Lord, but there's no pleasing you today,' Ella said with a sigh.

He was contrite. 'There *is* pleasing me as you put it. I did so enjoy that lunch. Everyone was so welcoming. Thanks, Ella.'

She smiled at him. 'Go on, they were delighted with you. All of them.'

'Were they?' He was childishly pleased.

'Oh yes, and Brenda says now that she's met you, she has less anxiety about the project. My parents don't think that you're a big bad dangerous Yank. My mathematics pupils love you to bits. You did yourself a lot of good!'

'I had a happy day.'

'So did I. Which is just as well, because I have a lot ahead of me,' Ella said.

'You do?'

'I do, Derry. I want to sort this whole thing out about Don's computer. Finish it, once and for all. And I wonder if I can do it from your suite in the hotel.'

'Sure.'

'You're very restful, do you know that? You don't say big long sentences when one word will do.'

'Good,' he said with a smile.

'I wouldn't be able to do this without you, Derry,' she said.

She was grateful that he hadn't asked her what she was going to do, but then Derry was a practical businessman. He knew he'd find out just as soon as he got to his suite.

'Why don't you make Muttie and Lizzie some sandwiches?' Cathy said as she let the twins off in her old home in St Jarlath's Crescent. 'I'll leave them some pavlova as well. Apparently Dee is on a diet and won't allow it to stay in her house overnight, in case she eats it.'

'Did you ever hate Muttie and his wife Lizzie?' Maud asked Cathy in her normal conversational tone.

'No, Maud, never. Did you?'

'Of course not.'

'Then why do you ask?'

'Something Derry said. He said he hated his father.'

'He said that?' Cathy was shocked.

'Not exactly, but nearly. He has cousins here, but he's not going to look them up,' Simon confirmed.

'They're called Kennedy and they're house painters here in Dublin,' Maud said, proud to have got the information.

'I know them,' Cathy said. 'They work with Tom's father.'

'Will we have a surprise party and bring them all together?' Maud suggested.

'No, Maud. I know I'm a dull stick, but believe me, that's not a good idea,' said Cathy, who decided she must ring Dee and tell her at once.

Ella and Derry made a pot of tea from the little tray in the room. 'First I'll call my parents, ask them if they're sure they don't want to take the money and run.' She made the call swiftly.

They wouldn't be happy to be paid off in this way, they told her.

Yes, of course, if there was compensation, if insider trading could be proved, then they'd be happy to have a share, but not this way.

'We liked Derry King,' her mother ended.

'And he you, Mother.'

She sat very still for a long time after that.

Derry sat equally calm, sipping his tea.

'Right,' she said eventually.

'Tell me what you're going to do.'

'I'm going to call his wife. Ask her what she intends to do. Does she want to have a life in Ireland again, does she own that place in Playa de los Angeles? It's the only one that's not owned absolutely by Don. Maybe he wanted that as a home for her and the children. Maybe he left her a note, too.' She was very calm.

'And then?' Derry King said.

'And then, depending on what she says, I will most probably call the Fraud Squad here and ask them to come to the hotel lobby and collect the laptop.'

'And what might she say that would change your mind?'

'If she says she will have nowhere to live and she can't bear the shame, I'll ask you to help me erase the stuff about her home.'

'Very generous of you.'

'I owe him that.'

'You owe him nothing. We've been through this.'

'Then you'll remember I want to behave perfectly.'

'He's dead, Ella. He doesn't know how well and perfectly you'll be behaving.'

'Please, Derry, help me.'

'How?'

'Sit beside me while I make the call.'

'You've thought it all out then?'

'Yesterday, all day. I made a tour of the past, pulled it all together. This is what I want to do.'

'Right, I'll sit beside you,' he said.

The phone only rang six times, but it seemed like ages. A man answered.

'Can I speak to Mrs Margery Brady, please?' Ella felt her voice faltering. Derry squeezed her for solidarity.

There was a pause. 'Who?' the man asked.

'Mrs Brady. Margery.'

'Where did you get this number?'

'Is this 23 Playa de los Angeles?'

'Yes, but ... this is not a number that anyone has ...'

The voice sounded familiar. Terribly familiar.

'Don?' Ella gasped.

'Angel? Ella, is that you? Angel?'

She couldn't find the breath to say a word.

Derry had an arm around her shoulders and was offering her a sip of water. She pushed the water away but held his hand very tight.

'Don, is that really you? You're not dead?'

'Where are you, Angel?' His voice was insistent, very anxious.

'You told me you were going to die, kill yourself,' she said, shaking her head in disbelief.

'I *was* going to, but in the end ... No good at finishing anything, me.' He gave a hollow little laugh. The laugh he gave when things were very serious.

'I thought you were dead, Don. Dead, you know, at the bottom of the sea. I wept over you everywhere, that you would never see this lovely autumn with the leaves changing, with the sun coming through the trees. I even wept for your sons, that they wouldn't know you ... and you never died ... you never died at all.'

'But that's good, Angel Ella, isn't it? We'll be together once I sort out this mess.'

'You never loved me, Don.'

'Of course I did ... do.'

'What had you intended to do, Don?'

'Wait until I could get the laptop so that we could sort it all out. Get our life together.'

She was silent.

Derry squeezed her hand harder. She had been holding the

receiver so that he could hear what was being said.

'Ella. Ella Angel, are you there?'

'You never loved me at all. Was it just sex? Was it because I was young? What was it?'

'We'll meet. Bring me the laptop. I'll tell you everything then.'

'I can't do that, Don.'

'Why not?' He sounded weak.

'Because I gave it to the Fraud Squad.'

'And the money for your parents? I can prove you took that.'

'No, I gave that back too.'

'I don't believe you.'

'Why not?'

'There would have been someone on to me by now.'

'There will be, Don, there will.'

'When did you give it to them?'

'An hour ago,' she said, and hung up the phone.

Chapter Fifteen

It all took much less time than they thought.

The detectives came to the hotel. Two quiet, unassuming-looking men, one a tall, dark man she had met before when she had lied about the computer.

'So it turned up eventually?' he said, looking at her.

'It did,' she said simply.

'And you are . . .?' he asked Derry.

Derry handed him a business card. 'Derry King, friend and business partner of Ms Brady.'

'And this is . . .?'

'A ticket and key for a safe deposit box. Don Richardson claims he left bank drafts or certified cheques there for me.'

'And you haven't opened it?'

'No.'

'If they were for you . . .?'

'He defrauded my father of money. They were a sort of apology, or that's what I thought.'

'All the more reason to take them, then . . .' The detective never finished a sentence, just left it hanging there and someone finished it for him.

This time it was Derry. 'Ms Brady and her parents, being very moral people, decided they couldn't just take money like that and say nothing. They are returning it to you.'

'Quite so. Very admirable.'

'And the password to the computer is Playa de los Angeles, like the city Los Angeles.'

'Ah, you just guessed this . . .?'

'Not exactly . . .'

'So Mr Richardson told you . . .?'

'Not exactly that either. He told me ages back that it was "Angel" and when I tried it recently it wasn't, so I tried words a bit like that and it opened.'

'Well done, Ms Brady.'

'But that's not the main thing . . .' she said, her words tumbling out.

'It's not?'

'No, the main thing is he's not dead. He's alive. I spoke to him this evening. He never killed himself at all.'

She looked from one face to the other to see the shock register. But to her surprise there was nothing at all.

'We never really thought he *was* dead,' said the detective. 'Didn't fit the pattern. Made no sense for him to kill himself.'

'I thought he was dead and I used to know him very well indeed,' Ella said.

'Yes, I'm sure.'

'You might have told me,' she said with tears in her eyes. 'Saved me all that heartbreak.'

'We didn't exactly see you since it happened. We asked you to keep in touch in case his briefcase turned up and you didn't . . . so how could we have told you?'

Derry intervened. 'But now the briefcase *has* turned up and Ella *has* been in touch, so is that everything?' His voice was smooth but with authority.

The two men responded to him. They stood up and shook hands. They thanked them for the co-operation and asked if Ella, and indeed Derry if he wished, would accompany them to the safe deposit box, so that the hand-over of what it contained could be authenticated.

'His name and address and contact numbers are all there,' Ella told them. 'He calls himself Brady, of all names. Isn't that a really nice bit of a laugh for all of us?'

There was real sympathy in the faces of the detectives. The whole thing was over in an hour.

Ella called her mother. 'It's done. It's given back. Well, given to the Guards, anyway,' she said in a dull tone.

'Well, I'm sure that's right. Thank you, Ella.'

'No, thank you, Mother, and Dad, too, for being nice and normal and believing someone I introduced you to. I will make it up to you if it's the last thing I do.'

'Stop, Ella.' Her mother noticed that the voice on the phone was shaking and tearful.

'And one more thing, Mother . . .'

'You're not coming home tonight?' her mother guessed.

'That's it. You're psychic,' she said.

'Don't get too upset, Ella. That's all I ask. The man is dead now, let him rest. We have no way of knowing how sorry he may have felt at the end. His mind disturbed and everything. We can't judge the dead.'

'The man is not dead, Mother. He's alive and well and living with his family in Spain.'

'No, Ella. He was killed in that terrible boat tragedy . . .'

'He faked it. He's living out there on Dad's money, and do you know what? He's calling himself Brady, Mother. That's what he's doing.' She sounded quite hysterical.

'Is Derry there?' her mother asked.

She handed him the phone. Ella could only hear his end of the conversation.

'Well, of course I will, no, have no worries. Certainly I will. No, she's actually much calmer than she sounded to you. I think it's just saying it for the first time to someone is the hard bit. No, she's in no danger, Barbara, believe me, she's not. And I too. Goodbye.'

She sat there unseeing. They were talking about her as a parcel. A package of nerves and reactions. Not a person.

'Do you know, Derry, the only thing that will hold me together over all this is very hard work,' she said.

'Good. I was hoping you'd say that.'

She was surprised. 'I thought you'd say talk, examine it, analyse it.'

'No, there's no point. We won't get to first base now, analysing what makes that guy tick. You've done all you said you would from this end. Now get on with your life.'

'And I can stay here?'

'Of course. Let's get down to work straight away.' He pulled a second chair up to the desk. 'Let's look at some of these stories. See how we could tell them . . . should it be table by table . . . have Mon and Mr Harris sitting down side by side, explaining how it all

began at one table, then move to another and get another story . . .
Or we could do it as an hour-by-hour thing . . . like the restaurant
starts to stir at about five a.m.'

Ella laughed. A real laugh. 'I don't think *anything* stirs in
Dublin at five a.m.'

'Now we're changing roles. You've been busy telling me how
modern it all is here.'

'Make it seven and we're more realistic.'

'Nonsense, Ella. Think about the garbage being collected, the
stuff coming in from market. It *has* to be earlier.'

'It would be interesting to see. We'll ask Brenda and Patrick
tomorrow night,' she said. 'Meanwhile, we'll go through the best
stories and the ones that will be hard to tell.'

'The guy from Scotland, Drew, he's not going to tell his own
tale, is he? Show himself up as a would-be thief?'

'Apparently he is, his luck turned that night, his fiancée admired
him so much for resisting temptation. Brenda says he's only
bursting to tell his story.'

Derry shook his head in amazement. 'Aren't people here quite
extraordinary?' he said in wonder.

'No, they're not. It's not just Ireland. It's the same everywhere,
in England, in the US, all dying to tell their story and have their
fifteen minutes of fame.'

'There's a danger that people will exploit them,' he said.

'Of course there is, but we're not that kind of business. Derry,
you're not having second thoughts on me, are you?'

'No, of course not. But talking about second thoughts . . .?'

'Yes?'

'I just wanted to say when your anger dies down, you'll
probably be relieved that he's alive. Don, I mean. It's only natural.
You loved him and he loved you. It has to be better that he's alive,
not dead at the bottom of the ocean. So, if you have second
thoughts about him and are glad he's still around, then that's
normal. That's all I wanted to say.' He looked oddly uncomfortable, as if he didn't really believe all this, but felt that it should be
said from a fairness point of view.

'No, I won't ever be glad about anything connected with him.
Whether he is alive or dead doesn't really matter to me. I think I
preferred him dead. I certainly don't love him or anything about
him. So there'll be no second thoughts. But I'm not going to spend

my life consumed with hate, either. That would really make me the loser.'

She thought he looked very pleased, but maybe it was just his pleasant smile.

When she awoke on the sofa yet again there was a note.

I've already gone to investigate this early-morning Dublin. See you tonight at Quentins, 7.30. Call my mobile anytime if you need me.
Love, Derry

Ella spent the day at Colm's restaurant on Tara Road.

'I don't know why you should think I should help you boost a rival restaurant,' Colm grumbled.

'Because I'm a neighbour's child, because you're not remotely in competition with me, and you love to talk about your pride and joy. I just want to know what's a typical day?'

'As if there ever was one. Come on in and have coffee and I'll walk you through it.'

By lunchtime, she thought she had understood the routine. It would be very visual. Derry would like it. Patrick and Brenda wouldn't object, their place was immaculate and all that backstage stuff would be something to be proud of.

'You look tired, Ella. Stay and have lunch. You've seen it all being cooked. Enjoy it.'

'No, I have a lot of things to do. I have to tell several people something but I want to rehearse on you, Colm. Just to make sure I can do it without crying.'

'Fire ahead.'

'Don Richardson's not dead. I spoke to him yesterday. He's in Spain, on the run.'

'Is it a secret?' Colm asked.

'No, not now.'

'Good. I'll tell Ria's ex-husband Danny that he might go out and kill him for all of us. Would that help?'

Ella laughed nervously. 'No, not really, but it did make me laugh. I don't suppose everyone else will be as practical as you are, Colm.'

She told Deirdre. Deirdre sat and listened with a stony face.

'Mother of God! Why couldn't he have done it properly? Did he wash up somewhere?'

'No, I don't think he tried it at all,' Ella said.

'And now of course you're taking him back?' Deirdre was anguished.

'*No*, Dee, I'm only telling you in case it was in the papers.'

'No! You are taking him back or going out to him, I know you are.'

'Oh, Deirdre, shut up. You're meant to be cheering me up, telling me some old song like "There Ain't No Good in Men". Not telling me I'm going back to him.'

'I wonder if Nuala knows,' Dee said.

'Let's tell her, then,' Ella said, her eyes dancing. And for a glorious moment Deirdre thought maybe it was going to be all right. That the one great love of Ella's life might not be able to seduce her back in again.

'Nuala! It's Dee.'

'No, Dee, I'm not going to talk to you. Last time you frightened me to death – I've had to blackmail them all with the threat of telling Carmel about your disgraceful antics with Eric to get them off Ella's back. Fine pair of friends you both turned out to be.'

'Shut up, Nuala. I told you if we had anything to tell you we would.'

'Did you?' Nuala was confused.

'Yes, and now we have. I have Ella here and now we do have news for Frank and his brothers.'

'You do?'

'Will I put Ella on?'

'Well, not if she's going to be cross with me,' Nuala said.

'Not at all. She won't be cross with you. Here's Ella now.'

'Hi, Nuala.'

'Oh, Ella, I'm sorry. I don't think Dee explained it all properly at the time.'

'No, Nuala, I'm sure she didn't. Have you got pen and paper?'

'Yes, I have.' Nuala sounded very nervous.

'Write this. It's Don's telephone number in Spain. Oh, and he's not dead, by the way. That was a mistake. He's alive, but he calls himself Mr Brady. I know, isn't it a scream? No, I'm not drunk, Nuala. That's the number and the other thing is that the Fraud Squad has his computer, with all the details, everything it contains.

Oh, and the last thing is that Dee would have gone the distance and told Carmel every last detail. She's been a marvellous friend.'

'Ella,' Nuala's voice was hoarse with fright. 'They're going to be in terrible trouble if it all gets out. Not only will they have lost money and property but there's a matter of tax, you see.' She ended in a near whisper.

'Oh, there often is, Nuala. Anyhow, we're all fair and square now.'

Ella hung up and they giggled as they had done for so many years.

'What I've been saying is getting easier to say as the day goes on,' Ella said as she walked into Firefly Films.

'I hate mystery statements,' Nick said.

'Don Richardson's alive and presumably coming back to this land in leg irons,' Ella said.

'You're not serious? Sandy and I once wondered if he might have staged it,' Nick said.

'You were right,' she said crisply.

'How did you find out?' Sandy asked.

'I spoke to him on the phone,' Ella said, and it didn't make her feel even slightly tearful. 'I spoke, and he called me Angel as he always did, and he had never died at all. Imagine.'

'Are you okay?'

'Yes, I'm fine, I'm fine, but I need to be kept very busy. Could I work here this afternoon until we all go to Quentins? I'm just a bit jumpy and I need to be with people.'

'Why did he ring you?' Nick asked.

'He didn't. I rang him, or rather his wife. I didn't know he was still alive.'

'And are you glad?' Sandy asked.

'I don't care, really and truly, I don't. Too much has happened to care.'

They believed her, got her a sandwich, and sat her down so that she could write out a type of running order that they might go through at tonight's meeting at the restaurant.

They watched her through the glass door, her head down over the paper as she planned out a very rough shooting schedule.

'Do you think she'll go back to him?' Sandy wondered.

'With any luck he won't be in a position to ask her.'

*

317

Cathy and Tom at Scarlet Feather heard from Ria and Colm that Don Richardson was still alive. Nora O'Donoghue heard it from them because she had gone into their premises to book a little wedding party. Nora was busy costing out the possibility of having canapés and wine in the back of a bookshop, which would let them have the premises free. There wouldn't be a huge number, but they had really very little money. Still, some things called for the equivalent of fireworks.

Cathy knew that the discussions were irrelevant since Brenda and Patrick had planned to give them a wedding present of a reception in Quentins. But they were only being told this much nearer to the time. Nora had been pushing Cathy for details of how many canapés each there would be for so many euros.

Then this news came suddenly out of the blue.

'I knew he wasn't dead,' she said calmly.

'How on earth did you know that, Nora?' Tom was sceptical.

'I saw him this morning,' she said simply, 'getting out of a taxi in Stephen's Green.'

Tom and Cathy called Deirdre to alert her.

'Is she sure? She can be quite odd, Nora O'Donoghue.'

'No, she's fine, she saw him, she said nothing and was going to say nothing because of Aidan, this guy she's going to marry, he was the one who knew him, taught Don Richardson's kids, and was conned out of money by him, she didn't want to upset him coming up to the wedding.'

'Thank God she mentioned it to you,' Deirdre said. 'Now we can alert Ella.'

'And maybe the Guards as well,' said Cathy.

Ella's mobile number was engaged. So Deirdre rang Nick at Firefly Films.

'Don't panic, it's okay, I can see her, she's in the next room talking away on the phone.'

'She's not talking to him, is she?'

'He doesn't have that number. It's a new phone.'

'What will we do, Nick?'

'Why don't you find Derry somehow. I'll tell her parents. It's not as if he's going to do anything in broad daylight.'

'It's just so that he takes nobody by surprise. Will you tell her, Nick? Gently, you know?'

'Sure thing, Dee,' he said. 'As soon as she gets off the phone.'

*

Ella was phoning Sasha, the girl who was now living in the Richardsons' Killiney house, the girl with Max the lovely baby, and whose uncle Michael Martin was a great friend of Don's.

'Do you remember me, Ella Brady? I came to visit you on Saturday,' she began.

'Well, am I glad you called.'

'You are?'

'I was looking everywhere for anyone who might tell me where you lived.'

'But why? What for, Sasha? I was just going to tell you that . . .'

Sasha interrupted. 'He's not dead, he never died. It was all a pretend suicide. He's alive, and he's coming back to look for you.'

'No, he can't, the police know, he wouldn't dare to come back here.'

'Well, he left his home in Spain last night. He'll be here today. He says if he can get to you first you won't sell him out.'

'But I've done it. I've given everything to the police.'

'He doesn't believe it.'

'Who told you all this, Sasha? Who says he doesn't believe it?'

'Michael Martin, my uncle. He told me to pack up everything of mine and Max's to have the place looking perfect in case Mr Richardson wants to stay here.'

'In his own house? But he's wanted for huge frauds. He wouldn't go there in a million years.'

'I know. That's why I wanted to find you. It's obvious he's not coming here, he's going after you.'

Derry King had begun his day at 5.30 when he walked to Quentins Restaurant to see if there was any sign of life and indeed he was proved right.

Eight large rubbish bags stood in bin containers, each bag tied and labelled. A private rubbish collector was removing them to a truck. The empty bins were left in the alleyway behind, some on their sides.

Derry nodded with satisfaction. This was one point he could score over Ella. She said no one was awake then.

She was such a courageous girl. She had faced everything so bravely. And there had been a lot to face. The only good thing was that this guy Don Richardson could not come back to Ireland now. It would be far too dangerous for him. So at least Derry didn't have to worry about Ella being in any danger. He went to get himself an early mug of tea. A small café not far away obliged. It was at times like this that Derry longed for a New York diner. Still, it wasn't too bad.

He nodded at the men sitting there. 'You're up early,' Derry said pleasantly.

'Big rush job, office block over there. We get treble time before seven o'clock in the morning,' one of them said.

'Nothing wrong with that kind of money. Did it take much negotiating?'

'No, Kennedys are tough but they're fair. If you do the work right, paint well and put in the hours, then you go home with a decent pay packet at the end of the week.'

'Kennedys?' he asked.

'That's us, well, that's the bosses.'

'Two guys called Sean and Michael?' Derry enquired.

'The very ones.'

'Well, isn't that a small world.'

'You know them?'

'No, my ex-wife met them a few years back, said they were good guys.'

'They're not bad at all.'

'Will they be round during the day, do you think?'

'Bound to be, they usually come in round seven when we're meant to be clearing out of the place. Will I tell them who was looking for them?'

'No, it's okay. I'll come back and tell them myself.' He had no intention of coming back. It was such an extraordinary coincidence that he should walk into his father's family by accident. What was anyone doing, calling this place a city? They were mad. It was a village.

Sandy called Tim and Barbara Brady to tell them that Don Richardson had been seen in Dublin.

'Thank you, Sandy. As it happens, Mr Richardson is here with me at this very moment. I'm telling him that we have no idea where Ella is and that you don't either.'

'She's here, Mrs Brady, don't worry. We'll get the Guards,' Sandy whispered.

The phone was hung up.

'Ring them again, Nick, quick, tell them he's in Tara Road.'

'They're not taking it as urgently as I thought,' Nick said. 'They

320

seem to think it's all a matter for Fraud, they don't think she's in any danger.'

'Well, can't we speak to Fraud?' Sandy said. 'They may think differently.'

'They've passed my message on,' Nick said. 'But I'll ring again saying where he is now.'

'We didn't expect to see you again, Don,' Barbara Brady said when she got over the shock of seeing him on her doorstep.

'I know, I know. But you *did* know I was alive? Ella must have told you.'

'Yes, she did, last night. She was very startled, shocked.'

'Is your husband at home, Barbara? I'd like a quick word with you both. It won't take long.'

'Tim isn't here. He's at the doctor. He doesn't sleep at all well, and there's a matter of his getting counselling.'

'I can't tell you how sorry I am.' Don looked sun-tanned but thinner than he had before. He had lost his lazy, easy confidence and his eyes darted around all the time.

'Yes,' Barbara Brady said bleakly.

'I have had so many regrets in this sad business. I truly did enjoy talking to him. He was a man of such integrity and a, well, a man of faith in a way.'

'He's not that now,' Tim Brady's wife said, looking around the small house they lived in, her face showing just how disturbed and upset the man of integrity and faith was these days.

'I did everything I could to make it up to him. I sent money. Ella surely told you that?'

'We couldn't take that,' Barbara said as if it were obvious.

'May I sit down, please?' Suddenly the great Don Richardson looked tired and even a little frightened.

'I'd prefer if you didn't, Don, it would be hypocritical to pretend that you are welcome here.'

'Ella?' he asked.

'I don't know, I really don't. She didn't come home last night.'

'Please.'

'I can't tell you what I don't know.'

'I'll only talk to her for ten minutes, in front of you and Tim if you like, or here in the house. Please, I have to ask her something.'

'I think you asked her enough over the years.'

'No, I'll tell you what it is. I know her. I *know* her, for God's sake. When I was talking to her last night, she said she had given in the laptop. She wasn't telling the truth. All I have to do is meet her and tell her how much she can save, for everyone, if she doesn't give it in. I can get it back together, that's what I'm trying to do. I can rescue people's investments, your Tim's, too.'

'I don't think she cares about the computer,' Barbara said.

'I agree with you and I don't believe she's handed it in.'

'She told me she had given it back.'

'She said given it *back*?'

'Those were her words. Then she said, "Well, to the Guards anyway".'

He was thinking hard. 'I still don't believe she would have done it. I know her voice, you see.'

The telephone rang. 'Can you answer it? It just might be her,' he pleaded.

But it was Sandy at Firefly Films.

He stood listening.

'Who was that?'

'Just friends concerned for her.'

'So they know I'm back, you can see I haven't much time.'

'Do you know that I don't give a damn how much time you have, Don Richardson, or how little? Our only daughter had the misfortune to love you and she has ended up a hurt, damaged girl as a result. She lives with a sense of guilt and shame on account of you, and the fact that her father is a shell of a man, disgraced and empty, and that I live in a prefabricated hut instead of that house over there. She has wept oceans over your leaving her to live in a marriage that she thought was over. She wept further oceans when she thought you were dead. *Now* do you understand how little I care about how much time you have or don't have? I do *not* know where Ella is, and if I did know, then by God I wouldn't tell you.'

'I'll go now, Barbara, and I won't say any more. I urge you not to, either. Remember, there is still the possibility that Ella may forgive me and come with me. I don't want her to feel that the door to her mother and father is closed.'

He was gone and Barbara Brady stood in her doorway shaking at the courage she had shown and her fear that Don Richardson might be right. Was it possible that, after everything, Ella would go back to him again?

Derry walked by Quentins again. This time there was activity inside. He knocked at the back door. 'I'm Derry King. I'll be meeting you tonight,' he said.

The tall dark man dusted the flour and sugar off his hands and gripped Derry's warmly. 'Brenda told me all about meeting you at lunch. I couldn't be there. Someone had to run the shop.'

'And it's an elegant shop I hear from all.'

'Well, thanks to you we're going to make it more widely known, certainly. Come on in, won't you?'

If Patrick Brennan was the slightest bit surprised to see a caller at 6.30 in the morning, he showed no sign of it. He was always here at this hour to do the pastry cooking. He was bad at delegating, he admitted, and just couldn't hand it over to someone else. This was his real skill, and what he enjoyed most. Today he had to make two lemon tarts, a chocolate roulade, a chocolate mousse, a tray of poached pears, a great bowl of chocolate curls, two litres of praline ice-cream and a raspberry coulis.

'But do you have to start so early?'

'Well, I do, really, you need constant exact temperatures for desserts. Later in the day the ovens are always opening and closing. It's not as good.'

And before the city woke up properly, Quentins seemed to be buzzing. A lad called Buzzo came in to hose out the dustbins in the lane and line them with heavy-duty rubbish sacks. He scrubbed out the kitchen and made a note of supplies needed.

'My brother used to do this at the start,' Patrick explained. 'But he's a family man now and he'll be going out to get us the vegetables, so we hired Buzzo. Poor divil, it's his only way of having a proper breakfast, getting a few euros together and still getting to school by nine a.m. He gets the money in his hand from me. I don't really approve, but if you had Buzzo's family ...'

'Drink, I guess?' Derry enquired.

'Oh, no. Drink they could cope with. Drugs, I'm afraid. Lives in a bad area. All his brothers are addicts and his father's a dealer.'

'His mother?'

'Away with the fairies, spaced out for years now.'

'No hope for the kid then?'

'He's survived so far. He's very bright, you see, so a few of us just make it easier for him to get by without having to be tempted by the drug money. Soon he'll be old enough to have a place on his own. He's gone down now to make tea and tidy up a bit for Kennedys' men, who are doing a job down the road.'

'Are they a good firm?'

'About the best. They did our last repaint job and I couldn't praise them enough.'

There was the sound of a horn outside.

'It's the linen, Mr Brennan. I'll take the sack down to them now,' Buzzo called out.

Yesterday's dirty tablecloths and napkins went off at speed down the lane and Buzzo returned carrying a large box of folded replacements. This had just been placed in what was called Brenda's cupboard when the meat arrived.

By now the chef trainee had arrived, so he took over and Buzzo, with his folded bank note in his pocket, was heading off for the second job of the day. It reminded Derry so much of his own early years, finding any job that was going and nailing it down. He wished he could tell Buzzo how well it had turned out for him, but kids hated these preaching speeches, so he would say nothing.

The trainee, who was called Jimmy and was a bit slow for Patrick's liking, was being hastened through his coffee. His job now was to cut up the meat and have it ready for Chef to cook when the time came. At the same time he was to make a stock with the bones, chicken carcasses and vegetables that were in the cool room all tied up in plastic bags.

And then Blouse Brennan appeared to check the list of what they needed. 'I'll have to buy courgettes. My own are ludicrous,' he apologised.

'That's all right, Blouse, a lot of places buy all their vegetables,' Patrick assured him.

Then the fish box came, from the fishmonger, and then boxes of wine from the supplier and the cheeses.

The assistant chef, Katie, said that there were three new cheeses today. She laid them out expertly on a marble-topped trolley in the cool room. 'That's three more to teach the waiters how to explain and pronounce. I'll have to ring up the cheese man and check myself first. We don't want to look like eejits.'

Derry smiled at her. If she were to say that to the camera, it would be very endearing. Ella had been right. Following a day in the restaurant was a good way to let the story unfold.

Ella! She was going to be fine. She had promised to ring if she wasn't.

Ella wanted to be alone. She needed to think. She did not need endless helpful voices of friends telling her she was all right and that it was all right and everything was going to be all right. None of these things was true.

Don Richardson was coming after her. Or was he?

Could she take Sasha seriously? She needed to talk to somebody. It wasn't fair to wear Derry down with it all again. Perhaps Don would go to her parents' house.

She called her mother. And discovered that he had just left.

'How was he, Mother?'

The question seemed to upset Barbara Brady. 'He was . . . well, he was all right.'

'No, Mother, I mean it.'

'Well, what do you want to know? He wasn't pale or anxious . . .'

'I mean, was he sane or did he look as if he were going to come after me with a cleaver?'

'He thinks he's coming after you with an offer you can't refuse. He thinks you're going back to him.'

'Then you've answered my question, Mother. He's far from sane and we must bring in the cavalry.'

She phoned the Fraud Squad. They had heard. He would be in custody by evening.

Dee wasn't able to come to the phone, her message said. Ella saw Nick and Sandy watching her covertly through the glass door . . . she couldn't wait like this in a trap until he arrived. She had to get out. But she knew they wouldn't let her.

Leaving her jacket over the back of her chair and her handbag on the desk so that they would think she was coming back, she took her telephone and her wallet with her. She slipped out to the bathroom and to the side door into the lane. They would be annoyed, but she had to be alone. She hailed a cab and asked to be taken to Stephen's Green. From the back of the cab she dialled directory enquiries and got Michael Martin's number. She got through straight away.

'Yes?' he said crisply.

'Tell him to stop looking. I'm on my way to Stephen's Green. I'll be beside the duck pond. I'll see him there.'

'Yeah, you and half the Guards in Ireland.'

'If they're there it's not because I'll have brought them,' she said and hung up.

'You okay?' the driver asked, looking at her in the mirror.

'I don't know,' Ella said. 'Why do you ask?'

'You're shivering. You've no coat. You look worried.'

'All of these things are true,' Ella agreed.

'So?'

'So I have to do something I don't want to do and I'm a little bit afraid,' she said.

'Take someone with you,' the driver suggested.

'I can't.'

'You've got a phone. Then tell someone where you're going.'

'But I don't want anyone coming in and interrupting it.'

'You're in a mess then, aren't you,' the driver said agreeably.

'I am indeed,' she said.

Derry King walked back to the building where the major painting job was taking place. He saw the professional sign for the painters. His father could have been part of this firm, lived in this city. Derry could have grown up here. But then, if he had, he might well have been like that boy Buzzo, cleaning out dustbins, making tea on sites before school. Like his own childhood in New York.

He saw two men walking towards a van with the name Kennedy on it. They stood discussing a sheaf of papers, some attached to clipboards. He watched them for a long time with a lump in his throat. They were square men like himself, same bristly hair, a little taller than he was, but they had the same lines coming out like stars around the eyes. You would not need a college degree in genetics to know that these were his relations.

He should be their friend. They were, after all, the sons of brothers. But there was so much to regret. To try to forget. He would walk way.

At that moment they looked over. He couldn't run.

'Sean? Michael?' he said.

'Well, Derry, you came to see us at last,' said one of them.

'You knew me?' He didn't know whether to be pleased or outraged.

'Of course we did.'

'Kim, I suppose?' he said.

'Well, she did show us a photo of you when she was here, but that was a while ago, and anyway, aren't you the spit of us?'

'That's right.'

Derry still seemed uneasy.

The bigger man said, 'Now it's easy for us to know you. There's only one of you. You don't have an idea which of us is which. I'm Sean and this is Michael, the brains of it all, and can we buy you breakfast?'

'I've been eating breakfast for hours,' he said with a half-smile.

'It's the one meal you can't overeat on, they say.' Sean was eager. Touchingly eager to treat the cousin who had ignored them for decades.

He looked from one to the other. 'You don't seem surprised to see me,' he said.

'Kimberly sent us a message saying you might be here and to look out for you,' said Michael.

'And one of the painters said there was a Yank who was the dead image of us, asking about us in the café,' added Sean.

And they laughed like old family friends as they went to Derry's third breakfast of the day.

Possibly ducks were not as content as they looked. Maybe they were up to their little feathered armpits with worry, but they looked fairly sound, Ella thought. As if they had it sorted.

She looked around. There was no sign of him yet.

She sat down on a bench and found a paper bag with the remains of someone's breakfast croissant. Normally she would have been appalled at the Dublin litter problem. Now she could give it to these quacking ducks as she pleased. Maybe it was what they called an Act of Random Kindness to leave the bag there.

She saw people moving around, some of them hurrying, others idling. None of them was Don. And yet she knew he would come. He had moved so quickly from Spain. He must be desperate to find her. Perhaps he had known she was lying when she spoke to him last night about having given the laptop in already. He must have flown out of Spain immediately, gone by London possibly. What passport had he used?

Suddenly she felt frightened. Why had she arranged to meet him here?

She dialled the number of Derry King's mobile. It was up on the screen, but she needed to press the green button for it to start ringing. Before she could do that she saw Don. He was moving towards her, arms out.

'Angel,' he cried. 'Oh, Angel, nothing matters now. I'm just so glad to see you again.'

*

327

Derry didn't know how the day passed, so much happened, so much was seen and noted. Even in his busiest days setting up his own business in the USA, he had not met so many people in the space of one day.

His cousins brought him back to their headquarters and explained the business from the ground up. How it had seemed such a great idea to hire themselves out to builders as master painters, to put a seal on their work as it were. But there were problems.

They told him unemotional stories about their own father, now dead, and their mother, who was in an old people's home and would love to see him, but maybe in another visit, not this one. They pushed him not at all and he felt he had known them all his life.

He went back to Quentins to follow how the day was unfolding there. He met the staff, saw them learning the names and nature of the new cheeses, watched the clever switching of tables as bookings changed minutes before lunch was served. And noted the clockwork precision of the kitchen, where everything had its own rhythm.

Derry saw Brenda on the phone and she told him she had just heard that Don Richardson was in Dublin.

'Does Ella know?' he asked immediately.

'Apparently so, she's safe at Firefly Films. With Nick and Sandy.'

'He didn't waste much time,' Derry said.

'No, I suppose he thought he'd better run in before the Guards got their paperwork ready,' Brenda said.

'If he sees her . . .' Derry began.

'He won't.'

'No, but if he does, do you think she might go back to him?'

Brenda noticed what she thought was more than a professional interest in the question. His face was very concerned. Wishing she believed what she was saying, she assured Derry that there wasn't a chance in hell that Ella would look at that man again.

'Hallo, Don.' Ella's voice was flat.

'Oh, my darling Ella.'

'No, Don, none of that.'

'But nothing's changed. There's been such hell and I know that I put you through it, but I had to. So that in the end we would be . . .'

'No, Don, you didn't. You didn't *have* to do anything.'

'It's going to be all right now, Angel. You and I can go away now. We'll get that money your mother and father wouldn't take, that will get us abroad anywhere, then with the computer we can get everything sorted out.'

She looked at him in disbelief. He really meant it. He thought it was possible that she would drop everything and run away with him.

What did he think her life had been like for all these months, what kind of grasp on reality did he have?

She looked at his face, wondering how he could be so confident and loving. He really did think she was going with him.

'I can't believe that you're here, Don, walking right back into the lion's den . . .'

'You didn't give it to them, Ella. I know your voice. I know everything about you, honestly I do. I know what you're like asleep and awake. I think of you all the time. I know every heartbeat. I can tell when you're lying, when you're frightened. I never knew anyone as well as I know you. I know every breath you take.' He was shaking now, trembling, and there was a heavy sweat on his forehead.

Suddenly she got frightened. She pressed the green button on her phone, which was behind her. She could hear the number being dialled. Please God, may Derry be there. Please may he hear me.

'Don, believe me, I'm not going away with you,' she began.

'You are of course, Angel Ella, and we'll be together as we were always meant to be.'

She could hear something click on the phone behind her. May it be Derry picking up.

'I didn't come out to meet you in Stephen's Green to talk about this, Don,' she said.

'Why *did* you come then, if you don't love me, want to go away with me to have a life together? Why else did you come?'

'To say goodbye and to say sorry, I suppose.'

'Sorry? You're not saying sorry for anything, Angel. You haven't given anything to anyone. It's all somewhere waiting for us to collect.'

'No. I gave it in.'

'Before or after you talked to me?'

'After,' she said, looking at the ground.

He smiled almost dreamily. 'I knew, I was right about that, that I could tell when you were lying.'

'Well, can you tell now? Can you tell that this much is true . . . that as soon as I put the phone down I rang the Fraud Squad and they came round and took the laptop. And we went and got the bag from the safe deposit. And they took that too.'

She looked at his face. He did believe it now.

'Why did you do this to me?'

'To have the courage to look you in the face and say it's over and you should give yourself up. Say you're sorry. Put your hands up. There has to be *something* that can be rescued. Do your time, give the boys some dignity in their father. And your wife, too, for that matter.'

His face seemed contorted now. 'Will you shut up. Do you hear me? *Shut up*, mouthing these pious wishes. Are you going to come in and visit me in the gaol for twenty-five years and wait until you are an old woman?'

She was very scared of him now, afraid that he would hit her. 'I'm only just up the road from you,' she shouted over her shoulder, hoping it would reach the phone behind her.

'What are you talking about?' he cried.

'I'm saying where I am to stop myself being frightened of you, Don, and the horrible look in your eyes. I'm in Stephen's Green beside the ducks. That's where I am, and I'm not afraid. It's the middle of Dublin City. You're not going to add to all you've done by hurting me.'

'Hurt you, Angel? Are you mad? I *love* you,' he cried.

'No, you never loved me. I know that now.'

'I came back for you . . .'

'You came back for your computer,' she said.

His eyes seemed very mad. Had they ever been like this before?

'Go away, Don,' she said in a weary voice. 'Please, go away.'

'Not without you.'

'You don't want me any more. I've given away what you thought I had. You should never have come back.'

'You are such a stupid, stupid fool, Angel.'

'Oh, yes, Don, I was, I know that now.'

He was very near her and he looked totally out of control. 'You could have had everything, Angel, anything you wanted.'

'I want you to go. Maybe you might even get away. Escape before they catch you. You've plenty of friends who'll hide you.'

'Not so many nowadays, Angel. Not without the computer.'

Then she saw people moving towards them. Out of the shadows, behind the trees and bushes of the park. The mother duck had taken the little ducklings away from the scene as if she knew it wasn't the place for them to be. A place where a grown man sobbed like a child to policemen and howled out, 'I did it for you, Angel. I did it all for you.'

And here Ella Brady trembled and shook in the arms of Derry King, who held her as if he was never going to let her go.

Chapter Sixteen

The meeting in Quentins that night was cancelled. There had been too much drama. No one could concentrate on a possible film documentary when real life itself had been so full of passion and fear. Over and over, people told each other the events of the evening. Nick and Sandy told Deirdre how they had run out to get a taxi to Stephen's Green when they heard from Derry what was happening. Brenda and Patrick told Tom and Cathy how Blouse had been crossing Stephen's Green on his way back to the restaurant and had seen it all. There was Mr Richardson crying out and roaring like a child.

Barbara Brady told anyone who would listen that she had finally found her courage and her voice possibly when it was too late. But she would remember for ever that she stood up to Don and told him she didn't care what happened to him in the future.

Sasha was told by her uncle Mike Martin that she was to unpack at once and re-establish herself in the Killiney house. Mike Martin himself was going abroad. Mr Richardson would not be coming back, and the best move was to establish squatter's rights immediately.

Nuala rang Deirdre to say that two of Frank's brothers had been in Stephen's Green also, in case the laptop was being handed over. They had been phoned by Mike Martin as a last-ditch stand. They had been horrified by Don's behaviour, and said that Ella had hired an American lawyer to protect her interests.

Square kind of a fellow called King.

There were photographs in the morning's paper of Don Richardson in custody and some eye-witness accounts of the scene. But there was one picture of Ella captioned 'woman being consoled at the scene'. Only those who knew her recognised her. Neither the press nor the public made any connection with Love-Nest Ella of many months back. Except Harriet, who had met Ella on the plane to New York. She might get a couple of hundred euros if she rang a newspaper and tipped them off. But still, Ella was a nice kid. She deserved a break.

And there were so many other ways of making money. The sharp-eared witnesses who were meant to have heard everything said that Don Richardson had called out over and over: 'I did it all for you.' This was hard to interpret.

Some of the feature writers said that he may have been calling out to his beloved wife who, it was understood, was still in Spain but expected imminently in Ireland. Some thought to stand at her husband's side. Others thought to answer charges.

Since the long-planned dinner in Quentins was postponed until everyone was calm enough to deal with things, everyone seemed to assume that Ella would go back to the hotel with Derry.

'I don't suppose there's a way you'd like to try the bed tonight?' he said.

'Jesus, no, Derry. I've been through enough today without considering that side of things,' she said.

'I didn't mean in bed with me in it, I meant you have the bed with me on the sofa.'

'Oh, I see,' she said. 'Sorry.'

And for some reason they found this very funny, and laughed all through the ordering of smoked salmon and scrambled eggs.

They played a game of chess as they had often done. They talked not at all about Don Richardson, where he would be tonight and what would happen to him. They didn't talk about Quentins either. In fact, they hardly talked at all.

And by the time Ella lay down on the sofa, which she insisted felt like home to her now, her eyes looked less frightened and her voice sounded much less shaky.

'I don't want to delay you in Dublin, Derry. We really *will* get down to work tomorrow.'

'I'm in no hurry to leave. There's a great deal to be done here,' he said as he kissed her lightly on the forehead and spread a rug over her.

'But America?' she said drowsily.

'Will survive for a bit without me,' Derry King said.

What could have happened in that week that made everyone change their minds about the documentary? And where did it start first?

Possibly in the kitchen of Quentins.

Blouse Brennan was going through the boxes of fruit. Expertly he was dividing them into the areas where they would be needed: limes and lemons at the bar, fresh berries over at the pastry table so they could be dusted with icing sugar and added at the last moment to desserts.

'I bet you they'll film you doing that, Blouse. You look very graceful,' Brenda said admiringly.

Blouse reddened. 'They won't have *me* in their pictures,' he said.

'Of course they will, Blouse, and out in the vegetable garden and with the hens, aren't you the most colourful part of it all?' Patrick reassured his brother.

But Blouse didn't respond to the flattery. 'I didn't think it would be nice to be in it as, well, I don't want people looking at me.'

'They'll be nice people, you know most of them, Nick and Sandy and Ella,' Brenda pleaded.

'No, I don't mean them.'

'Well, Mr King was in here, and he was the nicest man you could ever meet.'

'No, I mean real people, outside people looking at it. People like Horse and Shay back home. The Brothers who taught me, fellows who work on the allotments. I don't want them seeing me and knowing my business,' Blouse said, flushed and upset.

They knew not to let him get more distressed.

'Well, there's no question of you being in it if you don't want to, Blouse,' Patrick said.

'It would be a great loss, but it's your choice, no question of that,' Brenda agreed.

'Thanks, Brenda, Patrick ... I don't want to let you down or anything.'

'No way, Blouse,' Patrick said through gritted teeth.

Or it could have been in Firefly Films. They got the offer they had dreamed of from the day they started: to film one of Ireland's greatest rock bands all the way through from composing and rehearsing the songs up to a huge rock festival. They would be made if they could do it, but they would need to start almost immediately.

Nick was about to refuse. They were committed to Quentins.

Sandy said they should stall them for a week, a lot could happen in a few days and Derry King could easily change his mind.

Or it could have been Buzzo. He said he couldn't be seen in the film because nobody at school knew he worked here, and that his brothers would take any money off him if they knew he had it.

And Monica said that her husband, Clive, though the greatest darling who ever walked the earth, had been having second thoughts about their telling their love story. People were odd in the bank, no sense of humour. They might think less of Mr Clive Harris if they knew he had read books covered in brown paper about how to be attractive to the opposite sex. Regretfully, they would have to pull their story out.

Someone had told Yan the Breton waiter that if this film was successful, it would be shown everywhere, even in his homeland. Then his father would hear him saying for all the world to hear that they had not got on well as father and son. It was a very enclosed community. In his part of Brittany, people didn't air their problems in public. A million pardons, but he wouldn't be able to contribute.

And then Patrick Brennan finally had his annual checkup. He did all the stress tests on the treadmill and the exercise bikes. Then he sat down, still sweating mildly, to talk to the counsellor as part of the checkup.

'It's a stressful job, running a restaurant, of course, but once we get this documentary out of the way, we should be fine. We've promised to take time off together, delegate more.'

'When will that be?'

'Oh, a few weeks' time, I gather. It will be hell keeping the show on the road until then, but we have to do it.'

'Why, exactly?' asked the counsellor.

Brenda's friend Nora O'Donoghue was in the kitchen chopping vegetables. Brenda looked at her affectionately. She was such a handsome woman, with her piebald hair and her long, flowing clothes. She had no idea that she was striking and wonderful. Even there, as she washed the vegetables in a sink, laid them out on cloths to chop and dice, she looked like some happy goddess from a classical painting.

'I wish you'd stop that and come and talk to me, Nora.'

'Listen, I'm doing three hours' work for your husband, if not for you. Come and talk to me here while I work.'

Brenda pulled up a chair. 'Do you mind them filming you doing this?' she asked.

'They wouldn't want me, for God's sake, a mad old woman.'

'Oh, they would, Nora. You look lovely. I was just thinking it. Would you mind?'

'Not at all, if it's any help to you and Patrick. I'd be honoured.'

Brenda looked at her with a lump in her throat. What a generous-spirited person she was. She didn't care if her mother and awful sisters, if the students in the Italian class she taught, if Aidan's colleagues, saw her scrubbing vegetables in a kitchen. What a wonderful way to be.

'You're tired, Brenda.'

'Which means, You're ugly, Brenda.'

'No, it means, You're worried, Brenda.'

'All right, I am worried. Worried sick about this documentary and that we get it right.'

'You don't need to do it,' Nora said.

'If we are to amount to anything, then let us leave some kind of legacy after us.'

Nora carefully put down her short, squat, but very sharp knife and laid her hand on Brenda's. 'You? Amount to anything? Legendary, that's what they call you two already. How much more do you want to amount to? You've been giving legacies into people's lives and will continue to do so for ever.'

'You're kind to think we amount to a lot, Nora, but I don't see it that way. I thought this would sort of define us in a way.'

'Brenda, you have each other and all this marvellous place. In the name of God, woman, don't you have enough?'

Ella ran into Mrs Ennis, the school principal, in Haywards Café.

'I can't tell you how pleased I am to see you,' Mrs Ennis said.

Ella was surprised. She had left Mrs Ennis slightly in the lurch by leaving the school so quickly. Then Mrs Ennis, too, might have regretted her indiscretions about her own private life which she told to cheer Ella up.

'I was going to ask you, did you want any part-time work? I did try to call you, but none of your phone numbers worked.'

'Oh, I went into hiding for a while,' Ella admitted.

'But I gather from what I read in the papers that you're out now,' Mrs Ennis was matter-of-fact.

'Yes, that's right, I am.'

'Does teaching still interest you? You were good. The girls liked you.'

'I did like it, very much. It was more solid than anything else, in a way.'

'But maybe solidity isn't enough.'

'I think it is now. But I have to make a film documentary first.'

'How long would that take?'

'A few weeks, Mrs Ennis. I won't be part of the editing.'

'What's it about?'

'It's about a day in the life of a restaurant.'

'Why?' Mrs Ennis asked baldly.

Ella looked at her for a moment. 'Do you know, I'm not quite sure why. A dozen reasons along the line, partly as therapy for me at the start, I know that. Then a lot of other people got drawn in.' She seemed confused, thinking about why they were doing it.

Mrs Ennis was brisk. 'You know where we are, Ella. Ring us within a week if you'd like to come back to us. We need you.'

'You're very kind.'

'And the other business? All right about that?'

'Oh, yes. It's as if it all happened to someone else, not me.'

'Good, then you're getting better,' Mrs Ennis said.

Ella hadn't talked to Derry properly for three days. He was with his cousins morning, noon and night.

'You haven't had a fight with him?' Barbara Brady asked.

'You couldn't fight with Derry,' Ella said. She remembered his ex-wife Kimberly saying something similar.

When he rang later that day, he asked to see her. 'We have to talk, Ella. Can we have dinner at Quentins?'

'Will I get Nick and Sandy to come?'

'No, just you.'

It turned out that he had been eating there every evening with his cousins. Sean and Michael knew the place already and had come for special treats.

'I'm sorry you're going to turn all this into a sort of circus,' Sean had said bluntly as he looked around him.

'What do you mean?' Derry wondered.

'Well, when you have all these people appearing on television, they'll become celebrities and folks will come in to gawp at them. They won't be able to get on with their job like they did before. Before they became actors, I mean.'

'Ah, now, Sean, don't go discouraging Derry. This is his work, his business. You wouldn't like it if he were to go telling you how to paint a house,' Michael said.

'I wouldn't mind if he had anything interesting to say.' Sean was honest.

And that night, Derry told Ella all this. How the brothers had opened up his eyes about so many things. Filming wasn't his business, he assured them, selling was his business, creating needs for people, then filling them. That's what he was good at. He had spent time in their business and told them about ways they could expand. Sell paint as well as doing the job. Set up an advisory service after hours, in the evenings or Saturday mornings. Draw in the young couples, give them colour charts, do and don't lists. Make them your friends. You weren't doing yourself out of a market. There were two different worlds, those who painted and those who didn't.

And then, he said to Ella, he had listened to them as well. And understood what they were saying. He had grown to love Quentins, there was a possibility that a fly-on-the-wall would destroy it and the hard-working people there. He felt clear in his head about it. Now the only problem was to explain all this to Ella and to everyone else. He was amazed at how easy that turned out to be.

The only person who was confused and annoyed in the end was Deirdre. 'For week after bloody week I've been talking, sleeping, dreaming, breathing this documentary. It was going to be the making of everybody. And now suddenly, out of a clear blue sky, I'm meant to be overjoyed that it is *not* happening. No, Ella, give me some sense of being something rather than a nodding dog.'

'*You*, a nodding dog, Dee! Please!'

'No, I'm serious. It's all ludicrous. What happens when you go back to teaching, your man goes back to America, your other man goes to gaol, Firefly Films become rock groupies, Quentins misses out on immortality? Where's all the joy in that?' Deirdre was great when she grumbled. Which was never for long.

'Listen, cheer up. You're invited to a big party to celebrate.'

'God, what a mad crowd you are. Celebrating! Anyone else would be in mourning.'

'No, Dee, you eejit, it's for lots of things ... the new company, Kennedy and King. Derry's going in with his cousins. It's for Aidan and Nora's wedding party. It's for Nick and Sandy's new contract. It's for my getting exactly the job I want, part-time teaching, and I'm going back to university to do a doctorate as well, and it's for my father going to have a job as a financial adviser in Kennedy and King. And for so many other things ... if you can't celebrate all that, then you're only a miserable old curmudgeon.'

Deirdre threw her arms around Ella. 'I never saw you so happy. So that maybe is a reason to get a new party frock. Will there be anything there that I could get my nails and teeth into?'

'Lord knows, there might be,' said Ella. 'It's shaping up as a very unusual party.'

'Yes, Mrs Mitchell. I know it's inconvenient. Perhaps you could choose another night.'

'But my daughter-in-law ... well, my ex-daughter-in-law, tells me she's going to Quentins on Saturday night ... tomorrow.'

'But as I'm sure she told you, it's a private function, Mrs Mitchell.'

'Well, I had thought there might be exceptions for regular clients.'

'No, we *have* had this notice on the tables for three weeks, Mrs Mitchell, and in the newspaper.'

Brenda came off the phone and rolled her eyes up to heaven. 'Amazing how Cathy didn't kill that one dead. She's the most trying woman in Dublin.'

The next call was from Nora's mother. 'I don't know what you're thinking of to imagine that I and my family are going to a surprise party for Nora. I never heard such nonsense, and at her age. And at such short notice.'

'We had to keep it at short notice in case they heard about it.' Brenda's eyes rolled further around in her head.

'But I thought that this ceremony was going to be in a

bookshop. That's what Nora said, and we wouldn't have gone to that either,' Mrs O'Donoghue sniffed.

'We so much hope you'll be here tomorrow. It will be a great feast and every woman wants her mother there at a wedding party.'

'Huh, as if it were a proper wedding.'

'It will be a marvellous wedding. I'm one of the witnesses. So can I hope you all will come, or is this a definite no?'

Nora's appalling mother didn't want to rule herself out of what was being described as a feast. 'I can't say yes or no.'

'Well, we hope that's a yes. Meanwhile, not a word of any of this to Nora and Aidan.'

Brenda knew that the old bat would try to ring them and spoil it, but it was impossible now; Nora was staying in Quentins for the night and Aidan was at his son-in-law's house. Mrs O'Donoghue would not be able to find them now, no matter how hard she tried.

Maud and Simon were told that Hooves, their dog, could *not* come to the party no matter how rejected it made him feel. He had a collar the same as Derry King's dog had in America, but even that didn't get him in. They were warned by Cathy that two songs was the maximum, and could they be love songs?

Simon thought of 'Please, Release Me, Let Me Go'. But that was not suitable for a wedding, apparently.

Neither was 'Young Love, First Love, is Filled With Deep Emotion', which they knew, because the couple were not in the first flush of youth.

'Love,' Cathy said. 'You must know *some* song about love?'

They said they would do some research.

'Nothing to be sung without consulting me,' Cathy said. 'That's an order.'

Sean and Michael Kennedy were the first arrivals. They were trying out the canapés and looking at the banners on the wall. The menu was engraved for Aidan and Nora as it should be with wedding bells attached, but there was a banner for Kennedy and King too, and one for Firefly Films, and one for Ella's degree.

The sign writer had been busy tonight.

At the piano, two earnest-looking blond children sat beside an old man as he picked out the notes of a song and tried to teach it to them.

'We'd better write it down, Muttie,' the boy said.

'Everyone knows the words,' the old man protested. 'They're not words you'd be able to write down like, they're not in English.'

'Then why are we singing it?' the girl asked.

'Because Cathy says they must love it. She said it was a pity you didn't know it but you will if you concentrate.'

They concentrated heavily.

Derry came in a car to collect the Brady family.

'We're not really much for parties,' Tim protested, but Ella noticed he had dressed up smartly all the same.

'Can't have a party without my financial adviser there. I might revert to my father and get drunk and silly,' Derry said.

Ella smiled at him. He was able to make a remark about it, a joke even. At last.

'We wouldn't miss it for the world, Derry,' Ella's mother said.

Ella looked at the streets around her as they drove to Quentins. This was her world. There was no other and there never would be again.

Patrick made an appearance at the party in full chef's gear. 'Brenda is with them. She's taking the little party, just Aidan, his daughters and the son-in-law, down to Holly's for afternoon tea and they think they're going to the bookshop afterwards.'

'Wouldn't they be afraid Nora would get a heart attack when she finds the place closed?'

'No, don't worry.'

The Registrar was a kind man. He knew when he saw a party of only six people, a bride and groom tending towards middle age rather than extreme youth, that a ceremony of great dignity was called for. He looked from one to the other and stressed the importance of the day and the decision they were making in front of all present.

They thanked him profusely and asked him to join them for afternoon tea in Holly's. He was often invited to join the festivities, but never accepted. Today for the first time he was tempted. They were so touchingly happy, it made him blow his nose quite a lot. They had obviously travelled a long road to get to this day.

They drove to Holly's and got a great welcome. Photographs were taken in the garden under the huge trees. Tiny sandwiches and little cream cakes were served. Everyone was very relaxed. But the bride had her eye on her watch.

'We must be in time for the bookshop,' Nora said.

Brenda was delaying them. 'Ah, don't worry. It will start without us . . . they'll know we're on the way.'

'How many will there be altogether?' Aidan's daughter Brigid asked. She was in on the whole thing and thought it was so cool. In fact, totally cool.

'There will be fourteen altogether. I'd have loved to have asked more, but you know . . .' Nora said.

'It's the fourteen important ones anyway, and the others will understand. Don't start fussing, Mrs Dunne.' Aidan looked at her with great affection.

'Oh, God, you put the heart across me, Aidan. I thought your first wife had materialised down here in Wicklow.'

Nick, Sandy and Deirdre arrived together. They had been firmly instructed by Brenda to move among the guests talking and introducing. There were people from a lot of different worlds here tonight, and they needed someone to keep them together. Brenda would have done it effortlessly, but she was needed elsewhere.

Nick, Sandy and Deirdre got their first drink and began doing their duty, moving around and bringing the little groups together. Getting names and giving them.

'Aren't you a very lovely person? Are you an actress or a film star?' a man asked Deirdre.

'No, I'm not. I work in a lab and I'm as cross as a bag of weasels,' Deirdre said.

'And what has a gorgeous girl like you cross?'

The man was well-dressed, with bristly hair like Derry King's. Of course, it must be one of the painter cousins.

'Are you Sean or Michael?' she asked.

'I'm Sean. Imagine you having heard of us.'

'Everyone's heard of you. I'm Deirdre.'

'And what's upset you, Deirdre?'

'I paid four hundred euros for this dress and I look like the wrath of God in it.'

'You do not, you look lovely.'

Deirdre moved and examined herself in the mirror. With a very disappointed face.

A woman with the most amazingly brassy hair came over and watched her. 'It needs a scarf draped over it, something that picks up the colour,' she said.

'A lot of use that is to me to know that now. It looked fine in the shop.'

'Bet they draped a scarf over it for you?'

'They did, as it happens. I'm Dee, by the way, Ella's friend.'

'I'm Harriet, Nora's friend, and Ella's too. We met when she was going to America.'

'Oh, yes, she told me about you. You sold her a dog collar.'

'I can sell you a scarf now, if you want one. Just wait and I'll get you a selection. I checked my bag in to the cloakroom.'

In minutes Deirdre was transformed.

'I'll leave you now. He's one of the best catches in Dublin,' Harriet whispered.

'Who?' Deirdre felt disconnected from everything.

'Sean Kennedy, rolling in money and he's drooling over you.'

'I'm really meant to be mingling,' Deirdre said.

'I'd say you've mingled enough,' advised Harriet.

When they saw the notice on the door, Nora felt the tears coming down her face. 'Oh, Aidan, isn't that desperate? *What* could they mean, unforeseen circumstances?'

'They were so sure.' Aidan's face was bleak. 'And what did they do with the wine and the canapés?'

'Does it say anything else?' Nora wept.

Then they found a second note.

'It says the Dunne reception has been transferred eight doors down the street.'

'Which direction?' she sniffed.

'It says to Quentins,' Aidan said.

They looked at the others, who were beaming with delight.

'But we can't go to Quentins, not on a Saturday night. No, *Carissima* Brenda, even for a wedding. We can't do that on you.'

Now Brenda had tears in her eyes.

'I've a feeling it's going to be perfectly fine,' she said, and led the newlyweds eight doors down the road to Quentins.

*

343

Brigid Dunne had run ahead and when they came in the door, a man at the piano struck up with 'Here Comes the Bride', and after that everyone they could ever have wanted to see at their wedding appeared, to hug them.

Nora's hair was a triumph and her lilac-coloured dress with the dark royal purple chiffon sleeveless coat looked astounding. Harriet had got an immense bargain for her somewhere. No one would ever know how immense, not even the man whose lorry it was meant to have fallen off.

The twins approached. 'We are only allowed to sing two songs. Will we sing them now?'

'Of course,' Nora could hardly speak.

Simon and Maud liked things announced.

'The bride and groom have connections with Italy, what with the bride having lived out there for a long time and her teaching Italian here, so we thought they'd like "Volare".' Everyone in the room seemed to know it and joined in the chorus.

Maud announced the next song. 'It doesn't matter what age you are when you get married, your wedding day is meant to be your best day, so for this couple we are going to sing "True Love".'

The twins knew all the words, even the bit about the Guardian Angel on High with Nothing to Do. They looked round proudly as they sang. They were making a fine job of this, unlike 'Volare', which wasn't even English and everyone had drowned them out. So when they were doing it so well why was everyone weeping unashamedly? Simon and Maud found life more impossible to understand every day.

'Those two are extraordinary, they break people up all over the place,' Cathy said to Tom in the kitchen.

She had come in to sit down. Three times in the last two weeks she had gone to the hospital, certain that the baby's birth was imminent. Three times they had sent her home saying that there was absolutely no sign of anything. So she hadn't taken much notice of the pains earlier on today. She was so anxious to be at the reception. And she knew the hospital would only send her away again, but there was this pain, well, it wasn't a pain, more a downward dragging feeling. It had come on quite suddenly.

'Cathy, are you all right?' Tom asked suddenly.

'I must be, I have to be, but ...'

344

'But what?' He was ashen.

'But I think the baby's coming, Tom,' she said.

Blouse and Mary saw first what was happening. And knew there was no time to get an ambulance or to move them upstairs.

They moved instead to the storeroom and sat her down in a big armchair. Mary ran to her own quarters for sheets and towels. Blouse ran into the dining room to get Brenda and Patrick.

Ella came into the kitchen that moment and took everything in. 'Well done, Cathy,' she said. 'We'll be absolutely fine.' Her voice calmed the two, who were holding hands so tightly it looked as if they would never be prised apart.

'Couldn't be a better place, plenty of boiling water,' she soothed. 'Tom, get Derry to point out a Brian Kennedy to you. He's actually a doctor. You couldn't be in better hands. Quick now, but don't alarm them.'

Cathy's face was terrified. Mary and Ella calmed her. 'You couldn't be safer, Cathy,' they begged her.

Brenda was with them and then they began to believe it might be true. They leaned over her.

'Push, Cathy,' they all said. The baby's head was there.

Dr Brian Kennedy said by the time he came in, it was all over. The baby was born. Tom and Cathy had a son.

That was when Derry had come into the kitchen to find Ella. And the moment was frozen for ever in everyone's lives.

There should have been the noise of the kitchen, the ovens, the humming of the various appliances. There should have been the sounds of the party in the next room. They definitely should have been heard.

But they all remembered a moment of total silence before the little lungs of the boy who was going to be called James Muttance Feather gave a cry to say he was safely in the kitchen of Quentins and the world.

'I love you,' Cathy said to Tom.

And Mary said it to Blouse.

And Patrick Brennan said it to Brenda.

And Derry and Ella said it to each other at exactly the same time.